# ...AYAL OF

# RENEGADE X

## CHELSEA M. CAMPBELL

1<sup>st</sup> edition published by Golden City Publishing, 2015

Cover art by Raul Allen.

ISBN: 0-9898807-6-1

ISBN-13: 978-0-9898807-6-3

Books by Chelsea M. Campbell

Renegade X
*The Rise of Renegade X*
*The Trials of Renegade X*
*The Betrayal of Renegade X*

*Fire & Chasm*
*Starlight*
*Growing Up Dead*
*Harper Madigan: Junior High Private Eye*

# DEDICATION

FOR CHLOË AND KAREN, WHO GAVE ME ENDLESS PEP
TALKS AND KEPT ME FROM GOING TOO CRAZY.

# THE BETRAYAL OF RENEGADE X

# CHAPTER 1

"Only one more week of school," Gordon says at breakfast Monday morning, ruffling my hair and beaming at me like I just won the Olympics or something. He sounds both proud and relieved, like me getting through one whole semester at Heroesworth means he hasn't completely failed at being my dad. Or like maybe he thought I would flunk all my classes, or blow up part of the school, or do something else that would get me kicked out again.

Which is understandable, all things considered.

"I just want you to know how proud I am of you," he says. "How proud *we* are." He means him and Helen, my stepmom and the mother of my three half siblings.

"You did good," Helen says, grinning and squeezing my shoulder on her way to stop Jess from taking off her shoes again.

"It wasn't that hard," I tell them. "Blowing things up and getting expelled is *so* last season."

Amelia slumps into the chair across from me and glares. "He's not even getting straight *A*s," she whines. Amelia also goes to Heroesworth with me. We're in the same grade, but only because she got accepted slightly early. But that means it's her first semester there, too, only no one's acting like she deserves a lifetime-achievement award for it or anything, on account of her always getting good grades and never having been expelled. And I happen to know that she's not getting straight *A*s right now, either, so I don't know why she thinks that's a requirement for praise.

One benefit of being the black sheep in the family—or in this case, being the only half villain and going to an all-hero school—is that everyone expects me to screw up. So when I don't, it's like I performed a miracle.

Alex, my nine-year-old half brother, looks up at me adoringly and says, "I can't wait to go to Heroesworth, just like you!"

I gave him a dollar to say that. Though he's laying it on a little thick, which isn't what I paid for. I guess I can't expect quality at such low prices.

But apparently Amelia didn't notice how fake that sounded, because her mouth drops open and she gapes at me. Then her eyes narrow and her nostrils flare in and out. She grips her fork like she wants to stab someone with it—probably me—and jams it into her stack of pancakes. "*I* go to Heroesworth, too," she says. "Or did everyone forget?"

Helen gives her a sympathetic-yet-unenthusiastic smile. "We know, honey. But Damien's..."

"A screwup?" Little bits of pancake fly out of her mouth while she talks.

Gordon and Helen cringe at that, even though it's kind of true. Maybe a lot true. They both look to me, to see how offended and possibly horribly discouraged I am, now that my jealous little sister let the cat out of the bag. Like maybe I didn't know I wasn't a saint until just now.

I lean back in my chair, showing them how un-freaked out I am by that. "Amelia, I forgot. What's your grade in Intro to Heroism again?"

The blood drains from her face and she bites her lip. "That's the *only* class you're getting an *A* in. It's not that great."

"You didn't answer my question." Not only am I getting an *A* in that class, but Amelia's getting a *B*. Which really, *really* pisses her off.

"You still have to pass the final."

Piece of cake. Me and Riley have totally owned every mission in that class so far, no thanks to the rest of our group, and tonight won't be any different. Our current bad guy we've been studying through the school's criminal database and tracking around town for the past couple weeks is a kidnapper and a blackmailer with a record of not always keeping his victims in one piece. Or alive. Tonight, we catch him and get him off the streets once and for all, and that moment can't come soon enough.

"So do you," I remind her. "You never know—your *B* could become a *C*." Another mission means more fieldwork, which means Amelia messing up and not getting full points.

She lets out a little squeak of outrage.

Alex rests his chin in his hands and gazes up at me again. "You're the best brother in the whole world."

I make a slicing motion with my hand, trying to indicate he should cut it out. I only paid for one compliment, plus I don't want anyone getting suspicious.

"We should do something special next weekend," Gordon says. "To celebrate." He looks at me when he says it, clearly meaning to celebrate my lack of screwing up, though then he glances guiltily at Amelia and adds, "To celebrate *both* of you." Which just makes it that much more obvious that he hadn't meant her originally.

"Maybe we'll go out to eat Saturday night." Helen clears her throat. "You can bring Kat. If you want."

Which is a big deal for her to say, since only a few months ago, she wouldn't even let Kat in the house. Kat's a supervillain, and the granddaughter of Helen's nemesis. The one she defeated and killed years before we were even born, in the fight where she lost her superpower. She never got over it, and she's not exactly thrilled about me dating his direct descendant. Though at least I've finally convinced her that Kat's not evil.

"Thanks, but we kind of already made plans." Kat gets home from school on Saturday for winter break. I haven't seen her in weeks, and what we have planned isn't really rated for a general audience. "You guys can go without me, though. I don't want to get in the way of your happiness." I try to look as angelic as possible while I say that, like I really do care about them having a good time and not like I'm just hoping to luck out and get the house

4

to myself.

"Yeah, right," Amelia mutters.

"Another night, then," Gordon says. "We'll figure out a time that works for everyone."

It was worth a try. "Thanks, Dad."

"No problem, son."

Amelia pretends to gag in disgust.

Helen gives her a sharp look, silently scolding her for it. "You two better get going. You don't want to be late for school." She scoops up Jess and makes her put on her coat, telling Alex to grab his stuff and meet them in the car.

Gordon's phone rings, and he heads into the living room to answer it.

"I hate you," Amelia whispers, once we're alone. "And they're only being so nice to you because you messed up so much and they think you're a loser. You know that, right?"

"Wow, Amelia. You have such a sweet personality. No wonder you're so popular."

Her mouth turns extra sour at that. "You're barely passing this semester. *I'm* the one who's doing really well. I'm getting almost straight *A*s, and I'm treasurer of costume club."

"Good for you. And I wouldn't call three *B*s and an *A* 'barely passing.'" I might count the *C* I'm getting in our history class, but I don't see any reason to mention it.

"It's only one semester. You still have three left to go."

"Your point?"

"I just mean that maybe they shouldn't be celebrating

just yet. Because you still have a long way to go before you graduate, and just because you made it through one semester—which is supposed to be the *easiest* one—doesn't mean you're not going to fail later on." She shrugs, as if that's really obvious information and she just happened to be the one to tell me.

"Your faith in me is astounding." And I'm pretty sure one semester not guaranteeing my future is *why* Gordon and Helen want to celebrate—because there's a chance it won't ever happen again. Which is where they're wrong, because I've got this Heroesworth thing figured out. I might not get straight *A*s or have any extracurricular activities—not any school-sanctioned ones, anyway—and I might not fit in with all the *H*-bearing douchebags at that school, but I'm getting by. Which is good enough for me, and apparently it's more than good enough for Gordon and Helen.

"I was supposed to go to Heroesworth first," Amelia says, sounding more hurt than bratty for once. "I was always the oldest before. And now Dad doesn't even care if I follow in his footsteps or not. Just because you're older, and a boy."

"Maybe they'll do graduation in reverse alphabetical order and you'll get your diploma a few minutes before me." Since we have different last names.

She snorts. "*If* you even get yours."

"And anyway, it doesn't matter, because I'm not following in his footsteps. That one's all yours."

"You're going to Heroesworth."

"Yeah, but I'm not joining the League afterward."

She gets this look on her face that's half satisfaction and half disbelief. "Why wouldn't you want to join the League?"

"Uh, for all the obvious reasons?" Like that I'm half villain, I don't agree with most of their stupid rules, and I don't believe that signing their stupid League Treaty and promising to obey said stupid rules actually means anything. "The real question, Amelia, is why would *you* want to?"

"Because everyone joins up. Duh. Mom and Dad joined. Plus, all my friends are going to. And Zach."

"Yeah, but working in the League is pretty much all fieldwork. And we know how good you are at that."

She tries to kick me under the table. "It's only been one semester. I'm still *learning*."

"Only one semester. That means you've still got three more left to go. Fieldwork classes are required. And this is the easiest one. It's only going to get harder from here."

She scowls. Her chair screeches against the floor as she gets up from the table. "I'm going to school. *Don't* walk with me."

"I'm just saying that just because you made it through one semester doesn't mean you're not going to fail later on. Someone told me that. I can't remember who, but they sound like words to live by, don't you think?"

$$X \cdot X \cdot X$$

Brian, my least favorite member of our group, folds his arms and stands in front of the doors to the abandoned factory. His breath fogs in the cold night air. "We're not going in." He says it like he means it, like even after a whole semester he *still* thinks he calls the shots. Because having an *H* on his thumb supposedly makes him better than me.

Me and Riley exchange a look, and I know we're in agreement on this. There's no way in hell we're not going in there. Even if this wasn't our final mission for Intro to Heroism and a big part of our grade, and *even if* we hadn't just spent weeks preparing for this, we can't let this guy get away. He's kidnapped two kids—two kids who are locked up in this place right now, probably completely terrified—and is holding them for ransom. And after all the awful things we've learned about this guy and what he does to his victims, I don't know how Brian can even think about not doing this.

"Maybe he's right," Brittany says, shivering as she momentarily takes off her chunky purple scarf so she can rewrap it. "This place looks dangerous."

Brittany is a coward and an idiot. So is David, our other group member, who's staring at his feet guiltily. Like he's hoping we can just walk away from this, but knows it's the wrong thing to do.

And all of them can't wait to graduate from Heroesworth and join the League, so the citizens of Golden City can feel safe at night. Right. I bet five years from now Brittany's either a stripper or a housewife and David manages a gas station. Or maybe one of those hero-themed diners. I'm not sure which would be worse.

Brian nods, getting this smug look on his face. "We

don't know how many villains are in there. He doesn't always work alone."

I glare at him. "We know how many *victims*."

"It could be an ambush."

Riley sighs. He pulls the edges of his hat—a blue and white knitted cap with a snowflake pattern on it—down over the tips of his ears, which are turning red from the cold. "Our mission is to save those kids."

"And to not get killed," Brian whines.

*I'm* going to kill him if he doesn't shut up. "What were you expecting tonight? That he was just going to hand them over? That it was going to be all sparkles and rainbows?"

"Tracking this guy is one thing, but actually taking him on… Maybe we should call the League," he says, and I notice that, despite his smug bravado, his hands are shaking.

"*We're* here," Riley says. "Right now. We're not walking away."

"Maybe we should call them." David glances up real quick, then stares down at his shoes again. "This is what they do, right?"

Brian nods, like this is actually a good idea. "This mission is too dangerous. We need to call the professionals."

Unbelievable. Well, okay, not unbelievable, since it's not like this is the first time our other group members have displayed cowardice and idiocy in the face of danger. "Fine. You guys stay out here. We're going in."

"But—"

"*Move.*" I hold up my hand, letting electricity spark to life at my fingertips.

Brian's face goes pale. "You wouldn't."

"Try me."

He swallows, his eyes focusing on my hand.

Riley shoves him out of the way while his guard is down—meaning, unfortunately, that I don't get a chance to zap him—then flings open the door before any of them can try and stop us. Which is pretty unlikely, since it would mean actually doing something other than standing outside and whining.

We rush inside the building and into a hallway. It's dark, but there's faint light at the end of it, and sounds. A man talking, maybe some children whimpering.

There are footsteps behind us, and I'm about to turn around and tell Brian where he can shove it when Brittany whispers, "I'm coming with you."

Maybe there's hope for her after all. I'm upgrading her future potential to trophy wife and/or anchorwoman on the local news.

The three of us run down the hall. At the end of it is a big open room, lit up with a couple lamps and some Christmas lights. It's freezing in here, despite one measly space heater. Two kids are tied up and gagged in the corner, a boy and a girl. The kidnapper leaps up from where he was working on a ransom note and flings a trashcan and some random machine parts onto the floor as he takes off running.

Brittany's eyes are wide with relief. "That wasn't so bad."

"It's not over yet. You untie them," I tell her, jerking my head toward the two kids.

"We're going after him," Riley says.

Now Brittany's eyes are wide with shock, like she can't believe we'd leave her alone in a place like this, especially when there could be more bad guys lurking, but there's no way we're just letting him get away. Not when we're so close to catching him. Not when we've seen pictures of his victims before he got a hold of them, when they were still happy kids smiling for picture day and had their whole lives ahead of them.

Me and Riley take off in the direction the kidnapper went, the junk he threw on the ground hardly getting in our way. We run through the side door and down a hallway, catching up to him in another big room. The kidnapper has a flashlight, but he quickly turns it off when we get there. Not before we catch a glimpse of him climbing into a freight elevator.

I don't even have to think about it. The pictures of all those kids flash in my mind, and I know what I'm going to do. Because if that elevator gate closes, that's it, we've lost him, and who knows how many more kids he might hurt. But I can stop him. Lightning flares in my hands, the electricity loud and crackling.

"Are you crazy?!" Riley shouts.

"He's getting away!"

"You can't— That's breaking the rules! X, *don't*—"

But I'm already doing it. The lightning streaks from my hands to the kidnapper, just as he's closing the cage-like elevator gate. I can see his face in the glow from the electricity the moment he realizes what's happening. He reaches for something in his pocket, but he's too late. My electricity hits him, knocking him to the floor. It disappears, leaving us in darkness again.

Riley swears under his breath.

"Relax, Perkins. I didn't kill him." I just saved the day, and potentially a bunch of lives, is all. You'd think I'd get some credit for that.

"I told you not to do it!"

"He's a kidnapper. He's hurt *kids*. He's *killed* them. He was going to do it again. You know he was. I couldn't—"

"You couldn't follow the rules. Just this once, when it really mattered!"

"I couldn't let him get away! Is your grade really more important than people's lives?" Because, yeah, we're totally going to fail this assignment. Or at least I am. But it's worth it if this guy isn't out on the streets anymore. Getting an *F* doesn't really compare to making sure no more happy, innocent kids' lives get ruined because of him.

"The rules are there for a reason." Riley picks his way through the room in the dark.

I make electricity run along my hand, casting just enough light to see by.

We head over to the elevator. The kidnapper's lying on the floor, his limbs twitching a little. Riley opens the elevator grate and grabs the flashlight, shining it on the bad guy, who looks really sweaty and pale but is still, you know, breathing.

"You can turn that off now," Riley mutters, meaning

my electricity.

I do, but not because he told me to. I do it so I can take a closer look at the card in the kidnapper's hand. It's the thing he tried to get out of his pocket right as I was zapping him. Not a weapon, but a business card.

I pick it up and grab the flashlight from Riley so I can read what's on it. As soon as I do, I feel like I'm going to be sick.

"What is it?" Riley asks.

I'm tempted to tear it up. To fry the pieces beyond recognition. Or maybe just stuff them in my mouth and swallow them. Anything so he doesn't see what it says. But he's going to find out anyway.

I hand him the flashlight back, along with the card. It has the Heroesworth logo on it. It says that this guy is actually part of the League, that he's a superhero and a Heroesworth alumni, posing as a bad guy for our final.

Our apparently *staged* final.

Though, in my defense, all of our other missions this semester were real. With real-live bad guys.

At least, I'm pretty sure they were.

My mind races, thinking about how if this guy's a plant, then that means there's still a killer out there on the loose. But then I think about how all the research we did was through the school's database, and how he really looks like the same guy we've been tracking all over town. And there were only "before" pictures of his supposed victims. I thought that was because the "after" pictures were too gruesome, but... maybe there weren't any. Because there were no victims. Because this whole thing, from the

13

moment Miss Monk gave us the assignment, was completely fake.

The sick feeling in my stomach gets a lot worse. I feel like the ground's just been pulled out from under me. Like I'm falling.

"Great," Riley says when he's done reading the business card. "This is just great. This was only our most important project in Intro to Heroism, and you fried a freaking *superhero*!"

"I thought he was a kidnapper! I thought he'd killed kids!" Okay, so maybe I didn't save the day. Maybe there wasn't actually a day to be saved. But I think I showed excellent skill in bravery and pre-emptive attacks, which, in my opinion, should still count for something.

"I told you the rules are there for a reason! All we had to do was save those kids while following the League rules. That's all. But oh no, you couldn't do that. You couldn't just listen to me!"

I run my hands through my hair and take a deep breath. Adrenaline rushes through me and my blood runs cold. "He's still alive. There's that. Even if I'm dead." So dead.

"Correction. Even if *we're* dead. Or did you forget that this is a group project?" He shakes his head at me and gets out his cell phone to call 911.

It might be a group project, but I'm the one with the villain power. That I just used on someone from the League. I get out my phone too and contemplate calling my dad. Because if I'm going to get arrested again, I think maybe I should give him a heads up this time.

# X·X·X

"What were you thinking?" Gordon says when he comes to pick me up.

Not from the police station, though, since it turns out the fake kidnapper had to sign a waiver. Apparently this isn't the first time a superhero volunteer has been injured while helping out with a mission for Heroesworth. Though you wouldn't know that from the way the League members who came over to sort this out—conveniently already on their way, since Brian called them after all—were looking at me, like I was some kind of criminal. And I told Gordon I could get home on my own, but he insisted on coming down to the abandoned factory to get me.

"He was getting away." I climb into the car and put on my seatbelt. I guess the car is as good a place as any to get yelled at, since at least here the whole family can't hear him chewing me out.

"So you shot him." Gordon rests his hands on the steering wheel, even though he hasn't started the car yet.

"Zapped him. We should probably get going. This isn't a very good neighborhood. Fake kidnappers everywhere."

"He could have died."

"He's fine."

"They took him to the *hospital*."

"Okay, but he's going to be fine."

Gordon turns to look at me, a horrified expression on his face. "You don't know that, Damien."

"I knew what I was doing. And it's not my fault that he

wasn't a real kidnapper. The school tricked us. I didn't know the whole assignment was fake."

"And if he was a real criminal, that would justify using your villain power on him?"

"Don't say *villain power* like that." Like it's disgusting. "But yeah. Not to sound like Sarah or anything, but he'd killed kids. He'd tortured them. I thought he had, anyway."

"I thought things were different since you went back to Heroesworth." He rubs his palms against his forehead. So much for being proud of me.

"Things *are* different. Me and Riley pretty much aced all our other missions. I just didn't have to use my power until now."

His eyes go wide and he blinks at me. "You didn't *have* to use it. You *never* have to use it. And on a superhero..."

A few months ago, he was mad at me for hiding my lightning power from him and trying to pretend it didn't exist. Now he's talking like that's exactly what I should be doing. Like I should be pretending I only have my flying power—my *hero* power—even though I really hate it, mainly because flying means leaving the ground, which is one of my least favorite things to do. Or maybe that's why he wants to pretend that, since he knows I never use it, which means I'm much less likely to hurt someone with it. "I told you already, I didn't know who he really was. But you should know that being a superhero doesn't make you automatically a good person. He could have still been a murderer while having an *H* on his thumb, and I would have still zapped him."

"This is why the rules exist. I thought you would follow them when you went back to Heroesworth."

I laugh. "Yeah, right. Zapping that guy was way more important than the rules." Or at least it would have been, if the situation had been real. And I might not know the League rules that well, but I don't think there's anything in them that says, *Thou shalt not hurt a superhero, even if he deserves it.* They at least got that part right. "Can't you start the car? It's cold in here." Freezing, actually. I can see my breath fogging in front of me. I bunch the ends of my coat sleeves down around my hands.

He looks at me like I just asked him for a million dollars. "You put a man in the hospital. A *League* member. A *superhero*."

"So? A murderer who hurts kids doesn't deserve to be zapped, but you think I deserve to freeze to death for stopping him?"

"You broke the rules."

I shrug. "Those are your rules, not mine."

"I didn't think I even had to talk to you about not using your powers on *people*."

"Uh, superheroes use their powers on me all the time. But because I'm half villain that makes it wrong when I do it?" Typical.

"They use their powers on you to stop you when you get out of hand. Which shouldn't even be happening."

"And that's what I did to that guy. He was out of hand, so I stopped him. And I was successful. You have to give me that." Doesn't anybody appreciate an efficient bad-guy take down these days? And shouldn't he be relieved that if it had been an actually dangerous situation, I would have come out of it okay?

"You're not hearing me. I don't know how to make you…" He runs a hand through his hair, looking annoyingly like me while he does it. And like he might cry. Which is a bit overkill, if you ask me.

"Whoa, Dad. Calm down. I didn't do anything wrong."

"The fact that you think that *is* what's wrong."

"So just yell at me about it and get it over with." Not that I really want him to yell at me, but if he's going to do it, it might as well be now.

"So you can ignore everything I say? So you can get back to doing whatever you want?"

Pretty much, but I don't tell him that. "Let me help you. You're very disappointed in me and you don't know what to do because Amelia would never use her power to the detriment of others. Which is wrong, because she uses her power to steal stuff from me all the time."

He shakes his head. "This whole semester, since you went back to school, I thought you were following the rules."

"I wasn't *not* following them." I just didn't have a reason to break them.

"I thought you understood right from wrong."

"I do. Geez." I'm not a monster.

But you wouldn't know that from the way he's looking at me right now. "We shouldn't even be having this conversation. Superheroes should never have to use their powers on you, and you shouldn't have to use yours on them. That makes you sound like a…"

"Villain?"

He winces, which kind of hurts. "You had your chance to go to Vilmore, but you chose Heroesworth. I thought that meant something."

"It did. It *does*." Just not what he thinks. Deciding to go to Heroesworth doesn't mean I suddenly want to join the League or be some kind of Gordon clone or anything. "And if you're too upset to even start the car, maybe I should drive." I have my learner's permit.

"You should be the one who's upset here. You *hurt* somebody tonight. If you seemed like you cared, like you were at all shaken up by that, then..."

Then what? Then he'd know I'm not evil? He should know that anyway. "You'd rather I regretted it? That I used my power on someone when I *didn't* feel like it was the right thing to do? Because that sounds pretty reckless."

"Even if he was a criminal, even if you'd really had to use your power on him, you hurt another human being tonight. That should make you feel something."

"It's so cold in here I can't feel *anything*. Do you want me to drive or not?" And of course I feel something. It's not like I wanted to zap anyone. Well, maybe Brian. But the fact that I restrained myself from electrocuting my most annoying group member—which I have to do on practically a daily basis—and used my power to stop the bad guy instead should say something about me. Though if I told Gordon that, he'd probably only hear that I think about zapping someone every day, which wouldn't exactly help my case.

He puts the key in the ignition and looks me over, like

he's still trying to find some sign that I know what I did tonight was wrong. Which it wasn't. "I don't know what to say to get through to you."

"You don't need to get through to me. We just disagree." I reach out and turn the heater up to full blast.

"It's not okay for us to disagree on this."

I sigh and fold my arms across my chest. "Did you ever think that maybe you're the one who's not listening? You're not open to anything I say, and you won't even consider the possibility that maybe I have a point. You already decided how wrong I was before you even came down here. So if you won't change your mind about anything, why should I have to do any different?"

He grips the steering wheel, his jaw clenching in frustration. "Because I'm your *father* and that's just the way it is."

"Nope, not good enough. I'm going to need a better reason than that."

His eyebrows come together and his mouth twitches, like he really wants to argue. But in the end I guess he *doesn't* have a better reason than that, because he lets out a deep breath, his shoulders slumping in defeat, and eases the car into drive without saying anything.

# CHAPTER 2

"What time do you get in on Saturday?" I ask Kat on the phone Tuesday afternoon. I'm lying on my bed with my feet pressed against the slanting wall—the one I've banged my head on about five million times since Gordon forced me to move up to the attic a few months ago. I can hear clonking noises coming from Amelia's room next door, and she keeps stomping from her bed to her closet. It's probably wishful thinking, but it sounds like she's moving out.

"About two. But you can't come over right away because you have to give me a chance to hide your Christmas present."

"Or you could drop off your stuff and come over here, and I'll hide *your* Christmas present. In my bed, with no clothes on. If you know what I mean."

"Uh-huh. Isn't that what you got me for my birthday?"

Her birthday was last month. We hadn't gotten to see each other in weeks, and I stayed over at her dorm, even

21

though it was a weeknight. Needless to say, neither of us got to class on time, plus I had a forty-five minute train ride back to Golden City. I ended up missing a surprise group project in Intro to Heroism, which I suspect Miss Monk only assigned because I wasn't there. "You're forgetting First Mate Suckers." First Mate Suckers is the stuffed octopus pirate I got her. He has an eye patch and a peg leg and is really badass while also being soft and cuddly. And I know Kat didn't really forget about him because she posts pictures of him all the time, doing very non-piratey things like drinking coffee and taking tests.

"I didn't forget him," Kat says, pretending to sound offended. "I'm just pointing out that half your present is a repeat."

"It might be a repeat, but I don't expect any complaints. Plus, this time is different, because neither of us has anything we have to do the next day."

She clears her throat. "Actually... that's not quite true. Don't hate me, but I'm leaving again on Sunday."

I'm silent at first, the words not quite registering. "You're leaving."

"Only for a week. Everyone's going to this ski resort—"

"Everyone?"

"Liv's going, and Tasha was going to, but then her grandma got sick and she had to cancel. But Jordan and his new boyfriend are coming, plus his old boyfriend, Lucas, which is going to be *drama*. And June and Kelly and Cameron are going, too. And a couple other people, I think. My dad said I could go, and I know we haven't gotten to see each other much lately, but it's only for a week. That still leaves us two weeks of winter break."

But it was supposed to be three. We used to see each other every day, and even that didn't feel like enough. Now she'd rather spend some of her time off with her new friends, who she sees *all the freaking time*, instead of me? "That wasn't the plan."

"I know. But *everyone's* going, and they're going to be talking about this for forever, and I don't want to miss out. And we don't really have to be apart because you could come, too."

"It's a ski trip." That involves ski lifts and mountains and other high up places. Not to mention all her friends, judging me.

"You wouldn't have to ski. Not everyone's going to. Cameron's not. His power is making things warm, and he can't always control it. He said if he went skiing, everything would end up a big pile of slush. So you guys could hang out—I know you'd like him. And it's not like I'll be skiing the whole time. There's a lodge. There'll be snow and hot chocolate and a hot tub."

And feeling left out, and not knowing anybody, and listening to all her friends call her Katie, like she's a different person to them than she is to me. "What about the wedding?" My mom's getting married next week. And, despite hardly being invited, I'm going to be there. Kat's supposed to be my date, or at least she was, before something better came up.

She lets out a deep breath. "You don't have to go to the wedding."

"If I'm not there, then Mom gets to pretend I don't

exist." And she can act like Xavier, my perfect all-villain replacement, is her only kid. Like she has the perfect family she always wanted, that doesn't include me. And I was really looking forward to very publicly making out with Kat the whole time and offending all of Mom's guests. Which includes Kat's parents, so maybe that dream was never really going to come true, but it definitely won't if Kat doesn't even show up.

"Yeah, and that sounds like *such* a great reason to be there. Damien, you don't have to put up with her crap. You deserve better. And this ski trip is the perfect excuse to not go."

"She'll think it's because I know I'm not really wanted. Like I'm giving her space for her stupid big day that's all about her."

"So what if she does? Is it really worth putting yourself through all that? You could come on vacation with me. It'll be super romantic and Christmassy and stuff. We'll have our own room. For a *week*. My dad's paying for it, and he doesn't know you're going."

"That's because I'm not."

There are some angry noises coming from Amelia's room—an outraged squeak, followed by muttering—and then the whole attic shakes as she gets up from her bed and stomps her way to the door.

I turn over onto my stomach, in case that was the last straw and the rickety attic floor finally gives way. Because if I'm going to fall to my doom, I don't want to be taken unawares.

"Damien," Kat says, half scolding, half pleading.

"I don't know your friends. Not really." Though I hear enough about them.

"You could *get* to know them."

The stomping continues into the hallway, and then Amelia bangs on my door.

"They still call you Katie." I'm never going to get used to that.

"Damien!" Amelia calls, as if I couldn't hear her knocking.

"Go away!" I shout back.

"I know you're in there!"

So perceptive.

"Look, Kat," I tell her, "at least if I go to the wedding, I'm only going to feel left out for one day. Not for a whole week."

Amelia bangs on the door again. "I need to talk to you!"

"You'll like my friends," Kat says. "It's not like you haven't met most of them already. And they'll like you. I know they—"

The sound cuts off as the phone disappears out of my hand. As if some really awful person with the power to teleport things to herself just stole it from me.

I'm going to kill Amelia.

I get up from the bed and cringe as the floorboards creak and wobble beneath me. I'm currently trying to convince Gordon that the value of the house would increase significantly if he added on another room to the ground floor. I don't think he's buying it, even though I made graphs that chart how a modest investment now would result in lots of profit later. And by "made graphs," I mean I got my friend Sarah to make them, but still. The facts are there.

I fling open my door and glare at Amelia, who's standing in the hallway with my phone and her pink laptop.

"Give me that." I hold out my hand for my phone. "Now."

She sniffs, acting all offended, like she isn't the one who just stole something. "Not until you explain *this*." She points her laptop screen at me.

It's open to a picture of me and Zach that I posted on Facebook. We're waiting in line to get into *Heroes on Ice*. It's where superheroes reenact famous battles with supervillains to classical music, while ice skating. I wondered when she would notice it. "Oh, *that*." I ever-so-casually inspect the back of my hand. "Obviously Zach and I are dating behind your back. I knew you'd find out about our love eventually, but I didn't think it would be this soon."

Amelia scowls at me. "*I* was supposed to go with him. That was my ticket!"

"That he paid for. And you were sick. You couldn't go."

"So he took *you*? That was my birthday present! He bought them for us months ago, before they sold out."

I shrug. "The tickets were only good for that night. What did you want him to do, go alone?"

"Maybe. And you don't even *like Heroes on Ice*."

"I like things that are free. Well, almost free. I did have to put out."

Her mouth drops open at that. My phone rings and I grab it from her while she's still too stunned to notice. "Hey, Kat. I was just telling Amelia what an awesome boyfriend I am."

"Damien?" Crap. It's not Kat, it's my mom. "I'm so glad I finally reached you. You haven't been avoiding my calls, have you? Did you get my texts?! The supplies for the party favors aren't arriving for another *week*."

"Mom, this isn't a—"

"And there's no way we're going to be able to put them all together on our own in time, especially with all the million things I have left to do before my big day. I need volunteers, and I know you're on break from school soon. So I don't know why you didn't respond to my texts, unless you didn't get them."

"I got them, okay? But—"

"I have to double-check the seating arrangement, and call the caterers, because it turns out Taylor's cousins are all allergic to fish, and of course getting a suit at the last minute isn't going to be easy. But I have to make sure my little baby looks his best on my big day."

Amelia scrunches up her nose and smirks, obviously overhearing and thinking she means *me*. She doesn't know about Xavier.

I slip inside my room, shutting the door in Amelia's face to a muffled whine of "Hey!" "Is that seriously what you called me about?"

"I need a favor. Another one, besides help with the party favors. And before you say no, remember that it's my wedding day. I'm only going to have one, and... this would mean a lot to me."

For a second, I think she's actually going to ask me something important. Like maybe she really does want me to be a part of her "big day," even if it's just something small. Which is stupid, because all she's talked about for the past few months is how perfect this wedding has to be and how that means having her "little family" there with her. Her "little family" is her way of referring to her, Taylor, and Xavier. Her *new* family, the one that doesn't include me. And Taylor's the one who invited me, not Mom. Just because she hasn't *un*invited me yet doesn't mean she actually wants me there.

I tell myself that, but I feel a traitorous flicker of hope anyway.

Mom hesitates, like she thinks I might blindly agree to whatever it is if she waits long enough. But when I don't, she clears her throat and says, "I want you to... keep your distance at the wedding. From your brother," she adds, so I know she doesn't mean from her. Like we both don't know that Xavier's going to be glued to her the whole time.

I feel like I'm going to throw up. "That's the favor you want from me." So much for her wanting me around.

"Your brother's very sensitive. You have a tendency to upset him, and I don't want anyone causing a scene." My brother is only three months old, though he looks more like an eight-year-old kid, thanks to Mom's crazy growth formula. She also implants fake memories in his brain at night while he's asleep to try and make up for how fast he's growing, but I'm pretty sure that just makes him worse.

"And by *anyone*, you mean me." As if I'm the one who'll start screaming and throwing a fit at the drop of a hat.

"He can't help himself," she says, almost whispering. "Everyone's going to be there, all our guests, and I just want everything to go smoothly. It's a big day for us. For our little family."

I swallow. "But not for me."

She sighs, exasperated, like I'm the one being difficult and asking something outrageous of her. "Don't be like that. I'm stressed enough as it is—I don't need any difficulties from you. And Xavier's so excited that Taylor and I are getting married, and that he's going to be part of it. Just do this one thing for me. All I'm asking is for you to behave."

"Because *I'm* the awful one."

"So much goes into planning an *event*. One people will remember for years to come. I just want them to remember it for the right reasons. So I don't want anyone causing a scene or making a spectacle of themselves."

"How pissed were you at Taylor for inviting me?"

"*Damien.* That's not what this is about."

"Except you wish I wasn't going to be there, causing trouble, right?"

"I saw the news. I saw what you did during your final."

"Yeah, but you hate superheroes." Though that didn't stop her from sleeping with my dad in a filthy subway bathroom. "You should be proud."

"You made a big spectacle of yourself and ended up in the tabloids. I just want you to keep a low profile at my wedding. Don't upset anyone. You know how you are."

I clench my fist. Little sparks of lightning run along my spine. "So be quiet and stay out of the way." Maybe Kat's right. Maybe I don't need this.

"Is that so much to ask? On *my* big day?"

If she says the words *big day* one more time… "I don't upset Xavier—he upsets *me*."

"All the more reason to stay away from him. Just at the wedding. Someday, when he's older, you two will get along so well."

"So, in another month or two?" More like in another universe.

"And this wedding will be a good memory for both of you. It's going to be perfect."

"But only if no one knows I'm there." Because the only thing that could make her wedding actually perfect is getting to pretend she has one son, not two.

She makes a frustrated noise in the back of her throat. "Damien, you're not listening to me. I never said that."

"You didn't have to. I heard you loud and clear. Don't ruin the wedding. Got it." The sparks running up my spine get more intense, and I can feel all my hair standing on end.

"If you don't think you can do that—"

"Don't worry. It won't be a problem." Electricity flickers along my arm, building up underneath my skin. I try to hold it back, but I'm too pissed at her and it's not working.

"But if you're not sure, if you don't think you can control yourself, then maybe you shouldn't—"

There's a loud crackle as lightning surges into my hands. I drop the phone, not even bothering to hang up, just in time for it to not get fried.

And just in time to *not* hear how she was going to end that sentence, even though it's not hard to guess.

If I'm not sure I can control myself, maybe I shouldn't show up for the wedding.

## X·X·X

I grab my hooded sweatshirt from the hall closet the next day while I'm printing the article I found for Gordon. Since the direct approach involving future investments and rising real-estate values didn't work, I decided to try guilt. The article is about how several kids were traumatized for life by their parents trying to force them to get over their phobias. I'm going to put it in Gordon's desk drawer—not too obvious a place, but still somewhere he's likely to see it—because obviously I can't give it to him myself. That would be like admitting I *have* a phobia, plus he might not take it seriously, since he already knows I'm after something. And maybe this way he won't even know it was me who left it there. He might think it was Helen, quietly judging him for torturing his eldest son by pushing him off a building and then making him live in the attic.

Fortunately, I don't have any finals today and Gordon's at work and Helen's at the antique shop.

"What are you doing?"

*Un*fortunately, Amelia doesn't have any finals today,

31

either.

"Nothing," I tell her, hurrying to finish pulling my sweatshirt over my head and then catching the article as the printer spits it out onto the floor. And, most importantly, not letting her touch it, since her power only lets her summon things she's had her grubby paws on already.

"Is that for school?" She folds her arms over her chest and wrinkles her eyebrows at me. Like now she's the printer police.

"It's my confession of undying love for Zach. I was going to email it, but that just seemed too impersonal. I'm going to his house to give it to him."

She scowls at me. "Zach's *my* boyfriend. And he's at school. *And* you're not allowed to leave."

"Says who?"

"Dad. Obviously."

"Uh, he didn't tell me that." And I already made plans to meet up with Riley, so too bad. I head for Gordon and Helen's room with Amelia trailing behind. The door is ajar, and I nudge it open the rest of the way with my foot. I brace myself, still expecting a disaster area like my mom's room, even after living here for almost a year. But Gordon and Helen's room is nothing like my mom's. The bed is made and there's not even any laundry on the floor.

"He told you you were grounded, right?" Amelia says, still following me. "Because not leaving the house is what *grounded* means. And what are you doing in here?"

"Coming in without permission and touching everything they own. Your favorite hobby." I flash her a fake smile. "And I'm not grounded."

"Dad didn't ground you? But you failed your final."

"So if I bomb a test, I'm supposed to get in trouble?" Isn't failing its own reward?

"Yes. I mean... You broke the rules. Dad has to be mad, right?"

I shrug, sliding open his desk drawer and revealing the latest issue of *Heroes Monthly*. "Not mad enough to ground me. I think he actually, like, respects me for telling him the truth."

Amelia snorts. "Yeah, right. And saying you're not grounded is just what you'd say if you *were*, so that I'd let you leave."

"Let me leave?" I glance over my shoulder at her. "And how do you plan to stop me?"

"I..." Her mouth hangs open as she thinks that through.

I turn back to the desk and grab the magazine out of the drawer, intending to hide the article underneath it, since just setting it on top would be too obvious. But when I pick it up, a brochure falls out from between the pages and lands on the desk, face up.

*The Wellness Preserve—a relaxing place for troubled superpowered teens to rediscover themselves through a personalized therapy program, led by our highly trained staff.*

There's a picture of a guy and a girl standing next to a tree in the countryside with big smiles on their faces. The girl has a ball of fire badly Photoshopped into her hand and is making a big point of using it to roast a marshmallow, instead of the tree, I guess. And the guy is using his super strength to lift a giant log off of a dirt road.

There's also a quote from a satisfied parent. *I was at my wits' end with my daughter. I didn't know what to do. And then I found The Wellness Preserve.*

I stare at it in horror.

"Damien?" When I don't answer her, Amelia steps around me so she can see what I'm looking at. "Oh. My. God."

I open my mouth, but no words come out. I feel numb.

She smirks at me. "You were right. He *sure* respects you for telling him the truth."

"Shut up." Maybe it's someone else's, not Gordon's. It's in his desk, with his stuff, but it can't be his. He's probably just holding it for a friend.

"He respects you *so much* that he's sending you to live on a farm. That's what happened to Tiffany's cousin's dog when it peed on the floor. It had behavioral problems, so it 'went to a farm' and never came back."

My palms start to sweat. "That's not what's happening."

"That's what it *looks like* is happening. But don't worry, you'll probably be a lot happier out in the country, with more room to run around and chase rabbits."

"He wouldn't send me away." He promised. "This must be for you. Since I think we both know which one of us belongs on a farm."

"Well, he doesn't have to send you anywhere." Amelia points to the words *therapy program.* "I've heard about places like this. They can do your shock therapy at their facility while you live at home. It's a lot cheaper than the extended-stay option."

"I don't need shock therapy. Or *any* therapy. This brochure must have come with the magazine."

"*Heroes Monthly* doesn't come with brochures. And you have been messing up a lot lately. I'm not surprised he thinks you need professional help."

"This place is for nutjobs who use their powers to destroy stuff and can't control themselves." Messed up kids whose parents don't know how to deal with them and want to pawn their problems off on someone else.

"Yeah, and who does that sound like? You're doing badly in school, you're always breaking things with your power—"

"On accident. I don't destroy stuff on purpose. And I haven't done anything like that in months." That Gordon knows about, anyway.

"It still counts. You got arrested for it. And expelled. Plus, you zapped that guy the other night, and that was on purpose."

"That was different."

"You're always mouthing off and talking back and not listening. And people are still taking pictures of you, even though you're not the Crimson Flash's only kid or anything."

"Wow, Amelia. Jealous much?"

"You're not even that special. But everything you do ends up on the news, and that makes Dad look bad. So obviously he has to do something about you. Seeing that you put a superhero in the hospital was probably the last straw."

Before what? Before Gordon decides I'm a lost cause?

"He knows I wouldn't hurt anybody. I mean, not without a good reason."

"Yeah, well," she says, a smug smile spreading across her face, "he'll know that even better after you get your lobotomy."

# CHAPTER 3

I mash the buttons on the controller, but my heart's not in it. The dinosaur Riley's playing does a spinning attack and whomps me with its tail a bunch of times. Somewhere in my mind it occurs to me to block, but my thoughts don't reach my hands fast enough.

My alien clutches its chest and dies dramatically on the screen, even though it died from being beaten to death by a Tyrannosaurus, not a heart attack. Though it's also an alien, so maybe it doesn't actually have a heart in its chest, even if it's shaped like a human.

"Oh, boy," Riley says, with no enthusiasm in his voice. "I win *again*. It's like you're not even trying."

"I'm letting you win. It's your Christmas present." It's better than the one I'm getting, which is betrayal. From Gordon.

He makes a face. "I hope you saved the receipt."

Gordon's supposed to be the one who doesn't abandon me or pawn me off on other people. He's not supposed to be like my mom. And maybe he's not sending me away, but obviously he thinks he can't deal with me. Or just doesn't want to. At least Mom made it sixteen years. Gordon hasn't even made it for one.

Riley holds down the button on his controller and turns off the console. "Come on, X. You can tell me the truth."

"Okay, okay. Your real present is that I didn't get Sarah a better gift than you're going to get her."

"That's not what I— Wait, what do you think I got her?"

I wave my hand. "Something dumb. Probably a book. A book that *you* like."

He swallows, his voice wavering a little. "That's not true."

"A DVD, then. Probably a documentary."

"It's a boxed set. About the history of Golden City."

"Yeah, that sounds about right. You should know it was really hard finding something lamer than that."

He scowls at me. "We watched part of it on TV and then had to miss the rest. Sarah was really disappointed. She *likes* it."

"Sure. Whatever. It's still lame."

"What's wrong with it?"

"Besides being boring?"

"It's not boring. It's really interesting. And it won awards."

"Okay, so for your first Christmas with your girlfriend who you're really into, you're getting her a *documentary*. Do you hear how boring that sounds?" And I'm guessing he's not getting it for her so they can pretend to watch it while actually making out.

"It's not… It doesn't… Sarah's going to like it."

"Like it, but not love it." I lean forward and set my controller on the coffee table.

Riley opens his mouth to argue, but then holds back, thinking that over. "What did you get her?"

"A pair of socks."

"Seriously? You think the documentary that she wants to see is only a step up above socks?"

They're nice socks, pink with gray robots on them, but still. "You could have rented the stupid documentary and surprised her with it for, I don't know, one of your movie nights. How often do you rewatch crap like that anyway?"

He considers that for a second, then shakes his head. "She's going to like it. And don't think you can just change the subject. I know you feel guilty for what you did the other night, but letting me win at *Aliens vs. Dinosaurs* for two hours isn't going to make it up to me."

"That's where you're wrong, because I don't feel guilty."

He rolls his eyes at me. "Yes, you do. Just admit it."

"I *don't*."

"Okay," he says, not sounding like he believes me, "but you never lose that many times in a row, and I know you weren't just letting me win. Something's up."

"I didn't get enough sleep last night. It's an off day. I'll be back to kicking your ass tomorrow." I did have trouble sleeping last night, mostly because Amelia was blasting the radio and singing along really badly to pop music until one a.m., so it's not completely a lie.

Riley tilts his head, not buying it. "If you don't tell me what's really going on, I'm just going to have to assume it's guilt."

"For the last time, Perkins, it's not guilt."

"But it is something, then."

I glare at him. "It's *nothing*, okay?! So just *leave* it."

It comes out sounding meaner than I meant it to, and he blinks a couple times, looking kind of hurt. "Yeah. Sure. I just thought..."

We're silent for a minute, each of us on opposite ends of the couch. I drum my fingers against the arm rest and Riley pretends to read the back of the *Aliens vs. Dinosaurs IV* box.

I sigh. "You can't tell Zach. Or Sarah."

He glances over at me, then back at the box. He nods.

"I mean it."

"I know."

"I think..." I swallow, not really wanting to say it out loud. "I think Gordon's tired of dealing with me." I try to keep the fear from my voice, but I know it's there, and I know Riley hears it.

"Oh," he says.

"*Oh?* It's a big deal." I lean my head back against the couch. "I found a brochure. In his stuff. He was really upset the other night. About me zapping that guy. And now he has a brochure for this place for troubled teens. With superpowers. It's, like, practically advertising that they'll take your kids you can't handle and brainwash them into not using their powers to do anything bad."

Riley sucks in a slow breath through his teeth. "That

40

can't really be what it's for."

"You didn't see it."

"I know, but your dad wouldn't do that to you."

"It's aimed at parents who don't know how to control their delinquent teens with dangerous powers." I put a hand to my chest. "*I'm* a delinquent teen with a dangerous power. He wants to control me and he can't. And you should have seen him Monday night. He was freaked."

Riley bites his lip. "You probably just scared him, that's all. He's not going to send you away."

"No, but not everyone lives there. They have therapy programs. I looked through the brochure." Meaning I read every horrifying word before stuffing it back in that stupid magazine. I thought about stealing it, in the hopes that Gordon might just forget about it, but I was afraid he'd notice it was gone and come looking for it, and that seemed worse. Because then I'd know that he hadn't forgotten about it, that he was really considering this, and then he'd know that I'd found it, and that I knew what he was planning. And thinking about that made my chest get tight, like I couldn't breathe, and so I slammed the drawer shut and got out of there.

"Therapy's not so bad," Riley says, clearing his throat. "I had to go, after my dad died. Me and Zach. I didn't want to, but it turned out okay."

"That's different. Your mom wasn't scared of you. She wasn't worried that you were some psychopath who just goes around hurting people because you feel like it. As if she didn't know you at all."

"There's no way your dad thinks that about you.

Someone else could have given him that brochure. Maybe the counselor at school or something. It might not mean anything."

"He doesn't think he can deal with me. He's *giving up* on me." The words leave a stinging feeling in my chest. Maybe Riley's right and it's just a misunderstanding, but he didn't see the horrified way Gordon looked at me when he came to pick me up.

"You thought that guy was a kidnapper," Riley says.

"You told me not to do it."

"Yeah." He lets out a deep breath. "What you did was against the rules. But you didn't do it because you're crazy or because you go around hurting people. I know that. You dad knows that, too. He has to."

"He's going to send me to therapy so they can 'fix' me." Because he thinks I'm broken. "He—" My phone rings. It's Gordon. Of course it is. I almost don't answer it, but then I do anyway. "Hey. Dad."

"Damien." He hesitates, and my heart races as I imagine him saying that Amelia told him we found that brochure and that there's no point wasting time, now that I know about it, since I could be good and brainwashed before next semester even starts. Merry Christmas. "Dinner's at six. We're having meatloaf." He says that like nothing happened. Like he doesn't think I'm deranged or like he's considering getting me professional help.

"I hate meatloaf." Plus, Helen only makes that when—

"Your aunt and— Er, I mean, Helen's sister and her family are coming over."

I groan. Of all the people I want to zap, they rank

pretty high on the list.

"So." Gordon pauses. "I need you to be on your best behavior. Leah already thinks you put syrup in Belinda's hair last time."

"She pushed Jess! She made her *cry*."

He sighs, sounding worn out. "They're just kids."

"Yeah, but one of them's my sister." And the other one is a conniving five-year-old bitch who obviously gets away with murder. Or pushing three-year-olds. Whatever.

"Let me handle it this time. If anything happens," he adds, as if there's any chance that it won't. "Be home by five thirty."

"I can't." The words just come out, before I have time to think about them. There's no way I'm sitting through dinner with Leah and her awful family. While Gordon acts like he hasn't betrayed me, and Leah brings up seeing me in the news again, with that I-told-you-so expression on her face, and talks about me like I'm not in the room, and no one stops her and says, *He might be a problem, but he's* our *problem, and at least he doesn't torment three-year-olds like your stupid kids do.* "I'm staying at Riley's. I'm staying the night, I mean."

Riley glances over at me, raising his eyebrows, but he doesn't say anything.

Gordon's voice gets this gruff I'm-your-father tone to it. "Damien. It's a school night."

"Yeah, and Riley goes to school, too. Plus we don't have any classes until afternoon tomorrow. And he's helping me study for my Morality final. I really need the help, don't you think?"

"I don't know," he says, meaning me staying out tonight, not needing help with my morality, since we both know what he thinks about that.

"I can guarantee that I won't put syrup in anyone's hair."

He laughs, like he has any right to have a normal conversation with me. "You'll definitely be missed."

I'm pretty sure I won't, but I guess that's his way of saying I don't have to come home tonight.

He tells me to call him in the morning and says good-bye. I hang up and relax a little, sinking back into the couch.

"I don't have to stay here," I tell Riley. "I just said that so I wouldn't have to go home." I can always stay with Kat, at her dorm at Vilmore. It's forty-five minutes away and I'd have to take the train, but I could still get back before my afternoon final tomorrow.

"Yeah, I know," he says, picking up the second controller off the coffee table and tossing it to me. "But don't be stupid, X. Of course you can stay."

"You didn't have plans? I was pretty sure you'd be scrambling to find Sarah a better Christmas present."

"I told you. She'll like it." He shakes his head and presses the button on his controller to turn the console back on. "And no, I didn't have plans. Now shut up and play for reals—we can still get a few more rounds in before Zach comes home and kicks both our asses."

X·X·X

"And then Miles and I walked into the back room with our rayguns out, ready for anything, and..." The superhero guy, who apparently used to be best pals with Zach and Riley's dad, pauses in mid-sentence, trying to draw out the suspense.

We're sitting at the dining table, eating dinner, which is, thankfully, pork chops and not meatloaf. Zach, Riley, and their mom are hanging on this guy's every word, smiling and holding back laughter as he finishes up his story about the good ol' days, when he was partnered up with Zach and Riley's dad in the League and they used to go around hunting down villains. My favorite subject.

The guy—whose name is Curtis—grins real big and says, "Nah, you guys don't want to hear how it ends. How about I just stop there?"

"No way!" Zach says, his fork clattering to his plate. "You *have* to finish it."

Riley rolls his eyes at his brother. "Of course he's going to finish it."

Curtis spreads out his hands and leans forward. "So there we were, figuring we had the Thief King cornered in the back room of this diner. With who knows how many of his guys waiting for us. We knew it was dangerous, and we were both scared out of our wits, but neither of us would admit it. So we get our rayguns out and kick the door in, all ready for trouble, and there's the Thief King. Alone. Stuffing his face with an ice cream sundae, with chocolate sauce and peanuts all over it!" He slaps his hand down on the table and starts cracking up at his own stupid story.

The rest of them laugh, too. Riley even looks over at me, to see if I think it's as funny as they do, which I do not. And not just because I don't think it's crazy and hilarious that villains occasionally get caught eating desserts like regular people, but because it couldn't have happened.

Their mom leans her head back and sighs. "I forgot how much trouble you two used to get into."

Curtis notices I'm the only one not convulsing with side-splitting laughter and says, "That was a little hero humor, there. I guess it's not for everyone."

It's too bad Gordon's not here to see me *not* zap this guy. Even if I really, really want to. "It's an okay story, I guess. But it would be funnier if it was true." Which it's not. It can't be.

The laughter at the table dies down.

Riley shoots me a withering look, like he doesn't know why I always have to cause trouble.

"I assure you," Curtis says, trying to sound good-natured about it, "every word is the honest truth."

"The Thief King was deathly allergic to peanuts. Everyone knows that."

He kind of gapes at me for a second. "You sure?"

"Uh, yeah. It's common knowledge." At least it is for villains. I assumed it was for everyone, but maybe not.

He holds his hands out, palm up. "I mixed it up, then. It was a long time ago. Maybe it was sprinkles instead." He laughs at that, like that makes the story even funnier. Like he's going to tell it like that from now on.

So much for the honest truth.

Now that I ruined the mood, their mom gets up to start clearing the plates. Curtis puts a hand on her lower back, which suddenly seems really intimate and over the line, except she doesn't even flinch. Like it's normal for him to put his hands on her. Ugh. "Let me do that, Win," he says.

Zach cringes and Riley looks away. I raise my eyebrows at him, but he pretends he doesn't notice.

"No, I've got it," their mom says, not noticing how weirded out her kids are by what just happened. And me. Don't forget me.

Curtis gets up and follows her off into the kitchen anyway.

As soon as they're out of sight, I turn to Riley and say, "So, that guy's doing your mom, huh?"

He makes a face. "*No*. I mean, they... They've been on a couple dates, I guess. That's all."

"That we know about," Zach says. "She only just told us they were together last week. She wouldn't have said anything if it wasn't for sure. Which means they were already going out *before* that."

"He's got a point," I tell Riley.

"And she never dates," Zach adds. "It's only been three years."

"Three and a half," Riley corrects him, without looking up from an imaginary spot on the table he's staring at. "But... she wasn't going to stay single forever." He sounds more like he's trying to convince himself than anyone else. "And he's always looked out for us, ever since Dad died. It makes sense, kind of."

"But he's *not* our dad. It's weird. And gross. And he'd

better not be... you know. With her." Zach's face turns a little red and he clears his throat.

"He's a liar," I say, taking a drink from my water glass. "His story doesn't make sense."

Riley spreads his hands out on the table. "It's just a story."

"A fake one. When did he say it happened? Five years ago? Because the Thief King relocated to South America a year or so before that."

"So? Maybe he got the date wrong. And... he *likes* telling us stories about our dad. I figure he ran out of true ones a long time ago."

"So you don't care that he's a liar? Or that he's—"

"He's *not* doing my mom!"

He practically shouts that at me, right as his mom and Curtis come back in with a tray of brownies and a carton of ice cream.

There's a moment of really awkward silence. Zach squeezes his eyes shut, opening one eye slowly to survey the fallout. Riley hunches his shoulders and doesn't look at anyone.

Finally Curtis chuckles to himself a little and sets the ice cream on the table. Their mom follows suit with the brownies, as if everyone's silently agreeing to pretend it didn't happen. Except for Riley, who glares at me and mouths, *Thanks a lot.*

As if it's my fault he's so easily agitated.

"So, Riley," Curtis says as he takes his seat across the table, "tell me about what happened during your final. I hear there was some trouble?" His eyes go right to me as he says that part.

"Oh, leave the boys alone, Curtis." Their mom swats his arm. "It was one mistake. I seem to remember you making more than your fair share when you were their age."

"I didn't have a League scholarship on the line."

Riley swallows, looking guilty, as if what happened was in any way his fault.

"You know your mom can't afford for you to go to Heroesworth on her own. And you know why you have that scholarship. Don't dishonor him by losing it."

Yeah, no pressure. I don't know what scholarship he's talking about, but I can't help glaring at him. "Riley didn't do anything wrong. It was my fault. He just happened to be there."

"And by 'just happening to be there' and not stopping you, he broke a League rule. Heroes can't just let people go around hurting others. And he has a *League* scholarship to think about, and they don't look too favorably on that kind of thing. A hero needs to be aware of what company he keeps. His father would have never gone into battle with someone he couldn't trust. With a..." He trails off, apparently deciding it would be too rude to say *half villain* at the dinner table.

Zach sits up straighter, like maybe he's going to tell him where he can shove it, or maybe launch himself across the table in an attack.

Riley's eyes go wide. His voice takes on a defensive edge. "I trust Damien."

Curtis raises his eyebrows and tilts his head, like *Are you sure about that?* "As I understand it, none of the *heroes* in your group shot anyone. You were there with him, meaning it was your responsibility to stop him. He put you in a situation you shouldn't have been in, and now the League's putting you on probation for your scholarship. Your father and I never would have done that to each other." He gestures at me and Riley with his fork. "There's more to trust than knowing he won't shoot you while your back is turned."

"I resent that," I mutter. "I would so shoot him to his face."

Curtis ignores me. "You have to know he's looking out for you. That he's not going to do anything crazy and take you down with him."

"They're *sixteen*," Riley's mom says. "They're kids, not adults in the League. They're allowed to mess up sometimes."

"I trust Damien," Riley repeats. "He didn't mean to get me in trouble."

"Doesn't matter—it still happened." Curtis turns to me and says, "I don't mean to offend you, son, but you put our Riley here in a difficult position. How can he fight villains in the field if he's got to worry about the one on his team?"

I keep my fists clenched under the table as electricity surges in my palms. *Must. Not. Zap. Douchebag.* I open my mouth to speak, but then Zach beats me to it.

He gets to his feet and leans forward, pressing his palms into the table. "Damien's our friend and you don't even know him, so just shut up! You're not our dad and you never will be, so stop acting like it!" He turns and runs off to his room in a fit of drama, slamming the door behind him.

He may have picked that up from Amelia.

"Zach!" their mom shouts. She gets up to go after him.

Curtis shakes his head at me, like this is all my doing.

And I think maybe Mom's right. Maybe I do always have to cause a scene.

"The other heroes on our team might not have zapped anybody," I tell Curtis, "but they didn't go after the bad guy, either. Two of them wouldn't even come in the building to save those kids. And I might be a half villain"—and I might even be trouble—"but at least I'm not a coward."

And at least I know that, no matter what, I've always got Riley's back.

# CHAPTER 4

"Well," Sarah says, adjusting her glasses and pushing them farther up the bridge of her nose, "Curtis has a point—you *did* put Riley in a difficult position."

I can't believe her. "*Sarah*. You're supposed to be on my side."

"I am on your side." She pauses to peer into the store window at *Masquerade*, the upscale cape shop in the mall. It's literally a store that sells only capes. The one in the window is red velvet with white fur trim and is on a manikin dressed like Santa. I don't even want to know who would be lame enough to buy that. The store, like the rest of the mall, is decked out for Christmas with evergreen garlands, wreathes, and giant Christmas trees overloaded with ornaments. Sarah looks like she's thinking about going in, but then thankfully changes her mind and keeps walking. "But that doesn't make what Curtis said not true. Riley was supposed to stop you. In theory. That means he broke a League rule."

As if Riley would ever do that. At least, not on purpose. "Even if he could have stopped me"—which I'm pretty sure he couldn't—"there wasn't time. It's a stupid rule."

"But he was still *supposed* to stop you. Whether he wanted to or not."

"Okay, but I didn't know that." I stuff my hands in the front pocket of my sweatshirt.

"You broke the League rules, Damien. And you almost killed a superhero."

She should talk. She's the one who's always urging me to shoot first and ask questions later. Or at least she was, before she went crazy this fall and almost blew up a whole generation of supervillains. "I thought he was a murderer. And I didn't almost kill him. Geez."

"What if he'd had a weak heart?"

"A kidnapper with a weak heart? That would be his fault for choosing such a hazardous profession. And I thought you of all people would understand why I did it."

"I do understand, and that's why I know you shouldn't have done it." She stops in front of a bookstore that sells mostly movies and games, pausing just long enough for us to get jostled by some overly aggressive shoppers before deciding to go inside. One of them glances back at us, obviously recognizing me, but he keeps moving. Sarah chews her lip. "Maybe you should join my rehabilitation program."

She means the self-imposed one she made for herself after the incident at Vilmore. "Wow, *could I*? I didn't realize you were accepting new members."

"We could use some more volunteers at the retirement home," she says, leading me over to a wall of DVDs and not catching my sarcasm. "Though it would make more sense for you to work at one for superheroes instead of villains."

"Yeah, I'm not doing that. I don't need rehabilitation, and neither do you."

"Maybe not anymore. Oh!" Her eyes light up, and she reaches out and grabs a boxed set of DVDs off the wall. "This would be perfect for Riley."

It's a documentary. On the history of Golden City.

Right.

"Uh, Sarah…"

"We saw part of it on TV, but we couldn't watch the whole thing because we were going to the movies, and I know he was really disappointed about not getting to see the rest."

"Sure, but… You can't get him that."

She scrunches up her face. "But it's in my price range."

"Get him something cheaper. The more you save on him, the more you can spend on me."

"I already got your present. And you know how he loves historical documentaries. Even the boring ones."

*Especially* the boring ones. "You think it's boring?"

"It's really slow. And pretentious. That's the only reason it won any awards."

"You know, on second thought, you're right. It *is* perfect for him." And even more perfect will be rubbing it in his face that he was wrong and I was right.

Sarah grins and heads over toward the line for the

checkout stand, which is so long, it wraps partway around the store. "That's two presents down. No, wait, three. I forgot I got Heraldo that giant rawhide bone. I was going to wait to give it to him until Christmas, but he found it in my closet and chewed the wrapping paper off already." She hesitates, counting out the number of people she still needs to buy gifts for. "I only have four to go, unless... Do you think I should get Kat something?"

Do I think she should get something for my girlfriend who hates her guts and who actually refused to work with someone at school whose name was Sara-with-no-*h* because it was too much of a reminder? Yeah, I'm going to have to mull that over for a while.

"What did you get her?" Sarah asks.

A still from one of her favorite movies, *Vampire Aliens Attack*. It's from the best part, when the vampire aliens face off against the werewolves trying to defend the earth. But I don't tell Sarah that because I don't need her getting any ideas. "Listen, Sarah. About Kat."

"Her grandparents want her to call more. You should tell her that. I emailed her about it, but she didn't respond."

Kat's grandparents happen to live at the supervillain retirement home Sarah volunteers at. Since finding that out, she's made it her mission in life to become BFFs with them. Which has not improved the "Kat wants to kill her" situation. "I don't know how you haven't noticed this, but you and Kat? Not friends. Not even a little."

"Not yet. She's going to come around. Eventually. And a Christmas present from me might help that. As a sign of goodwill."

"It won't. Kat doesn't want to be friends with you." Kat's never been crazy about Sarah, since Sarah and I went out for, like, two seconds while me and Kat weren't together. And then Sarah broke into Kat's dad's company this fall—while she was messed up from the effects of her personality enhancer going wonky—on her mission to entrap villains, who she was sure were all criminals. Then there was Homecoming, where she actually shot Kat with a homemade shockwave gun and sent her to the ER. And there was the incident at Vilmore, where she almost destroyed a generation of villains and also tried to kill me, and I can't say any of that went over well with my supervillain girlfriend. And even though I've told Kat that Sarah wasn't herself when she did any of that, I can still see why Kat can't just shrug it off and pretend it never happened. She doesn't really know Sarah—not the *real* Sarah—and Sarah's desperate attempts to make it up to her and become her bestest friend have only made it worse.

"But," Sarah says, "that's only because she thinks I hate supervillains, and I don't."

"That's *a* reason. I wouldn't say it's the only one."

"I'm really improving on my open-mindedness, so if something happens and I go crazy again, I won't try to hurt any villains. Or you."

"Sarah, that's not going to happen." The line moves forward, like, an inch. I check the time on my phone. "It was my fault, and I've got control of my lightning power now."

The woman in front of us kind of glances over her shoulder when I say that. I see the moment of recognition in her eyes when she sees who I am, though she tries to hide it. She pretends she's being super casual as she hurries to get out her phone and starts texting someone.

"It was my invention," Sarah says. "And my biases about justice. Maybe you won't trigger a malfunction again, but something else might, and I have to be ready for it. I'm really trying to change, and to make up for what I did."

"You don't need to change. Or to make up for anything."

"But if I did, maybe Kat wouldn't hate me."

"You can't make someone like you, Sarah. And trying to force it just makes it worse. You know that."

The lady in front of us glances back again, still texting like crazy. Then the guy who's sort of in front of her, sort of to the side, notices she's focused really intently on something and looks over. His mouth actually drops open and he nudges his wife and his teenage daughter, jerking his head at me. Then they all stare.

I flash them my most cheerful smile, even though people pointing and staring at me wherever I go is getting pretty old. But at least it pays well. "Pictures are five dollars. Ten if you want to be in it, too." Twenty if they want me to make my hands go all electric, but it's too crowded in here to offer that one.

The parents turn around, looking kind of embarrassed, though their daughter's eyes light up. Offering up photo prices gets some curious looks from other people nearby, until they recognize me, and then I can see them considering it.

"Special holiday discount," I tell them, even though those are my usual prices.

Sarah rolls her eyes at me as a crowd starts to gather. People actually step out of the line to come get a picture with the Crimson Flash's infamous half-villain son. Though I'm not sure if all of them realize who I am yet, just that there's a celebrity in the store.

There's a big gap between Sarah and the rest of the line now. What would have been at least a half-hour wait is probably down to only ten minutes. She looks over at me, and I gesture for her to get going. "I'll catch up with you later."

"Okay," she says. "But if I don't see you, you'll be at my demonstration, right? I need a volunteer from the audience, and if you can't do it, I need time to figure out someone else."

Sarah's unleashing—I mean, unveiling—a new invention on the unsuspecting senior citizens at the retirement home, now that she's deemed herself "rehabilitated" and is working on projects again. I think I'd make a pretty obvious plant, what with being under eighty, but I don't have time to argue about it right now, since there's a growing crowd of people anxious to take pictures of me. And even though I'd really like to double-check that this new invention of hers isn't the exploding type, I just nod and say, "I wouldn't miss it."

I swivel back and forth in Zach's desk chair, being careful not to knock over the stack of paperbacks on the floor. They're all fantasy and sci-fi novels. Some are new, and some have yellowed pages and bent spines, but pretty much all of them are based on TV shows and video games.

"It's not fair." Zach's sitting on the edge of his bed, staring at his phone. He's looking at his mom's Facebook page, at a picture she posted earlier of her and Curtis eating pizza during her lunch break. It's a cutesy double selfie that practically screams, *Look how in love we are!* Zach's mom is grinning, squished up close with Curtis, who has a glob of tomato sauce on his nose that he either doesn't notice, or thinks is funny somehow. Ugh.

"Moms shouldn't date," I tell Zach. "And if they do... it shouldn't be with *that* guy."

"The other day, she said she had to run to the store. But she had this big smile on her face, like she was looking forward to it. And she was gone for hours. I know she was meeting Curtis."

Riley appears in the doorway, scowling at me with his arms folded. "You're sure Sarah said it was boring?"

I told him about her getting him the same DVD set earlier and that he'd better step it up. "Boring *and* pretentious. Don't forget that."

"But..." He sighs and stalks off to his room across the hall. Then I hear him typing at his computer, presumably shopping for Sarah's new Christmas present.

Zach turns off the screen to his phone, like he can't even look at his mom being happy with Curtis anymore. "He was supposed to be our dad's best friend. And best friends don't…"

"Sleep with their dead best friend's wife?"

He nods. "She says it's just casual, but it's more than that. Everyone can tell. Amelia even told me I had to bring her to their wedding. Their wedding! They'd better not get married." He makes a face.

"Or have another kid."

"*What?*" A look of pure horror washes over him.

Oops. "Er, I mean, I'm sure they won't do that." Just because my mom did doesn't mean they will.

"Curtis doesn't have any kids. And me and Riley only have a few years before we're out of school."

"Listen, Zach, just because they could get married and have a kid doesn't mean they will. Sure, it seems like things are going well now, but Curtis is a douchebag. Your mom's going to see that eventually. You said she hasn't dated since your dad died, right? So she's just using him to test the waters. It's going to get old." Hopefully.

He perks up. "You think so?"

Riley appears in the doorway again. "What do you think about a soldering iron? Sarah said she could use a new one."

"God, Perkins. Could you be any more hopeless?"

"Go away," Zach says. "Damien's hanging out with *me.* He was just about to tell me something important."

Riley glares at me, ignoring his brother. "It's a really nice soldering iron. It's a great gift."

"Yeah, for someone who *never* wants to get in her pants."

His face turns bright red and he looks away. "It's

thoughtful. Sarah will appreciate it."

I roll my eyes at him, then tell a disappointed Zach that I'll be back in a few minutes. I push past Riley and cross the hall to his room, sitting down at his computer and closing all the tabs he has open for stupid crap like low-level robotics kits and a desk organizer.

He follows me, shutting the door behind him and then coming to peer over my shoulder at the computer screen. "The soldering iron is practical, plus I know she needs a new one. She'll use it all the time."

"It's *too* practical."

"You got her socks."

"*Fun* socks. Socks she'll actually *like*. And I only got her those so I wouldn't show you up."

"Fine. I won't get her the soldering iron."

"And no desk organizers." I swivel around and give him an accusing look.

He holds up his hands. "Okay, okay. Let me think for a minute." He sits down on the edge of the bed, his forehead wrinkling in thought.

I click through a few more tabs and notice his email is open. There's a message from the League, labeled *IMPORTANT INFORMATION ABOUT YOUR SCHOLARSHIP.* I swallow. "Hey, Perkins... About what Curtis said the other night."

"He was being a jerk."

"Yeah, no kidding. But what did he mean about you having some scholarship?"

"It's from the League. I got it because of..." He takes a deep breath. "The League gives out scholarships to kids

61

who have a parent who died in service to the city. So..."
He waves his hand, trying to sum it up.

"So, because your dad died, they're paying for you to go to Heroesworth."

"Pretty much."

"And now? Curtis said you were on probation." Because Riley supposedly broke one of their stupid rules.

He stares at the floor, not looking at me. "It's not a big deal."

"Except that if you lose it, you can't go to school anymore, right?" How am I supposed to get through another year and a half of Heroesworth if he's not there and I only have idiotic douchebags to work with?

"That's not going to happen. I'm only on probation. As long as I keep my grades up, and as long as I don't break any more rules, I should be fine."

"Except you're not the one who broke a rule." He shouldn't be punished for what I did.

"According to the League, not stopping you counts."

"And you're okay with that? You think that makes any sense?"

"We were the only ones there. It's not like anybody really knows whether I could have stopped you or not."

"Uh, yeah, they *do*." I hold up my hand, making electricity wash over it in waves for a second. Riley can turn invisible. I can zap things. And he was somehow supposed to stop me? "The League really expects you to... what? Take a shot of lightning to the head to protect some murderer?"

Riley scowls. "He wasn't a murderer. That's the whole

point. We were wrong about him. Heroes out in the field could be wrong about the criminals they're chasing, too. And they're—*we're*—not supposed to let other heroes hurt unarmed citizens. That rule is there to protect people."

"From *League members*." Because even they know that signing some stupid piece of paper doesn't really mean they can be trusted.

"Everyone makes mistakes. And you know what happened to Sarah, and she would never hurt anyone."

I don't agree with that, but I get what he's saying. "That wasn't her mistake. It was mine." If I hadn't accidentally zapped her stupid personality enhancer, she never would have gone on some crazy villain-hating spree. "Just like this was."

Riley rolls his eyes at me. "Come on, X. Don't be like that. You didn't know."

But even if I had, that wouldn't have changed anything. "And what if I screw up again and get you in more trouble?"

"You won't. And you wouldn't have this time if you'd just *listened* to me."

"But if I do, you basically get kicked out of school." Which means no joining the League, which is, like, his whole future.

"So don't break the rules." He makes that sound so simple.

"Yeah, but—"

"No *buts*. You're my friend, and we were *owning* that class. We make a good team. You messing up once doesn't change that, so just shut up about it."

"But—"

"Seriously, X. I mean it. It's not like you're going to make the same mistake. Everything's going to be fine."

Except it wasn't a mistake. I mean, assuming the situation had been real, like we thought it was. And that was a rule I actually *knew* about. What happens when I break one on accident?

But Riley's smiling at me like he doesn't care that I screwed up, because we really do make a good team. I messed up and got him in trouble, and he's still my friend, and he still wants to work with me. So I smile back and say, "Yeah, you're right. Everything's going to be fine." Even if I don't really believe it.

## X·X·X

"Damien." Gordon walks into the living room later that evening, waving a brochure. Only *walks* might not be the right word. It's more like he's trying not to stomp.

I stop doing my homework and set down my binder next to me on the couch, giving him my full attention. "What's wrong, Dad? You sound like something's bothering you."

He scowls. "I found this in my desk."

"Oh?" I say that all innocent, like I don't know what he's talking about. And no, it's not the same brochure I found. It's not the one about sending superpowered kids to some camp that's not-so-secretly an asylum.

"Did you make this?" He holds the brochure out to me. It's glossy, full color—really professional looking. So I'm not sure why he thinks I made it. Well, other than the picture of him I used for the photo on the front.

In the picture, he's standing there in his Crimson Flash outfit, with his red cape billowing out behind him. On the top of the brochure, it says, *If you've got severe bowel problems made worse by your superpowers, don't worry— you're not alone. And at the Super Sanitarium, we're here to help.*

I raise an eyebrow at him. "I think you need to be more selective about which companies you agree to be a spokesperson for. Unless you really do have severe bowel problems. I mean, don't sell people false hope."

He glares at me. I can hear his teeth grinding. "Let me put it another way. I *know* you made this brochure. Now I want to know why."

"I don't know what you're talking about."

"Damien."

"I just hope you're getting the help you need at this place."

He takes a deep breath. "Is this because of the... If you have a problem, you need to come to me and talk about it. Instead of attempting to punish me for it."

*Attempting?* "So you're saying you don't feel like you've learned your lesson?" I pick up my binder and write that down, shaking my head.

"*No.* That's not what I..." He clears his throat. "You found the brochure I brought home, didn't you?"

"Yeah. Thanks for coming to *me* when you had a problem. Instead of, you know, going behind my back and making plans to have me committed."

He sighs and sits next to me. "I was only thinking about it."

"*What?!*"

"About suggesting therapy. That's all. I thought it might help."

"Help with what?"

He looks away. "To help you make better decisions for yourself."

If anyone here needs to make better decisions for themselves, he just proved it's him. "I don't need help making decisions. But even if I did, aren't you supposed to teach me that? As a parent, I mean. I guess parenting's just not for you, huh?"

"My job is to make sure you learn how to make the right choices, and if I can't get through to you about it, then that means finding another way."

"Okay, then there's no reason to send me to that place, because, lucky for you, I already *am* making the right choices. Your job is pretty much done." When he just sits there, scowling at me, I add, "You should be happy about that."

"Doing what's right isn't about doing whatever you want, regardless of the consequences."

"I *wasn't.*"

"You broke the rules, on purpose. You attacked an unarmed man. And you don't think there was anything wrong with that. Now, I understand wanting to protect those kids, but you need to learn when it's okay to use your power and when it's not."

"Let me guess. The times when I'm supposed to use it

are... never?"

"You shouldn't think it's okay to use it on people."

Wow. He's seriously telling me what I should *think*? And he makes it sound like I go around zapping everyone I see. "Uh-huh. And before you say you think I'm crazy and need to take a semester off to 'rediscover myself' in group therapy, let me ask you this. Do you want the whole city to see that brochure with you on the cover? Because don't think that's my only copy."

"I don't think you're crazy. And I'm not sending you to therapy."

Good, because high-quality color prints don't come cheap. "Too expensive?"

"It wasn't the right choice. I want to get through to you, but I realize replacing one institution with another and inflicting more rules on you isn't the way to do it."

"*And* you were afraid I'd zap them all and you wouldn't get a refund when I got kicked out. It's okay—you can admit it."

He shakes his head, then claps me on the shoulder before getting up. "Just come to me next time you have a problem, all right? And, please, consider your decisions before you act on them. Villainy might be about doing whatever you want, but being a hero is about following the rules."

# CHAPTER 5

I get one of Mom's guests to take a picture of me and Zach under all the sparkling icicle lights and real boughs of holly, in front of a ten-foot-tall Christmas tree at the wedding. We're both wearing black tuxes with green accents. Just like Mom wanted, since all the guests are supposed to dress up in red and green for her perfect Christmas wedding.

"I'm Marianna's son," I tell the wedding guest as she hands me my phone back. She's got gray hair and a red velvety dress that makes her look kind of like a Christmas stocking. I think she's one of Taylor's aunts, though I don't know which one.

"Her son?" she says, glancing across the room at where my mom is pretending to dance with Xavier, as if that will somehow confirm what I'm saying.

"Her other son. You might have seen me on the news. And this is my good friend, Zach."

"His *hero* friend," Zach adds, holding out his hand to

shake with her.

She doesn't take it. Her eyes dart to his thumb, even though the lighting in here is too dim to actually tell whether he has an *H* or not.

"He's only fifteen," I tell her, meaning he's not old enough to have his letter yet. "I like them young."

"Oh. That's…" She looks around, maybe hoping to spot someone she knows so she can get away. "I really have to… go. But it was very, um, nice meeting you."

"Actually," I say, before she can run off, "can you do me a favor? Another one, I mean. Can you tell my mom you saw us here? I'm not allowed to talk to her."

Her forehead wrinkles and her mouth drops open a little. Instead of answering me, she acts like she didn't hear and disappears off into the crowd.

The lighting in the picture she took of me and Zach isn't great, but you can definitely tell it's us. I post it to Facebook and write, *On another date with your boyfriend*, tagging Amelia so I'm sure she'll see it.

"You didn't tell me you had another brother," Zach says. He means besides Alex.

*That's because I wish he didn't exist.* I shrug. "He's the all-villain son Mom wished she'd had instead of me. She didn't even get pregnant with him until after she kicked me out, but she fed him some growth formula she invented, so now he's way older than he should be. It's like she just can't wait to replace me. We… don't exactly get along."

"Oh." Zach chews his lip, thinking that over.

"Uh-oh." I catch sight of Mom making her way over

here. The bright red hair and the huge white dress are kind of a giveaway. "That's my mom. You know what to do." I glance around, but Zach's already gone invisible. He and Riley both have the same power, and most of the time it seems pretty lame, but once in a while it comes in handy.

"Damien." Mom has this big fake smile plastered all over her face, and she says my name through gritted teeth. Her hair is done up in this twisty shape on top of her head, with some curly strands left loose to hang next to her face. Her dress is stark white and has tons of tiny, sparkly snowflake beads sewn onto it. She's left Xavier behind to come talk to me. "What are you doing?"

"I don't know what you're talking about. I'm here, staying away from Xavier, just like you said."

"You know that's not what I mean. I've been hearing that you're here *with* someone."

"Yeah, you knew I was bringing a date."

"Someone who's not Kat." She looks down her nose at me, even though I'm taller than her.

"Kat's on a ski trip. She couldn't make it."

"So you brought someone else."

"I didn't want to mess up your plate count. Why, is there a problem?" I grin at her.

She folds her arms, the fake smile melting into a scowl. "You said you would behave. At *my* wedding."

She says that as if I might have a dozen weddings to go to and can't remember which ones I promised to behave at. "How am I not behaving? Unless…" I put a hand to my chest and pretend to be shocked. "You don't have a problem with me bringing a *guy* as my date, do you?"

"*Damien.*"

"Wow, Mom. For a woman who's had two kids out of wedlock, each with different fathers, you'd think you'd be more open-minded."

She narrows her eyes at me. The snowflakes on her dress sparkle in the white icicle lights. "That's not it. I know you're with Kat."

"So you're only okay with it because you know I have a girlfriend? Way to be socially conscious."

"That's not what this is about."

"Really? Because you obviously have a problem with me bringing him, and I don't know what else about him could possibly be bothering you." I tap my chin, pretending to think that over.

"Don't act like you don't know what I'm getting at."

I gasp. "Is it that he's a *hero*?"

"When I said not to upset your brother, I assumed you wouldn't also be trying to upset *me*."

She should really know me better than that by now. "Is there something upsetting about having hero genes? I didn't think it would be a problem, since I'm half hero, and having me, your firstborn son, at your wedding doesn't bother you, does it? There's nothing inherently offensive about me existing, is there? Or is it that your guests think I might be sleeping with him? Because we all know how offensive a villain sleeping with a hero would be."

Her face and part of her neck turn an angry red. "I told you not to cause a scene."

"How am I causing a scene? You're the one who came over here to harass me about my date. I was minding my own business. It's not my fault if you invited a bunch of narrow-minded people who have a problem with non-traditional couples."

There's a high-pitched squeal, and then a screech of "Moooommmmmyyyy!" Xavier comes running over, looking like he's about to cry from being away from her for more than two seconds. His hair—which is the same bright red as hers—has been gelled down so much, it looks like plastic doll hair. He grabs her arm, more like a toddler would than an eight-year-old, at least until he spots me. Then he launches himself toward me, throwing his arms around my waist and practically knocking me over. "Damien!"

I don't hug him back. I know this is where I'm supposed to, because he's a little kid and he's my brother, and if it was Alex or Jess glomping onto me right now, I wouldn't even have to think about it. But it's Xavier, my replacement, and it's kind of all I can do not to push him away.

Zach reappears next to me, giving me a curious look as he watches me standing there awkwardly. "This is your brother?"

Xavier steps back, leaving a smear of snot on my jacket, and scowls at Zach. "Who's this?" He has a screechy, demanding voice that reminds me of nails on a chalkboard.

Zach smiles and waves at Xavier. "Hi, I'm Zach. Damien's friend."

Xavier ignores him and says, "Mom, tell him to stop *looking* at me."

"Xavier, sweetie," Mom says—and I feel a twinge of jealousy when she calls him that—"that's not how we talk to our friends, remember?"

"But he's *not* my friend. And you told me Damien wasn't going to be here!"

I raise an accusing eyebrow at her. I guess she figured it would be too hard to keep Xavier from seeking me out if he knew I was here.

"Well, that's... he surprised me," Mom says, putting a hand on Xavier's shoulder and drawing him closer to her. "I didn't know."

Xavier wipes his nose on the back of his hand. "He was supposed to be my best man."

"Ring bearers don't have best mans, sweetie."

He looks at her like she's insane. "I could have had one, if I wanted. It's my wedding, too." Then he turns to me and says, "Grandpa was looking for you. So was Grandma, but Mommy said you weren't here."

A cold, sick feeling spreads through my stomach when he talks about my grandparents. *Our* grandparents. I've talked to them on the phone a couple times over the past few months, but I haven't seen them in person in about a year. And it's bad enough that Mom lied to Xavier about me not being here, but to them, too? I glare at her. "Wow, I guess I really should have RSVP'd, huh?"

"I'm staying at their house tonight," Xavier says. "Maybe you could stay over, too. I'm Grandma's favorite person in the whole world, so she'll make cookies whenever I tell her to."

"Great." I've been their grandson for almost seventeen years, but I haven't even seen them since last Christmas. And now Xavier's staying over at their house and is my grandma's favorite person. Right.

He picks up on my sarcasm and tilts his head at me, like he can't figure out why I would have said that that way. "Why don't you want to go there with me? It won't be perfect unless you go, so you *have* to. Mom, tell him he *has* to." His voice gets extra whiny when he says that.

"*Damien*," Mom says through gritted teeth, as if this is my fault.

Zach exchanges a look with me, like maybe now he can see why I'm not crazy about Xavier.

Xavier watches us, unable to interpret what's going on. His eyes water and his chest starts heaving in and out as he takes deep breaths. "Stop it! Stop being mean! You're *my* brother, and you have to come to *my* grandparents' house with me if I tell you to!"

*His* grandparents' house? Little flickers of lightning run along my back, but I keep it under control. And I think I keep my voice pretty calm when I say, "I don't *have* to do anything."

Mom puts an arm around Xavier and starts petting his hair, even though it's so plastered down it's basically a shell. She whispers something soothing to him, then glares at me from behind his back and says, "Damien. You *promised*. Tell your brother you'll spend time with him."

I promised I'd stay away from him, not have a sleepover. It's kind of the opposite.

"Oh, look, someone I know," I say, spotting Kat's parents over at the refreshments table. Normally I wouldn't go out of my way to talk to them—well, to her dad, anyway—but given the circumstances, I'd rather be talking to *anyone* except Mom and Xavier. "Come on, Zach." I grab his arm and pull him along.

"Damien!" Mom scolds. "This isn't what we talked about."

I ignore her and walk away a little faster.

"So that's your brother?" Zach says.

"Yeah. You want to trade?" As if I would ever do something that awful to Zach.

He makes a face. "You don't really think my mom will have another kid, do you? Because, I mean, that's what people do, isn't it? They get married and have another kid." He swallows, looking pretty disgusted with that idea.

Which is understandable, since Curtis is a douchebag and couldn't help but have douchebag offspring. "I didn't think my mom would. She wasn't even going to *tell* me I had a new brother. But that doesn't mean your mom will."

We get to the refreshments table. Kat's Mom sees me and smiles, waving us over. She has a small plate in one hand with carrot sticks and some tiny sandwiches on it. "Oh, Damien—there you are! Your mother told us you weren't here."

"She's pretending I don't exist." I smile at them, as if I didn't just say my own mom is purposely lying to everyone about me even being at her wedding.

Kat's dad pulls his cell phone away from his ear, stuffing it in his pocket. "I was just calling Kat. To see how she's doing on the trip." He looks me up and down suspiciously.

And I think we both know he was calling her to see if I was there, holing up with her and sharing her bed for a week, because Mom said I wasn't around. "This is my friend, Zach. He's my date, since Kat couldn't be here."

"Hi," Zach says.

Kat's dad gets this self-satisfied smile on his face. "She said she's having the time of her life."

Great. "She's just saying that so you won't worry." She's probably devastated without me.

"She's there with all her friends. Her *villain* friends. Having fun." There's an unspoken *without you* at the end of that sentence.

"It's only a week. I could have gone, but I had to be here. For the wedding."

He gives me a really skeptical look. "Did you? Your mother didn't even know you were here."

"*Tom.*" Kat's mom glares at him, like she can't believe he said that.

I clench my jaw. "Kat and I are fine. I don't need to go on vacation with her."

"Right," he says. "You keep telling yourself that." He claps me on the shoulder.

I take a step back. "Well, this was *so great*, catching up with you, but I have other guests to see. Come on, Zach."

"It was nice meeting you," Zach says to them—even though I'm pretty sure it wasn't—before hurrying after me into the crowd.

As soon as I'm far enough away that I don't think her

dad can see me, I get out my phone to call Kat.

"He was probably just being a jerk," Zach says. "Kat wouldn't have the time of her life without you, right?"

"Of course not."

Unless she was on some awesome vacation with all her friends and I stayed behind like an idiot.

Her phone goes straight to voicemail—she probably turned it off in case her dad called her again. I'm considering leaving a message when a familiar gruff voice behind me says, "There you are. We've been looking for you all night."

I look up and see my grandparents for the first time in about a year.

Grandpa comes up to me like he's going to hug me, then reaches over and zaps me behind the ear with his finger.

"*Ow.*" I glare at him.

"Still got it," he says, laughing to himself.

My grandma hugs me for reals. She smells like lavender and lemons, and she's dyed her hair cotton-candy pink. The last time I saw her, it was dark blue. She says she was an attention-getting redhead her entire life, and she's not about to let a little thing like her hair turning gray stop her from turning heads. "What do you think?" She moves her head from side to side.

"Very cool. Though I'm surprised you didn't dye it red and green to match Mom's colors."

"It's good for your mother to not get everything she wants. Who's this?" She nods at Zach.

"I'm Zach," he says. "Damien's friend. He goes to

school with my brother."

"Your *friend*, huh?" Grandpa says, looking Zach over. "What happened to that Katherine girl you were seeing?"

"Nothing. I'm still with Kat. She just, uh, couldn't be here."

"You can tell us the truth," Grandma says, leaning in close. "I've known a few boys who were 'just friends' in my day. But maybe you keep that Kat girl around, too? We want to have great grandchildren. I'm not saying we want them *now,* obviously. That Xavier's enough of a handful as it is. But don't go burning any bridges. Maybe you and Kat get back together someday, and then you knock her up and come back to this handsome guy here, eh?"

"Wow, that's, um, really great advice." And by that I mean it's the worst advice I've ever heard. "But me and Kat are still together. Really."

"Well, all right, then." She sounds almost disappointed that I won't be putting her crazy plan into action.

"You should come over some time," Grandpa says. "If that so-called father of yours will let you. And if he won't, I've got a thing or two to say to him." He pounds one fist into his open palm, electricity washing over both of them.

Zach stares at him, his mouth hanging open and his eyes going wide in complete adoration. "That is *so cool.*"

"I don't need my dad's permission to go to your house," I tell them. "And he *is* my dad." Whether they like it or not.

"You want to see something really cool?" Grandpa asks Zach, acting like he didn't hear me.

"*Yes.* Damien never wants to show me his lightning

power."

Grandpa holds both hands out, palm up, and makes electricity arc between them, like an electric rainbow that touches down on each hand. He moves his hands farther apart, then closer together, the arc moving with them. Then he claps his hands together and the lightning disappears.

"Whoa." Zach glances over at me, as if he's wondering if I saw that, and also like he's maybe wondering why I never do anything that awesome.

Grandpa cracks his knuckles. "It's all in the wrist."

"We saw you on TV," Grandma says.

Who didn't? "Don't tell me. You think I shouldn't have made a spectacle of myself."

She looks at me like I'm insane and puts a hand on her hip. "Honey, you know my philosophy. What's the point of doing *anything* if you're not going to make a spectacle of yourself?"

Grandpa puts a hand on my shoulder, steering me a little ways away, then glances around, as if he's making sure no one's listening. "Should have finished him off."

Well, that's a first. "He wasn't really a kidnapper."

"He was a superhero. Trying to teach you how to hunt down your own kind, isn't that right?"

"That's not— I mean, sort of." I sigh and shove my hands into my pockets. "I'm half hero, too, you know. And I've told you before, I *want* to go to Heroesworth."

He makes a grunting noise that's part acknowledgment, part skepticism. "They punish you for what you did?"

"I broke the rules, so, yeah. But I still passed the class,

and—"

"And you believe in these rules, do you?"

I glance away. "I'm not joining the League, if that's what you mean."

"And if that kidnapper had been a villain, they would have given you a pat on the back for it. Because a villain, now, he's dangerous. I've been around the block more than a few times. Been on a few of the League's wanted lists. I know how this works. And now they've got you hunting down villains." He shakes his head in disgust, and I think if we weren't at a wedding, he might actually spit.

"It was staged."

"This time. But I've been hearing things, like that my grandson's been getting in everyone's way. For that damn school of yours."

"I've only been on a few missions. It can't be *everyone.*" I scuff the bottom of my dress shoe against the floor. "And anyway, it's not like I knew any of them."

"Not yet. But sooner or later, you're going to run into someone on our side that isn't just a random face."

"You mean like *Mom*? Like when she almost got me and all my friends killed in some stupid attempt to take over the city?!"

"I find it interesting that it was this superhero you zapped and not any of the others. Any of the *villains.*"

"I didn't know he was a superhero."

Grandpa sort of half shrugs at that, as if he doesn't believe me. "You might think you don't have a choice, that you have to pretend to be one of them. But you don't."

"I'm not pretending."

He snorts. "Well, you're deluding yourself, then."

"This is my life now. It just is. It doesn't matter if you don't like it."

"All right," he says, still sounding skeptical. "But that school isn't looking out for you. You're just as expendable to them as any other villain. And when you go too far one of these days, when you piss off the wrong people, I'm not going to be able to smooth it over. And that school of yours, those heroes you know, they're not going to stand up for you. So you be careful, all right?"

"Yeah, sure."

"I mean it." He wraps an arm around my shoulders and hugs me. "I wouldn't want anything to happen to my favorite grandson."

## X·X·X

Mom has this long banquet table set up for her and the rest of the wedding party, so she can face her entourage of guests while we eat dinner. There's even a lighting scheme directed at her to maximize the sparkle of her dress. Taylor's sitting on her left and Xavier's on her right. He keeps pawing at her, trying to climb over onto her lap, even though he's way too big for that. She laughs nervously and sits him back down in his chair, whispering something in his ear that only makes him frown.

Me and Zach are sitting at one of the small round tables scattered throughout the reception hall. Unfortunately, there's assigned seating, and since I was supposed to be here with Kat, that means we're sitting with her parents. I poke my fork at the sliced turkey on my plate. Mom decided to go with a "Christmas dinner" theme, so it was turkey or ham. Both options came with mashed potatoes and gravy, a side of cranberries, and some green beans. There's also a basket of rolls on our table. It's actually pretty good, though that doesn't mean I'm not counting down the minutes until we can get out of here. Dinner, then cake, then leave.

Technically, we could leave right now. But that would be leaving early, and I'm not giving Mom the satisfaction. But I figure anytime after they serve the cake is fair game.

"So, Damien," Kat's mom says, "how is, um... How are things at school?" She sounds a little worried, and I figure she must have seen the news. Or Kat told her about it.

Kat's dad raises his eyebrows at me, as if he's curious to know the answer, too.

"School's over. I passed all my classes." I shrug. My grades aren't as good as Kat's, especially since I botched my Intro to Heroism final, but they're not too bad.

"I guess you were serious about not wanting to join the League," Kat's dad says, meaning because I zapped that guy.

"For the millionth time, I *didn't* know he was a superhero. But yeah, I was serious about that." I glance over at Zach, to see his reaction, since I know he plans to join the League someday.

Just like Riley and all the other heroes I know.

Zach's watching the conversation while shoving a forkful of ham and mashed potatoes into his mouth, but he doesn't give any signs of being offended or anything. I mean, it's not like I've made it a secret that I'm not joining.

Kat's dad gives me a stern look. "But you're out there learning how to capture villains."

"*Criminals*. I'm learning how to catch criminals. They could be anybody."

He waves that away. "That's not what I'm getting at. What I mean is that you're already doing the League's bidding. And from what Kat has told me, it doesn't sound like you can be a professional hero if you don't join. So what I don't understand is what kind of career you think you're going to have. You're already committing the crime, so to speak. It seems like refusing to join is shooting yourself in the foot."

Kat's mom touches his arm. "I'm sure Damien has other plans. There must be other career options." She gives me a questioning look.

"Yeah. I..." I turn to Zach, as if he might have the answers.

"You could be on TV like your dad," he says.

No way in hell. Well, the TV part I don't have a problem with. It's the being on TV *like my dad* that's the issue. "Zach, if I ever have the desire to dress up in a bright red cape and teach safety to kids on television, I give you permission to have me committed. In fact, I kind of insist on it." Besides, my dad only has that show because of his work in the League.

Kat's dad opens his mouth, like he's going to say something else, but then someone clinks a glass, drawing everyone's attention to the banquet table.

Taylor's best man, a guy who's been his BFF ever since they roomed together when they were students at Vilmore, is holding up a champagne glass. "I'd like to propose a toast to the newlyweds! I've known Taylor for over twenty years, but I've never seen him as happy as he is today."

Mom and Taylor both have huge smiles on their faces. A couple people in the crowd make *aww* noises, and everyone raises their glasses in a toast. Mom clinks her glass of red wine against Taylor's—I guess champagne wasn't good enough for them—and then Xavier forcefully climbs onto her lap, bonking into the glass and making her spill it. All down the front of her white wedding dress.

A gasp of horror runs through the room. Mom's mouth hangs open as she stares down at herself.

"You should have let me sit with you," Xavier says in his demanding, screechy voice, only this time he doesn't just sound demanding, but spiteful. "You deserved it."

An angry scowl I recognize all too well spreads across Mom's face. The lasers in her eyes flash, though she manages to keep them in check. She grabs Xavier's arm and pushes him down into his own chair, which starts him screaming bloody murder. His face turns bright red, and he shrieks and shrieks, threatening to burst everyone's eardrums.

Everyone's gaping at Mom and Xavier, even her wedding party. The best man's eyes are wide, and he looks pretty horrified, like maybe he spoke too soon about Taylor being happy. Grandma, who's Mom's matron of honor, shakes her head and rolls her eyes, sharing a knowing look with Grandpa. Which I'm pretty sure means Xavier *isn't* her favorite person in the whole world.

Not that I'm keeping track or anything.

Taylor quickly stands and takes Xavier's hand, trying to lead him away from the banquet table. Mom's staring at all her guests in shock, her face almost as red as Xavier's, as if this just might be the most embarrassing moment of her life.

The most embarrassing moment of her life that I'd like to point out *was not my fault.*

I didn't ruin her wedding.

Precious Xavier did.

Xavier's fighting against Taylor, now kicking and screaming. One of his wild kicks hits Mom in the side, hard, and she cries out. Or at least I think she does, because it's still hard to hear over Xavier. But the kick seems to bring her to her senses, and she gets up and helps Taylor grab their awful son and drag him out of the room, into the hall, where Xavier's screams are at least muffled.

The silence in the reception hall is super awkward. A couple people cough. Everyone at the banquet table still looks stricken, like they can't believe that just happened, except for my grandparents, who look like they've seen it all before.

There are murmurs running through the crowd, and I catch the words *embarrassing, awful,* and *ruined,* to name a few.

And then some idiot stands up and clinks his glass with his fork, and that idiot is me. And I have to admit that part of me wants to just let Mom's wedding be ruined, because she made such a big deal about it, and because she was so sure I was going to be the one to screw it up. But letting it stay ruined just for spite would make me as bad as Xavier—well, almost—plus I want everyone here to see what a charming, amazing older son Mom has. One who is obviously way better than his replacement.

This is where I'm supposed to say something brilliant about my mom that makes everyone forget what just happened and that the wedding might be sort of ruined. Everyone's looking at me, because I clinked my glass for a toast, and they're waiting for me to say something.

I clear my throat. "My mom is..." I glance over at the door to the hall, where she and her "little family" ran off to deal with Xavier. "I mean, I'm her son—her *other* son that you probably don't know about—and I just wanted to say..." To say what? Toasts are supposed to be positive, right? I'm not sure how many positive things I have to say about her. "She's, um, she's a great..." The word *mom* sticks in my throat. "...scientist. And, I mean, she... I lived with her, for sixteen years, and when Taylor proposed, I wasn't very happy about it."

Everyone is still staring at me, only now like they're kind of worried *both* her sons are a little unstable. The best man and one of the bridesmaids look like they're considering whether or not to stop me before I say something awful and *really* ruin the wedding. Mom must have warned them about me.

"But," I add, "now..." Now I'm still not happy about it. And I kind of wish I'd stayed seated and kept my mouth shut. I could still be eating dinner right now instead of realizing I have nothing good to say about my own mother at her wedding. And I know I should just lie and say something nice and meaningless and get this over with, but I can't. I can't even think of a fake compliment for her.

I'm silent for what feels like forever, still struggling to find something to say. Then Zach stands up beside me and comes to my rescue. "But now you're really happy for them," he says. "Because they make such a good couple."

"Right. And, um..."

"*And* you've probably never seen her so happy, right? I know I haven't." That gets some smiles from the audience, even though Zach's only ever seen her today. But they don't have to know that. "And they've got their whole lives ahead of them, and it's so great that they're going to get to be together for that."

"Yeah. That."

"So let's toast." He raises his glass. "To your mom and your new stepfather. Who are going to have lots of awesome years together."

We clink our glasses, followed by everyone else, so that the whole reception hall fills with the sounds of tinkling glass. There are some *awws* and a *What a cute couple*, that I think are meant for me and Zach. People are smiling and eating and chatting again like nothing bad happened. There's still some muffled whining coming from the hallway, but no one's paying attention to it.

I slump back down in my seat at the table, realizing I'm probably the last person who should have stood up to toast them. But at least it's over now.

# CHAPTER 6

Sarah smiles nervously as she stands in front of the rec room at the retirement home before her demonstration starts. She's got several rows of chairs set up, though there are so many people from the actual retirement home here for this thing that me and Kat and Riley have to stand off to the side. Almost everyone seems to actually know Sarah, and more than one person offers her a few words of encouragement before finding a seat. I figured there would be at least an okay crowd for this, since there's probably not that much to do around here, but I wasn't expecting it to be standing room only.

"We're so proud," Kat's grandma says, standing next to us and beaming across the room at Sarah.

Kat looks like she's going to barf. "Proud of what? That she hasn't murdered everyone here?"

Riley shuffles his feet and leans against the wall. "She's never actually murdered anyone. And she doesn't hate supervillains." Though he looks like he kind of does, what with the way he keeps glancing over his shoulder and checking the time on his phone. If I didn't know better, I'd think being in a room full of supervillains—ones who probably don't have that great of control over their powers and who probably also really hate superheroes—was making him nervous.

Kat's grandma clucks her tongue, as if Kat's being crazy unreasonable. "Sarah's a lovely girl. Jerry and I have spent so much time with her these past couple months, it feels like she's part of the family."

So much so that she even sewed her a homemade Christmas stocking, which Kat was livid about. Apparently she only makes them for family members and really close friends. Everyone in Kat's family has a personalized stocking from her, and it's a big deal. And now Sarah has one, too.

"And," Kat's grandma goes on, "I haven't seen you around here in months. Sarah's here several times a week."

Kat gapes at her. She's too stunned to speak at first. And then Sarah calls for everyone to sit down because it's time for the demonstration, and Kat's grandma hurries off to her saved seat.

"I have school," Kat finally says. "I don't even live in the city. She knows that."

I squeeze her hand. "And you have an amazing boyfriend you can't help wanting to spend all your free time with. It's not your fault if other people don't have that."

"*Hey*," Riley says, scowling at me.

"What? I said *other people*. I didn't say Sarah. I don't know why you'd assume that, unless you think you're not an amazing boyfriend and that she doesn't want to spend time with you."

"Grandma kicked me out last time I was here," Kat says. "She told me I didn't have a good enough poker face to play with them. She said she could always tell what my cards were. It was really mean."

"What, and she didn't want your money?"

"She said I was making her look bad."

To be fair, her grandma's right—Kat doesn't have a very good poker face. But last I checked, that wasn't a requirement for being someone's grandkid. Not being the illegitimate offspring of a random hookup between your superhero dad and a supervillain, on the other hand, *is* apparently a requirement, since Gordon's parents refused to even come to Thanksgiving because I was going to be there. They didn't say that, exactly—they made up some excuse about going to see some relatives across the country—but it's not like we didn't all know the reason. Well, except for Jess, since she's three, and Alex, since he thinks I'm too awesome to ever even consider that his—I mean, "our"—grandparents might not want to see me. And even though they're not going anywhere for Christmas, they've made it really clear that they've only got presents for Amelia, Alex, and Jess, and that they're the only ones they want coming over for the family get-together, other than Gordon and Helen, of course. Which, I can't help but notice, just leaves me.

"Okay," Sarah says at the front of the room,

commanding everyone's attention. "If you look at your programs"—she holds up a bright orange flier—"you'll see that first off, I'm going to tell you a little bit about my invention. Then I'm going to demonstrate it."

"She made programs?" I whisper to Riley. "I thought this was only going to take a couple minutes."

"She just wants to do a good job."

Sarah clears her throat. "There have been problems lately with residents losing control of their superpowers."

I notice Riley glance around, like he's afraid someone might actually lose control right now and kill him.

"The specialized safety walls might protect others from these accidental attacks, but the person who loses control isn't so lucky. Even if someone is immune to their own power, that's only while they're using it, and only if secondary effects like fire or smoke inhalation don't get them. And if they get tired or lose consciousness, then they're in trouble. You all remember what happened to Edna." A knowing murmur runs through the crowd, and Sarah bows her head in a moment of silence.

Kat gives me this look while everyone's eyes are closed and mouths *What the hell?*

I shrug, since this is the first I'm hearing about it. I mouth back *Not her fault.* Probably not, anyway.

"So, to address the problem," Sarah says, when the moment of silence is over, "I made this." She holds up what looks like some kind of rubber sports watch. A homemade one, but still, there aren't even any wires sticking out of it. She must really care what these people think, because she's apparently gone all out. "It simply detects when the wearer releases any kind of superpower energy and sends out an alert to the nurses. This way, if someone has an accident, it doesn't have to be deadly. And I made it out of the same substance used in the walls, so the device itself is superpower resistant."

Kat bites her lip, her forehead creasing, like maybe she thinks that actually *is* a good idea and is annoyed that Sarah thought of it.

"Now for a quick demonstration," Sarah says. "I just need a volunteer from the audience." There's a pause, and then several hands go up. She ignores them, jerking her head toward me. "I said, I need a *volunteer*."

Oh, right. Me. I raise my hand.

Sarah smiles and points to me. "You. The young fellow in the blue sweatshirt."

Young fellow? I think she's officially been spending way too much time in this place. I start to go up to the front of the room, but Kat grabs my arm.

"Seriously? You're volunteering for this?"

"I'm a plant," I say out the side of my mouth, trying to keep quiet about it. Not that it really matters.

Kat apparently doesn't care if anyone hears her, though, because she says, really loudly, "Are you crazy? She almost *killed you* with her last invention!"

Sarah's face goes red. There's some more muttering from the audience, and all eyes are on either her or us.

"I told you," I start to say, "that wasn't—"

Kat cuts me off. "It wasn't really her. I *know*. But why can't he do it?" She points to Riley. "He's her boyfriend. If it's not dangerous, then why isn't he her test subject?"

"I need a supervillain," Sarah says. "Renegade—er, Damien's—power is more suited to my purpose. No one's going to invisible themselves to death. Sorry, Riley," she adds, as if he might be offended that his power won't accidentally kill him.

"No problem." He waves it off.

"See," I tell Kat. "It's not dangerous. It doesn't even explode." Well, I hope not. I still haven't had a chance to ask her about that.

"I don't care. You're not doing it." Kat hooks her arm around mine with no intent to let go. She tells Sarah, through clenched teeth, *"Find someone else."*

Then someone in the audience says, "I'll do it," and makes his way to the front before anyone can protest. It's Kat's grandfather.

"Thanks, Jerry," Sarah mutters, quickly glancing over at Kat, then away again.

"No," Kat says. "Someone else can—"

"Don't be ridiculous," her grandfather says. "It's just an alert bracelet."

Sarah straps it to his wrist and then stands back. "Okay. Now just use your power, and it will take care of the rest. For anyone who doesn't know," she tells the audience, "Jerry's ability is fire. So it's a good one to demonstrate with, because this is exactly the kind of situation I'm worried about. Someone with a dangerous power accidentally using it and then getting trapped in their room. Everyone else would be okay, because of the safety walls, but no one would even know the person inside needed help. Not until it was too late."

Kat's grandpa holds up his arm, inspecting the alert bracelet or whatever it is. "What do you want me to light on fire?"

"Nothing right now," Sarah says, as if that was a completely normal question. "Just make some flames."

Kat clutches my arm tighter, obviously not liking this one bit.

Her grandpa makes fire come to life in his hands. As soon as he does, the watch face lights up and starts blinking and making a loud warning noise. A noise that's echoed down the hall in the nurses' station.

It's hard to hear, because the alarms are so loud, but I think Sarah says, "Oh, good, it works."

Some people from the audience start clapping, like they don't know what else to do, and the rest cover their ears.

"All right," Sarah says, practically shouting to be heard above the alarms. "You can stop now."

Kat's grandpa stares at his hands, which are still covered in flames.

"You can turn your power off now!" she says again, louder this time, as if he just didn't hear her.

"I'm trying! It's— This thing won't let me! How are you supposed to stop it?" It might just be me, but it looks like the flames in his hands are getting higher. And I'm not an expert or anything, since I'm still not sure if exploding is on its list of possible actions, but I don't think Sarah's gadget is supposed to keep people from turning off their powers. Or whatever it's doing.

"You push the button!"

"What button?"

Sarah reaches over and presses something on the side of the watch thingy. It doesn't turn off. Her eyebrows come together and she starts to look worried.

"I can't make it stop," Kat's grandpa says. The flames in his hands are definitely getting higher now. "I'm losing control!"

"Oh, great," Riley mutters, as if he knew all along something like this would happen.

The flames blast out of Jerry's hands and start spreading across the floor.

Sarah has to step back, unable to keep messing with the device to turn it off, on account of her volunteer being on fire.

"I'm fine," Jerry assures everyone, not sounding completely convincing. "No need to worry." That's great for him and all, since he's immune to his own power, but the rest of us aren't exactly fireproof. In fact, some of the audience members have started evacuating.

Riley swears and gets out his phone, presumably to call 911. Again.

"I don't understand!" Sarah clutches at her hair. "I don't know what went wrong—the device isn't supposed to mess with anyone's powers, just trigger the alarm."

Kat glares at her, like this is all her fault, which I guess it kind of is. "It wasn't enough for you to try and kill my boyfriend—you have to try and kill my grandpa, too?"

"I didn't—"

"Do something!"

Sarah glances around the room for a solution. Then she sucks in her breath and points at the ceiling. "Renegade, zap the sprinklers!"

Kat scowls at Sarah using my superhero name.

"Got it, Cosine!" I say her sidekick name out of habit, before I have a chance to realize that it might piss off Kat even further. It probably does, but I have more important things to worry about.

I zap one of the metal sprinkler heads, and then *another* alarm goes off, this one even more blaring, and water rains down on us. It puts out the fire and soaks everyone's clothes. The alert bracelet stops blinking and sending out alerts or whatever, and Kat's grandpa is finally able to turn his power off.

"Are you okay?" Kat asks him.

"I was all right the whole time," he says. "I just couldn't stop the flames."

Right. He certainly didn't *look* okay, when he was busy freaking out.

Kat's grandma, also completely soaked, comes up and takes his arm. Some nurses and other retirement-home staff hurry into the room to assess the damage.

"I'm sorry," Sarah says, taking the bracelet back and staring at it in extreme disappointment.

"It's all right," Kat's grandpa tells her. "No harm done."

Kat's grandma gives Sarah a reassuring smile. "You meant well."

Sarah looks to Kat. "I'm sorry. I really—"

Kat turns her back to Sarah without saying a word and storms out of the room.

"Kat, wait." I glance over at Sarah and Riley, then hurry after her.

She stops in the hallway when I put my hand on her shoulder. Her eyes are wet, like she's about to cry. "I hate her," she says, wrapping her arms around herself. Water pours off of her clothes and puddles on the floor.

"It was an accident."

"I know. And I still hate her. And you didn't have to call her Cosine." She sounds especially hurt by that.

"That's just... I was in superhero mode. She's my sidekick." Sort of. She's on a self-imposed hiatus right now, after what happened last fall.

Kat winces. "We were supposed to be a team."

"We are."

"Not like that. Not, you know, working together." She leans her head against the wall and sighs. "I hate that I'm never going to have that with you." Her eyes really are watering now, and she rubs her palms against them and sniffs.

I swallow, feeling like a jerk, even though I don't know what I was supposed to do differently. "Kat." I put my arms around her, and she leans into me. The water in our clothes squishes together. "We're always going to be a team."

"Except that I'm a villain and you're a hero."

"That doesn't have to mean we can't ever work together."

But she gives me this really skeptical look when I say that. Hopeful, but skeptical, like she knows it's never going to happen.

I'm on the phone with Kat Christmas morning, after the ripping-open-presents frenzy. The space under the Christmas tree seems really empty now, especially since Helen's already gathered up all the discarded wrapping paper and shoved it in a garbage bag to recycle later. I'm sitting on the couch with my feet on the edge of the coffee table, while Alex plays with his new toys and watches some Christmas movie on TV. Jess is curled up next to me, hugging the stuffed aardvark I gave her while also watching the movie. Amelia's in her room, Helen's in the kitchen, on the phone with her sister, and Gordon's outside shoveling snow out of the driveway so they can go to his parents' house. He tried to get me to go do manual labor with him, but I pretended I was already on the phone and didn't hear him, even though I hadn't actually called Kat yet.

"What did you get?" Kat asks. She already told me she got a new set of scrapbooking supplies—Vilmore edition, for all those school memories, I guess—a new set of skis (probably to encourage her to go on more trips without me), and an electric kettle, which was a gift from her aunt, and which her mom has warned her is a fire hazard no less than four times already, as if she thinks Kat will burn down her entire dorm and maybe the rest of the school, too.

I told Kat it would be a shame if I'd saved Vilmore from Sarah's lightning machine only to have a plastic teapot do the job instead.

"I got the worst present ever," I tell Kat. "Amelia got a cell phone."

"Wow. The gift that keeps on taking. So, your parents have completely lost it?"

"Apparently." Amelia's been begging for a cell phone the whole time I've known her, and Gordon and Helen have always said no way, despite pretty much everyone in the universe having one, since Amelia's glued to the phone enough as it is. I guess they changed their minds. "There was much squealing and shrieking when the wrapping paper came off." There's still the occasional squealing coming from her room, where she's calling everyone she knows to brag and give them her new number. She even texted it to *me*, as if I care, and as if I won't make sure she regrets it later.

"What did you really get?" Kat asks.

"A hooded Heroesworth sweatshirt." A present that says, *We're so happy you're going to hero school. Please don't get kicked out again.* At least it wasn't an all-expenses-paid trip to psycho camp, which I was kind of dreading. I even checked the pockets on the sweatshirt, just to make sure there wasn't some hidden envelope with my group therapy itinerary or anything. There wasn't.

"Your parents know you so well. Did you also get one of those pennant flags so you can display your school spirit on your wall? Or maybe some notebook paper and pencils, the better to get *A* pluses with?"

My parents might not know me at all, but Kat sure does. "They got me a new comforter, for my bed, with matching sheets and pillow cases. I think that was meant to be a present for both of us."

She laughs. "Tell them I said thanks, but if it's red and

100

gold, I'm sending it back."

Red and gold are Heroesworth colors. My sweatshirt is dark red with the Heroesworth logo embroidered in gold thread over the heart. Thankfully, my new bedding isn't from the school store. "It's dark blue. It's soft. You'll like it."

Jess leans into me, resting her head against my upper arm. "Soft," she says, petting her stuffed aardvark, which is, in fact, very soft. Then she jams its long snout into me, pretending it's biting me. I can tell because she makes chomping and chewing noises while she does it.

I'm not sure if aardvarks can bite people. Or if they even chew. I always kind of thought they sucked up ants like a vacuum cleaner. Which, now that I think about it, is probably not true. That would be like snorting ants, which sounds kind of painful.

"Do aardvarks have teeth?" I ask Kat.

Jess says, "*Yes*," at the same time as Kat says, "Probably. The better to chew their ants with."

Gordon opens the front door, stomping the snow off his boots out on the mat before stepping inside. "Time to get ready," he announces. "Alex, put your toys away. Jess, get your shoes on." He claps his hands, indicating they should get going.

Jess pretends the aardvark is clamped onto my arm with its teeth and has to pull really hard to get it to let go. Then she trudges off to get ready. Alex shoves his toys off toward the wall, then glances at Gordon to see if he can get away with it. Gordon gives him a stern look, and Alex sighs dramatically as he gathers up his stuff to dump it in his room.

Gordon shouts for Amelia to come down. Then he turns to me. "Off the phone. Come on."

I'm not sure who he's talking to, so I ignore him and keep talking to Kat. "Do you want to come over and test out the new bedding?"

"What, you're not even going to wash it first? And you should come over here, since I can't really leave, what with it being Christmas and all. And don't tell me you'd rather stay home alone, because that's just sad. *And* I know it's not true."

"Damien." Gordon stands in front of me, trying to get my attention. "I said get off the phone and let's go."

That's not actually what he said. "Hold on," I tell Kat. To Gordon, I say, "*What?*"

"We're leaving. You need to get your shoes on." He grabs my new Heroesworth sweatshirt and tosses it at me, like I'm Alex or something and incapable of getting my own coat, which I don't even need because I'm not going anywhere.

"*You're* leaving. I'm not." They're going to Gordon's parents' house. My supposed grandparents who made a point of inviting everyone except me.

"We're *all* going. I don't care what they said." A muscle in his jaw twitches. "You're my son. You're part of this family, whether they like it or not."

This from the man who could barely tell them I existed a few months ago. But today he's decided I have to be part of the family. "Yeah, I don't think so. I have plans." And if I wanted to spend Christmas where I'm not wanted, I would have gone over to Mom's house.

"You're canceling them." He actually grabs my phone out of my hands, says, "He'll call you tomorrow," and turns it off. *Off!* Seriously!

"What the hell?!"

"You can have this back in the morning, when it's not a holiday." He's using his gruff "I'm your father and I know everything" voice. Which, naturally, I really, really hate.

"So you gave Amelia a phone, but now you're taking mine?" So unfair.

"If you'd put it away when I told you to, you wouldn't have lost it." He says that like it's a fact, some simple truth that's obvious to everyone. "You need to start understanding that there are consequences to your actions."

There's an edge to his voice, so I know he's not just talking about today. He's still hung up on what I did during my final. Great. So we're back to that again. "Uh, yeah. Have you thought about the consequences of *yours*?"

"It's Christmas. You're not missing Christmas dinner with the family. And... they need to know that when they invite us over, it's all of us or none of us."

He sounds pretty serious about that. So much so that I wonder if maybe he really *does* understand how awful this might be. "So, if they refuse to even let me through the door?"

"Then we *all* get back in the car and go home." He puts a hand on my shoulder and sighs, like he's worried that might be a real possibility. "Now go get your shoes on. It's time you met your grandparents."

# CHAPTER 7

Gordon's parents live in a white two-story house with a nice garden out front—or at least what looks like it would be a nice garden, if it wasn't covered in snow—and a fenced-in backyard. It looks so generic and clean and non-threatening that it belongs in a magazine. One that advertises great American living. The perfect place to raise your 2.3 kids and the family dog.

Actually, Gordon and Helen sort of had 2.3 kids before I showed up. Maybe that's why they always act like I'm going to go dig up the neighbors' yard if they don't keep tabs on me.

Or, you know, that I'm going to zap some poor, unsuspecting superhero who's pretending to be a criminal.

Gordon's mom answers the door. She has a big smile on her face for a split second, and then she notices me and her mouth goes all tight and disapproving. She doesn't *say* anything. She just acts like I'm not there, greeting everyone else by name and not acknowledging me.

Blood-wise, this woman is just as much a part of my genetics as my other grandma, the one I've known my whole life, and that's just weird. Like, this woman who hates me so much for existing makes up a fourth of my genes. And her husband, who I'm assuming hates me just as much, if not more, makes up another fourth.

But she lets us in the door, which is more than I expected. And more than Gordon expected, too, apparently, because once we're inside he gives me this relieved look.

We're not the only guests at this family gathering. Not that I'm a guest so much as an uninvited crasher. But it's not just us—Gordon has two brothers, one older and one younger, and they're both here. Them and their wives and their combined total of five children.

Gordon's brothers—my uncles—look a lot like Gordon. Their kids look... Okay, not *like* me, but kind of. On my mom's side of the family, everyone has red hair and I stick out like a sore thumb. But here, almost everyone has dark hair, like Gordon's and Alex's and kind of like mine. There are other similarities, too, like how their faces look and something about their noses. I look like I belong here, even though I don't.

My new family members don't look pleased to see me, either. They look like they're just as weirded out by our similarities as I am.

One of Gordon's brothers comes up to him as the rest of the family starts to mingle. Amelia talks to a couple of the older cousins—two boys who look around fourteen or fifteen and who may or may not be brothers—and Alex and a younger boy cousin instantly become engrossed in some handheld video game. There are two girls, a couple years younger than them, playing with a wooden train set by themselves. Jess clings to Helen's leg while Helen catches up with her sister-in-laws and admires the fake Christmas tree.

I just sort of stand next to Gordon because I don't know what else to do. If I had my phone, then at least I could text everyone I know about how stupid this is. Or get online and check Facebook or something, instead of standing around like some loser who has nothing to do and doesn't know anybody.

Gordon's brother seems kind of worried about me being here—though not worried enough to put down his glass of eggnog—and gives Gordon a questioning look.

"Damien," Gordon says, putting a hand on my shoulder and steering me closer to him. "This is my older brother Ted. Your, um, uncle."

Uncle Ted makes a sour face, like he can't believe Gordon just tried to introduce us instead of explaining why he brought me. "Can I talk to you?" he asks him, indicating they should talk somewhere more private, where I won't be able to hear.

As if I don't know they're talking about me and about how Gordon should have left me behind.

I make my way over to the fireplace, where Amelia's talking to her cousins. Our cousins, I mean, except that I've never met them. They wrinkle their noses in disgust and take a step back as I come over, as if they're going to catch villainy from me.

I look them in the eyes, sizing them up and not backing down. The one on the right is a few inches taller than his brother or cousin or whoever, and he has the same green eyes as me and Gordon. They're also both wearing Christmas sweaters with pictures of snowmen in bright red scarves, so I'm going to guess they're brothers. That, or their moms both just happen to hate them.

"This is Damien, my brother," Amelia tells them, rolling her eyes to show them how little she appreciates this fact. To me, she says, "Have you met Nolan and Devon?" As if there's any possibility that I could have met them before now. And she obviously didn't think they knew who I was, either.

Nolan and Devon are watching me kind of warily, like they think I'm completely unstable and might suddenly attack them. At the family Christmas party. In front of everyone.

As if I wouldn't have the patience to wait until there were no witnesses.

"I want my phone," I tell Amelia.

She scoffs, really playing it up for them. "I don't have it. This is *my* phone." She hugs her new phone, which of course she's been clutching this whole time.

"Uh, yeah, I know." Even if I didn't already know that it wasn't my phone, it's sparkly pink and has the letter *A* on it, formed out of silver bling stickers. "Gordon has mine."

"And let me guess. You want me to get it for you? Dad will know it was me, and then he'll take my phone, too."

"No, he won't. If he even notices it's gone, I'll tell him I stole it."

"Yeah, right. I'm not risking getting in trouble for you."

"Come on. You know he'll never believe you did it."

This should be the point where she starts asking what's in it for her. But she's too busy showing off to her cousins to act like she'd ever consider it. "You're as bad as Alex," she tells me, giving them a look like, *Brothers. What can you do?*

Both of them still seem kind of nervous, like they don't want to get too close to me.

"Don't worry," I tell them. "It doesn't matter if you stand right next to me or across the room. I can zap you just as easily."

The shorter one, Devon, stands there with his mouth hanging open.

Nolan glares at me. "If you even think about it, I'll—"

"You'll what?" If he has his power yet, I'm guessing it's flying, like Gordon and almost everyone else in his family. Or at least all the boys, which unfortunately includes me. I just happen to have two powers, on account of my mixed parentage. Nolan, who's 100% hero, does not. And even if it turns out he has some other, more violent power, I still think I can take him.

Amelia laughs nervously. "He's not going to zap anyone. He was just *kidding*. Right, Damien?"

Nolan doesn't break eye contact with me, but he gets this look on his face, like he thinks she's deluding herself and has no idea how evil I am. "You've already zapped one superhero. What's to say you wouldn't do it again?"

"Uncle Gordon shouldn't have brought you here,"

Devon adds, even though his brother is the one who's bravely getting in my face about it. "We all saw what you did on the news. There's no way you're really related to us."

"I know, I can't believe it, either," I tell them. "Seems kind of weird that I'm related to such prejudiced douchebags."

Nolan's nostrils flare. His hands are fists. He looks like he's *this close* to punching me in the face.

"Go ahead," I tell him. "Hit me. On Christmas. At your grandparents' house."

"I'm not starting anything," he says. "I'm—"

He doesn't get a chance to finish—he's too startled by the glass of eggnog Amelia just poured down his back. "Oops," she says, standing there holding her now empty glass. A glass she didn't have a couple seconds ago, so she must have used her power to get it. I wonder whose glass it was and kind of hope it was Ted's.

Nolan's snowman sweater is wet and dripping. He turns toward her, gaping, like he can't believe she would betray him like that. Him, her all-hero cousin she's known her whole life, as opposed to me, her half-villain half brother she hasn't even known for a whole year.

Amelia swallows, her face going pale, like she's a little worried about what she just did. "It was an accident," she lies.

Helen and the other two moms come over to see what's going on. One of them, a brunette also wearing a Christmas sweater—though this one has Santa on it instead of a snowman—purses her lips and tells Nolan he'd better go get cleaned up.

"What happened?" Helen asks. She eyes both me and Amelia suspiciously.

"Nothing," Amelia says, staring at her shoes. "I just tripped is all. Sorry, Nolan."

"Yeah, right." He glares at her before storming off to try and get the eggnog out of his clothes.

"Come on, honey," their mom says to Devon. "Why don't you, um…" She hesitates, trying to think of a polite excuse for him to not be anywhere near me. "Why don't you go see if you can help Grandma in the kitchen?"

Devon looks torn between whining about having to help and being grateful for an excuse to get away from us. In the end, he looks put out about it, but hurries off to the kitchen without any real protest.

Their mom watches me and Amelia carefully, as if she's not convinced that it really was Amelia and not me who "spilled" the eggnog. Even though Amelia's still holding the empty glass.

"It was just an accident," Helen says.

Nolan and Devon's mom makes a *hmph* noise. "I didn't want to say anything in front of the kids, but I don't know if bringing that boy was such a good idea. I can't believe you let Gordon talk you into it."

She won't say that in front of her already prejudiced kids, but she'll say it in front of me and Amelia?

Helen scowls and looks like she's about to tell her where she can shove it, but she doesn't get the chance because Gordon comes storming out of the hallway, where he went to go talk to his brother. His face is kind of red and he looks really pissed. He comes over to us, and I hope it's to say that we're going home, but it's not. Instead he tells Helen, "Do you have any idea what Ted just said to me? He actually had the nerve to—" He suddenly notices that I'm standing right there and that maybe he shouldn't repeat whatever awful things Ted said about me. "Damien. Why don't you go check on Alex. You, too, Amelia."

"I can see Alex from here," I tell him. "He's still playing video games. He's fine."

Gordon sighs and starts to lead Helen off, so they can talk alone, when his mom comes in from the kitchen. His brother Ted and an older man I've never seen before— who must be his dad—follow her over to us.

"I didn't want to say anything," his mom says, in a voice that clearly indicates she's been *dying* to say something, "but Ted's right, Gordon. We didn't invite that boy for a reason."

"It's Christmas," Gordon says.

"Exactly." This from his dad. "We all want to enjoy the holiday and have a nice family get-together."

His mom shakes her head. "He's already caused trouble and made a scene."

"As I just told Ted," Gordon says, giving his brother a dirty look, "he's my son and he's part of this family, whether you like it or not."

"He threw eggnog at my son." Ted says this like it's the one unforgivable crime in the universe. Like he would have given me a fair chance if it wasn't for this eggnog incident.

Amelia steps forward. "That was me. I threw the—I mean, spilled—that eggnog. It wasn't Damien."

Ted doesn't even acknowledge that she just spoke, let alone what she said. "He threatened my boys."

Gordon quickly glances over to me, then tries to hide it by staring down his family instead. "Damien's a good kid."

His mother gives a disdainful sniff. "You're acting like we didn't all see those news reports."

"The boy's a menace." His dad shakes his head sadly, like it's too bad. "It's one thing for you to decide you don't care about your own family's safety and bring him to live with you. But it's another to bring him here and—"

"Damien wouldn't hurt anyone." Gordon's voice burns, and he sounds like he believes that more than anything. "What you saw on the news was a misunderstanding. He thought that man was a criminal. Damien only zapped him because he thought the lives of two kids were on the line. He knew he'd get in trouble for it, but my son is the kind of person who doesn't think about the consequences for himself when innocent people are in trouble. You would know that if you'd spent any time with him at all, instead of judging him and acting like he doesn't deserve to be here. And, Ted, it was just eggnog, for crying out loud!"

They all gape at him.

"He stays," Gordon adds, and then turns away from them and storms off out the sliding glass door into the backyard.

*Whoa.* I hurry after him, sliding the door back open almost as soon as it shuts. There's snow on the ground and

I can see my breath and I don't have my coat on.

Gordon whirls around, probably expecting that one of them's come to argue with him some more. When he sees it's me, his face softens and he lets his shoulders relax. "I'm sorry you had to see that. Ted can be kind of a jerk."

"So can his kids."

"Did you really throw eggnog on him?"

"Amelia did. Because…" Well, I don't have to tell him that me and Nolan were on the verge of a fistfight. "He didn't like me very much."

"Maybe we should have stayed home. We could have had a much quieter Christmas. But I wanted them to know that they don't get to decide if you're part of this family or not. I know that's hard and probably not the Christmas you wanted, but—"

"No, it's okay." It was worth it, to hear him defend me like that. "And I really appreciate you admitting I did the right thing during my final. Especially, you know, to them."

He blinks at me, like he can't quite make sense of that. Then understanding flashes in his eyes and he shakes his head. "I was defending you."

"Yeah, but it's cool that you've come around. That you finally see my side of it."

"No, I mean I was defending you and *that's all*. I didn't want them to only know the side of you they saw on the news. But what you did is still wrong."

"What? But all that stuff you said, about that guy being a criminal and those kids' lives being on the line—"

"I can see why you wanted to help them. But it's still

not okay that you used your power on someone. That you broke the rules." He tilts his head a little, looking almost sorry for me that I don't understand that. "Just because I didn't want the rest of the family to know about our problems doesn't mean we don't still have them."

# CHAPTER 8

Itake my time getting to third period the first day of
the new semester. Third period is Advanced Heroism,
which I have with Riley. We're finally going to be working
in pairs instead of groups, and we even get to choose our
partners. I haven't actually been to the class yet, but this is
apparently common knowledge, plus the teacher, Mrs.
Deeds, sent out a really cheerful email outlining the basics
of the class and telling us how crazy excited she is to start
working with all of us.

And I know I said all that stuff to Riley about not
wanting to jeopardize his scholarship, but he was right—I
was just being stupid. Or at least I hope I was, because I'm
still not convinced I won't accidentally get him in trouble
if we keep working together. But the alternative of *not*
working together, especially when we finally got rid of the
rest of our annoying group, seems pretty stupid.

I'm hoping I won't have to actually say out loud that he
was right and I was wrong. A real friend would let me sit

down next to him like I never said anything dumb and just assume we're working together because we make such a great team, right?

Admitting I was wrong can be my backup plan.

But when I walk into class, it's obvious that that's not going to work, because someone's already sitting in my seat. All the desks are these tables that seat two people. Perfect for a class where everyone's working in pairs. And there's Riley, sitting at one of them, flipping through his notebook, and next to him is some guy I don't know. He's got sandy-blond hair and a black T-shirt for a band I've never heard of. And his backpack's got patches that look like flags from around the world stuck all over it with safety pins.

I don't have any idea who this guy is, but he's sitting in my spot, and that can't mean anything good.

The table next to Riley is still empty, so I walk over there and sit down, really casually, like I didn't notice that I've been replaced. And okay, maybe I haven't been. Maybe I should give Riley the benefit of the doubt. Except that I can tell, just by looking at them, that I'm not wrong.

Riley jumps when I sit down at the next table over.

"Thanks for saving me a seat, Perkins." I drop my bag on the floor, but I don't start getting out my stuff yet.

He clears his throat. "This is Mason. He just moved back to town. We used to be friends, back in junior high, before he left."

Mason leans forward to peer past Riley at me. Some of his hair flops into his face, and he smooths it back with his hand.

"Mason, this is Damien," Riley says.

"Hey," Mason says, nodding his head. And I don't know if he's been living in a cave or what, but there isn't that usual *I know I know you from somewhere* look I've seen on countless strangers' faces ever since that video of me blowing up part of the school went viral last September. He gets up and goes out to the hall to refill his water bottle, which is stainless steel and has a bunch of pretentious stickers on it encouraging people to be eco-friendly and take care of the Earth.

"You can catch up later," I tell Riley, once Mason is gone. "Class is about to start." I jerk my head toward the empty seat next to me, indicating he should come sit where he belongs.

"Actually..." Riley leans down to retie his shoe, even though it wasn't undone. "I thought you didn't want to work with me."

Great. I can already tell where this is going. "You convinced me I was being stupid. And I *did* want to work with you—I do, I mean. I just thought—"

"Maybe you were right. About my scholarship being in danger. I've had a lot of time to think about it over the past couple weeks."

"But *you* were right. About us making a good team. Do you really want to go on dangerous missions with that guy?"

Riley glances over at Mason's empty seat and his douchey backpack with the flags on it. "We were pretty good friends before. We always thought we'd work together, when we got to Heroesworth."

"You didn't even know he was coming back to town, did you?" They couldn't have been that close.

"His family traveled a lot. We lost touch." He shrugs. "But he's here now, and he doesn't really know anyone else."

Oh, right, and I'm so popular, I'll just pair up with one of my many other friends. "Come on, Perkins. You can't bail on me now. We had *plans*."

"I can't lose my scholarship. If I do..." He presses his hands against the desk and shakes his head. "That's my whole future. This, I mean. Heroesworth, and then the League. What would my mom say? If I lost it? I can't do that to her."

What would *Curtis* say, I think he means. And okay, yeah, maybe his mom would be plenty upset, too. She'd probably say she was disappointed or something, or maybe not say anything at all and just start crying because her eldest son ruined his entire future in one fell stroke. One fell stroke of being friends with a half villain. Which, personally, I don't think the League should punish him for, but nobody consults me on these things. What with being a half villain and not part of the League and all.

"You were so sure I wouldn't screw things up for you," I remind him.

He scratches the side of his face, looking guilty. "I had more time to think about it. And we can work together again after this semester, when I'm not on probation anymore."

"Next semester is *next year*." And no, we won't be able to work together then. I know how this goes. He partners up with Mason now, and then that's it, they're a team for the next year and a half. Longer, probably, since they'll both join the League after they graduate. Just like they probably planned back in junior high, when they were BFFs.

"If I get in trouble again, I get kicked out of school. I can't let that happen, and Mason, he's…"

"What?"

"More like me. We're on the same page."

"You haven't spoken to him in years. And now you're going to go on dangerous missions with him, no questions asked?" Maybe I can't promise I won't break the rules and get Riley in trouble again, but I can promise that I'm watching out for him. I don't know what Mason's power is, but I know he can't zap bad guys.

"It's one semester."

"Great." *So* not great. "You're ditching me, and now what? Who the hell else am I supposed to work with?"

I glance around the room, surveying my prospects. Even if I didn't hate everyone else at this school, it looks like everybody already has a partner anyway. The only seat not taken is the one next to me. It's against the rules to work alone, and there's a moment where I wonder if the teacher will force me to be a third wheel in somebody else's group, and if Riley and Mason will even volunteer to have me, since I'm obviously not on the "same page" as them. But then, right on cue, Amelia hurries into the classroom. Her face is flushed and she's huffing and puffing, like she ran here. She hesitates in the doorway, taking everything in. Probably looking for a seat that's still open.

Then she spots me. She looks really relieved to see someone she knows who doesn't have a partner, even if it's me. Then she forces a scowl onto her face as she stomps over and flops down in the empty chair, sealing my fate.

## X·X·X

Mason's power is light. He actually said, in this really pretentious tone, that he considers himself "a light in the darkness. Literally." This was supposed to be impressive or something. Riley nodded on in approval, like anyone calling himself that isn't a complete and total douche. This is what I have to put up with at lunch, not just today, but for the foreseeable future, since apparently Mason not really knowing anyone else means he also has to eat with us.

His lunch is all vegan and organic. He makes a big point of telling us that. He even offers me some of his quinoa and tofu, which I decline, despite his spiel about how good for me it is.

If he actually cares about what's good for me, he shouldn't have stolen my partner for Advanced Heroism. A situation he should enjoy while he can, before he gets what's coming to him. Mainly me, forging his paperwork and getting him transferred to the other class. Then Riley will be partner-less and I can ditch Amelia.

"And after Paris and Berlin," Mason says, "we spent some time traveling around Africa, helping to build schools in a bunch of different villages." Did I mention that he spent the past couple years traveling around the world with his family? His tone says it's no big deal, but there's this smugness to his eyes and the way his mouth curves a little that says he knows better and is not-so-secretly bragging. Ugh. "One night, when we were on the *Cote d'Ivoire*—that's the Ivory Coast," he adds, looking directly at *me*, as if he's assuming I won't know what he's talking about, or that I even care, "the lighthouse went out. But luckily I was there. I used my power to light it up even brighter than if it had been working. I saved *lives*."

Like we've never saved a life before. This *is* hero school, after all. "Riley and I save people all the time." Him being a human lighthouse is no big deal.

"Sure," Mason says, as if he doesn't believe me. Or like he doesn't believe I have a real part in it. Like it's just Riley doing all the hero work while I stand around and look stupid.

"Wow." Riley stares in admiration at Mason and all his supposedly amazing work overseas. "Nothing we do at Heroesworth really compares to *that*."

"Right, it's all just hum-drum, everyday rescues over here. Just fighting bad guys and putting ourselves in harm's way. I know that can't compare to safely standing in one spot and turning on your power, but it's all we have." I sigh and give Mason a fake apologetic look. "You're going to be bored out of your mind." So he should probably just transfer now, or go back to backpacking around the world with his parents or something.

"It's different," Riley says. "What we're doing here at

school… It's what *everybody's* doing."

"No, it's what everybody's *trying* to do. We're better at it than them."

"But there are plenty of other heroes in Golden City. If we don't stop some criminal, somebody else will. Mason was the only one around who could do what he did. I mean," he adds, glancing up at Mason, "it's got to be pretty different, coming back to town after all that."

"Yeah," I mutter, "civilization is the worst."

"It's fine," Mason says. "There's still plenty of good to do around here."

Riley shakes his head, like he thinks Mason is only being nice and doesn't mean it. "I just wish we could do something like that. Something that really *mattered*."

"Geez, Perkins. I had no idea our work catching fake kidnappers meant so little to you."

"You know what I mean."

I'm about to tell him that no, I *don't* know what he means, when Amelia comes up to our table. She clears her throat really loudly, as if we didn't all turn to look at her already. "I need to talk to you," she says, taking the seat next to me, uninvited.

"You can talk to me at home. Or, better yet, never."

"It's about Advanced Heroism." She stops there, waiting for me to say something.

"And?"

She glances over at Riley and Mason, then back at me. "Can we talk alone?"

"You heard her," I tell Mason. "This is a private conversation." Apparently.

Riley gets to his feet, even though I didn't say *he* had to leave. "Come on, Mase. I was going to give you a tour of the school before lunch is over anyway."

Mase?

"Yeah, okay." Mason grabs his stupid backpack with the flags all over it. He nods at Amelia, saying hello and good-bye in one douchey head bob.

Amelia watches them leave.

"Can we get this over with?" I check the non-existent watch on my wrist. "I have places to be, you know."

"I just wanted to say... About Advanced Heroism. I thought, maybe..." She picks at a spot of crud stuck to the table, which is kind of gross, since who knows where it came from.

"Let me guess. You don't want to work with me? Don't worry. The feeling's mutual."

Her mouth drops open a little. Then she shakes her head. "Fine. Never mind."

"Okay. Great. Conversation ov—"

"I saw you picking up transfer papers. At the office, right after class."

"I didn't see any point in wasting time." The sooner I get rid of Mason, the better.

"I know you don't want to be my partner."

She says that like it's some big secret, as if we aren't both annoyed at being stuck with each other. "Yeah, and I'm sure I was your first choice, too."

"I'm not that good at fieldwork." She winces, like it's physically painful to admit she's not perfect at everything.

"You don't say."

123

"And I don't want to get murdered by a supervillain. In a dark alley. Or in some underground lair, or wherever. And you zapped that guy on your last mission, like it wasn't even a big deal, so..."

"So you think I'm going to *murder* you?"

"Not *you*." She gives me this frustrated look, like she can't believe how stupid I am. "But somebody else might. A criminal or a supervillain or something. Somebody I'm supposed to catch. And I know you're going to transfer, and I know you really don't want to work with me, but you're my brother, and I thought, maybe, if I *asked* you..." She pauses and stares really hard at the table. "But never mind, okay? Just forget I said anything."

I stare at her in disbelief. "You *want* to work with me?"

"I didn't say that. And I don't care what you do. Transfer to the other class. It doesn't matter."

"Except that you might get murdered by bad guys. If I'm not there to zap them."

Her face turns a little red and she bites her lip. "I don't need your help."

Right.

"I was just being *nice*," she adds, though I'm not sure what part of that she thought counted as "being nice." "Working with you would probably mess up my GPA anyway. It's probably a good thing you're transferring."

She doesn't actually look at me while she says any of that, which kind of makes it unconvincing. "I'm not the one who was getting a *B* last semester."

Her nostrils flare. "You might have had a better grade than me, but then you went and screwed it all up. I can see why Riley doesn't want to work with you anymore."

"That's not what happened."

"You might be better at fieldwork than me"—she shrugs, I guess to emphasize how unimportant it is that I'm better than her at something—"but I can't trust you not to suddenly do something crazy, like zap somebody, and get us both in trouble. Just like you did to Riley."

"I didn't *do* anything to him."

"You got him in trouble."

"Not on purpose. And a minute ago, you wanted to work with me *because* I zapped somebody. Because you're afraid of getting murdered by supervillains. So which is it?"

"I don't know." She sighs and rests her chin in her hands. "But if your own best friend can't trust you, then how am I supposed to?"

# CHAPTER 9

Sarah stares at her plate of Justice Fries and Hero Sauce, not making eye contact with me. It's been like this all night. Me, her, and Riley are sitting in a booth at one of the superhero-themed diners downtown. It's Friday night, but it's after nine so it's not too crowded. She and Riley are sitting across from me, and I feel kind of like a third wheel, especially when Sarah won't even look at me. And I'm still mad at Riley for choosing Mason.

And because I would never have chosen to eat at a place like this in a million years. Well, except for that one time me and Kat came here and I made the waiter—who was sweating in his polyester superhero costume, complete with its own cape—translate the theme names of every item on the menu. When he said, in a really exasperated voice, that the Liberty Burger was just a hamburger, I gasped and asked if that meant it was still all-American.

"Sarah. It's *fine*." I try not to sound too frustrated when

I say that. I take a drink from my milkshake—the Golden City Salted-Caramel Swirl—so she doesn't see how annoyed I am.

She shakes her head. "It's not fine. You're mad."

"I'm not mad." I'm not. Or, at least, not at her.

She gives me this skeptical look. "I almost burnt down the retirement home. I thought I was better, and I wasn't. And then... I just made things worse with Kat. I shouldn't have called you Renegade."

"I think saying you almost burnt down the retirement home is giving yourself too much credit. Jerry was the only one on fire, and he's fireproof." Or at least while he's using his power. "No real harm done."

"A couple of the guys at the home said they'd take a look at my alert bracelet. They used to be in R&D before they retired. I don't usually accept outside help—"

"When do you even get offers for that?"

"—but this is for the good of the retirement home. It's going to save lives."

"Right. And, anyway, I called you Cosine, which was..." Worse than her calling me Renegade? A mistake? Neither of those things, as far as I'm concerned, but Kat was obviously pretty upset about it. "If you've been picking up on any anger vibes coming from me, you should know they're aimed at your boyfriend. Not you." I glare at Riley, just to hit it home.

"Seriously?" Riley sets down his all-American Liberty Burger. "It's been a week."

"Yes, seriously." I don't know why he expects me to have forgotten already that he betrayed me. "And it's been four days."

"But I told you why. And this isn't permanent, X. I thought you understood."

"Riiiiight."

Sarah glances back and forth between us. I'm sure she's heard all about it already. "If you're not mad, then why have you been avoiding me?"

"I was busy," I mutter. "With school."

"During break, I mean."

Now it's my turn to look away. I play with the straw wrapper from my milkshake, rolling it up into a little ball and then untangling it again. Obviously I spent my time with Kat, while she was still home. And obviously she wasn't exactly thrilled with the idea of hanging out with Sarah again. And maybe I could have called, but I didn't want to have to tell Sarah no if she invited me over or something. It would seem like I was mad at her, which I'm not, plus she's my friend. And if I didn't tell her no and went over to hang out, then Kat would be pissed at me. And not telling Kat about it would feel like lying to her, so there's no way I wouldn't have told her. So, yeah. Maybe I was avoiding Sarah.

"I hardly get to see Kat. And she was gone for part of break, so... You know."

Sarah nods. "I saw Kat's face when I called you Renegade. She hates me, and she hates that I'm your sidekick."

"You're on hiatus," Riley reminds her. "You're not his sidekick right now. And even if you were going around patrolling for bad guys, it would be all three of us, wouldn't it?"

Before we were friends, Riley tried to steal Sarah from me and get her to sidekick for him instead. And by the time we decided we didn't hate each other's guts, Sarah decided she was taking a break from superheroing for a while. So we never actually discussed all three of us working together.

"I don't know if I can work with you," I tell Riley. "I have to think about my reputation. I wouldn't want to be seen with you and have someone think I'm some straight-up, League-abiding do-gooder. I might lose my vigilante funding. So, you know, maybe ask me again next year when I've had some time to think about it."

Riley throws down the Justice Fry he's holding, which is remarkably similar to a plain, regular French fry. It lands in the middle of his blob of ketchup—er, I mean Hero Sauce—getting totally covered in it. "This is why I'm not working with you this semester. Because you never cut me any slack. *You* mess up, because you can't be bothered to follow the rules, no matter what the consequences are for anybody else, and then you expect everyone to just let it go. But *I* choose to do something you don't like, that I wouldn't even have needed to do if it wasn't for you screwing up, and you're all over me about it."

"I did something you didn't like, *once*, and you replaced me."

"*Boys.*" Sarah gives us both stern looks. "Don't. This is history repeating itself."

Whatever. "I'm not going to go back to breaking his fingers, if that's what you mean." Me and Riley are still friends. And while I might be considering taping a small dead fish just inside his locker, where he might not notice it at first, that doesn't mean I'm going back to my old ways of wishing he didn't exist.

"*Finger*. As in just the one," Riley corrects me.

"I'm not talking about that," Sarah says. "I mean like Curtis and your dad."

Riley scrunches up his forehead. "My dad and Curtis worked together for years, ever since they were at Heroesworth. They were best friends."

I turn sideways and lean against the wall, putting my legs up onto the booth bench and stretching out. "Let me guess, before they were partners, one of them ditched his half-villain friend after their first semester together and never worked with him again?"

"I didn't ditch you!"

"I heard Curtis and your mom talking," Sarah goes on. "The other night, when we were in your room, watching that documentary I got you, and I went to go get some water. They were in the living room, talking kind of quietly. They shut up when they noticed me, but before that, Curtis was saying he wished he'd been there more for Miles, and your mom was comforting him. She was saying Curtis didn't need to feel guilty, that he was always a really good friend to your dad and to your family, but Curtis didn't seem to think so."

The anger drains from Riley's face. He swallows, looking kind of uncomfortable. "It's called *survivor's guilt*. I feel it, too, sometimes. A lot, I mean. So does my mom. It's not really surprising that Curtis worries about it. He was supposed to be there that morning, when there was that bus bombing, but he was late for work, and my dad went out without him. If he'd been there, maybe he could have done something."

"Yeah, but the way he was talking… it sounded like he and your dad were in a fight. When it happened. So the last things they said to each other weren't very nice."

"I never heard that."

"Well, he sounded pretty upset about it. And now you guys are fighting."

"We're not going to die," I tell her. "We've got plenty of time to be pissed at each other." I say that last part playfully enough, expecting Riley to at least smirk at it. But instead he gets this really serious look on his face.

"My dad didn't know he was going to die that day. If they were in a fight, maybe they thought they had more time, too."

"Yeah, well, we can't live our lives like we think we're going to die tomorrow. I'm not going to pretend I don't care that you abandoned me."

"I didn't abandon you." Riley's voice is quiet, like he really means it this time and isn't just saying it out of some defensive reflex. "I'm sorry, X. I mean… you know."

"And I'm sorry you mistakenly think that douchebag is a better partner than me. Oh, wait, no, I'm not."

"See," Riley says, suddenly annoyed again. "This is what I'm talking about."

Sarah finishes chewing the Justice Fry she stuffed in her mouth. "Just promise me you guys still have each other's backs."

"Of course we do. And, Sarah, even if my dad and Curtis were fighting… Well, it's not like they weren't still watching out for each other. It's not the reason my dad died."

Sarah looks like she has something to say to that. Like she really wants to argue with him. But then, whatever it is, she seems to think better of it and keeps her mouth shut.

"We're not even working together this semester," I tell her, trying to sound reassuring. "He's got Mason now." And I've got Amelia. "What could possibly go wrong?"

X·X·X

"What if we don't find anything?" Amelia whines. "How are we supposed to know if it's a front or not?"

We're on our way to scope out a laundromat that's rumored to be a front for the Red Bandit, a supervillain who specializes in black-market goods. Our first mission is just simple recon, but the way Amelia's acting, you'd think we were storming some villain fortress of doom.

"And," she says, "what if it *is* a front and we get caught? What if they have guns?!"

"Wow," Kat says on the phone, "that's, like, the second time she's asked that."

"Third," I correct her. "She won't shut up about it."

"Some people can't take a hint."

Amelia lets out a high-pitched scoff. Her breath mists in the air. "Are you guys talking about me?"

"*No.*" I roll my eyes at her, like she's being ridiculous.

"Seriously," I say into the phone, "it's like she thinks we're going to be forced to show our thumbs at the door."

"You *are* talking about me!"

"If you have to show your thumbs," Kat says, "then you'll know it's a front and you can go home."

"Exactly."

Amelia stops on the sidewalk in front of me, waving a hand in my face.

"That's really annoying. Can't you see I'm trying to have a conversation?" She of all people should understand how important phone time is.

"You're supposed to be paying attention. We're *almost* there. And we still don't know what we're doing in all the scenarios."

"What scenarios?"

She throws out her hand and starts counting on her fingers. "Not finding anything, finding supervillains, finding supervillains with rayguns, finding supervillains with powers, getting attacked, getting captured, getting *killed*—"

"Whoa. You have a plan for if we get killed? Won't we be out of commission at that point?"

Kat laughs. "I think she means she has someone on standby, ready to tell the press your tragic story if you guys don't come back."

"I don't have a plan for getting killed!" Amelia says. "I don't have a plan for *anything*. We're supposed to be figuring this out, but instead you're on the phone. With a *supervillain*."

She says that like talking to a supervillain makes me

extra irresponsible. "Wow. Just because we go to Heroesworth doesn't mean you get extra credit for being letterist."

"That's funny," Kat says, "because I *do* get extra credit for it. Double points for making the enemy my sex slave, but only if I have proof."

"So that's what those pictures were for. I thought you were just going to sell them on the internet."

"It was a difficult decision, but my future is important. That extra credit now will pay off more in the long run."

Amelia stomps her foot on the sidewalk. Right on a crack, too, as if she doesn't care whose back she's breaking. So careless. "Get off the phone! You're supposed to be listening to me!"

I'm not sure why she thinks that.

"It's okay," Kat says. "I have to go to my psych class anyway. Let me know how it goes. I want a full report on how many quarters a load of laundry costs. I want to know how it compares to the machines in my dorm and if I'm getting ripped off."

"You probably are. I mean, where else are you going to go? They've got you where they want you."

"Yeah, they do, but I still hate not knowing."

We say good-bye and then hang up. Amelia's shoulders slump in relief as she sees me put my phone away. "*Finally.* We're supposed to be working, and we don't have anything figured out yet, and—"

"First of all, nothing's going to happen. We're just checking it out. It's a place of business. Anyone can walk in off the street and wash their clothes or whatever."

"Oh, my God! We forgot to bring laundry! We're going to look suspicious. Maybe we should go back."

"We're not going back."

"I could call some up." She flexes her fingers, looking like she's thinking really hard about whether she wants to use her power to summon her dirty clothes.

"It's not a crime to show up to the laundromat empty-handed. Nobody's going to even be looking at us."

"People are *always* looking at you."

True. "Okay, then maybe you should go in alone."

Pure terror spreads across her face. "Mom and Dad aren't going to be very happy if you let me die in a laundromat, you know. Or *anywhere*," she adds, as if I might have been getting ideas about where it was okay to let her get killed.

"I was kidding." Like I'd trust her to do this on her own. She'd take one step through the door, panic, and start shouting that she was just a random superhero, trying to do her laundry, which, by the way, she forgot, so maybe she should run home real quick.

"Yeah, right," she mutters.

"Come on. Let's just get this over with."

"But we don't have a *plan*."

"We go in, we get our info, and we get out. What more is there to know?"

"*Everything.*"

"Whatever. It's going to be fine. And this is only our first mission. You might want to tone down your freak-out level, so you can save it for when we're actually in danger."

# X·X·X

The laundromat seems pretty full for the middle of the day, though there are still some machines open. It's warm in here and the windows are steamed up. The whole place smells like a weird combination of overly flowery laundry soap, dampness, and grime. A couple heads turn when we walk in, and then everyone goes back to reading or staring at the machines. Waiting.

There's a change machine in the corner and a vending machine that sells little boxes of detergent. There's also a big wad of pink gum on the floor that I narrowly avoid stepping in.

"Well?" Amelia whispers, ducking into the corner with the machines.

"Well what?"

"We should buy some soap. So we look natural."

I glance across the room, at all the bored people not paying any attention to us. "How does buying soap make us look natural?"

"Because then we have a reason for coming in here."

"Yeah, but having a box of detergent and no laundry is weirder than having nothing."

Amelia takes off her pink coat and wads it up, like she's going to wash it. "I'm just trying to make this work. Since we don't know what to do."

"Speak for yourself. I know exactly what to do."

"You do?"

"We should split up."

136

"*What?*"

"We can get this place checked out faster."

"That's what they always say in horror movies. We'll cover more ground, but one of us will end up dead in a basement."

I can't believe her. And I have a whole semester of this to look forward to. Possibly the rest of my time at Heroesworth, since it's not like Riley's going to un-ditch me, despite what he said about working together next year. "Look, Amelia, the sooner we look around, the sooner we can leave. So just go, okay?"

"But—"

"This isn't a horror movie. Besides, even if it was, the whiny virgin girl always lives."

She scowls at that, then stands there, watching me for a minute. Hoping I'll change my mind. Or maybe she's trying to figure out a reason why we should stick together. But it's fieldwork, not hand-holding class, and eventually she makes a *hmph* noise and storms off toward the washing machines.

I lean against the wall and get my phone out. I think about texting Riley, to remind him what a jerk he is for ruining our plans—and my life, at least for the next four months—but then I think he and Mason are probably having a great time on their mission, since they're both on the same page or whatever, and the last thing I want to do is remind him what an awesome time he's having without me.

I text Zach instead.

*Any chance you can start at Heroesworth, like, NOW?*

He doesn't start until next year, assuming he gets in, which I'm pretty sure he will. As Amelia's pointed out, if they'll let me in, then they don't exactly have standards. And sure, Gordon pulled some strings, but my mom was sleeping with the dean of Vilmore when I originally applied there and I *still* didn't make the cut.

Of course, even if he did go to Heroesworth, it's not like we'd be in the same grade. And if it was somehow possible for us to be partners, he'd probably pick Amelia.

*Riley's a jerk for ditching you,* Zach writes back. *And Mason's a monkey wrench AND a screwdriver.*

*A what?*

*A tool. Only, like, he's such a tool he's a double tool.*

I laugh. *He was traveling the world as a human flashlight. But Riley thinks he's so great.*

*Lightning > flashlight. Riley doesn't know what he's missing.*

Except he does know. That's why he's missing it. *Were they really BFFs back in the day?*

There's a pause. Kind of a long pause.

*Zach. Come on.* I haven't known Riley that long, I guess, but there's no way he was better friends with Mason than with me. If for no other reason than Mason's obvious toolness.

*Mason was over all the time,* Zach writes. *It was so annoying. They were always talking about going to Heroesworth together and being partners in the League. Even though Mason is super boring.*

Now it's my turn to pause. The way Zach tells it, I'm the one getting in the way of *their* plans. And now they can work together, like they always wanted, and then join the League, leaving me behind.

*That was all before he moved away,* Zach writes, trying to reassure me. *Riley hasn't even emailed him in years.*

I'm still trying to think of what to say to that when I hear a familiar squeal of "Oh, my God! I'm *so* sorry!"

I look up from my phone. Amelia seems to have accidentally bumped into some guy. He must have dropped whatever he was holding, because she scrambles to pick something up off the floor. "Sorry," she repeats, sounding embarrassed. Light glints off the metal thing he dropped, which she holds out to him. "I can be really klutzy sometimes."

He snatches it away and grumbles at her before turning and heading for the door.

"I said I was sorry!" Amelia calls after him.

I'm surprised she was even getting a *B* last semester, what with her amazing stealth skills. I may have underestimated how much of a liability she is. Why bother working in pairs if your partner is going to stumble into people and attract attention to herself? Why not work alone? It would be less dangerous, not to mention less annoying.

*Amelia's totally botching this mission,* I tell Zach. *At this rate, we're not even going to pass this class.* Then I'd have to retake it, and me and Riley wouldn't be able to be partners even if we wanted to. Though maybe I'll do so badly—on account of Amelia, of course—that I'll get sent back to Intro to Heroism, just in time to be in Zach's group next year.

*She told me \*you're\* botching it,* Zach writes. *She messaged me and said you're just standing there, texting.*

Another message comes in, only this time it's from Amelia. I knew nothing good would come from her having my number. And what, *now* she's concerned with being quiet, after all the commotion she made by bumping into someone? I glance up from my phone before opening the message, scanning for Amelia, but I don't see her.

Typical. She'd better not have given up and gone home. I can't picture her sneaking off, both because this is a school assignment and because she wouldn't miss an opportunity to tell me to my face why I'm the reason our mission is a bust. But I don't know where else she would be.

*I did it!* her text reads. *I'm in the back room. :)*

*What? What back room?* What the hell is she talking about?

*There's a door. Front right corner. I stole the key from that guy and went in!*

*Who told you to do that?* Geez. After all her whining about how we had to plan for every possible scenario, she just runs off without telling me?

*I took the initiative.*

*Get back out here.*

She ignores me. *There's a hallway that leads to an office. I'm going in.*

*Wait.*

She doesn't answer right away, and my mind races, jumping to conclusions. Maybe she put her phone away. Maybe she's not talking to me because she doesn't want me to tell her no. Or she could be in trouble, or—

*Uh-oh,* Amelia writes.

And I don't know if that's supposed to be a mild *uh-oh,* like, oh no, the door is locked, or if it's supposed to convey the worst, but it *is* my cue to freak out.

*Amelia?*

I stare at the screen, willing her to answer. And there could be a legit reason why she's not saying anything that doesn't mean she's in danger, but I get this awful feeling that that's not the case. If I'm wrong, she can make fun of me and say I ruined the mission all she wants, but if I'm right... I shove my phone in my pocket and sprint for the door to the back room. I fling it open and run in, electricity already twitching beneath my skin.

"Damien!" Amelia calls out when she sees me, a look of horror on her face. A tall man in a business suit stands behind her. He's got a tight grip on her forearm and is holding a raygun to her head.

My blood runs cold, but my electricity runs hot. Lightning flows into my hands. I'm not sure what I'm going to do, because zapping the guy holding a gun to my sister's head—his finger curled on the trigger—might not be the best idea. Then a man's voice behind me says, "Don't try anything."

I can hear him breathing, and I can tell he's got a weapon pointed at me by the way Amelia's face turns pale and her eyes well up with tears.

She starts to tell them to leave me alone, but her captor shoves the end of his raygun into the side of her head, and her lip trembles and she doesn't say anything.

"Amelia! *Call* it!" I make eye contact with her, willing her to understand. Because she's touched the raygun, she can summon it to her. But she doesn't move, either too panicked to understand or too afraid they'll shoot me as soon as she does.

"We know who you are," the guy behind me says.

"Yeah, who doesn't?"

"Take her away." He makes a gesture with his free hand that I can just see out of the corner of my eye. The guy holding Amelia nods and starts to drag her off down the hall. Panic flickers in her eyes.

"You can't do that!" I scream at them. "You—"

"Shut up! I have to bring you in alive, but nobody said anything about her. So keep your mouth shut and cooperate. Now come on, let's go." He points in the opposite direction of where they took Amelia. "The boss wants to see you."

# CHAPTER 10

I consider zapping the guy behind me, but there's still the issue of him having his finger on the trigger. Which I'm assuming he does, even though I can't see him, and even though he said he was supposed to bring me in alive. Electricity crackles along my arms, and all my instincts are telling me to blast him. I could do it without looking. Maybe I could duck right before, so his gun wasn't pointed straight at me.

Or it could all go horribly wrong, and I'd end up dead, and then there'd be no one to save Amelia.

And then I'd also never find out why some criminal who owns a laundromat wants to see me. I remember my grandpa's warning, about pissing off people we know. But there's a chance this boss guy just wants his picture taken with me, right? Or wants me to be their new spokesperson in a commercial? Maybe I can charge him extra for hazard pay.

I'm still mentally playing out all the possible ends to

this scenario when we get to our destination. It's an office.

"Go on," the guy with the raygun says, indicating I should open the door. I get the feeling that normally he would fling it open and push me in himself, if I wasn't covered in electricity. "Don't keep him waiting."

I could make a run for it. Drop to the ground, zap him, and run like hell. Then figure out where they took Amelia. And I can't help wondering how this situation would be different if it had been me and Riley instead. But Riley can turn invisible. He wouldn't have got caught in the first place.

And he probably wouldn't want me to do anything stupid, like risk getting killed. In the back room of a laundromat, no less. That is *not* what I want it to say on my obituary.

So I open the door, ignoring the spark when I touch the knob, and step inside.

"He's all yours, boss," the guy with the raygun says before leaving and closing the door behind him.

The "boss" is sitting behind the desk, in one of those big leather rotating chairs, with his back to me. Like this is a James Bond movie and he's going to turn around and be petting some cat. Or one of his eyes will just be a big diamond or something. So, definitely someone eccentric. And possibly theatrical. Who knows who I am. But that could be anybody, considering how many people have seen those videos of me on YouTube. Or on the news. Which really only supports my theory about him wanting me for a commercial.

"Damien," he says.

I know that voice. It sounds, just a little bit, like mine. "*Grandpa?*"

He swivels the chair around to face me. Thankfully, he doesn't have a cat or a diamond for an eye or anything. But he does cluck his tongue. "What did we talk about?"

"Since when do you run a laundromat?" I thought he was retired. And how much running does it really need? Doesn't it kind of run itself? "This is supposed to be a front for the Red Bandit. Not you." Obviously if I'd known it was him, I would have figured out a way to get a different assignment. Or at least done a better job of not getting caught, which probably would have involved making Amelia wait outside, because I really don't want the lecture I know I'm about to get.

Grandpa laughs and slaps his hand on the desk. "A front for the Red Bandit! That's exactly what everyone is supposed to think. He works for me."

"So this is a front of a front."

"Something like that. And don't think you're getting out of answering my question. You know what we talked about."

"Where's Amelia?"

"Who?"

"My *sister*! One of your guys dragged her off. He had a raygun to her head!"

"Oh, she'll be fine."

"I'd like more reassurance than that."

"Since when do you not trust your old grandfather?" His eyebrows come together and his mouth turns down. "As if I don't know it's that damn school. Trying to change you, turn you against your own."

Yeah, like he didn't just take my sister hostage. "Tell them not to hurt her."

"They're not going to. She's a kid, like you. We're not monsters. You used to know that." There's an edge to the way he says that, like me being concerned for Amelia, after they pointed a freaking gun at her, is proof that I've been brainwashed.

"Call them."

"Have a seat." He gestures for me to grab the extra chair pushed up against the wall and then picks up his cell phone.

I wait for him to actually dial before pulling the chair over. It's made of bright orange plastic and is really uncomfortable.

Grandpa tells his goons not to hurt Amelia. And not to scare her too much. He sounds pretty put out about it, like this is seriously ruining his day. Then he hangs up. "Now, you want to tell me what you're doing here?"

"We were doing recon. That's all. It was an assignment."

"Well, you weren't doing a very good job of it. Got yourselves caught pretty easily. What do they even teach you over there?"

"It wasn't my—"

"In my day, at Vilmore, we knew how to sneak around. How to blend in. We didn't get in trouble—we *caused* it."

"Great." I slump down in my chair.

"That's right, it *was* great. And you tell me you want to go to that school, and I'm supposed to stand by and let it

146

happen, when they're not even teaching you the basics? You're lucky it was me in charge here. Anyone else might not be so lenient. It pisses people off, you know."

He pauses, waiting for me to take the bait. I humor him, but only so we can get this over with. I try to sound as bored as humanly possible when I say, "What does?"

"You. Poking into everyone's business. You're a villain, but ever since you got that *X* on your thumb, you've been acting like you don't know where you belong. You think it's with heroes, but I don't buy it. It's not like everyone doesn't know who you are. You being famous, being the son of the Crimson Flash—I'll never know what your mother was thinking with that one, by the way—"

"That makes two of us."

"—and turning your back on villains, attacking them and training for the League... People notice."

I sit up straight. "I'm not training for the League." I told him that already.

"Doesn't matter what you plan to do. Heroesworth teaches League standards. It trains up new recruits and spits them out. And you being a cog in that machine means something. Everyone sees *my* grandson on TV, betraying his own kind. It's shameful, but I don't care how that looks for me. I have a reputation—everyone knows who I am and what I stand for. But I don't want to see you throw away your potential and make a fool out of yourself."

"Can we stop pretending this isn't about how I look to your friends? Because I'm not going to drop out of the school I actually want to go to just because it makes you look bad." Especially since no other schools will have me.

"My point is that one of these days, you're going to wake up and realize you're making all the wrong choices."

"They're my choices to make."

"You have no future as a hero. Plain and simple. The League's never going to have you."

"But I don't *want*—"

"Not wanting to join implies that you have a choice. They're not letting in a half villain, no matter who your father is. So you get through this school of yours, where they don't even teach you how to do recon without getting caught, and then what?"

"Then I marry rich, obviously. Kat's doing way better than me in school—I'm sure she'll be able to keep me in the high quality of living I'm accustomed to. And I'll repay her in sexual favors, to keep things fair, since you know I'm not a mooch."

Grandpa pretends he didn't hear me, though I catch an eyelid twitch of disapproval. "You can train all you like, but you'll never actually be one of them. What's the point of preparing for a future you'll never have?"

"Don't worry. My future is secured. Kat knows what she'll be missing if she doesn't lock this down."

"So your future is with a villain." He folds his hands on top of the desk, his fingers interlocking, and gives me this know-it-all look.

"I was joking. I mean, I *am* going to marry Kat, but I'm not going to be her sex slave full time. Just on the weekends."

"There's a reason you didn't joke about your future

with heroes, and that says everything I need to know."

"It doesn't. I have a future with them." I just don't know what it is. "They're my friends, my family."

"Friends who are going to join the League. Family who are going to look down on you when you don't. When you *can't.*"

"They're not going to abandon me. Not like Mom did. If you want to talk about who I *don't* have a future with—"

"Don't lump me in with your mother. You have other family, Damien. You have me and your grandmother. And in a few years all your friends are going to move on, without you. Maybe you'll marry Kat, but she'll have a career, and you won't. And you'll hate that. You might want to go to Heroesworth now, because you don't want to feel left out, but it's only a quick fix. You're going to end up feeling left out for the rest of your life if you stay on this path, and that's why I've come out of retirement. To give you another option."

"You've... *what*?"

He spreads his arms out. "Welcome to the truth."

"You want me to work at a laundromat? After I realize what a washed-up hero I am and that my whole life is a failure? Then you want me to work *here*?" Way to paint a bright future full of opportunity. "If this is your truth, then I don't need it."

He laughs. "Not *truth—Truth*. With a capital *T*. The laundromat is just a front. I don't want you to work there."

"Oh. Well, good, because even if I don't know everything my future holds, I know it doesn't involve working in a place like this." Forever. Because this is apparently the next step down from professional hero.

"The Truth is the organization I'm building. The *villain* organization." He pauses to let that sink in. "You don't have to have trained at Vilmore to join. Especially when your grandfather runs the whole thing."

"A villain organization." With a dose of some good-old-fashioned nepotism.

"The heroes have the League. It's about time we had an equivalent. Past time, if you ask me. It's something I've been thinking about for years, but there was always a reason not to do it. I was too busy, or I couldn't risk the attention from the League. But now I'm retired. And I have my grandson's future to think about."

"You think I'm going to join your villain organization?"

"The Truth."

"Right. Okay. The Truth. What do you guys even do?"

"We stand up for villain rights. Heroes have always treated us like second-class citizens. Well, no more. I'm giving villains a voice, and we're going to be heard." He meets my eyes. "You could make a difference here."

Me, making a difference for villains. Who have to put up with heroes treating us like crap. Like we're diseased or something. I can't say it's the worst idea I've ever heard. Even if it's not an option. "My dad's the Crimson Flash."

"Don't I know it."

"I can't join your organization."

"Can't join ours, can't join theirs. Doesn't leave you with much, now, does it?"

Erg. I hate how he sounds like he's right. I mean, he's

*not.* I don't know why yet, but I'm sure there's a reason. "I can't drop everything, my whole life, just because you want me to."

"Because of your father? Because he expects you to play nice and not do anything inconvenient for him?"

"I didn't see you standing up for me when Mom kicked me out."

His eyes narrow. "Your mother didn't tell us what happened. It was months before we knew you didn't get your *V*, and by then you were already living with him. But don't think I was happy about that, or that I wouldn't have taken you. You should have called."

I look away. "I didn't know how you'd react. To me being half hero."

"It was your mother's fault, not yours. I don't know where we went wrong with her."

"And he's my *dad*." Is it such a crime that I maybe wanted to get to know him? "Whatever he expects from me, I think I caused him enough trouble last semester."

"Because you take after me." He grins and holds up a hand, making sparks. "There's nothing wrong with being a villain, Damien. Nothing wrong with it at all. I always hoped you'd inherit my power. My brother's son inherited his. He taught him all about it. And his granddaughter. I missed out on that with your mother."

"Yeah, well, there's always Xavier." I wonder if he'll get a power when he's *actually* old enough, or just when he's grown that much. Though I feel a twinge of jealousy when I think of him getting the same power as me. I do *not* want to hear Mom gushing about what an amazing ability lightning is, as if I don't have it. And I don't really want him sharing it with Grandpa, either.

Grandpa scoffs. "Let's not think about that little monster getting any worse. Right now, we're talking about you. Those heroes don't like you using your lightning. They're making you ashamed of it. I can hear it in your voice."

"Did Mom tell you I can fly? Because I can."

He laughs. "I'd heard. But I know how you feel about heights."

"I just mean that if I *did* fly, you'd make me feel ashamed of it, too."

"Maybe." He sighs. "And I like to think at least it wouldn't be on purpose. But the reality is that you don't fly. Maybe you can, but you don't. You use your lightning. You get into trouble, living with your father and going to that school, because they don't understand you. They want you to live by their rules—they want to change who you are, so you fit into their world. I don't know how you can be happy with that, and I hate to see you wasting your talents. Or having to suppress everything that makes you *you*. Your father may have taken you in—I'll give him that much—but there are consequences to staying with him. I want you to know that you have another option. You always have a place with me and your grandmother. And I'd like to make sure you always have a place in villainy."

I open my mouth to argue, but then I swallow back the words. Because he sounds like he really means it. "Thanks, Grandpa. It's nice of you to offer, but I'm okay where I am. Really."

He looks like he doesn't believe me about that, but he just nods. "Your grandmother and I only want what's best for you. I don't want to see your life get ruined because of your mother's mistakes. Golden City has plenty of heroes, whether you join them or not. The League has plenty of cogs. But the Truth needs villains who will fight for what they believe in. We need passionate people dedicated to equality. Not someone who can recite a list of rules. You won't make a difference as a hero. But as a villain, you could change the world."

He makes it sound so simple. And I'd be lying if I said it wasn't tempting. Making a difference in the world for villains? Being somebody? "I..."

"You don't have to decide right now. Here." He opens up his desk drawer and pulls out a small envelope, then hands it to me. "It's an invite to a little event we're having. You can meet everyone, see what we're about. And it's catered. Free food." He wiggles his eyebrows, like that's the most tempting thing he could have told me.

*I can't.* That's what I should say. It's not what comes out. "I'll think about it."

"That's all I ask." He picks up his phone and sends off a text. When it chimes that he has a new message, he gets up from behind the desk to show me to the door. "My associates will see you and your sister out. Oh, and one more thing before you go. We're a fledgling organization, and I would hate for the Truth to be snuffed out before it really got legs. You know the last thing the heroes want is for us to have a voice. So I can trust you not to say anything to anyone, can't I?"

"Yeah, of course."

"No one. Absolutely no one. I mean it."

"What about Mom?"

He rolls his eyes. "God. *Especially* don't tell your mother."

I smile at him.

He puts a hand on my shoulder and says, "I love you, Damien. Remember that."

X·X·X

It's *really* hard not to text Kat as soon as we get out of the laundromat. I even get out my phone, twice, on the way to the bus stop, ready to type, *I've found the Truth, ask me how*, or, *You'll never believe what happened on our mission today*. But I resist. Just barely. Though I'm pretty sure that when Grandpa said to tell "absolutely no one," he didn't mean Kat. Right?

I keep expecting Amelia to chew me out for not listening to her about making plans for each scenario. Because, after what just happened, she might decide winging it didn't work out too well. And she might blame me for that, even though it's not my fault. Because when I said we didn't need to plan, I didn't realize her default move was going to be wandering off and doing something stupid. But other than a quick, "Uh-huh," when I asked her if she was okay, she doesn't say anything. She stays a few stomps ahead of me the whole way to our stop, and then marches onto the bus and snags a window seat. She folds her arms and makes a point of staring angrily out the window when I sit next to her.

We're right by the heater, which is on full blast. I start sweating and unzip my coat. The whole bus smells like damp wool and old sweat. Gross, but somehow comforting.

"Look," I tell her, "I knew working together wasn't going to be easy, but if we're going to survive this semester—literally—we need to lay down some ground rules. For one thing, we—" I glance over at her and stop talking. Her lower lip is quivering, her face is red, and there are tears streaming down her cheeks. "Amelia?"

She puts her face in her hands to muffle a hiccuping sob. "How... how can you be so..." She has trouble talking while crying so hard. "...so calm? After what just happened?!"

Heads turn. An old woman across the aisle glares at me.

I ignore them. "Did they hurt you?" My heart speeds up. Maybe Grandpa was wrong about what his goons would or wouldn't do to her, even after he called and told them to leave her alone.

She shakes her head. "I thought they were going to kill you!"

"*Me?* They said they wanted me alive."

"They said they had to bring you *in* alive. Everyone's seen you on the internet and on TV, and they know who you are and who Dad is, and then they took you, and it was all my fault."

Wow. She must be really freaked out if she's admitting she screwed up. I consider, just for a split second, asking her to put that in writing.

Her shoulders shake with another big sob. "I was too scared to try and help you. But I should have *done* something."

Everyone's staring at us. "We're *fine*," I tell them, making eye contact with the old lady, who's still glaring at me, like she thinks I've done something horrible to make Amelia cry.

I lower my voice, conscious of everyone still probably listening in, if not actively watching us. "Everything turned out all right. So, you know. Cheer up or something."

"I'm not an idiot. I know we got caught because of me, and that the only reason we got away is because of you." She looks over at me, checking for confirmation. "So if I'd been there by myself, I still would have gotten caught. But I wouldn't have gotten back out." She sniffs really loudly, to keep the snot from dripping out of her nose, and wipes her eyes with the back of her coat sleeve. "And you haven't even told me what happened. What did they want from you? Was it the Red Bandit? Why did they let us go?"

Yeah, I was kind of hoping she wouldn't ask about any of that. "They wanted my autograph, obviously."

"For *reals*. Just tell me, Damien. Because whatever they did to you, it was my fault. So I should know about it."

"They didn't do anything to me." Not that I'd tell her if they did.

Which she must know, because she meets my eyes, looking pretty skeptical. Hers are red from crying, her eyelids puffy. "Don't lie, okay? It's just making it worse."

But I can't tell her what really happened. I promised Grandpa. And telling Amelia would be like telling the whole school, if not the whole city. "It was someone I knew. Through my mom."

"What did they want?"

"They chewed me out a little. For turning my back on villainy." No big deal. Just taking me captive at gunpoint so my grandpa could tell me he thinks I'm ruining my life.

"They didn't want anything from you?" She frowns. "Who was it?"

I stare at my knees. "Just someone who owed my mom a favor." Which I'm pretty sure isn't true, considering that my grandparents have to put up with Xavier and have had him stay the night at their house before. Mom must owe them, like, a million favors from that alone.

Amelia scrubs at her cheeks with her sleeve. "That's all?"

"They just wanted to scare me. So I'd think about the choices I'm making."

"Oh." She exhales, like she finally believes that they weren't trying to murder me. Then she scowls all of a sudden and smacks my arm really hard.

"*Ow*. What the hell, Amelia?"

The old lady across the aisle tuts disapprovingly.

"Those guys scared me, and it turns out you were fine!"

"You'd rather they hurt me?"

"No. But I was really worried. I thought I'd gotten you in trouble, and..."

"And you never would have forgiven yourself for getting your favorite brother killed? It's okay—I know the

157

truth. You don't have to say it."

She kicks my foot. "Shut up."

"Even if it was real, Amelia, we would have gotten out of it." Somehow.

She doesn't look like she believes that, but she gives it to me anyway, nodding and leaning her head against the window.

# CHAPTER 11

"The Truth?" Kat says on the phone, and I can practically hear her wrinkling her nose at it. "That sounds *so* pretentious."

"I think it's supposed to be pretentious. All activist groups have to sound pretentious. It's, like, a rule or something." The floor creaks as I make my way over to my dresser. It's morning, and I'm usually downstairs by now— to avoid anyone seeing me navigate the stairs, not because I actually like getting up early or anything—but then Kat called me back. Her phone was on silent last night, so she didn't see that I'd called until she got up.

"So they're an activist group?"

"Yeah. A secret one. For now, anyway." I grab my new favorite T-shirt from my drawer. It's black with a red and white warning sign on it that says, *DANGER. HIGH VOLTAGE.* And as if that wasn't awesome enough, there's a glow-in-the-dark lightning bolt on the white part that's only visible when you turn out the lights. Kat got it for me for Christmas. "Hold on," I tell her. "I have to put on the best shirt in the world."

She laughs. I set my phone down while I take off my pajamas and change into the shirt and some jeans.

"An activist group," Kat repeats after I finish getting dressed. "That stands up for villain rights."

I sit down on the edge of my bed, wedging my phone between my ear and my shoulder so I can put my socks on. "He wants me to join. It's... He doesn't think I have a future. You know, as a hero."

"Wow."

"I told him I was marrying you and that you were going places and would be able to keep me in the lifestyle I'm accustomed to. Possibly better than the lifestyle I'm accustomed to." What with my current living situation involving an attic/deathtrap, where the floor's one wrong step away from crumbling beneath me. Sure, Amelia's lived up here for years without falling through, but that just means it's that much more worn out.

"Your plan for the future is trophy husband?"

"*Your* trophy husband. It's a perfectly attainable goal, but he acted like it didn't count."

"Old people just don't understand how gender roles are changing for our generation."

The stairs creak with Amelia's familiar stomp, and then there's a knock on the door. "Damien! Mom wants to know why you're not downstairs yet. We have to go!"

"Go away!" I'd tell her I'm on the phone, but then she might try and steal it from me again.

She makes an outraged *hmph* noise and then stomps off.

"Anyway," I tell Kat, "he doesn't think I have a real future. If I stay at Heroesworth and don't join up with the Truth or whatever." I try to play it off like it's stupid and not important, but really I'm hoping she'll tell me how wrong that is and that of course I have a future. Maybe she'll even have a suggestion about what that future might be, since I have no idea.

Kat's quiet for a minute. "You're thinking about it. About joining up."

"I didn't say that."

"You didn't have to."

"I told him no." I sigh, letting my shoulders slump. "If he'd done this a year ago, then I probably would have jumped at it. But now?"

"Are you going to tell your dad?"

"Geez, Kat. Just because I turned down the offer doesn't mean I'm insane. Besides, I promised I wouldn't tell anyone."

"You're telling *me* about it right now."

"That's different. I trust you. And Gordon would tell the League. That's exactly what Grandpa doesn't want."

"But... Okay, don't take this the wrong way, but you live with your dad, not your grandpa. You go to hero school. Shouldn't you maybe warn them? About the Truth?"

There are more footsteps on the stairs. Slower and heavier this time, which means it's Gordon.

"If the League knew that villains were trying to stand up for their rights, they'd try to stop them. I can't believe you're saying I should rat them out."

"I know. But it isn't just about heroes versus villains if people you care about might get hurt."

"No one's getting—"

Gordon knocks on my door. "Damien?"

"No one's getting hurt," I tell Kat, keeping my voice down.

"How do you think they're going to fight for villain rights?" she says, lowering her voice to match mine, even though she's not the one in danger of being overheard.

"I... He didn't mention that part."

"Damien?" Gordon says again. "It's time to leave."

"Just a minute!"

"Can you really picture your grandpa leading some peaceful protest?" Kat asks. "Or starting a letter-writing campaign?"

Nope. "Kat, listen, I, uh, have to go." I get up from the bed, making my way to the door.

"Uh-huh. Don't change the subject."

"I'm not. I'm going to be late for school."

"Hero school. Full of heroes who don't know what's coming to them."

"Aren't you supposed to be the villain here?"

"Just— Oh! Liv got coffee for all of us. I have to go."

"Uh-huh."

"Just think about what I said, okay?"

I promise her I will, and then we hang up.

When I open my door, Gordon scowls at my high-voltage shirt, like it's not even a little bit funny, let alone hilarious and awesome. He looks like he really wants to say something about it, but he restrains himself. "Is

162

everything okay?"

"Fine."

He raises an eyebrow, like he doesn't believe that, but then lets it go. "Helen and Amelia just left. I said I'd drive you."

"I can walk. It's okay." I don't need him clocking how long it takes me to get down the stairs and then acting all disappointed that his plan of forcing me to live in the attic hasn't magically cured me of my fear of heights.

"It's cold out. And you're already going to be late." He looks me over, a worried expression on his face. "You were really quiet last night. You hardly said anything."

"Amelia said enough for both of us." All she could talk about was what happened at the laundromat. The way she tells it, you'd think we'd almost died or something. Though her retellings conveniently leave out the part where she got us caught.

"I can tell when something's off with you. Are you and Kat—"

"We're fine."

"Then did something happen yesterday? That you're not telling us?"

I told them the same thing I told Amelia, that our captor was someone my mom knows, just trying to scare me. "Did I mention that Amelia botched the whole thing?"

He runs a hand through his hair, not liking that answer. "I know it must be a strange situation to be in, getting recognized by villains while on a hero mission. Especially if they don't agree with the choices you've made."

"Dad, I don't know if you've noticed this, but *nobody*

agrees with the choices I've made. Not even you."

"That's not... There might be a few things that we disagree on, and I don't always understand why you do what you do, but..." He smooths out his shirt and clears his throat. "I was trying to say that if you have any questions for me, I'm here."

"Actually, there is one thing. And I want you to tell me the truth. Don't hold back or sugarcoat anything. Okay?"

"Of course."

I squeeze my eyes shut for a second, unable to believe I'm really asking him this. "Do you think I have a future as a hero?"

"*What?*"

"You heard me. And don't say I can join the League, because you already know how I feel about that."

"You might change your mind."

"I won't. And that's not the point. Just tell me, realistically, where you see me in five years."

He leans against the door frame, his forehead wrinkling. "You've got plenty of time to figure out what you're going to do. You're only sixteen. It's not like you have to decide right now."

"I'll be seventeen next month. And don't avoid the question. You said you wouldn't hold back."

"All right. The truth is, I don't know any more than you do. I didn't know where I'd end up when I was your age, and I wasn't half villain, and I didn't have the whole city watching to see what I'd do. So I don't expect you to know. Your friends and your sister might plan to join the League, but that doesn't guarantee them success. And it doesn't mean they know what job they'll have after they join, or if it will make them happy. No one can say where their lives will really take them."

"Great. So you think I have no future at all. Let me put in a formal request right now for Alex's room as soon as he moves out, since I'll obviously still be living here."

He laughs and shakes his head, like he thinks I'm just being dramatic. "You'll be fine. Now come on. Grab your stuff and meet me downstairs. You're late enough as it is."

X·X·X

Riley shoves his open notebook at me in Advanced Heroism third period. He's sitting at the table next to mine, so it's not exactly discreet when he passes his notebook across the gap between our desks and clears his throat.

There's a note at the top of the page. *What happened to you yesterday??*

The teacher, Mrs. Deeds, is at the whiteboard at the front of the room, talking about how impressed she is with how all our missions went. Well, with how most of them went. Amelia's sitting next to me, listening to Mrs. Deeds, but she glances over when she sees the notebook and tries to read it. I turn my shoulder and keep the page out of her view.

*You already know what happened,* I write back. Because I know Amelia was on the phone with Zach for at least an hour last night, recounting every little detail of our mission. And there's no way he didn't tell Riley as soon as they hung up.

Riley waits until the teacher isn't looking and then slides his notebook back to his desk. He scribbles on it some more and passes it back. *I know what you told Amelia. I want to hear what really happened.*

I look up from the notebook and raise my eyebrows at him. Does he seriously think I'm going to write down all my secrets in the middle of class? Leaving an easily confiscated paper trail? Not that I'm sure I want to tell him what really happened. I don't *not* want to, but it's one thing to tell Kat. It's another to tell someone who can't wait to join the League and has had all their rules memorized for years.

Riley tilts his head in response, like he knows I'm hiding something and should tell him anyway.

I roll my eyes at him and write, *If you wanted to know what happens on my missions, you shouldn't have ditched me.*

I'm in the middle of passing it back when Mrs. Deeds suddenly looks right at us and says, "Damien. Riley."

I freeze. Maybe if I don't draw any attention to it, she won't notice the notebook. Even though she obviously knows we were passing notes and is calling us out on it.

She looks at us like we're supposed to do something, like we're supposed to already know what it is. Then she says, "Come up here and tell the class about your missions."

Oh. So, this isn't about writing notes in class, then. We get up from our seats. Amelia kind of half scowls, half pouts, like she doesn't know why Mrs. Deeds would only call up one of us. Mason gives Riley a questioning look, probably wondering the same thing.

Mrs. Deeds smiles once we're standing in front of the class, doing her bidding. "I've singled you out as examples of what to do on a mission, and"—she looks straight at me for this—"what *not* to do. Riley, your mission was particularly successful, and your partner wrote in his report that most of that had to do with your actions. Would you like to tell us about it?"

Riley lets out a deep breath, seeming relieved that this isn't about us getting in trouble, and maybe kind of touched that he and Mason are still such amazing BFFs. They share a look, and Mason gives him a nod of approval.

Barf. And meanwhile, Amelia's smirking at me, probably because she realized that me being up here isn't a reward—it's some kind of punishment.

"Our mission," Riley tells the class, "was to stake out the Golden City Museum, to check for any weak points in security before the new exhibit goes up. But while we were there, we sort of noticed a suspicious guy trying to do the same thing."

"Don't be modest," Mrs. Deeds says. "Mason already told me what you did in his report."

Riley glances down at his feet, then back up again. "I might have noticed the guy first. And I was the one who apprehended him when he ran. After he realized we were onto him, I mean. He went tearing through the museum, pushing people out of his way. He looked like he was heading for the main entrance, but I took a chance that he was just trying to throw us off, turned invisible, and took a shortcut to the side entrance that's past the Egyptian wing."

A couple people nod. Everyone is watching him tell this story, totally entranced.

"I got there first, and when he came running for the door, I tackled him to the ground. Security wasn't too far behind him, so I didn't have to detain him long."

Mrs. Deeds is practically giddy with delight over one of her students doing something so supposedly awesome. She looks like it's all she can do not to hop up and down. "*And?*"

"And it turned out he was an art thief the museum had been trying to catch for months. But it's not like I knew that or anything."

"Still, you caught him without much trouble, despite how well he'd eluded the authorities before. And," she adds, addressing the whole class, "that's why I'm nominating Riley Perkins for the Heroesworth Award for Bravery in the Field. You'll be attending the ceremony at the Heroes' Gala next month."

*Seriously?* I glance over at Riley. His mouth is gaping open, and he looks like people do in game shows when they find out they just won a fabulous new car. Mason beams at him, Amelia's already not-so-secretly texting Zach about it, and a bunch of people start clapping.

"Wow," Riley says, after the applause dies down. "I've never been nominated for anything before."

"You deserve it," Mrs. Deeds tells him. Then, to everyone else, she says, "It's not every day that a mission turns out so successful, and I don't expect that sort of thing to happen every time. But I do want you all to note that it was Riley's determination to go above and beyond what was required of him that brought about that success. And now..." She looks over at me, the smile on her face wilting, like she just got a whiff of fresh dog poop. "Let's hear a firsthand account of the class's least successful mission."

"What?" She can't be serious.

She gets this stern look on her face. "Didn't you read the syllabus? This is what we do after each mission, so the whole class can learn from each other's experiences. Why don't you start by giving us an overview of your goal yesterday, and then you can tell us where you think you went wrong."

Shouldn't Amelia be up here for this? I'm not the one who screwed everything up. The one time it's not my fault and I *still* have to answer for it. "We were checking out a laundromat that was supposed to be a front for the Red Bandit. It wasn't." I shrug.

"And?"

*And* I really want to zap pretty much everyone in the room right now. Even Riley, who's supposed to be my friend, because he's still looking all starry-eyed about getting nominated for a useless award. A nomination he got without me, because apparently he and Mason make a better team.

But I don't say any of that, because that would be pretty stupid. "And it really doesn't matter what else happened because nobody got hurt and we're still here and everything."

Mrs. Deeds purses her lips and shakes her head. "You got captured by supervillains and compromised your mission. Do you want to tell us why that was?"

Um, no? Why would I ever want to tell them that? "Obviously I wanted to fail, so I'd have something to work for the rest of the semester. And to make Perkins here look good, of course."

Mrs. Deeds scowls at me. "From what I understand, these were villains you knew. Because you're half villain yourself."

A murmur runs through the class as people start whispering about that and giving me dirty looks, as if she just said I sold out the entire school instead of that I maybe happened to know some people.

Riley's paying attention now, watching me.

"Okay, fine. You got me. It was all a set up. They were going to help me sell Amelia on the black market, but it turned out there weren't any buyers, so they 'let us go.'" I make exaggerated finger quotes on that last part.

"Hey!" Amelia says, glaring at me.

"But I can say with absolute certainty that it's not a front for the Red Bandit. So I think that was a pretty successful mission."

Mrs. Deeds is obviously not impressed. She looks back and forth from me to Riley, probably wondering how the two of us ever worked together. Or maybe like she gets why Riley has a new partner. "Is that why you didn't use your *ability*"—her lip curls on the word—"to stop these villains when they pointed weapons at the two of you? Because you knew them? We all know you didn't hesitate to use your power on that unarmed superhero last semester, so I find it strange that you refused to do so in this situation."

"You mean why didn't I use my lightning to fry some guys who had their fingers on the triggers?" I absently hold up a hand and let some electricity wash over it. I don't even think about it until some people in the audience gasp, and I notice that everyone looks pretty horrified. Everyone except Riley and Amelia. And Mason, which just makes me hate him more, because it's like he doesn't think he's in any danger from me. Even though I obviously have a dangerous power and he stole my partner and I hate his guts.

I make my lightning go away, though the class doesn't stop looking horrified. "That was a free sample," I tell them. "I normally charge admission for the lightning show. If anyone wants to see more or get their picture taken—for a small fee, of course—I'll be available after class."

"No, you won't." Mrs. Deeds has her arms folded across her chest and this really harsh expression on her face. Which really undermines the email she sent out at the beginning of the semester, about how she was so happy to be working with *all* of us. "You're reporting to the office. Now." She grabs a notepad from her desk and writes something down—presumably a message about how awful I've been, and that I've been conspiring with villains to sell my sister on the black market. She tears it off and starts to hold it out. But then she pulls her hand back, like she just realized she doesn't want to make contact with me. Like I might zap her or something.

Riley comes to her rescue, snatching the paper from her and saying, "I'll make sure he gets there." Then he practically pushes me out into the hall.

I shove him off me as soon as we're out of the room. "You'll make sure I get there? What the hell was that?"

"I was trying to help you. Before you made it any worse." He glances up and down the hall, which is empty, since it's the middle of third period. "Did you really know those villains?"

I hate that he's even asking me that. "Their leader knew my mom." I also hate that I'm lying to him. Sort of. And I don't want to see the doubt in his eyes as he considers that statement, so I stare at a student-made mural on the wall. It's of a superhero and a government official—probably the mayor—both smiling and each holding one end of a giant golden key to the city. Propaganda at its best.

"And you couldn't have just told Mrs. Deeds that?" Riley asks. He sounds kind of pissed at me. Or maybe just worried.

"Amelia was the one who screwed up and got us caught. But you didn't see Mrs. Deeds calling her up to be humiliated about it. She'd rather blame the half villain."

"You didn't have to give her a reason to." He reads the note, then hands it to me. "She's recommending you for suspension."

"Wow. Good thing you're not associated with me anymore, right?"

He gives me this disgusted look. "You could get kicked out again, X. If you keep this up."

If I don't play along and let everyone treat me like I'm a criminal, he means. "That's easy for you to say. You're catching bad guys and winning awards."

"It was just a nomination."

"Yeah, but think about it. If I'd done what you did, I wouldn't be getting anything for it. And if you were still partnered up with me instead of Mason, you wouldn't have gotten anything for it, either."

He opens his mouth to argue, then doesn't. "Okay, maybe that's true. And it sucks if it is. But we still have almost a year and a half left here. Can't you just... not push people so much? And it wouldn't kill you to play by the rules for a while. Just until we graduate."

"And then what? I don't need a degree from Heroesworth to patrol the streets with Sarah. Which we both know is about the only hero work I'll ever be qualified for." And Sarah doesn't have an *H*, either, so she won't be joining the League like everybody else. Even if she really wants to.

Not that Kat would be okay with me choosing that particular career option.

"Actually," Riley says, absently scratching the side of his face and not looking at me, "Sarah will be in college then. So—"

"So it's just going to be me."

Riley shoves his hands in his pockets and doesn't say anything.

Which is all the answer I need.

# CHAPTER 12

I get sent home for the rest of the day. Mrs. Deeds wanted me to get suspended—she recommended several days in her note—but the dean rolled his eyes and said she was overreacting. Though not overreacting enough for him to send me back to class.

I had to call Gordon, and he had to come pick me up, and now I'm sitting in the car with him in the school parking lot. He took off work to come get me, after he already had to drop me off today.

He presses his hands into the steering wheel, even though he's not driving yet—though he did at least turn the car on so we don't freeze to death this time—and sighs.

I fold my arms and slump down in my seat. "If you're going to lecture me about how stupid that was, you might want to call Riley first and compare notes, so you don't have any overlap."

"You could have just told her what happened."

"See, that's exactly why I told you to talk to Riley. He said the same thing."

Gordon tilts his head a little and gives me this look, like the fact that he and Riley both told me this should mean something. "Damien. Debriefing is an important part of the process. How is anyone supposed to trust you if you don't tell the truth?"

I glare at him. "Mrs. Deeds read my report, and Amelia's. She already knew what happened. She just wanted to try and humiliate me in front of everyone. Amelia made mistakes and got us caught, but Mrs. Deeds didn't call *her* up to talk about it. She wanted to make the half villain look stupid, even though I'm the one who got us out of it. So, no, I couldn't just play along and tell the truth, because I couldn't give her the satisfaction."

"So you thought it was better to tell her you were working with the bad guys?"

I shrug. "She'd decided she wasn't going to trust me before she brought me up there. She didn't respect me, so why should I respect her?"

Gordon thinks about that. "I knew going to Heroesworth would be hard for you." He looks over at me, concern on his face. "But I thought it would be the other kids who wouldn't accept you."

"Yeah, you were totally off base with that. I have so many friends, I can't even remember all their names. I don't want to sound like I'm bragging, but I'm pretty sure I'm going to be voted most popular for the yearbook."

"Damien."

"What?"

He shakes his head. "I was trying to say I never expected that kind of behavior from your teachers. They're supposed to be adults."

"Adults who work in a school that's supposed to be all hero. They can be letterist all they want and no one will notice."

He gives me a long look, like he's considering how much truth to that there is. I think he's going to try and tell me that I must have it wrong, that I've just misidentified all the ways my supportive superhero teachers have tried to help me. So when he opens his mouth to say something, I cut him off.

"I don't want to talk about it. I use my powers to stop someone I was told kidnaps and murders kids, and I end up on the news like it's the worst thing I've ever done. Riley uses his power to catch someone who just happens to look suspicious, and he's getting a freaking *award*."

"He's getting an award?"

I shrug with one shoulder. "He was nominated. Because I wasn't there. I'm sure he'll win." Just as long as none of the judges see him hanging out with me or anything.

Gordon twists up his eyebrows. "Riley turns invisible. He doesn't hurt anyone. Him using his power is completely different from you using yours." His gaze falls to my high-voltage shirt, and he gets this worried look, like he thinks I really might not understand.

"They might be different, but that doesn't make it fair. Riley didn't have to try and catch that guy. It wasn't part of his assignment. But he did what he thought was right, just like I did."

"He didn't hurt anyone."

"He could have. He was invisible, and he tackled some guy. What if him being invisible, like, caught the guy off guard so much that he slipped and hit his head? He could have gotten seriously hurt, or maybe died or something. And that's ignoring the fact that Riley could have gotten hurt, too. But all the bad guy did was steal art. And before you say anything, I know that stealing is a crime. But stealing some paintings isn't worse than torturing and murdering innocent kids. You get that, right?"

"Damien, that's not—"

"The point? It *is*. Because if Riley had accidentally hurt that guy while using his power, he would have still been a hero for it. But I use my lightning just enough to stop some murderer—who was *fine*, by the way—and I'm public enemy number one. And yeah, he wasn't a real murderer, but I had every reason to believe he was, and all I did was take him down. I knew what I was doing. I wasn't hurting him—not that badly, I mean. But I could have. You don't think I wanted to? If he really was a killer, then he would have deserved whatever he got from me. But I held back. And I know using my power at all was against the rules. But what I did and what Riley did weren't all that different."

We're both quiet for a while. Eventually, Gordon says, "Have you—"

"The last twenty-four hours have really sucked, okay? So let's just drop it. You can lecture me about how crazy you think I am tomorrow." Or maybe the next day. Or next week. Or preferably never.

"I was just going to ask if you've had lunch yet."

Oh. "I'm not hungry."

"Okay. Get out of the car."

"What?"

"Come on." He unbuckles his seat belt and opens his door. "I took off work, you're out of school, and we have all afternoon to spend together. That doesn't happen very often. The roads are clear, and if you don't want lunch, then we can at least practice driving."

"You want me to drive? I mean, I'm supposed to go home and think about what I've done or something. I thought you'd be mad, not want to spend time with me."

He looks almost hurt by that. "What happened yesterday wasn't your fault. And what happened today... Maybe you could have handled it better, but it wasn't right for your teacher to interrogate you like that. I'm glad you stood up for yourself. And of course I want to spend time with you."

## X·X·X

We drive for a while and then end up getting lunch anyway, because I lied about not being hungry. We go to the same diner I was at with Riley and Sarah before. Because it's apparently Gordon's favorite restaurant. Of course it is. Though they do have a sandwich named after him, and not just because he's kind of famous, but because he used to order it so often when he'd come here for lunch, back before he even had a TV show. Which I have to admit is kind of cool, even though I'd rather eat dirty socks than ever order a sandwich named after my dad.

"Amelia was so afraid of the vacuum cleaner when she was little." Gordon laughs good naturedly and takes a bite of himself—a toasted turkey sandwich with some kind of special sauce—while he reminisces. "At first she would just run and hide, but then she decided to stand up for herself and would scream at it whenever we turned it on."

"That's so hilarious," I tell him, setting down my Liberty Burger as I pretend to be as amused by that story as he is. "I bet it's not as funny as when you were potty training her, though, right?"

His eyes light up. "Actually, there was this one time when we were at the store, and a fan stopped Helen for an autograph, and Amelia took her dirty diaper off right in the middle of the frozen aisle and handed it to them. A complete stranger!" He starts to laugh again, then catches himself and clears his throat. "I'm not sure your sister would appreciate me telling you that."

"No, no, we're cool. I just want to know about all that time I missed." Mainly any embarrassing stories Amelia wouldn't be able to live down if someone were to spread them around school. You never know when you're going to need to blackmail someone, and she already used her power to take back all the baby pictures of her that I stole.

"Well, maybe keep that one between us."

"Of course. I won't mention it." Not unless provoked, anyway.

Gordon smiles. "This is fun. I'm glad we're doing this."

"Any time you want me to get kicked out of class, just say the word."

He takes another bite of his sandwich, thinking about something. "You know, what you said earlier—"

One of the waitresses at the front of the diner suddenly screams. We both turn to look and see her drop her tray, dishes clattering everywhere, and hold her hands up, as if someone's pointing a gun at her.

Which is exactly what's happening. A guy in a black ski mask stands at the front of the diner, around the corner from us. He shouts, "Nobody move!" and gestures with the gun to the cashier. "Start emptying it. Now!"

The woman behind the counter turns pale. Her hands shake so bad, she almost doesn't get the cash register open.

My heart pounds. Lightning crackles up my spine and along my arms, hidden by my coat sleeves. The high-voltage shirt is particularly appropriate right now.

And then, before I can blink, much less zap the guy, Gordon gets to his feet, drawing way too much attention to himself, considering that there's a robbery going on. And especially considering that the bad guy was ignoring us. "Look at me," Gordon says, talking to the guy with the gun. "You don't want to hurt anybody."

The robber guy really seems like he disagrees. He narrows his eyes and points the gun at Gordon.

"Are you insane?!" I whisper. Really loudly.

Gordon shifts his eyes over toward me, then away again.

"Your kid's right," the robber says. "Don't be a hero." Gordon's wearing plain clothes, because he wasn't filming today, so the robber doesn't know who he is and hasn't recognized me yet. If he's even going to—he might be one of the, like, three people in Golden City who haven't seen the videos of me.

Gordon takes a step forward, like he didn't even hear him. "Drop the gun. You don't have to do this."

"Shut up! I said don't move!"

Electricity surges in my hands. I ball them into fists, not sure what to do. Because if I don't do *something*, I'm going to lose control. But zapping the guy with his finger on the trigger isn't any better of an idea than it was yesterday. Especially when it's pointed at my dad.

Gordon actually takes another step toward the guy. Like he has a death wish or something. What the hell does he think he's doing? He has flight, not superspeed. He can't dodge a bullet.

The robber guy's hand is trembling. "Stop! If you come any closer, I'll shoot!" He cocks the gun, meaning business.

This time Gordon doesn't move. He holds very still.

I can*not* die in a superhero-themed diner. With my dad, who was eating himself.

Now would be a really good time to pull out one of Sarah's gadgets and cause a distraction. Except she's been on hiatus for three months and hasn't made me anything. So I have to improvise.

Gordon shifts his eyes toward me again. Like he's trying to tell me to do something.

There's a pass-through into the kitchen. I blast electricity toward the grill. Flames leap up from the greasy hamburger patties and strips of bacon. One of the cooks shouts and jumps back.

The guy with the gun turns to look. And that's when I zap him. A little harder than I meant to, because all the adrenaline rushing through me makes my lightning harder to control. But I don't kill him.

The robber drops to the floor, twitching. Gordon rushes over to him and kicks his gun away.

I march up to Gordon, keeping an eye on the bad guy in case I need to zap him again. "What the hell is wrong with you?! You were just going to, what, sacrifice yourself?" I can't help thinking of Riley's dad and how he gave himself up to save that bus full of people. And how much Riley wishes he hadn't.

"I was thinking of you," Gordon says.

I hold up my hands. "I have *lightning*! I could have just zapped him in the first place! Which I was going to, if you hadn't gotten in the way. And saying, 'Hey, son, could you zap that bad guy over there?' before you jumped into harm's way would have been way easier than trying to communicate silently because there's a gun pointed at you!"

"Actually... I wanted you to escape out the back and call the police."

"Wow. And here I thought you didn't want anyone to end up *dead*."

"I acted out of instinct. It's my job to protect people."

"So, you thought I was too dangerous to do anything? Is that it?" That better not be it. I get that he doesn't trust me to use my lightning power without hurting people, but... Okay, no, I don't get it. And if he tells me he'd rather risk his freaking life than let me use my villain power, I'm going to seriously lose it. "Don't tell me you were scared for that guy." I point to the robber on the floor.

Gordon looks me in the eye. "Damien, I honestly just didn't think about it. I'm not used to having someone around who can…"

"What? Kill people?"

He sighs. "Who can take care of themselves in a dangerous situation. I thought you'd… I don't know what I thought. But you're my son—I'm supposed to protect you, not the other way around." He looks down at the robber on the floor. "I hate for any situation to come down to violence, but—"

"If you even try to say you wish I hadn't done that, or that I could have hurt somebody—"

"—you did good."

"Oh."

"And…" He looks away, kind of guiltily. "I might have judged you too harshly before. About what happened with that superhero last semester."

"You what?" I blink at him. "That must be the crazy talking. I know you just almost died, but don't say anything you don't mean."

"Damien, I *do* mean it. What you said about your situation being similar to Riley's…" He takes a deep breath and puts a hand on my shoulder. "You were right."

Those three little words I've been waiting to hear. And it might just be the adrenaline, but I feel really good. Like maybe we understand each other better than I thought.

"Thanks, Dad," I mutter, not wanting him to know just how important it was to me that he said that.

The guy on the floor twitches. He seems pretty out of it, but he manages to look up at us and say, "I did it for the Truth."

The warm, happy feeling disappears and my blood runs cold. My mind races, thinking maybe I misheard him. Even though I know I didn't.

Confusion spreads across Gordon's face. "That's a strange thing to say. The truth?"

"The Truth will be heard," the robber guy mumbles, his voice partially drowned out by approaching police sirens.

"What truth?" Gordon asks.

"He's pretty messed up," I tell him, kind of hating myself for it. And for how quickly the lie comes out of my mouth. "He probably doesn't know what he's saying." His eyes look kind of unfocused, so he really might not. Even if I do.

Some guy who knows about the Truth tried to rob this superhero diner. He could have shot Gordon, or me. And maybe there is something to what Kat said, about how I should warn him. But maybe Grandpa has a good explanation for this. This guy might not actually be associated with the Truth at all. I should find out, before I blow Grandpa's secret.

Except that, after everything we've been through today, it feels wrong to keep this from Gordon. Not saying anything after all this is kind of like lying to his face. But then the police rush in, asking Gordon what happened and who stopped the bad guy. And he beams at me, all proud and stuff, and says, "My son saved everyone. He's a hero."

So I swallow back any doubts I have about not telling him what I know. Because Gordon isn't disappointed in me for once, and the last thing I want to do is screw that up.

He thinks I'm a hero. So why remind him that I'm a villain?

# CHAPTER 13

"That's never going to happen again," Grandpa says on the phone Saturday. "You have my word."

I'm sitting on my bed up in my room, because of course I can't have this conversation downstairs where someone might hear me. Even though it's kind of freezing up here in the attic. It's so cold, I actually have on my Heroesworth sweatshirt I got for Christmas, because all my other coats are in the hall closet by the front door.

"How did it happen in the first place?" I ask him. "Because that's two days in a row now I've had a gun pointed at me, no thanks to you."

"Damien. You have my sincerest apologies about that. The first time was necessary, but the second... That shouldn't have happened. I didn't sanction that. You think I'd do all this work and get villains organized to stand up for their rights, and then blow the whole thing by having my guys go out and commit petty thievery? We've got better things to do than that."

I'd like to believe him. I *do* believe him, as far as them having better things to do goes. "It was a superhero diner."

"So?"

"So, I think it was more than petty thievery. I think it was a hate crime."

He laughs at that, as if that couldn't possibly be what happened. "One of those tourist traps? They're just for out-of-towners. Real superheroes don't eat at places like that."

"My dad was there!" And me. Not that I picked that place or anything, but I can still do the math. He doesn't think I'm a real superhero. Or he just doesn't want me to be one.

"I'm sorry," Grandpa says grudgingly. "But I promise we didn't have anything to do with it. We're not responsible."

"Then who is?"

"Some idiot who got it into his head that being pro-villain means being anti-superhero. You know how it is—I tell my guys about the Truth and bring them in on it. Then they bring in their guys, and so on. That's how I'm building this organization, with people I can trust. But I can't always control who *they* trust, and somewhere down the line someone made a mistake. They trusted the wrong guy, and he not only flew off the handle, using the Truth as some excuse for a robbery, but he pointed a gun at *my* grandson. You don't get much stupider than that."

"So, you're saying you don't have control over everyone in the Truth."

"That's not what I said."

"But how can you be sure this won't happen again? No one got hurt, but they could have, and—"

"I'm taking care of it."

"What does that mean?"

"It means you have nothing to worry about."

I'm thinking over my answer to that when there's a knock at my door. "It's me," Sarah says on the other side.

I tell her to come in. Then I tell Grandpa I have to go.

"Wait a second," he says. "I want you to know what a great job you did yesterday. You shouldn't have had to be in that situation, but that guy would have tried to rob that place whether you were there or not. And because of you, everything turned out all right. No one got hurt, and no one found out about the Truth."

"Are you praising me for being a hero?" I motion for Sarah to have a seat on the bed.

"The way I see it, you kept our secret from getting out too soon. Thanks to you, villains still have a chance to be heard. So you can call that whatever you want, but I know what you've done for villainy. Think about that."

I don't promise him anything. I just tell him I have to go and hang up.

"Are you okay?" Sarah asks me.

I slip my phone in my pocket. "You mean because I stopped an armed robbery yesterday?"

"You said this was an emergency."

"No, I said it was urgent."

"That means it's an emergency."

"It means I needed you to come over here right away."

"Like an emergency. And you never want to hang out on Saturdays, because that's when Kat comes home. So I figured it must have been something really serious."

I roll my eyes at her. "Kat's stuck at school this weekend. I mean, not that I can't hang out with you even if she's not. But I called you here to talk about the future." I stand up and clear my throat, holding my arms behind my back.

Sarah's forehead wrinkles. "I don't think you should drop out of Heroesworth. You don't have anywhere else to go."

"What? Who said anything about dropping out?"

"I just figured, because your mission went so badly..."

"It was *one* mission, Sarah."

"I know." She sounds relieved. "That's what I'm telling you. So don't give up. You still have a future, and you never know what could happen."

"I was talking about *your* future."

"Oh." She looks away and picks a piece of fuzz off my new comforter.

"Yeah. Because your so-called 'award-winning' boyfriend informs me you're going to college after high school is over."

"He hasn't won yet. He was just nominated. You know that."

"Focus, Sarah. He said you were going to college, but I've called you here today to rethink that decision."

"But—"

I clear my throat. "Exhibit A." I point to her. "You're already successful in your chosen field. What can some school really teach you, anyway?"

Sarah's expression sours. She scoots back onto the bed and draws her knees up. "I'm not successful. I keep hurting people, or almost hurting people."

"Someday you're going to get over that and realize you're not a maniac. And don't think I'll be above saying 'I told you so,' because I'm not."

"And it's not my chosen field. They don't really teach gadgetry at college, but I was going to maybe do robotics. Except now I'm not. Because..." She splays her hands out in front of her, palm up, and studies them. "I just don't think it's a good idea. I might do math instead. Or art history."

"Art history? Sarah, you can't major in art history."

"You can. I checked. All the schools on my list have it."

"That's not what I meant." I sigh and sit down on the bed with her. "You're not interested in art history. And you're really good at making things."

"Things that explode."

"Well..." She's got me there. "That's not the only thing you're good at. I think going to college would be a waste of your talents. Not to mention a waste of time that you could be spending as my sidekick instead. Why put all that money and effort into school when you could join the working world right off the bat? With, you know, your dream job."

Sarah looks at me like I'm crazy. "My dream job isn't being your sidekick."

"We'll work on a new title."

"It's not even a job. We don't get paid."

Right. I was hoping she wouldn't notice that part. "Riley's going to join the League, but I'm still going to be here for you."

"You don't want to be alone, you mean." She gives me this skeptical look, like she's got me all figured out. Which maybe she does.

"Sarah, Sarah, Sarah. This is about you, not me. I'm just telling you that even if Riley's going to abandon you and join the League, you can still count on your best friend. Which is me."

"Joining the League isn't the same as abandoning me. Riley wouldn't do that." She pauses. "He's not abandoning you, either."

I wave that away, dismissing it, as if it had never even occurred to me. "I don't care what he does with his life. We're not even working together anymore—I don't need him."

"You say that, but you failed your mission and then got kicked out of class."

"I didn't fail the mission. But even if I did, it was Amelia's fault. And I only got kicked out of class because our teacher is a letterist bitch."

"So you don't care that Riley might be getting an award? For work he did without you?"

"Where are you getting this stuff? Of course I don't care."

Helen shouts from downstairs, her voice muffled. "Damien! You have a visitor!"

Yeah, I know. She's a little late with that. And why can't she just text me?

"I'll admit that me and Riley made a good team," I tell Sarah. "But so do the two of us."

"You don't need my gadgets anymore, since you have lightning."

There are footsteps on the stairs. I guess because I didn't shout back at Helen that I heard her, so now she's coming to tell me in person.

"Don't reduce yourself to just being about the gadgets, Sarah. All Riley can do is turn invisible, but I still find ways for him to be useful."

Sarah's eyebrows jump up. "That's not how he puts it."

There's a knock at the door. "I heard you!" I shout at Helen. Then, to Sarah, I say, "It's not your gadgets that are important. Maybe I don't need them anymore, to attack bad guys. But I do need *you*."

The door opens. I'm about to tell Helen that I said I heard her—I didn't say to come in. But it's not Helen standing there. It's Kat.

"Kat!" I jump up from the bed. I don't know why. Somewhere in the back of my mind, I think it will make me look excited to see her, which I am. But I'm pretty sure it just makes me look guilty. Even though I haven't done anything to be guilty for. It's not a crime for me to hang out with one of my best friends. "I thought you weren't coming home this weekend."

"Our teacher extended the deadline for our project, so I thought I'd surprise you." She bites her lip, glancing back and forth from me to Sarah, looking hurt. "You need her?"

I swallow. "It's not what it sounds like."

"Really? Because it sounded like you were talking

about doing superhero stuff together."

"Oh. Well, then it kind of is what it sounded like."

"He was just upset," Sarah says, "because he's not going to have anyone left after everybody graduates."

"*Sarah.*" I say her name through clenched teeth. "You're not helping."

Kat glares at me. "Nobody, Damien? Seriously?"

"I, uh, didn't mean you. I mean, I thought you'd have something else to do, after you graduate, and you're not a superhero, so—"

"Neither is she!"

"I know, and of course I want to work with you, too. It's just... Sarah's my sidekick, and you're going to Vilmore. You can't waste that on doing superhero stuff. Plus, your dad would kill you."

"And it's not a real job," Sarah adds. "It doesn't even pay."

"Again, Sarah, *not helping.*" I motion for her to shut up.

"I think one of us should go," Kat says. She glances at Sarah, then turns to leave.

"Kat!"

She hurries out of the room. I follow her, not even pausing to avoid the especially creaky floorboards, which I think is pretty brave of me. Though then Kat practically runs down the stairs, and I hesitate at the landing, which is kind of the opposite of brave.

Crap.

I take a deep breath and keep going, because there's no way I'm letting my stupid fear of heights stop me from going after her. I take the steps a lot slower than she did, though pretty quickly for me, even if my stomach drops when one of the wobbly boards actually *slides* a little beneath me. My heart races as I hurry down the rest of the stairs, telling myself not to think about it.

Kat's already out the front door when I get to the bottom. Alex actually turns away from the TV to watch the drama, and Helen's not-so-subtly giving me this sympathetic-but-accusing look, like she thinks *I* must have done something to cause Kat to flee the house.

Which maybe I did, but I didn't mean to.

Thankfully, Amelia doesn't come stomping out of her room to gawk. Which probably just means I was wrong about her being home and not that she, like, respects my privacy or anything.

Kat was in such a hurry to get out of here, she left her striped pink and black scarf draped across the back of the couch. I grab it as I run past and out the door. I hope Kat didn't drive here—she has her license—because there's no way I can catch up to her if she did.

The old-but-not-so-old-it's-unreliable car her parents got her for her birthday is in the driveway. She's sitting in the driver's seat, not going anywhere.

I open the passenger door and get in. "You forgot your scarf."

"Thanks." She lets out a long breath. Her gaze flicks over to me. "I thought I'd have more time, before you got here. Because... you know. The stairs."

"I made record time. Though step number twenty-two almost slid out beneath me."

"It did not."

"It did. I nearly died."

A grin slides across her mouth real quick, then disappears again. "I'm sorry I freaked out. But that really hurt. I mean, you *need* her, Damien? You're supposed to need *me*."

"I do need you."

"Not just in the bedroom, I mean."

I roll my eyes at her. "Kat, seriously. The bedroom stuff was furthest from my mind."

"Uh-huh."

"I need you for lots of reasons."

"Just not that one." She takes a pair of gloves out of her pocket and puts them on. "The two of us were supposed to work together. Me and you. We were supposed to go to Vilmore and be partners in crime."

"Are you mad I didn't go to Vilmore?" After I saved the school last semester, they offered me admission and a full-ride scholarship. I could have practically lived with Kat in the dorms and made our dream of working together come true, but I turned it down. It was the right decision, but that doesn't mean I don't realize what I gave up.

Kat shakes her head. "It would have been cool if you went there, but I get why you couldn't. I'm okay with that. I just... It hurts to see you living our dream with somebody else. I know we have to work with different people at school, but you were trying to set up a whole future with her."

"She's my sidekick."

"I'm *so* tired of hearing that. And the fact that you didn't even think of me, when you were thinking about your future…" She presses her hands to her face.

I put my arm around her and draw her closer to me. "Kat, of course I think about you being in my future. But until I can offer a competitive salary, along with a top-notch health and dental plan, I think you can do better. I mean, Sarah's right—it's not exactly a paying job."

Kat drops her hands. "You won't be alone after graduation, Damien. You know that, right?"

"Everyone's going to join the League. Except you and Sarah. But you're going to have some awesome villain job when you get out of school—I know you will—and Sarah's going to college for some reason. And even if nobody goes anywhere, they'll still be *going somewhere*, you know? And then there's me."

There's a knock on my window, startling both of us. Sarah's standing there, shivering a little in the cold.

I push the button to open the automatic window. "Hey, Sarah. Sorry I took off."

Kat rolls her eyes, like it's ridiculous of me to be apologizing.

"It's okay," Sarah says. "But it's starting to snow, so I should get going and walk Heraldo. It takes forever to get him into his dog booties, but he loves chomping at snowflakes."

"Okay. Do you need a ride?"

Kat glares at me.

"I mean," I add, "I can get Helen to take you home."

"It's okay," Sarah says. "I'm going to walk." She leans forward, peering into the car at Kat. "It was good seeing you again. And Damien doesn't really need me. I'm sure he wouldn't have said it if he knew you could hear him."

"Sarah!"

Sarah gives me a thumbs up before ducking her head back out the window, like she thinks what she said was actually helpful or something. Then she heads off in the direction of her house, pausing once to turn and wave good-bye at us.

"Kat, listen, I—"

"I should go, too," Kat says, cutting me off. "I can't drive in the snow."

"I'll go with you. We can hang out at your place, or walk back over here."

"I think I should just get home." She stares blankly out the windshield while she says it, not looking at me. "By myself. Sorry, Damien."

"But..." She came home this weekend to see me. Me, her favorite person in the whole world. And now after only, like, ten minutes together, she's leaving.

I stare at her for a while, not quite believing that this is happening. Then I get out of the car.

# CHAPTER 14

Grandpa's party is way classy. It's black tie and is at a really nice, villain-owned hotel. There's no sign outside the door to advertise it or arrows pointing where to go or anything. It's all really secret and cool. The invitation has instructions to go up to the guy at the front desk and say, "Golden," which is the name of the room the party's in. I'm pretty sure the guy recognizes me when I come up to him, because he gets that shocked look in his eyes, but he doesn't say anything. He just asks for my invitation, shines a special light on it to reveal a seal of authenticity, and then says, "Right this way," as he leads me down the hallway toward the party.

He never once mentions my name, even though I'm pretty sure he knows it, and he never says anything about the Truth. And if he's secretly taking pictures of me to post on the internet later, he's doing it awfully discreetly. Grandpa's really kept this whole thing under wraps. I'm surprised it wasn't an elaborate costume party with required face masks like in the movies.

The ballroom is full of people, all wearing tuxes and fancy dresses. I'm scanning the crowd, looking for Grandpa, or at least for someone I recognize, when I catch a glimpse of bright red hair. She's not wearing a wedding dress this time, but Mom still stands out in a crowd. I quickly turn around, so maybe she won't see me, but it's already too late.

"Oh, Damien, there you are!" Mom says as she hurries over to me, dragging Xavier by the hand. "Your grandfather said you'd be here."

"Let go!" Xavier whines, trying to pull his hand away so he can get to me. "You're not allowed to hold onto me unless I say so!"

"I think maybe Grandpa needs a hearing aid, because I told him I couldn't make it." It's really annoying that he didn't believe me. And that he was right. "And he wasn't even going to tell you about it, so what are you doing here?" Even if he did tell her about it, there's no way he'd let her bring Xavier.

"Is that any way to greet your mother? Honestly. I'm his *daughter*. Of course he told me about it."

I raise my eyebrows, giving her a skeptical look. She's got on a green dress I've seen her wear a million times that also has a dark stain across one boob, her stockings have a huge run going up the side, and Xavier isn't even in a suit, just a black T-shirt and some blue pants that come up a little short. And he's only wearing one sock.

"All right. Your grandmother told me. She said she couldn't babysit tonight and also that she couldn't be bothered to think of a fake excuse. Hmph."

"So you brought him here?"

"And speaking of babysitting..." She tugs on Xavier's arm, yanking him forward. "Taylor had to visit one of his aunts in the hospital—it's an emergency—and your grandfather's busy, and your grandmother refuses, so—"

"No. No way. I'm not—"

She shoves Xavier's hand into mine before I can make a run for it. "I'll just be a minute! I haven't been to the bathroom in over four hours."

"Mom, wait! You can't—" But she's already disappeared into the crowd, like she couldn't get away fast enough. Or maybe she really does have to go to the bathroom that bad.

Xavier's hand feels small and sticky in mine. I glance down at him. Not only is he not in black tie, like he was at the wedding, but his hair is wild and sticking out all over. He stares in the direction Mom went, his lower lip sticking out.

"She's coming back," I say, more to myself than to him.

"I *know*. Let go of me. I'm not a baby."

I drop his hand, which seems to surprise him. I make a face and wipe my palm on my thigh.

"Hey! You're... you're not supposed to let go."

"And you're not supposed to exist, but we don't always get what we want."

"I could get lost! Or *stolen*. And then Mommy will hate you."

"Or she'll realize she's better off and that I did her a favor." I shrug. Plus, as far as her hating me goes, I think that ship has sailed.

Xavier gapes at me, unable to comprehend how little I care about what happens to him.

"If you don't want to get lost or stolen, I suggest you go find Grandma." I walk off into the crowd, looking for Grandpa. He's the one who invited me to this thing, and even though he's going to gloat about how he knew I'd show up, I still want him to know I'm here.

"Wait!" Xavier's footsteps follow me.

I don't even look back at him. "Her hair's pink right now. She shouldn't be hard to find." And just because she said she wouldn't watch him doesn't mean she'll abandon him in a crowded room. Not like I'm doing.

Grandpa's standing near a piano—a piano that someone is actually playing—holding a martini and talking to a couple of his friends. He spots me right away and motions for me to join the group.

He smiles at me, sounding more proud than gloating. "You made it."

Xavier comes up beside me and tries to make me hold his hand again, but I make a fist and don't let him.

"This is my grandson, Damien," Grandpa says, introducing me to his friends.

They nod and say hello, taking turns shaking hands with me. "We've heard a lot about you," one of them says.

"Who hasn't?"

"Actually," Grandpa tells his friends, "if you'll excuse me, I need to have a few words with my grandson." He puts his arm around my shoulders, so it's clear he means me and not Xavier. Not that there was any confusion.

The other guys say they'll catch up with him later and wander off to find their wives.

Grandpa elbows me in the ribs. "How do you like the party? Pretty fancy, huh?"

"Is that what you wanted to talk to me about? Because if you're going to say I told you so because I showed up—"

"I'm not. I'm glad you're here."

"Oh."

"*Stop it*," Xavier screeches, still trying to shove his hand into mine. "Stop trying to lose me!"

Me and Grandpa both make disgusted faces at him. I consider making my hand spark, because that would at least get him to stop touching me, even if it probably wouldn't do anything to shut him up. But, thoughtful and amazing half brother that I am, I decide to warn him first. Even if I really, really don't want to. "If *you* don't stop that, I'm going to zap you."

He scrunches up his face, angry and red, sucking in a breath like he has a lot to say about that.

I hold up my hand and make electricity flow across my skin.

"You can't do that to me," he says, though he doesn't sound that confident about it. He glances up at Grandpa, like he's checking to see if he's going to step in and tell me I'm out of line.

He's not.

I glare at Xavier until he scowls and shoves his hands in his pockets.

Grandpa smiles at me. "I want to talk to you about your future."

"Look, just because I showed up, it doesn't mean—"

"It doesn't mean you're joining the Truth. I know." He sighs. "But you're here. You made the effort to come to this shindig. Tell me why."

I raise my eyebrows at him. "Uh, you invited me."

"Don't be smart about it. And don't look at me like you think I'm going senile. You're not here just because I invited you. I'd like to hear your reasons."

"It's not going to change anything."

"We'll see. And speak up."

"I just... You said you were sticking up for villain rights, and that I could make a..." A difference. But I catch myself before admitting that's something I care about. I don't want him thinking I actually do want to join, even if I kind of do. "I support villain rights. Obviously."

"Why?"

"Geez, Grandpa. You *know* why."

"Humor me. It's my party, my organization. I want to know."

"Uh, because I'm a villain? And I live with heroes. I spend all day with them at school. And they *don't* care about us having rights. You should see how they've rewritten the history books. They make it out like villains have never done anything worthwhile or contributed to society, like we're all just here to get in their way and cause trouble. They give themselves all the glory. And they act like villains are diseased or something."

"And that bothers you. Enough for you to come here."

"Of course it bothers me! I mean, I don't care what they think about me. The kids at school and stuff. But, yeah, the way heroes act like all villains are automatically evil and that they're better than us? That pisses me off. A lot. And I knew things weren't great for villains, like, before I went to live with heroes. But even my family, the people I *know* care about me and don't hate me for supposedly being half evil, they still say and do letterist stuff all the time. My friends, too." I shrug, like it's no big deal. "But, Grandpa, I can't join the Truth."

"*I* can join," Xavier says in his most annoying nails-on-the-chalkboard voice. "You should have asked me instead."

I glare at him again. "Did I mention I'd zap you for talking?"

He glares right back but doesn't say anything.

"Damien." Grandpa puts a hand on my shoulder. "Listen to yourself. You live with heroes who supposedly care about you—"

"They *do*."

"—and even they don't treat you like an equal. What hope is there for the rest of us?"

"It's not like that."

"But you're staying out of a group that supports villain rights because of them. That doesn't sound like they're really looking out for you."

"Grandpa—"

He holds up a hand. "Hear me out. Your only reason why you can't join—not even that you don't want to, but that you can't—is because your father's a superhero. The man who wasn't in your life for sixteen years, who didn't raise you."

"He didn't even know about me."

"Because he had random relations with *my daughter*, a complete stranger, and it never occurred to him that there might be consequences." He cracks his knuckles. "He wanted to pretend it never happened and let your mother deal with the results all on her own. Some hero."

"I don't think…" Okay, maybe he did want to pretend it never happened. But I know he would have been there if Mom had told him about me. "He's around now, okay? And I don't want to screw things up for him again."

Grandpa puts a hand to his temple, like I'm giving him a headache. "So instead you're screwing up your life. And your future. He shouldn't want that for you."

"He doesn't." My voice is quiet. I don't know if it's true or not. I can't imagine Gordon wanting me to screw up my life, but he and Grandpa have totally different ideas of what that means. "I want villains to have rights, okay? But I can't do this. I'm trying to be a hero and to not make trouble for once. You made this organization partially because of me, but I didn't ask for that. So, I'm sorry, but I can't be part of the Truth."

"Yeah," Grandpa says, sighing and looking at me like I'm a huge disappointment. "That's what I thought."

## X·X·X

This is the first time we've had to have partners in Rescue Strategy fifth period. It's the only other class me and Riley have together besides Advanced Heroism. The teacher says to pair up for the assignment today, and Riley looks over at me like he expects us to work together.

And okay, yeah, we sit next to each other and are mostly on speaking terms. But that doesn't mean I'm not still pissed he picked Mason over me.

"Come on, X," Riley says when I glance around the room, looking for someone else to be partners with, even though no one is even getting out of their chairs, just turning to the person next to them. "Don't pretend we're not working together." He sounds really put out about it.

"You shouldn't make assumptions about who I'm working with. Just like I shouldn't have assumed we were working together in Advanced Heroism. I mean, it's not like we *made plans* or anything."

He rolls his eyes at me. "Will you get over it already? It's not like I *wanted* to ditch you. Er, not that that's what happened. I didn't ditch you, and if we'd been working in teams of three—"

"I get it," I snap. "You don't have to say it." If we'd been working in teams of three, he would have included me. But when it was only two? He picked Mason. Who he hadn't seen or talked to for years. So obviously we weren't as good of friends as I thought we were. He can say it was because I zapped that superhero during our final and endangered his scholarship—and maybe it was partly because of that—but he was the one trying to convince me we should still work together. At least until Mason showed up. "Are you sure you can afford to do this assignment with me? I wouldn't want you to risk your GPA."

"Let's just get it over with. Everyone else has already started."

It's true. Pretty much everyone in the class is bent over their sheets of paper, scribbling stuff and discussing the question on the board.

The teacher, Mr. Hernandez, wanders over to us, giving us a suspicious look. "Is there a problem here?"

I open my mouth, but Riley glares at me. "We're working," he says, scrambling to get a piece of paper out of his binder.

Mr. Hernandez nods in approval and goes off to annoy another group.

The question on the board is about what we would do if we had to rescue two people at once, but we only had time to save one of them. We're supposed to talk it over and figure out what our plan would be.

Riley carefully writes down the question on the piece of paper, even though it's on the board. "This one's easy. We split up. There's two of us and two of them."

I shake my head. "That's what *everyone's* going to write."

"There's a reason they're all writing it."

"Uh, yeah. The reason is that they're idiots. It's too obvious."

He sighs. "You're making this too difficult."

"Let me guess. Your best friend Mason would just go along with it. Because you're both 'on the same page.'"

"You don't get it. Mason wouldn't just go along with it. He'd *agree* with me. He wouldn't be looking for ways to cause trouble."

Is that really what he thinks I'm doing? "He'd agree with you, but then he'd just stand there. Why were you the only one who went chasing after that guy at the museum?"

"That wasn't—"

"Next scenario," Mr. Hernandez says, grabbing a marker and writing on the whiteboard as he talks. "Not only do you have two people you need to save at the same time, but it turns out both rescues are a two-person job. No splitting up—I saw a lot of you writing that on your papers. *And* one victim is the person you care about most. The other is the person your partner cares about most. If you can't agree on which one to save, they both die. What do you do?"

"See?" I tell Riley, gesturing at the board. "It was a trick question."

"I was the one who spotted the guy at the museum. There wasn't time to talk it over. The guy saw me notice him, so he took off, and I followed."

"And Mason saw you running after some guy, and he… what?"

"He went and got security. And don't look at me like that. It all happened really fast. There was nothing he could do."

"If you were really on the same page, you wouldn't have needed to talk anything over. If *I'd* been there—"

"You would have run after him with me. I know, X. But you know what else you would have done?"

I swallow. "Mason having a lame power doesn't make him a better partner than me."

"You would have zapped the guy."

"Come on—give me more credit than that. I wouldn't

208

have—"

"Yeah, you would. You would've zapped that guy, who was unarmed, and I would've lost my scholarship." He rubs his face with his hands and breaths out through his nose.

"I don't just go around zapping everyone who looks suspicious. Geez. And before you say anything about what happened at the diner on Friday, that guy was definitely armed. He was pointing a gun at people, including my dad. So if that's what you're getting at—"

"It's not. Let's just work on the assignment." His eyes flick down to the paper. "Who do you care about most?"

"Kat. You're not even going to ask if I'm okay?"

"Sarah already told me." He writes down her name, then adds Kat's next to it. "She said you were fine. And trying to convince her not to go to college."

The teacher stands in front of the whiteboard and waves a hand to get our attention. "Three more minutes, people!"

"You say that like it's a bad thing. Sarah doesn't need to go to college. Plus, if she becomes my sidekick full time, she won't leave town. You should be on board with this."

"Just because she's going to college doesn't mean she's leaving. Two of the schools on her list are in Golden City. Come on, we only have three minutes to figure this out."

"We don't need three minutes."

"Right." He sounds a little relieved. "Because we're saving Sarah." He starts to circle her name.

"*What?* Why would you think that?"

"Because you care about Sarah, too? Sarah's the most

important person to me, and you're her best friend, so, if you do the math—"

"Whoa. This isn't about math, Perkins. You can't decide whose life is worth more based on math. Unless, in this scenario, Kat is pregnant with my unborn lovechild and you're killing two people by not even considering rescuing her. Three, if it's twins. I don't even know how you can be so heartless."

"That's not—" He tightens his grip on the pencil he's been using to write with. "Nobody's pregnant in this scenario. It's just them. And Kat can take care of herself."

"Yeah, so can Sarah. That's not the point. Everybody needs help sometimes."

"Okay, fine. Sarah's more useful to society."

I gape at him.

Riley glances away. "You know she is."

"What, as opposed to Kat, because she's a supervillain?"

He ducks his head. "That's not what I meant. But Sarah's a genius. She invents really amazing things."

"Really amazing things that have a tendency to blow up."

"Really amazing things that *you* rely on. Sarah's brilliant."

"And you think that makes her better than Kat."

He sighs. "I was just trying to say that if we're being objective about this—"

"Time!" Mr. Hernandez shouts. "How many of you came up with an answer?" He scans the room for raised hands. "Anybody?"

Everyone looks at each other. Nobody raises their hand.

Mr. Hernandez folds his arms and gets this smug grin on his face, like that's exactly the result he expected.

Which really annoys me, because we didn't come up with anything, either.

"I've been teaching this class for ten years, and nobody's ever—"

The door opens, interrupting him, and another teacher pokes her head in. She seems really frazzled, and there's urgency in her voice. "Turn on the TV. Quick! It's on every station!" She ducks back out into the hall, not even closing the door all the way, and her hurried footsteps echo as she runs to the next classroom.

I share a look with Riley.

"What's going on?" he whispers.

"How should I know?"

Mr. Hernandez's face goes pale. He grabs the remote off his desk and turns on the TV.

And there, on the screen, is a dark, grainy video of two superheroes interrogating a supervillain. The supervillain is tied up, unable to move. One of the heroes is holding a club. The other raises his hands and shoots bright beams of energy at the villain, who immediately starts screaming.

Then the image dissolves and words appear on the screen:

*This is the Truth. It's time to believe.*

# CHAPTER 15

My heart races as more images appear on the screen. A couple of superheroes kicking someone on the ground. A written account from an anonymous villain of her treatment while in League custody. The camera zooms in on some key phrases:

*They didn't feed me for four days.*

*Later, they determined I was innocent and debated what to do with me.*

*I almost didn't get out alive.*

A cold, unsettling feeling creeps up my spine. I glance around the room, gauging other people's reactions. Pretty much everyone is staring in horror at the screen.

Someone says, "That's a lie. Villains are *liars*."

Heads turn toward me.

I ignore them, keeping my focus on the TV. There are a couple pictures of villains right after being released from the League. Black eyes. Broken bones. Burns.

My stomach churns, empty and sick. I never trusted the

League, but somehow this is worse than I expected.

Riley's hands are shaking. He looks over at me, but I pretend I don't notice.

Other kids are starting to mutter that it's fake. Everyone knows the League doesn't do this kind of stuff. *Villains* do. It would be just like them to stage something like this.

Photos could be set up. Written accounts could easily be faked. But these are real. I recognize some of the superheroes in them. Not anyone I know, but people I've seen on the news sometimes. They wouldn't pose for pictures like this. And there's something so visceral about the images, I don't know how anyone can question them.

Then a video comes on. I swallow when I see myself on the screen. I'm at Grandpa's party. Dressed up and obviously there on purpose. You can see the top of Xavier's head, but all the focus is on me.

I can feel everyone in the room staring at me again. Riley leans in and whispers, "What's going on, X?"

But I don't have an answer for him. I sit and watch, just as stunned as anyone.

Well, maybe not quite as stunned as them. I do have some idea of what this is, at least. I just don't know why it's happening.

In the video, I say, "I support villain rights. Obviously."

Grandpa's questions are cut out, so we never hear his voice. It jumps to me answering him.

"Uh, because I'm a villain? And I live with heroes. I spend all day with them at school. And they *don't* care about us having rights."

An angry murmur runs through the classroom. Sweat prickles along my back and sparks ignite beneath my skin. I can't believe this.

"You should see how they've rewritten the history books," I continue in the video. I'm clenching my fists as I'm saying it, giving away how much it matters to me. "They make it out like villains have never done anything worthwhile or contributed to society, like we're all just here to get in their way and cause trouble. They give themselves all the glory. And they act like villains are diseased or something."

I can't believe Grandpa was *filming* me. Without asking. And now he's broadcasting it on every channel.

The video jumps past Grandpa's part again, going straight to me, practically shouting, "Of course it bothers me! I mean, I don't care what they think about me. The kids at school and stuff. But, yeah, the way heroes act like all villains are automatically evil and that they're better than us? That pisses me off. A lot. And I knew things weren't great for villains, like, before I went to live with heroes. But even my family, the people I *know* care about me and don't hate me for supposedly being half evil, they still say and do letterist stuff all the time. My friends, too."

It ends right there, before I tell Grandpa I can't join the Truth. I don't know if that's a good thing or a bad thing. Me saying I can't join might have taken some of the edge off what I just said—*maybe*—but it would also be an outright admission that I knew about the Truth before all this.

Though maybe that's not exactly a secret now, either.

It stops on a freeze frame. Xavier's head is tilted back as he looks up at me. Words dissolve onto the image:

*The son of the Crimson Flash believes in the Truth.*
*Do you?*

## X·X·X

I find Gordon in his dressing room at the TV studio. I didn't even have to ask where he was—as soon as I stepped foot in the building, everyone stared at me, until someone pointed down the hall, knowing exactly why I must be here.

Gordon's pacing the room when I come in. He looks a little startled to see me and glances at the clock on the wall. He frowns but sounds more tired than mad when he says, "You should still be in school."

Technically, that's not true, because school got out two minutes ago. But I couldn't have gotten here this fast unless I left early. I couldn't exactly stay for the rest of fifth period when pretty much the entire class was glaring at me like they were three seconds away from finding some torches and pitchforks. Plus, Riley was giving me this wide-eyed look like he couldn't believe what I'd done and was expecting me to fill him in. Which I wasn't really looking forward to anyway, and I certainly wasn't going to do it in front of the angry mob.

I expected Gordon to be pissed at me. Maybe not "my son just blew up part of the school and got arrested and expelled" pissed, but still mad. Probably a lot mad. Even though I didn't have anything to do with that broadcast

215

and I was only stating my opinion. But he couldn't know any of that. And, given his lack of pissed-off-ness, I'm not actually sure he saw that video, even if everyone else in the studio obviously did.

"So," I say, clearing my throat and bracing myself for the worst, "you didn't see the—"

"Of course I saw it." His face is pale, and he's giving off this really weird vibe, part anxiety, part sadness.

"Okay, well, I know this looks bad. But I can tell you who's behind it." If Grandpa's going to sell me out, then I can do the same to him. I tried calling him about a million times on the way here, but he kept sending me to voicemail. Finally he sent a text that said, *It was for your own good.*

Yeah, right.

I expect Gordon to look shocked or pleasantly surprised, like he knew he could count on me after all. But he just stands there, waiting, like he's worried I'm going to say it's *me* or something. As if I'd have time for that.

I raise an eyebrow at him. "Don't you want to know who I was talking to in the video?" I mean, Grandpa pretty much threw me under a bus for his own gain, so it's not like I don't want to return the favor. But I was kind of expecting at least a little bit of excitement over this. "Come on, Dad. I'm giving you an exclusive."

"You lied to me." Gordon sinks down into a chair, his head in his hands.

"Not exactly, but—"

"When we were at that diner. The perpetrator said he tried to rob them in the name of the Truth. Did you know?

Did you know what he meant?"

Well, this isn't going how I planned. "Yeah, I'm getting to that. If you'll just let me—"

"You didn't say anything! You knew this was going to happen, and you didn't tell me. That's *lying*, Damien."

"I wanted to tell you."

"But you didn't."

"I couldn't. I promised, and, no, I *didn't* know this was going to happen. I knew about the Truth, but that's it." Mostly.

He sits up, watching me carefully. "I'd really like to know what's going on here. I thought you wanted to be a hero, and now..." He lifts up a hand, then lets it fall to his lap in defeat. "You joined some villain terrorist group."

"Whoa. First of all, they're not a terrorist group."

He tilts his head, challenging that.

"They haven't hurt anybody. And second, I didn't join. And I'm not going to." Especially after the crap Grandpa pulled today. "So relax a little, okay?"

He scowls at me. "Don't tell me to relax. My son was on TV today supporting a terrorist movement against the League. After lying to me and keeping secrets. Because what? Being a villain is more important to you than your own family?!"

I can't help wincing at that. "I have *two* families, remember? My grandpa—I mean, Alistair Locke—"

"I know who your grandfather is, Damien."

He says that like it should be obvious, but it's news to me. "He started the Truth. He wants me to have a future in villainy. I told him no. But he asked me to keep it a secret, and I couldn't betray him. So, yeah, I didn't tell you."

"But you meant what you said in that video."

He looks me in the eyes, and I glance away. "I didn't know he was recording me. Or that he was going to make me the Truth's spokesperson without my permission." And without any payment.

Gordon sighs and pinches the bridge of his nose. "I wish you'd come to me about this."

"Why? So you could tell the League, and they could make sure no one ever heard of the Truth or about how villains are treated like crap every day? That's exactly what the League wants—to shut us up, so they can keep oppressing villains. And I know they have their precious rules and everything, but you saw those pictures. Where were their rules then? Is it okay to attack an unarmed villain as long as you really, really don't like him?! Everyone acts like I did the worst thing ever when I zapped that superhero, but you know they wouldn't have even blinked if that guy had been a villain. If I'd zapped a supervillain, it wouldn't have made the news."

Gordon stares at me, his mouth gaping a little. "Damien, I meant I wish you'd come to me about *this*. You said in that video that even the people that care about you are..." He hesitates, not wanting to say it.

"Letterist?"

He nods. "You've obviously got a lot of pent up anger about it. And I'm sorry if I've—if we've—been contributing to that."

"Wow." Did he really just apologize to me? For being

*letterist*? "But it's okay. I know you're not doing it on purpose."

He gets up and puts his hands on my shoulders. "It's *not* okay. I don't want you to feel like an outsider in your own home. It's bad enough that you have to deal with that at school, but I want all my kids to feel safe when they're under my roof."

"So, you're not mad?"

He looks at me like *What do you think?* "Of course I'm mad. You still lied to me. You might not have joined your grandfather's terrorist group, but you agree with him. You made that very clear in that video, and the fact that you didn't know it was being recorded just shows how truthful it was. You chose to keep his secret for him, instead of coming to me about it. You assumed you couldn't trust me, and that you *could* trust him, even though he's—"

"A villain?"

"He's a murderer." He pauses a second to let that sink in. "He's killed people."

He says that like it's going to shock me or something. As if I don't know Grandpa's work history. "Gee, I'd sure hate to be around someone who's killed people. I certainly wouldn't want to be around them every single day, or live in the same house with them, or eat the food they've made. That would be a crime in itself, don't you think?"

"Helen's not a murderer."

"She's killed people." Like Kat's grandfather, for instance. Not that he didn't deserve it or anything, but still.

Gordon gets this really defensive look on his face and

steps back. "She was in Special Ops in the League. It was her job to take out dangerous criminals who couldn't be dealt with any other way."

"That the League decided to kill, you mean. But what gives them the right? The League decides some villain should be taken out, and that makes it okay to murder them?"

"It's not something they just *decide*." Gordon's got his shoulders back and his chin tipped up, in full-on stern-but-self-righteous mode. "They have rules in place. There's a series of criteria a villain has to meet, as well as certain circumstances. The League doesn't send Special Ops after a criminal lightly."

"But the League decides what the criteria are, right? They still decide what the limit is and when to send out their team of assassins."

"Of course they do. I know what you're getting at, but the League is the only organization qualified to make that call."

"Says them. I get that it was Helen's job to take out criminals the League decided were too much of a threat. What I don't get is why that's okay, but Grandpa doing the same thing for villains makes him a murderer."

Gordon's eyebrows come together and one side of his face sort of twitches. He takes a deep breath, like he has to calm himself before he even tries to answer that. "Villains kill innocent people."

"My grandpa didn't."

"Not according to the League. We'd have put him away a long time ago if we had the proof. But that's the difference between us and villains. We need evidence before we condemn someone. Before we go after them. Villains only need a means. And your grandfather's superpower gives him that means. It makes it easy for him."

He means Grandpa has lightning. Just like me. "See, you don't even know when you're being letterist."

"I'm not being letterist—I'm being realistic. Your grandfather is... not who I'd want you to choose as a role model. And the fact that you trusted him and kept dangerous secrets for him—"

"Just because you don't like the idea of villains finally having an organization of their own doesn't make it dangerous!"

"—it really hurts. And the Truth *is* dangerous." He gives me this look of pity, like he feels sorry for me for believing otherwise. "It's already destroying reputations."

"By exposing the truth. If those superheroes in the pictures didn't want a bad rep, then maybe they shouldn't have done what they did."

He holds up a hand. "Maybe. But we don't know what really happened. All we know is that some pictures were shown out of context, and now prominent members of the League are going to be harassed and brought under suspicion."

I can't believe him. "So you really think that heroes treat villains in a safe, unbiased manner?"

"I didn't say that."

"No, but it's what you meant." And if there'd been pictures of villains torturing heroes, he wouldn't have thought twice about the context or given them any benefit of the doubt.

"I just think that the Truth is going to be trouble, and I don't want you involved with it."

"I'm *not* involved with it."

"Everyone in Golden City is going to believe otherwise. And when it gets out that your grandfather's the mastermind behind this…"

"It's not evil for villains to want rights."

"I know," he says, his voice hushed. "But when the Truth starts doing more than ruining reputations—when things get violent—I think you're going to regret being associated with it."

He sounds so sure about that, that things will escalate. Kat pretty much said the same thing, that Grandpa's not the type to do things peacefully. So I don't argue with him, because it's probably true. But that doesn't mean that what the Truth stands for, what they're trying to accomplish, is automatically wrong. "I wasn't trying to be associated with them. Grandpa took that video without me knowing."

"But you were there with him. You said all those things, and it's obvious you meant it. You chose that. Just like you chose to keep secrets for a man who's killed superheroes. With lightning," he adds, as if I didn't know that part.

"I'm not my grandpa."

"No," Gordon says, sounding relieved, "you're not. And I really hope you stay that way."

# CHAPTER 16

People glare at me at school the next morning. They make a point of bumping into me really hard in the halls. Gordon and Helen thought maybe I should stay home. Just until this "blows over," as Gordon said. I pointed out that that could be never, and I'm pretty sure Helen agreed with me. She just also agreed with Gordon that a school full of superheroes who all watched that broadcast might not be the safest place for me right now.

But I don't care how much the kids at school hate me. I'm not giving them the satisfaction of not having to deal with me.

Someone jostles me again, this time with an elbow aimed at my ribs. I try not to wince or show any sign that it hurts, even though it does. A lot. I kind of succeed, but then someone else flat out shoves me, and I accidentally crash into Amelia, who gets squished against the wall.

"Ow!" she yelps, glaring at me. She dusts off her arm where I ran into her, as if I'm covered in filth or something. She takes her time readjusting her backpack and says, "You *don't* have to wait for me."

I lean against the wall, out of the way of the crowd. Maybe if I just stay here until the bell rings, I'll be able to get to class with some dignity intact. "Come on, Amelia. What kind of brother would I be if I didn't wait for you?"

"The good kind." She says it all snotty, and I know the only reason she walked into the building with me was because Helen was watching, since she insisted on driving us to school. But then Amelia glances over at me, looking worried for a second. "You're not going to zap anyone, are you?"

"Wow, you think so highly of me."

"I just mean, because everyone's mad at you. And pushing and stuff. I've seen you get freaked out before."

"Do I look like I'm freaked out?"

She bites her lip, looking me over. "Not yet."

"It was a rhetorical question. I'm not going to zap anyone." That's just what they want me to do. Not that anyone here wants to get zapped, but if I did lose it, then at least they could point to me and say they always knew I was bad news. And I'd probably get kicked out of school again.

"And you're not going to blow anything up?"

"*No.* Just go to class already."

Amelia opens her mouth, like maybe she's going to protest. She hesitates, then says, "Who was that boy?"

"What boy?" I ask, even though I know exactly what she's talking about.

"The one in the video. He had red hair."

My stomach knots up. No one in Gordon's family knows about Xavier, or that he's my all-villain replacement. "I don't know. Just some kid."

She doesn't believe me. It's obvious from the way she scrunches up her eyebrows and takes a step closer to me. "He was staring up at you. And he was standing *really* close. You knew him."

"I was watching him for his mom, okay? He's a relative, but I don't know him that well."

"Oh." She sounds like she wants to believe me, but like something about that doesn't sit right with her.

I hate that she can tell that I'm lying. Or at least keeping something from her. I could just say, "That's my brother," because it's not like she would know Mom had him after I left and used some weird growth formula on him. But I can't help feeling that it would be obvious that Mom likes him better than me. What with him actually living with her and everything.

Before Amelia can ask any more questions, I tell her I have to get to class and head down the hall, not waiting for a response. I get a few more shoves, and one girl actually tries to trip me, but I avoid her. Riley's waiting for me outside the door to my first-period class, even though his is all the way across the school.

"You're going to be late," I tell him.

He looks mad. A little relieved to see me in one piece, but still mad. "I want to know what the hell happened. I tried to call you yesterday."

"You and everyone else I know."

"I get that you're probably in trouble, and that maybe

you couldn't answer your phone. But that's why I'm here now. *Tell me* what's going on."

"Later, okay? You're going to be late for class, and that's probably going to look bad for your scholarship or whatever."

He clenches his fists in frustration. "Will you let that go already?!"

"I didn't mean it like that." Well, maybe a little. "Just... I'll tell you at lunch."

"Tell me now, X."

"Why? Because you're worried I'm part of the Truth and you don't trust me anymore? Or you don't want to be seen with me?"

He shakes his head. "I know you're not part of the Truth."

"How? You saw that video, just like everybody else."

"Because you wouldn't. I know you wouldn't."

I could have. I was tempted. Really tempted. And only a year ago—maybe even only six months ago—I would have been all over it. But Riley's so sure I wouldn't have done it. Maybe he's right, or maybe he only thinks that because it's what he needs to believe. Either way, his faith in me feels misguided.

"Listen, Perkins, I—"

I don't get to finish what I was about to say, because someone comes at me from the side and slams me into the wall.

"*You,*" the guy who just pushed me says. He's taller than me. A lot bigger, too, and he has this look in his eyes like he really wants to kill me. "You're going to pay for that little stunt you pulled."

I assume he means that video of me, which wasn't really a "little stunt." If it was a stunt at all, I'd say it was a pretty big one. "Yeah, now's not really a good time for me. There are, like, a ton of people in line ahead of you who want to tell me I suck, and you can't just cut in front of them. You'll have to take a number and try again later."

Riley's eyes go wide, and he motions for me to shut up.

Which is probably a good idea, but it's also not going to happen.

The guy glares at me. "You think you're so smart, but all you villains are exactly the same. *Worthless.*"

"Great. Another fan. Autographs are five bucks."

"He's kidding," Riley says.

"Yeah. For you, ten bucks."

The guy shoves me into the wall again, and this time I bang my head. "My *dad* was in those pictures!" he shouts, even though I wouldn't think he'd want to advertise that.

"I guess villain-hating runs in the family."

A couple people have stopped to see what's going on, though none of them attempt to break it up. No teachers appear either, despite us being right next to a classroom.

"My dad taught me everything I know. He wouldn't do those things."

"Really? Because you're about to attack a villain right now. Did he teach you that, too?"

"He taught me not to back down from a fight. Especially one involving a villain."

A fight *he* started. "You don't want to mess with me. Seriously." Lightning prickles beneath my skin, and I let it cover my arms and collect in my hands.

I hear Riley swear under his breath. Like he thinks I'm actually going to use it, when really I've got everything under control.

The guy—who someone in the gathering crowd just referred to as Brad—makes a really ugly, very unimpressed face. "No, *you* don't want to mess with *me*." He holds up a hand, which starts glowing. I've seen this power before. It's an energy ray that burns like hell and could actually, you know, kill me.

I'm so going to die right now. Why did Riley let me say all those things? Why did Gordon and Helen let me come to school today?! I wonder if I can somehow leave a message for Kat, telling her I love her and could she make sure there's a good turnout at my funeral. And to serve pirate-themed cupcakes. First Mate Suckers can do the eulogy.

"I'd prefer to punch you in the face a couple times," Brad says, making his hand glow even brighter, "but I can make do with this."

Crap.

How is this actually happening? I'm supposed to be the dangerous one at this school.

"Stop!" Riley shouts, stepping between us, even though there's not a whole lot of room between my lightning and Brad's ball of energy. "Just let it go."

"He doesn't belong here," Brad says. "And if you like villains so much, maybe you don't belong here, either." He raises his hand to fire, whether Riley's in the way or not.

I make my lightning die down long enough to shove

Riley out of danger without zapping him. He stumbles into a couple people in the crowd. There's nowhere for me to go, and if I use my lightning, I'll get expelled. For good this time. And Brad's still going to mess me up either way. I can't help the zaps of electricity that run along my arms and up my back, making crackling and snapping sounds. My hair stands on end, making my head tingle. Maybe I should just let him punch me in the face and get it over with, but I'm not sure I could keep from zapping him. And it won't matter who started the fight or that he had a huge part in it—all anyone will take from it is that the half villain used his villain power again. This time on another student.

Brad doesn't look smug or anything when he realizes he's got me. He just looks disgusted, like he thinks this really is what I deserve and beating me up is just part of his daily chores. The energy in his hand grows. He's going to do it.

And then I hear running footsteps, and someone shouts, "Shut your eyes, Ry!" and the whole hallway gets blindingly bright. So bright, I can't see *anything*. My eyes snap closed, and blobs of color appear behind my eyelids.

"Not okay," the voice says scoldingly, I think to Brad. And this time, I recognize it.

I'm not sure which is worse: getting burned to death with energy rays, or getting saved by Mason.

Using his stupid light power.

In front of *everybody*.

"I don't want to hear it." I glare at Riley. We're in his car, on our way to his house after school.

He scrunches up his eyebrows, not taking his eyes off the road. "I didn't say anything."

"But you're going to."

"Okay. Would it be so bad to admit that Mason totally saved your ass this morning? Because he did."

"That's why I don't want to talk about it." The last thing I need is Mason showing me up with his lame ability. Which is *not* better than lightning in any way, even if it was maybe useful just this once.

"You could at least, I don't know, go easy on him." His eyes shift over to me real quick, then back to the road.

"What's that supposed to mean?"

"I'm just saying that you don't have to make jabs at him all the time. Or roll your eyes whenever he's talking."

"It's not my fault everything he says is pretentious."

Riley sighs as he slows down to turn the last corner toward his house. "You would have gotten expelled today if it wasn't for him."

"He shined a light. Big deal."

Riley smacks his hand against the steering wheel. "It *was* a big deal! And I'm not asking you to like him. But after today, you can see why he makes a good partner."

Better than me, he means. "Because he showed up at the last second?"

"Yeah, because of that. And he doesn't pick fights."

"Geez, Perkins. You were *there*. You know I didn't start that."

"No, but you didn't have to antagonize him so much,

230

either."

"So, what, I was just supposed to stand there and take it?"

"I don't..." Riley trails off as we pull up to his house, and it's pretty obvious why. Curtis's car is in the driveway. Riley hesitates after getting out, and for a second I think he's going to say we should go to my house instead. But he doesn't.

"Wow," I tell him as we follow the stepping stones that lead across the yard. "I really thought your mom would have moved on by now."

"He's not so bad," Riley mutters, but the stiff way he holds his shoulders makes it pretty clear he doesn't believe that. Not that I couldn't have guessed anyway.

"Yeah, you sound real thrilled about it."

He shrugs. "He makes my mom happy."

"I find that extremely hard to believe."

Riley ignores me and unlocks the front door. "We can talk in my room, okay?"

I still haven't explained how I ended up in that video for the Truth. It was too crazy at lunch time, plus everyone kept staring at me, and Mason wouldn't shut up about what happened this morning. Plus, Riley's not the only one who deserves an explanation. "Sarah's not here yet."

"Yeah, but..." He glances over at Curtis's car. "We should go to my room anyway."

"He's been dating your mom for a couple of weeks, and he's already controlling whether or not you have friends over?"

"It's not like that. But everyone in Golden City heard what you said yesterday, X. And not everyone agrees with it."

Oh. "So you don't want to be seen with me. In your own house."

He scowls. "I stood up for you this morning. I ate lunch with you. And I shared my textbook with you in Rescue Techniques because you forgot yours. So shut up about me not wanting to be seen with you and don't start anything."

He doesn't wait for me to agree before going inside. Curtis is talking on his cell phone while shuffling through a stack of folders on the dining table.

"I don't see the Trentons' file," he says, right before he looks over at us. His forehead immediately wrinkles with disapproval. "Hold on, honey. Riley's here." He starts to cover the phone with his hand, then changes his mind. "Actually, let me call you back in a minute. And I'll check the cabinet one more time. I'm sure it's there."

Riley hangs his coat up on the wall, along with his knit hat and scarf. Then he motions toward his room, meaning we should hurry before Curtis gets the chance to talk to us.

Too late.

Curtis hangs up and clears his throat. "Riley." He says that all authoritative, as if he has any right to tell him what to do. "What's going on here?"

*What's going on here?* Is he serious with this crap?

"We're going to hang out in my room. What are *you* doing here?"

"Your mom thinks she left a file behind this morning.

The Trentons want to look at more townhouses. I did an early patrol today, so I had time to help her out. And it's a good thing I came by." He glances at me, then at Riley. "I know you saw that broadcast yesterday. So what's he doing here?"

"Damien's my *friend*."

"He *was* your friend. Before he betrayed the League."

You tell someone your honest opinion *once*, and this is what happens. "The League betrayed themselves."

Curtis's face gets kind of red, and he twists up his mouth, like something tastes bad. "I want him out of this house. You're too young to know better, but this is for your own good. You'll thank me later."

Riley gapes at him in shock. "It's not your house."

"I'm the adult here, Riley. This is how it works."

"You don't make the rules. You don't even live here. And you might be dating my mom, but that sure as hell doesn't make you my dad."

The front door opens right as he says that, and Zach walks in. I can tell from the look on his face—kind of scared, kind of excited—that he heard the whole thing.

Curtis sighs. "You know your dad wouldn't approve of this. He believed in the League. What do you think he'd say if he were here right now? Do you think he'd be happy that you're friends with a villain? With a *terrorist*?"

"Whoa! I am *not* a terrorist." Why do people keep thinking that?

Zach stands next to me. "You want to talk about what Dad would want? Because I'm pretty sure he wouldn't want you sleeping with our mom!"

Curtis winces at that. "Zach, stay out of this."

"No. Damien's my friend, too. We actually *want* him here. And if he says the League did all those things to villains, then it's true and they deserve it!"

"*Zach,*" Riley says.

"And that's exactly why I don't want him here. He's a bad influence on you kids. Your mother and I talked about this, and—"

"You *what*?!" Riley clenches his fists. "You talked to her about us? Behind our backs?!"

Curtis holds up his hands, motioning for Riley to calm down. "She was worried about what she saw yesterday. So we decided it would be best if you didn't see him anymore."

"*You* decided, you mean," Zach snaps. "Mom wouldn't say that."

"Well, she did. And until further notice, you two aren't going anywhere except school and back. You can still have friends over," he adds, as if that makes it okay, "but only ones we've met and approved of. Riley, we're happy to have Sarah and Mason come by anytime. And Zach..." He hesitates, like he doesn't want to finish that sentence. "We feel it would be best if you stopped seeing Amelia."

ah

# CHAPTER 17

"Come on, Amelia." I'm standing outside her door later. "I need to talk to you."

"No!" she shrieks. "I'm never speaking to you again!"

I'm about to say that at least *something* good came from all this, but I stop myself. She's been crying in her room for about half an hour, after spending at least that long crying on the phone with Zach. Peppered with intermittent shouts at my wall about how much she hates me and that this is all my fault.

Which it *isn't*—it's clearly Curtis's fault—but listening to it is making my exile to my room kind of unbearable. Not that I'm officially exiled or anything. Gordon and Helen "aren't mad" at me, they just look at me like they don't know who I am, which makes me feel like I'm about to throw up. And like I don't belong here.

I tried to ignore all that and got Alex to play dinosaurs with me for a while. He got some new ones for his birthday last month, and the whole collection now includes three T-Rexes, his old Velociraptor, a Stegosaurus, and the Brontosaurus I got him, which he tells me isn't a real dinosaur anymore. So we've been pretending that it's an experiment gone wrong. Specifically the Velociraptor's experiment, since he gave up the spy business, married the Stegosaurus, and started a mad science lab. The T-Rexes are all brothers and also cowboys—one's the sheriff—and their posse is always trying to take down Velociraptor and co. Which was recently made a lot easier, since they discovered that Velociraptor has a lot of unpaid back taxes.

That's how it usually goes, anyway. Today neither of us was really that into it. Velociraptor wasn't devious enough, the T-Rex brothers caught him too easily, and they weren't even that thrilled about it. Eventually I looked up at Alex and said, "I'm *not* part of the Truth."

He shrugged one shoulder and said, "I know," but unenthusiastically, like he either didn't believe me or didn't care, because I still said those things. I still said everyone who cares about me is letterist.

We were quiet for a while, our hearts *really* not into the game now. Then he made an excuse, saying he had homework to do, even though it's Friday, and gathered up all his dinosaurs and disappeared into his room.

That just left Jess, who I'm pretty sure isn't mad at me or having any conflicted feelings about what I did or didn't do, but she was taking a nap.

And Riley's not allowed to hang out with me anymore. And Sarah's helping out with Bingo at the retirement home tonight. She did call me, at least, when she got to

Riley's house. She put me on speaker phone and I was able to explain everything that happened. They got pretty quiet after that, and the suspense was killing me. Finally, they said they didn't hate me or anything—though kind of begrudgingly—and Sarah said she understood why I kept my grandpa's secret. Riley didn't get a chance to say much of anything, because right then his mom got home and he couldn't get caught talking to me on the phone.

But no matter what they *said*, I still got the feeling things were a little different between us. Like they had a lot to process before they could really decide how they felt about all this.

So.

My exile isn't official, but it might as well be. It's Friday night, but Kat's not coming home this weekend. She didn't say it was because of that incident with Sarah last Saturday, but she didn't really need to, either. I tried to call her a few times this week, but she didn't pick up. The only time I really talked to her was after Grandpa broadcast that video of me, when she called to see if I was okay and to find out what was going on. At least she's mad at me for a different reason than everybody else. It's kind of refreshing.

But that does mean that while I'm stuck here, it's really hard to block out the sound of sobbing and the occasional yelling at me coming from the other side of the wall.

So even though Amelia says that she's never speaking to me again, I open her door and come in anyway.

She's lying face down on her bed, though she quickly sits up so she can scream, "Get out!" Her eyes are red and puffy, making them look extra beady as she narrows them at me.

I close the door behind me and lean against it. I can't believe I'm doing this. "It's going to be okay, Amelia."

"No, it's not!" She hurls her pillow at me. Her aim is pretty terrible, though, so it misses and hits the door with a *thwack*.

"It's not like he broke up with you." I know this not just because Zach wouldn't do that, but because I could hear almost every word of their conversation, or at least Amelia's side of it.

"He just can't see me or talk to me anymore! We don't even go to the same *school*." She reaches for her pillow— either to hug it or throw it at me again—and remembers it's not there. She uses her power to teleport it over to her. I get ready to dodge, but she buries her face in it instead. Her words come out muffled when she says, "He's going to forget about me."

I sigh and make my way over to her, wincing as the floorboards creak. I sit down on the edge of her bed. "He's not going to forget about you. And how long can Curtis really ban him from seeing you, anyway?"

"I don't know—how long can you go without screwing up?"

"He's just their mom's stupid boyfriend."

"But his mom agreed, too." Amelia sniffs dejectedly. "I thought she liked me! But they don't think I'm good enough for him now, because I'm related to *you*."

I thought their mom liked me, too. Obviously she didn't like either of us more than Curtis. "They'll get over it."

"Not before Zach forgets about me. And don't say he won't, because that's what boys do. If you don't see them for too long, they forget about you and go after someone else. Someone they actually see every day."

"Uh, you know I'm still with Kat, and I don't see her every day."

Amelia shakes her head. "That's different. She's more... *memorable* than me." She makes a vague hourglass shape in the air with her hands, as if that looks even remotely like Kat, and as if Kat being hot is the only reason we're still together. "And you get to call her all the time and she can at least visit you on weekends. But even with all that, I bet she still worries about it. About all the girls you *do* see all the time."

"Kat knows she has nothing to worry about." But I can't help thinking about last weekend, when Kat overheard me practically begging Sarah to be part of my future plans. Which I wouldn't have done if I knew Kat was coming home, but I guess that's part of the problem. Maybe a big part of it. I swallow, a guilty ache spreading through my chest. "I mean, I wouldn't do that, and neither would Zach."

"Not on purpose, but it happens. It happened to Tiffany's sister, Leslie, when her boyfriend went away to college this year. He was totally in love with her before he went. They spent *all* their time together. And"—Amelia glances back and forth, then lowers her voice—"they'd even had *sex*." She pauses a second to let the gravity of that sink in. "He swore nothing was going to change between them, and at first he called and emailed all the time. Then he just stopped. And *then* he brought a different girl home for Christmas! He didn't even tell Leslie they were broken up first! And when she confronted him about it, he said he needed someone who was there, at school with him. Who wasn't still in high school and who was going through the same stuff he was. Like that was supposed to make it okay."

"Just because that guy was a selfish douchebag doesn't mean Zach is. Besides, you and Zach don't exactly have a long-distance relationship."

"We're not going to have *any* relationship if I never get to see him."

"I think *if* is the key word here. You really think his mom and Curtis are going to lock him up and never let him use the phone or the internet? Even if they say they're gong to, it won't last. It's too much work—they'll get lax about it. And, worst case, Zach can turn invisible."

"So?" Amelia raises an eyebrow at me.

"So, it's kind of hard to keep tabs on someone you can't see."

She stares blankly.

"I'm talking about sneaking out. You're allowed to leave the house, and they can't really stop him. Problem solved."

Amelia doesn't look too happy about it, though. She chews her lip for a second, then scratches at some of the tear tracks on her face. "You think he'd really do that? Just to be with me?"

Well, that and to defy Curtis. "I don't think he's going to just give up and find someone else because it's easier."

"I guess you're right," Amelia says. "I mean, he's still friends with *you*, and there are tons of people it would be easier to be friends with. Way easier."

"That's not what I was getting at. I'm a great friend, and totally low maintenance."

But she's smiling now, and her eyes don't look as red. "If he can put up with you, then he's not going to give up on me."

"Zach doesn't have to 'put up with me.' Zach, like my many other friends, thinks I'm awesome."

She's already reaching for her phone. "You can go now."

"Wow. That's the thanks I get?"

She scoffs. "Why should I thank you? You're the one who caused the problem."

I'm also the one who hooked her up with Zach in the first place, though neither of them knows that.

Amelia holds her phone in one hand and makes a shooing motion with the other.

But I just sit there, staring at my knees. How is it that Amelia has people to talk to and I don't? When did that even happen?

"Damien?"

"I..." I almost blurt out the whole thing, about Kat being mad at me, because I don't have anyone else to talk to about it. Or anyone else to talk to, period. But the last thing I need is to tell Amelia my business. And it's not like I don't know why Kat's mad. I'd be pissed, too.

"You should call her," Amelia says, even though I didn't tell her anything. I guess my problems are that obvious.

"But—"

"No *buts*. You love her, right?"

"Yeah, of course I do."

"Then call her already!" She rolls her eyes at me. "Boys are so dumb sometimes."

"Okay. Um. Thanks, Amelia."

"Whatever." She motions for me to leave again without looking up from her phone.

## X·X·X

I sit on my bed and dial Kat's number. I listen to it ring, willing her to answer. She's been avoiding me, but even if she hadn't, it's Friday night, and she practically lives with all of her friends. She's probably way too busy to—

"Hey." Kat picks up on the fourth ring. She sounds happy I called.

"Kat." Relief washes over me, and I slump down so I'm half-lying, half-sitting on my bed. "I thought that maybe you were…"

"Hey, get chips while you're out!" Kat shouts at someone. "Barbecue!" Then, back to me, "Sorry, Damien, Liv's getting party supplies. What were you saying?"

"Nothing." It comes out bitter. *Of course* she's having a party. Instead of coming home to see me, because I totally botched everything last time she made the effort.

"Oh." She sounds disappointed.

Neither of us says anything for a while.

Then Kat breaks the silence. "Damien, maybe I'd better

go. People are starting to show up."

"No, wait!" I can't just let her hang up. Not without saying what I need to say. "I really missed you this week."

She lets out a slow breath, like she was hoping I'd say that. "Me, too."

I think about what Amelia said, about worrying that Zach will forget her. "I think about you all the time. About what you would say if you were with me. And I know you so well, it's almost like you're there, but you're not. And I hate that I don't get to see you. I *hate* it. But even worse is not getting to talk to you, Kat. And if I had to pick one person to spend my future with, it would be you. No question. Even if it meant never seeing anybody else ever again. And I know I've been screwing things up lately. And maybe I don't know how to fix it, but you're my best friend. I love you. More than anything, and—"

"Will you come over?"

"To your dorm?"

"Yeah."

"When?"

"What do you mean, when? *Now.* You should come over now. I mean," she adds, "if you're not busy."

"I think I can shuffle a few things. But aren't you having a party?"

"Sort of. Some of our friends are coming over. The boys are bringing pizza, and we're going to watch zombie movies and hang out. We do this pretty much every weekend, but me and Tasha and Liv are hosting this time, so we got to pick the movies."

"Oh. You're sure you want me to come?"

"Uh, yeah. I know you don't really know anybody, but..." She swallows. "I really want to see you. And maybe you could stay the night?"

"I'll be there."

"I love you, Damien. I'm sorry about this week."

"Don't be. I'll see you in an hour."

"I'll tell them not to start the movie until you get here."

We say good-bye and hang up. I change into my high-voltage T-shirt, throw a change of clothes in my backpack, then head downstairs. Gordon and Helen are watching a sitcom on TV. They barely glance over at me as I get my toothbrush from the bathroom, then grab a hooded sweatshirt from the closet, even though I have to walk past them twice. I come stand in the living room, ready to tell them I'm spending the night at Riley's when they ask. Which I know they will, because it's pretty obvious I'm leaving.

They don't ask, though. I stand there for what feels like forever, and they don't say anything. I clear my throat. "I'm going out."

Gordon gives me that weird "I hardly know my own son" look he's had ever since he found out I knew about the Truth. I think for a second that he's going to say I have to stay home, that everybody in Golden City hates me and it's not safe to be out at night, or that we need to talk more about what happened. But he just says, "Okay," as if he could care less where I'm going or what I'm doing.

"I'm going to Riley's," I tell him, even though he didn't ask. "I'm spending the night." I hold up my backpack as proof.

Gordon nods in acknowledgment, then goes back to staring at the TV.

"I'll be back tomorrow, if anyone cares." I hesitate, giving him one last chance to tell me not to leave. Not because I don't want to go, but because his indifference makes me feel like someone just punched me in the stomach. But nobody says anything. So I leave.

# CHAPTER 18

"Park Place, with two hotels on it." I hold my hand out to Tasha, one of Kat's suitemates. "Pay up."

"Not again," she mutters, counting out her Monopoly money.

"I also accept properties if you don't have the cash. I'm flexible like that."

She glances over at her property cards, then sorts through her bills again.

There are six of us playing: me, Kat, Tasha, Jordan, some girl named June, and Cameron. He's the one Kat told me about, the one who wasn't going to ski because he makes things warm all the time. What she didn't mention is that his last name is actually *Frost*, which I think is kind of an important detail, what with it being so ironic. A couple of guys—Nathan and Blake—are playing video games on the couch and slowly finishing off the last of the pizza. Liv's in her room with *Tristan*, of all people, because he's apparently her boyfriend now. Ugh. And how convenient that he's going out with someone who lives with Kat, so he can be over all the time. He glared at me when I first got here, his mouth twisting up in a sneer, but then he gave me a half-assed shrug and said, "Hey."

Which was weird, because he hates my guts and I hate his, and I could tell he wasn't exactly happy that I'd shown up. But maybe he's actually, like, respecting the fact that Kat chose me and not him. Or maybe he really has moved on and doesn't care about our feud anymore. I find either of those options hard to believe—he obviously still hates me and he seems like the type to hold a grudge—but whatever.

Tasha finally pays up, handing over almost all of her money. I've got piles of it, all four railroads, the electric company, several high-end properties, including Park Place and Boardwalk, plus a few others of varying value. All of them have at least one hotel. It's too bad this game isn't played with real money, because I'm totally killing it.

"Ugh," Jordon says, stretching his arms behind his back. "Can we just admit that you won and stop playing?"

Kat shakes her head, grinning. "Don't give in to him. We'll never hear the end of it."

"I just don't see the point of going back and forth for a couple more hours when we already know how it's going to end."

"We don't know that," June says. "Not for sure." But she looks down at her three property cards and meager stack of cash and doesn't look too convinced.

Cameron throws his cards in the middle of the board. "I'm out. Jordan's right—there's no point. Besides, if we're going to watch another movie"—he checks the time on his phone and yawns—"we should do it now."

"We're waiting for Liv." Tasha glances over toward the bedrooms. "She said she wanted to watch it."

"I think she's kind of *busy*."

"Someone go knock," June says, her voice hushed, as if she's afraid Liv might hear her from the other room.

No one volunteers.

Kat gets out her phone. "I'll text her. And if she doesn't answer, we'll watch it without her."

Tasha starts putting away all the Monopoly pieces. Cameron holds his hand out to me. "Good game."

"Thanks." I shake with him. He doesn't hesitate or flinch or anything. Like he's not even considering the fact that I could electrocute him. Like he trusts that I'm not some evil psychopath out to get him.

And his hand *is* really warm.

It's refreshing. The trusting me thing, I mean—not the warm hand thing. It's also a relief. Nobody here tonight has looked at me like I'm the scum of the earth, or like I shouldn't exist. Like I don't *deserve* to. And I know it shouldn't feel weird to be treated like a real person, but a weight lifts from my chest that I didn't even know was there.

Cameron wanders over to the couch and tells the guys he'll play winner if there's time. Kat's texting furiously with Liv, which probably means Liv's skipping the movie.

Tasha finishes putting the game back in the box and shoves the lid on. "This goes on the top shelf." She glances between me and Jordan. "One of you boys gets to put it away, because I can't reach."

Jordan wiggles his eyebrows at her. "Get Nathan to lift you up."

"Shut *up!*" She smacks him on the arm and then glances over to the couch real quick, where Nathan's playing video games. He doesn't look like he heard.

June comes and stands next to me. She looks really nervous, and I figure she's about to say something unpleasant, like that being half hero makes me not good enough for Kat or how dare I show up for this party and kick ass at Monopoly when everyone knows I'm that traitor who goes to Heroesworth. She doesn't *seem* like the type to say something like that, but I can't think of what else it would be.

"Hey, um, Damien?"

For someone about to tell me off, she doesn't sound too sure of herself. Maybe she just wants to see the *X* on my thumb but thinks it's rude to ask. I decide now's as good a time as any to go find the bathroom and avoid this situation altogether. I'm about to make an excuse to leave when she says, "I just wanted to thank you."

"I don't— Wait, what?" My mind races, trying to come up with what I did that's worth thanking me for. "You *wanted* me to obliterate you in Monopoly?"

Her cheeks turn a little red and she sucks in a deep breath before launching into her explanation. "I know it couldn't have been easy for you, because Katie says you live with your dad, and he's a... you know. Hero. A famous one, and everybody's always watching you. So I know it was probably really hard for you to say all that stuff. But…" Her voice gets tight and her bottom lip trembles a little. "My mom wasn't in that video, but she got taken by the League last year. For being out at night and 'looking suspicious.' That's what they said, anyway. She has telepathy. That's her power, but it only works on heroes, and I think they knew that. Like they'd been studying her or something. They wanted—" She breaks off all of a sudden, her eyes going wide, like she just realized where she was and who she was talking to. "I'm sorry. You probably don't want to hear about it. You're, like, famous."

I swallow. Me, too famous to talk to her. Like her mom getting abducted by the League is too small potatoes to even listen to. "What did they do to her?"

"They were afraid she'd use her powers on them. She'd never done anything before—she's a *veterinarian*. She didn't even go to Vilmore. But they thought that even if she wasn't planning to spy on heroes, other villains might get her to help them, or that maybe they already had. Of course my mom wouldn't do that. She'd been approached before and said no. But the heroes didn't care. She could hear their thoughts, and she knew they were too scared of her to let her go." June's quiet for a few breaths, and I can tell it's hard for her to keep going. "They falsified reports that said she'd tried to attack them, that she'd pulled out a raygun when they approached her on the street 'just to talk.' That's how they justified bringing her in, at least on paper. Then they tortured her, to find out what she knew about them already."

"Did she…?" I can't bring myself to ask if she escaped,

or if something worse happened.

"She got away. She's okay now. Mostly." June clenches her fists and looks up at me. "But I wanted to thank you. For standing up for us. It means a lot, especially since everyone knows who you are. My mom cried when she saw that broadcast, exposing what heroes *really* do. So, just... thanks." She looks embarrassed, like she's taken up too much of my time.

"Yeah," I tell her, trying not to look as stunned as I feel. "No problem."

## X·X·X

Me and Kat don't even make it halfway through the second movie before sneaking off together. Kat loves zombie movies, but she loves me more, and when she pinches my arm and turns her head toward her room, I squeeze her hand in silent approval. We slink away down the hall, and I'm already kissing her and running my hands under her shirt when she presses her door closed and locks it behind us. It's only been a couple weeks since we last did this, but after everything that's happened between then and now, it feels more like months.

The lightning bolt on my high-voltage T-shirt glows bright in the dark. It looks really cool, and I almost hate to take it off.

Almost.

Kat unbuttons my jeans and I unhook her bra. We practically tear the rest of our clothes off, and then we have sex in her bed. It's a little bit weird that there are so many people just down the hall, and that they all must know what we're doing in here. But it could be hours before they leave, so I decide I don't care.

Afterward, we just lie there for a while, because neither of us has to go anywhere or answer to anyone. I can't remember the last time we got to do that. Even when I stayed over for her birthday, I had to scramble to get to school the next day. And whenever we're at my house, well, we usually only have a small window of time.

Now that I think about it, maybe it's never been like this.

Kat rests her head on my chest and drapes her arm over me. I can feel her breathing, in and out, her breath warm on my skin. And it's really stupid, but I think this might be the best moment of my life.

I should have gone on that ski trip with her. We could have had a whole week together like this. And yeah, everyone calls her Katie, and it's super annoying. But whenever I call her Kat, her friends look at us like I must know something about her they don't. Like I'm not just her boyfriend, but someone special and important. Which I am, obviously, but it's cool that they notice.

"I made a mistake," I whisper.

"No, you did fine," Kat teases, and I can feel the muscles in her face twitch as she smiles.

"Not *tonight*. Not this. But, Kat. I think I really screwed up."

She must hear in my voice that I mean it, because she goes tense. "Damien, what are you talking about?"

It's more than just the ski trip. I sit up and run my

hands through my hair. The peaceful feeling I had is gone, and maybe that's my fault, maybe I can't just accept good things when they happen to me, but this is big, and I can't pretend I'm not thinking it. "I should have gone to Vilmore."

"You what?"

"Seriously, what the hell was I thinking?"

"Uh, you were thinking that you wanted to be with your family." Kat reaches past me and turns on the lamp on her nightstand. We both wince at the sudden brightness.

"My family? I bet I could stay here again tomorrow night and Gordon wouldn't even notice. No one would care if I didn't come home."

"That's *so* not true." Kat shivers and grabs her shirt off the floor.

"Okay, maybe not. But it would just be another excuse for them to be pissed at me."

"Did something happen?"

"You mean, besides everyone thinking I'm some kind of psychopath terrorist because of that video?"

"You meant what you said. And if your family didn't know you felt that way, then maybe it *needed* to be said. They'll get over it."

"A full-ride scholarship. And I threw it away." The enormity of that hits me, like it took this long for it to sink in. Or maybe it was because at the time, not taking it sounded like a good idea. It's only now, when everything's falling apart, that I'm not so sure. "That was my whole future."

"Whoa, Damien." Kat puts her hands on my knees and looks me in the eyes. "It was *a* future. That doesn't mean it was the only one."

"What if it was? I mean, what am I going to do? As a hero?"

"I don't know. But that's not the point."

"If my whole family getting to know me is just going to make them hate me, then I should have stayed away."

"They love you. It's obvious they do. And what about your friends?"

"Riley and Zach aren't allowed to see me anymore. Plus, Riley didn't even want to be partners with me." And Kat doesn't want me hanging out with Sarah. "I just make trouble for them."

"You think if you went here, you wouldn't cause any trouble?" She gives me a really skeptical look. "It's kind of what you do."

I laugh. Just a little. "I probably wouldn't cause *as much* here."

"Yeah, right. You'd pick fights with every guy who flirts with me, or anyone who says something bad about heroes, because people do. It's a school for villains, and like it or not, you're still half hero. And you wanted to go to Heroesworth. You said yourself that going to Vilmore didn't feel right anymore."

"I know. And it was true. It *is*, I mean. I just miss you, Kat. I want you to be part of my future, but we're going in completely different directions."

Not just because she's a villain and I'm trying to be a hero, but because she's going to actually be successful, and

I'm not sure I see that happening for me anymore, no matter what school I go to.

Kat gets quiet. She takes my hand and entwines her fingers with mine. "You know how much I wish we were on the same path. It hurts that we're not. And I *hate* that you and Sarah are a thing."

"We're not 'a thing.'"

"You work together."

"I work with Riley, too."

"But you haven't made out with him."

"That you know of." I wiggle my eyebrows at her.

She elbows me in the ribs.

"*Ow.*"

"Riley also didn't try to kill me." She sighs. "You know why I can't stand Sarah. And if you weren't a hero, if you'd changed your mind and come to Vilmore, *we'd* be partners. Just the two of us. You'd know all my friends, and we could do our homework together and go to the same dining hall. But, as much as I want that, that doesn't mean you made the wrong decision."

"I have to tell you, you're not really selling me on this. You're kind of just rubbing it in."

"My point is, it sucks that we're apart so much, but we're making it work. And if you hadn't stuck it out with your dad, you never would have forgiven yourself. Deep down, you wouldn't. Especially after what happened with your mom. You need him."

"Take that back. I don't *need* Gordon. I let him give me food and shelter and stuff for his benefit. It makes him feel good about himself, like he's finally doing the right thing by me."

"Uh-huh. That's so what's going on. And anyway, I meant emotionally."

"Well, that's where you're really wrong, because I don't."

She shrugs, not believing that. "He needs you, too. They all do."

"Sometimes I think me and him are never going to get along. It's like, things are only good between us if he thinks I'm doing exactly what he wants. He doesn't listen to me. He doesn't *get* me. And just when I think he might be starting to, he says something completely stupid that totally ruins it."

"Still. Just because it's not easy doesn't mean it wasn't the right choice. I think you know that."

I lean my head back and let it thunk against the wall. "Maybe. But I can't take him looking at me like he doesn't know me, like I'm just some villain exchange student who lives in his house." It's been almost a year. I should be more than that to him, even when he's mad at me.

"Maybe you should tell him that."

"He doesn't listen to me, remember?"

"But if you don't bring it up, then you're not even giving him a chance. How can he listen when you don't say anything?"

"Don't be on his side, Kat."

"I'm not. I'm on yours. That's why I think you need to talk to him."

# CHAPTER 19

I'm lying face down on the couch Saturday night, flipping channels on the TV. I hate everything that's on, and it seems like anything I might want to watch doesn't start for at least twenty minutes.

Amelia suddenly looms in front of me, her phone in one hand. She snaps a picture of me sprawled on the couch with my face smashed into the armrest, then smirks at her screen. "You're awfully mopey for having been at *Riley's* last night."

"It's really hard to be away from Zach. You wouldn't understand."

Her nostrils flare in and out in outrage. I have a pretty good view of them, what with her standing over me like that. She leans in and whispers way too loudly, "I know you went to see Kat."

She acts like wanting to see my girlfriend is so scandalous. I point the controller at her and hit the mute button, but of course nothing happens.

"You can't even go to Zach and Riley's house anymore. And Kat posted on Facebook that she cried when she said good-bye to you earlier."

I lift my head at that and prop myself up on one elbow. It was so hard to leave today—I ended up missing the train, twice. We were lying on Kat's bed, and I had my arms around her, and I kept saying I should go, but I couldn't bring myself to actually do it. And yeah, there were tears in her eyes when I finally did get up to leave. And when we said good-bye at her door, she threw her arms around me, and we just stood that way for a while. She said she wasn't crying, but my shirt was wet and her shoulders were shaking and we both knew that really she was.

"Did *you* cry?" Amelia asks.

"Why do you have to be such a heartless bitch? This is why Zach's mom doesn't want him around you."

"That means you did." She snickers, like she wasn't sobbing over not getting to see Zach last night.

"Only because I had to come home to you." For the record, I didn't actually cry. But I still felt like complete crap, like every part of me was heavy and empty at the same time.

She opens her mouth to say something else—something smug, from the look on her face—but then Gordon walks in and holds up his car keys. "I'm making a run to the store. Damien, do you—"

"*Yes.*" I jump up from the couch and take the keys from him. Gordon might not be my favorite person right now, and I might not be his, but going to the store with him

258

beats staying here with Amelia.

We put on our coats and get in the car. I'm in the driver's seat, which I still can't believe, even though I've had my permit for a couple months now.

Gordon doesn't say anything until we're about halfway to the store. Then he clears his throat. "Damien, I want to talk to you about something."

I almost look over at him, to see if his expression is as serious as he sounds, but I decide I can't risk taking my eyes off the road. "If this is some kind of trick and we're actually going to an asylum or something, you really shouldn't have let me drive."

"What?" He sounds amused, though I still don't feel comfortable looking over. Maybe at the next stoplight. "Why would you think that?"

"You don't always think things through."

"That's not what I meant."

We get to a red light, and I can finally glance over at him. He looks worn out, maybe kind of nervous, but not "tricking my son into checking into a shock-therapy program" nervous.

"Take a left here," he says.

"The store's in the other direction."

"We're taking a longer route."

"Why?"

"Because I want to talk to you. And because you hate turning left."

Only when there's traffic, which there is. "Turning left is overrated. Turning right three times is just as good."

"You'll be fine. Put your blinker on."

I do it and grit my teeth, waiting for the light to turn green.

"I actually have two things I want to talk to you about. After what happened last week, I really don't think you should go to school on Monday." He waits for me to say something. "Damien? Did you hear me?"

"Can't talk. Have to concentrate."

The light turns green, and all the cars from the opposite side of the road start going. People behind me squeeze into the space on my right so they can go past. The wind from all the cars whooshing by rocks the car a little, and I'm pretty sure we're going to die here.

"Go after this next car," Gordon says.

"There's no room."

"There's plenty of room. Just trust me on this. It'll be okay."

Yesterday, he hardly looked at me, and now he wants me to trust him?

The car goes by, but I chicken out, and then after what feels like forever, the second car finally goes past. Just as the light turns red.

Great. "I'm going to turn right. Like a sane person."

He shakes his head. "You need to learn how to do this."

"You want me to do everything your way. And now we're stuck here."

"We're not stuck."

"And I'm going to school on Monday."

"I don't think that's a good idea. You're getting into fights. It's not safe."

"It was one fight, and I'm *fine*. Nothing happened."

"You don't have to prove anything. If that's what this is about."

"It's—" The light turns green again. There are about a million cars coming from the opposite direction. It looks like there's never going to be enough space for me to cross. "It's not."

"Two more cars, and then go."

"I can't."

"You can. Just— Now! Go now!"

Damn it. I don't have time to think about it. Somewhere deep down, I must actually trust him, because I do what he says. I press on the gas and turn the wheel, and I'm not sure why my body is letting me go through with this, because now I *know* we're going to die. And even though he's the one who told me to go, it's going to be all my fault somehow.

There's a car coming straight for us. My heart pounds and lightning crackles across my skin. But then I press harder on the gas to speed up, and we make it past.

"You did it!" Gordon sounds super proud of me, like I just saved ten burning orphanages all at once.

The fact that we're not going to die tonight slowly registers. "I did it. And I'm going to school on Monday."

"Damien."

"We're starting new missions this week! We're going to track down some notorious boat thieves. That practically makes them pirates. It's rumored that they have a bunch of stolen artifacts on their current boat, too. I mean, seriously. I'm *not* missing that."

"You like fieldwork."

It's not a question, but I answer it anyway. "Yeah, it's exciting. And it's the thing I like most about Heroesworth." Kind of the only thing, but I leave that part out. "It makes all the other crap I have to deal with there actually bearable. So I'm going on Monday."

"Well…"

"If I miss that, then what's the point? It's the only part of school I'm looking forward to. Even if I don't go for a while, I'm going to have to go back eventually. So don't make me miss out on the one thing I actually like."

"I'll think about it."

I turn right at the next corner to head toward the store. "You said you had two things you wanted to talk about." As soon as I say that, I regret it. Anything he wants to talk about is probably something I don't want to have anything to do with, so why bring it up?

"Oh. Right." He clears his throat again. He sounds really nervous.

I wonder if he knows where I went last night and if this is going to be some kind of belated sex talk, even though he already knows me and Kat have been doing it for months. And *I'm* not the one with an illegitimate love child, so I'm not even sure he's qualified to talk to me about it.

"Your birthday's coming up. In a few weeks."

"More like four. It's on the twentieth."

"I know what day your birthday is, Damien."

I shrug. It's not like he was there or anything.

"And I know I've missed all of them so far." He says it quietly. "I'm not proud of that."

I glance over at him and almost wander into the other lane. "It's okay. Really."

"It's not. That's *sixteen years* of your life, and I wasn't there."

"Think of it this way. That was sixteen years without me causing trouble for you. You're lucky you only have to deal with me for two." Two and a half, probably, since I won't have graduated yet when I turn eighteen.

He doesn't say anything. There's a tense silence in the car, and I think I might have actually hurt him. "I thought maybe we could do something together, just the two of us. Anything you want to do. We could go to a game, or—"

"How about a strip club?" I pull into the grocery store parking lot and find a space with no other cars around it.

"A..." He splutters, trying to come up with a reason why we can't, until he finally says, "You're not old enough."

"Like anyone's going to card me if you're there. Just a father and son, enjoying ogling strange women together, right? Come on, you said anything I wanted."

He squirms, his embarrassment fighting sixteen years' worth of guilt.

"I'm just kidding, Dad. The only thing I want for my birthday is for us to go into the backyard and throw a baseball around."

He looks relieved for a second, since he doesn't have to find a way to tell me that when he said "anything," he didn't really mean *anything*. Then he realizes I'm making fun of him and scowls. "I'm serious about this. So, if you think of something you want to do, let me know. And of course you can have a party."

"Yeah, that's not happening." My last two birthday parties were complete disasters. Plus, I'm a bit lacking in the friends-who-are-allowed-to-see-me department.

"Oh." His shoulders deflate.

"I mean, I think Kat's throwing me a party at her house," I lie, just because he looks so dejected about it.

"Maybe we can have a family thing. We'll at least do cake. And if there's something you want, something big, we can talk about it. Like a car? A used one. Or a computer?"

I stare out the window, not looking at him. "You don't have to feel guilty, okay?"

"Amelia got a computer for her birthday."

"That's different." They got her a laptop because they wanted to. Because they actually like her for some reason. Not because Gordon missed most of her life and was trying to overcompensate. "Seventeen's not an important birthday."

"It's important to me."

"Not to me. So don't worry about it." I'd rather get nothing than a present that shows just how little he understands me.

"Damien, I'm going to worry about it. You'll be eighteen next year. An adult, legally speaking. This is the only birthday I'll spend with you while you're still a kid."

"A kid? I drove us here." Not to mention the things I did with Kat last night.

He sighs and leans his head back, running his hand through his hair. "You'll be eighteen next year."

"You said that."

"And then you'll graduate. You'll get a job, and you'll move out to live with your friends. I'll only see you at Christmas, and only when you don't have something better to do. Before you know it, you'll have your own family, and then we won't see each other at all."

"Uh. Way to plan out my whole life there."

"It's how it goes. It'll happen with you, and with Amelia, and eventually with Alex and Jess. The difference is that I missed out on the first sixteen years of your life. We've only got these two years."

"You don't know that."

He tilts his head, giving me a look that says we both know better. That I'll be out of the house as soon as possible.

"Okay," I say, giving in. "I guess we can at least have a cake."

# CHAPTER 20

"This is how we're going to play it this time." I'm sitting in Advanced Heroism on Monday, since Gordon decided I could go to school after all. We've still got a couple minutes before class starts, and I'm trying to give Amelia some guidance on what is and isn't okay to do on a mission. "First of all, *don't* wander off and get caught by bad guys."

"Uh-huh."

She's not even looking at me. Her eyes follow Riley as he comes in the door and sits down at the desk next to ours.

"Amelia?" I snap my fingers. "Are you listening?" I'm pretty sure she should be writing this down.

She acts like she doesn't even hear my question and leans across me to talk to Riley. "Here," she says, tossing him a piece of paper folded up into a thick square. "Give that to Zach. And you'd better not read it."

"Of course not." Riley acts like he doesn't know why

she even has to say that.

I wonder how difficult it would be to steal that note from him in fifth period. "Okay, now that that's over, let's discuss what we're going to do. And by *we*, I mean *you*. You're going to what? That's right, *not wander off*."

Amelia blinks at me. Then she looks at Riley again, like she's waiting for something.

"Oh! Right." He starts digging through his backpack. "Zach almost didn't get a chance to give it to me this morning. He was getting ready to leave while I was in the shower, and—" Amelia snatches the piece of paper out of his hand as soon as he finds it, effectively cutting him off.

Unlike her note, Zach's isn't folded a million times. Just once, in half. She opens it and starts reading.

"You can read that later," I tell her. "This mission is important. It has *pirates*. And if you screw this up for me or botch it in any way, I will never forgive you. I, your favorite brother, will hold a grudge as long as I live."

She glares at me. "Will you *shut up*?"

Mason hurries into his seat next to Riley, sitting down only seconds before the teacher walks in. "Almost didn't make it," he says, pretending to wipe sweat off his forehead. "I was advising Brad on how he could have better handled expressing his feelings last week."

"You *what*?!" I can't believe him.

Riley just gapes.

"It's okay." Mason gives me a nod of acknowledgment, like this whole thing was no big deal. "I've done mediator work before."

"Wow," Riley says, stunned.

"I explained to him how that video might have looked to villains who saw it, and how they might feel just as angry and confused as he did. We discussed how villains are human beings, too, and how we only have one Earth that we have to share with each other."

Ugh. I didn't think it was possible to hate him any more than I already did, but he just proved me wrong. "You talked to Brad, the same guy who was going to kill me last week, about *that*?"

"You're welcome."

I clench my fists under the desk. "I don't need you fighting my battles for me."

He holds up a finger. "There was no fighting involved, X. You know, the verbs you use say a lot about how you think. Change your verbs, change your mind. That's what I always say."

Did he just call me *X*? Rage flares in my chest. Electricity twitches up and down my spine. "I'm going to electrocute you."

"Exactly. That's a perfect example of a verb to stop using."

"No, I'm actually going to electrocute you if you ever call me X again."

"Huh? Oh. I guess I did call you that. I must have picked it up from Ry." He shrugs. "I didn't even notice."

He'll notice when I *murder* him.

Mrs. Deeds starts passing out info sheets to everyone. Riley waits until she goes by before saying, "It was just a mistake. It's not worth getting worked up over."

"I understand that you're upset," Mason says, in a

soothing voice you might use on a wild animal or an escaped mental patient, "but the fact that your immediate reaction when you got angry was to threaten to hurt me indicates a deeper issue. Like I told Brad earlier, the only way to work through our problems is to first identify them, then confront them. We do that by talking. We're all just human beings here, trying to survive and make sense of the world around us. That means we have a lot in common—we just have to find those connections with each other. So if you ever want to work through anything, I'm here for you, X. Er, I mean, Damien. You can talk to me."

I'm so pissed at him right now, I can hardly see straight. My vision is actually blurring a little, and I can *hear* the crackle of electricity.

Amelia scoots her chair farther away from me. Riley looks worried.

Unfortunately, Mason doesn't notice any of that and keeps talking. "It can be hard to open up to people, even to a trained mediator like me, but you'll feel better if you do. And from what I've seen from you so far, I would hazard a guess that you've got some deeply rooted abandonment issues. You don't want to let those fester."

I take a deep breath, really hoping I don't blow something up. "All right, Perkins, that's it. I was going to go easy on you during this mission. Maybe form an alliance, share some info, but now? Forget it."

Riley's eyebrows come together. "What? What did I do? And this isn't even a competition."

"For starters, you're friends with *him*. And I don't care

what he did or did not do for me last week, because if he says one more word to me, there's a good chance that someone in this room will die. Okay? And it might not officially be a competition, but we all have the same end goal. Only a few teams are going to get to actually take down the pirates, and I don't know about you, but there's no way I'm missing out on the action."

Riley rolls his eyes. "They're not pirates."

"They're thieves on a boat with treasure. It's close enough."

Mrs. Deeds takes her place at the front of the room and announces that class is starting. "I know you're all excited for this next project. Like it says on your info sheets, this segment is going to be very hands-on and will take up the next three to four weeks. Unless some of you really excel at fieldwork."

She beams at Riley when she says that, even though it's obviously going to be me. I mean, granted, I do have Amelia on my team, weighing me down, but I think a few rules and a lot of busywork will keep her from causing too much trouble.

"This assignment is going to be a little different than what we've been doing up till now. We're going to have one team of three. Hopefully no one feels that's unfair, but if you do, come speak to me privately and we'll figure something out."

One team of three? Me and several other people glance around the room, trying to spot whoever this extra person is. I don't see anyone, though. Maybe they're only in the process of transferring in and aren't here yet.

"We're also going to be working on the same project, instead of having individual missions. During the next few weeks, you'll be doing extensive research, learning new methods of observation and tracking, and putting together a comprehensive report. You're encouraged to share information with each other, but only the two teams who complete their tasks the most efficiently—that is, quickly while keeping a high standard of quality—will have the honor of capturing our criminals and recovering the stolen goods."

I lean over and whisper to Riley, "That could have been you."

"What makes you so sure it won't be?"

Mrs. Deeds smiles at the class. "You'll see on your info sheets a list of the stolen items. We're going to spend the rest of today doing some research on them, so take your things with you and head to the computer lab."

There's the sound of chairs moving and people loading their stuff into their backpacks as everybody gets ready to leave.

"Amelia?" Mrs. Deeds says, coming over to us. "You'll be joining Riley and Mason's group this time."

"For today?" Amelia asks.

"For the rest of the project. Possibly the rest of the semester."

Wow. I guess Mrs. Deeds paid more attention to Amelia botching our mission before after all. And since Riley supposedly did the best, she's making him and Mason take her on, in the hopes that she learns something. Which is kind of like saying she's not going to learn anything from me, but I can let it slide, since this could be worse. She could be making me and Riley trade partners, sticking me with Mason. Barf.

Amelia looks over at me, confused about what's going on. She hesitates, then says, "Okay," and grabs her stuff.

"So I'll be working alone?" I ask. She said there was only going to be one team of three, not two.

Mrs. Deeds purses her lips in a weird, almost pitying expression. "I'm afraid you're not going to be participating in the rest of the missions."

"Wait, what?!" She didn't just say that, did she?

"The school doesn't feel that you're the kind of student we want representing Heroesworth when out in the field. Considering the incident last semester, when you attacked that League member, and that public statement you made recently about supporting the Truth, *and* the way you've behaved in my classroom, you no longer have the privilege of doing fieldwork. And it *is* a privilege, not a right."

That's why she put Amelia on Riley and Mason's team? Because she was *benching* me? "So, what, I only get to do the research part?"

She shakes her head, still giving me that pitying look, which is really getting on my nerves. "You'll be given an alternative assignment."

"Alternative." That sounds bad. And like it definitely doesn't involve capturing pirates. "Like, what? A computer simulation?"

"No." She goes over to her desk and picks up a gigantic three-ring binder full of paper. It looks heavy, and when she drops it on my desk, it lands with a loud *thud*. "You'll spend the rest of the semester completing these worksheets." She opens the binder to the first page.

*Think of a time when you did something for someone else without expecting or receiving a reward. How did that make you feel? Name three selfless acts you can complete on a daily basis.*

"You're not serious."

Mrs. Deeds looks down her nose at me, her mouth stretching into a thin line. "We take the reputation of this school very seriously. You've never done anything but tarnish it, despite being given multiple chances to clean up your act, and you should count yourself lucky that you're getting an alternative assignment at all. You can thank the dean for that. I would have been happy to fail you."

I look down at the binder again, thinking maybe it won't be that bad. But then I turn the page and see this:

*Imagine that a supervillain moves in next door to you. He laughs maniacally at all hours of the night and has been using the mailboxes on your street for raygun practice. The rest of your neighbors are getting worried but are afraid to confront him. As their resident superhero, they ask you to handle the situation. Describe in at least three paragraphs how you would deal with the villain and make the neighborhood safe again.*

Mrs. Deeds gives me a fake smile. "Is there a problem?"

I flip the binder closed and give her a fake smile right back. "Nope. No problem at all."

"Good," she says. "You can work on it in the library. Now, if you'll excuse me, I need to join the rest of the class in the computer lab. We've got an important assignment to work on."

$$X \cdot X \cdot X$$

Alex finally agrees to hang out with me again on Wednesday afternoon. I'm at the dining table, staring at my stupid worksheets, when he comes home from school. The worksheets are just about the most boring, tedious assignment I've ever had, and thinking about them is giving me a headache. So I look up at him and say, "Do you want to go to the park?"

He stands there for a moment, like he's considering whether or not he's still mad at me. But then he nods and drops his backpack in the middle of the floor. "I have homework I'm supposed to do, though."

"Yeah, me, too. I won't tell if you won't."

He grins, despite the fact that I can see he's trying not to.

On our way to the park, I text Sarah to see if she wants to meet us there, since she'll probably be walking Heraldo anyway. Alex is totally in love with Heraldo, after playing fetch with him for the first time a couple months ago. He would throw a stick and then they'd both race to get it. For some reason Alex enjoys throwing sticks covered in slobber and getting muddy dog prints all over himself.

"Sarah's coming, too," I tell him when she texts back.

His eyes light up, and I'm glad his hands aren't muddy, because he's got that excited look Heraldo always gets right before jumping on me. "Does that mean Heraldo's going to be there?"

"She said she's bringing him. And some treats you can feed him," I add, when another text comes in.

Alex says, "Oh, my God!" and looks like this is the best news he's ever heard. Then he suddenly gets this serious look on his face. "Did you ask her?"

He means about getting a puppy if Heraldo ever has kids, something he made me swear I would ask Sarah about. "I already told you. Boy dogs don't have puppies."

"I know that." He rolls his eyes at me, like I'm the one lacking in sex education. "But he could have puppies with another girl dog."

"He's fixed."

"Can't he get it reversed? Sam's dad got fixed, but then he got it reversed so they could have Sam's little brother."

"It doesn't work that way with dogs."

"Oh." He kicks a rock so that it goes skittering ahead of us on the sidewalk.

"Besides, Gordon and Helen wouldn't let you have one anyway."

"I could convince them."

I hope not. Not that I have anything against Heraldo, but... he's kind of gross. And gigantic. And I enjoy not living with him or any of his hypothetical offspring.

It's a nice day out, even though it's still really cold, so there are a bunch of people at the park. People are out jogging, or walking their dogs, or just sitting on benches, talking.

Heads turn when we go by, which isn't necessarily unusual, but it feels different this time. The hushed whispers sound more on edge than excited.

Alex picks up on it, too. "Everyone's looking," he says, keeping his voice quiet.

I guess that's what happens when you appear on TV and cause yet another scandal. "Ignore them."

"It's because you're a villain."

Does he think I don't know that? "*Half* villain," I correct him. "And it's because they think villains shouldn't have rights." I say that part really loudly, and several people glance away.

Alex shoves his hands in his pockets and walks faster. "Why did you have to say that?"

"Because they were being letterist douchebags."

"And when you were on TV? Why did you have to say *that*?"

Man, I really wish Sarah would show up right now. I look around, just in case, but don't see her. I think about all the things I could tell Alex, like that I didn't know I was being filmed, or how no one was meant to hear it, but none of that makes it any better. "Someone had to say it."

"No one at school wants to play with me anymore. And Joey asked for his birthday invitation back. I thought you were a hero now."

"I am." I'm trying to be, anyway.

Alex takes a breath and holds it for a second. Then he looks up at me and says, "Do you like your villain family more than us?"

"No, of course I don't. But it's not about that."

There's the sound of heavy footsteps running toward us. Two guys. One's holding a raygun, and the other has his hand out in front of him, like it's a weapon. They're dressed in everyday clothes—business casual—but they must be superheroes.

"We're with the League! On the ground!" the one with the raygun shouts.

At me.

I actually glance over my shoulder, to see if there's some serial killer standing behind us or something, but there's no one. Just me and Alex, and somehow I doubt they're this afraid of a nine-year-old kid.

"Hey, I didn't *do* anything."

"I said *on the ground*!" He waves his raygun at us.

Alex whimpers and moves closer to me. I start to reach for his hand, but the guy who doesn't have a raygun—because, presumably, his superpower is something way worse—shouts, "Step away from the boy!"

"What the hell? He's my brother!"

The two heroes exchange a look, like *Yeah, right.* One of them jerks his head toward us and the other nods.

Raygun guy makes a grab for Alex, jerking his arm and dragging him toward them. Alex shrieks.

Adrenaline rushes through me. I feel like someone just dumped a bucket of ice water down my back. Lightning surges in my hands. "Don't *touch* him!"

Alex tries to fight against his captor, but of course he can't. Tears well up in his eyes. "He didn't do anything!"

"He's a villain," raygun guy explains. "That's enough."

"But he goes to hero school," Alex says, his voice really small.

"It's new League policy. All villains are to be considered armed and dangerous," the other guy tells him.

He looks at the electricity in my hands with this self-satisfied smile on his face, like I'm proving that villains really should be thought of that way. "His presence on public property is disturbing the peace. We have to bring him in."

Alex's face is wet. More tears slide down his cheeks. He looks so terrified. And not of me, like these douchebags want him to be, but of *them*. Of this whole situation.

"Let him go!" I shout. Electricity crackles uncontrolled across my skin. It's like Homecoming all over again, and if they don't let him go, I don't know what I'm going to do. There's no ceiling to blow up this time.

Raygun guy, who still has a grip on Alex, leans over and tells the other one, "Shoot if you have to."

"No!" Alex screams.

I'm shaking all over. I feel like I'm going to be sick. I don't know what the hell's going on, only that it's *bad*. "I'll go with you," I tell them. "Just leave my brother alone!"

"We can't leave a minor unaccompanied. Stop using your villain power and come quietly or I'll be forced to shoot."

I can't. I try, but I'm too freaked out, and I don't trust them. I'm pretty sure they want to shoot me anyway, whether I stop using my power or not.

And then Sarah's voice says, "*Stop*." At first I think she's talking to Heraldo, who lets out a couple deep barks, but then I realize she means the heroes who are holding me at gunpoint and practically kidnapping my little brother. She tells Heraldo to stay, then steps in front of them, so she's between them and me. "You can't do this."

Heraldo growls in agreement.

I don't think I've ever been so happy to see him in my life.

"Get back!" the second hero shouts, holding up his palm.

"He's a known villain," the raygun guy says. "And he's using his dangerous villain power in a public place."

"He wasn't before you pointed a gun at him." She wasn't here for that, but she knows me well enough to know what must have happened. Only a few months ago, we were in this same situation, only she was the one pointing a gun at me. "That's against League rules."

"Not anymore. Any known or suspected villains are now considered armed and dangerous and should be viewed as the threat that they are. Now, I'm going to have to ask you again to get out of the way. For your own safety. Otherwise, we'll have to bring you in for obstructing justice."

I can't see Sarah's face, but I still catch the moment of shock when she hears that stuff about the new League policy.

"I've asked you nicely to stop," Sarah says, sounding annoyed. "So this is really your fault." Then, before anyone thinks to do anything, she whips some gadget out of her coat pocket. There's a loud whirring sound, then a *pop*. And suddenly the superheroes get this confused look on their faces. Their arms go slack, so they're no longer pointing any weapons at us.

"Come on!" Sarah shouts. "I don't know how long it will last!"

She grabs Alex's hand and takes off running. Me and Heraldo chase after her, though he's faster than me and is soon in the lead.

"What was that thing?!" I ask her.

"Stupefication gun! But it's still in the early stages, and... damn! It happened again." She holds up the gadget, which looks kind of like a tiny megaphone, except there's a hole in the side of it, like something in it exploded.

"What do you mean, *again*? Who have you been testing it on?!"

She makes a gesture to indicate she's too out of breath to answer that. Conveniently.

The four of us keep running until we're sure no one's following us. Maybe Sarah's gadget stupefied them for longer than she thought, or maybe they decided it wasn't worth it to come after us.

"Short-term memory loss is one of the possible side effects," Sarah explains when I bring it up. "That's another issue I'm having with it, which is why it's still a work in progress."

"Again, Sarah. *Who* have you been testing it on?"

"Don't look at me like that. Dad volunteered. He's excited that I'm getting back into inventing stuff again."

I can't imagine why. Her gadgets have so far gotten him kidnapped and tortured—by my mom and Taylor, no less—and turned her into a crazy, villain-hating vigilante who tried to commit minor genocide. Not that I'm not glad she's making gadgets again, but at least I know better than to volunteer.

"Are you okay?" I ask Alex.

He shakes his head, then sort of crumples and throws his arms around my waist. He buries his face in my stomach and sobs loudly, his whole body shuddering with each gasping breath.

I put a hand on his back and exchange a look with Sarah. What happened back there was so messed up. And that's League policy now? Attack any villains, or suspected villains, you see on the street, even if it means endangering and kidnapping a little kid?

"I wouldn't have let them take you," I tell him.

But that just makes him cry harder, and in between sobs he says, "I—want—to go—home!"

"Okay." I try to take his hand, but he refuses to let go of me, which kind of makes it difficult to go anywhere. Then Heraldo slurps the side of his face, and he calms down enough to start walking. Sarah and Heraldo accompany us, and Alex clutches my hand with a death grip the whole way home.

# CHAPTER 21

Gordon knocks on my bedroom door later. I don't want to talk to him, which he should have realized already, since I didn't even come down for dinner. Apparently he can't take a hint, so I take a page out of Amelia's book and yell, "Go away!"

It works just about as well on him as it does on me, because he opens the door and comes in anyway, which is really annoying.

I sit up on my bed and glare at him. "Just write my punishment on a piece of paper and slip it under the door."

"You're not in trouble."

I raise an eyebrow at him. He obviously doesn't understand this parenting thing at all. "Alex almost got kidnapped on my watch." By the *League*, who could have done who knows what to him. I mean, he's not a villain, but they didn't necessarily know that. And maybe they wouldn't have hurt him, but screaming at us, pointing weapons at me, and dragging him away from me in the park was damaging enough.

"It wasn't your fault."

"It happened because of me. Because I was with him. He almost got seriously hurt." If Sarah hadn't shown up, I don't know how much longer I could have controlled my lightning.

Gordon sits down on the edge of my bed. "He's a little shaken up, but he'll be all right. You kept him safe." He says that so sincerely, my stomach twists, like it's tying itself into knots.

"I don't think you realize how dangerous the situation was."

"I know it must have been scary at the time, but I checked it out, and they are part of the League."

"And that makes you feel better because...?"

"They wouldn't have hurt him. They would have brought him in, called me, and then I would have picked him up."

"You *hope* they wouldn't have hurt him. He doesn't have 'Property of the Crimson Flash' tattooed on his forehead or anything."

He shakes his head. "I've been part of the League for almost twenty years now. I *know* they would have taken care of my son."

One of them, anyway. "And what about me?" I rub my hand across the bedspread, the soft blue one they got me for Christmas. I push it in one direction, then back again, feeling the fabric shift.

Gordon doesn't say anything right away. "What they

did to you was out of line and uncalled for. I don't support this new policy. You have to know that, Damien." He looks at me, his eyes pleading. "And I'd like to think they wouldn't have hurt you, either."

"But you don't believe that, right?"

"Things are changing. I don't know what to believe. But I know you and Alex got home safe, and for now, that's all that matters."

"He could have gotten hurt. He could have *died*."

"The League wouldn't have—"

"Not because of them. Because of me!" I hold up my hands, even though there's no lightning now. "I could have zapped them."

"But you didn't. You made the right choice, and I'm proud of you."

"It wasn't a *choice*."

"It may have felt that way, but you could have chosen to use your power on them. Even though you knew it was wrong."

"No, you're not listening. I didn't *decide* not to zap them. I was so freaked out, I couldn't control it. Maybe if they'd stopped pointing weapons at me I could have, but they wouldn't. They were trying to take my brother, and if Sarah hadn't shown up when she did, I don't know what would have happened." I stare at my palms, imagining how it might have gone. "They had a hold of Alex. If I'd zapped them, he would have been hit, too." And even if he wasn't, watching me zap those guys—and then getting in serious trouble—wouldn't exactly have helped the situation.

"You didn't lose control. Nobody got hurt, and everything's okay."

Except that the world is totally screwed up by this new League policy. "Everyone knows who I am. They know I'm half villain, and that makes me a target. And as long as I'm a target, I'm dangerous to you guys." To pretty much everyone, really.

He gives me a look, like he thinks I'm just being dramatic. "You haven't hurt anyone. And you're not going to."

"You sound so sure of that, but not that long ago you were going to send me to psycho camp, because you thought I couldn't control my power."

"It wasn't psycho camp, and I was only thinking about it. I was frustrated about what happened, about the decision you made, and... It doesn't matter now, because I was *wrong*."

I press my hands between my knees. "If that's the way you feel about it."

"It is. I trust you to make the right decisions."

"The right decisions, or the decisions *you* like?"

There's frustration in his voice when he says, "The right decisions." I can tell he wants to make the argument that they're the same thing, but he holds back.

"I hope you mean that." Because he's not going to like what I'm planning to do tonight, even if it is most definitely the right thing.

"I do." He claps me on the back. "Now, stop torturing yourself over this and get some sleep."

"Okay," I lie.

He smiles at me as he gets up to leave, and I wonder if I'll ever see him again.

### X·X·X

I stuff my phone charger into my backpack, along with as many clothes as will fit. I double-check that my phone and my wallet are in my pockets. There's nothing else that I *need*, though I look around my room and kind of wish I could bring the framed picture of me and Kat at Homecoming, in our bathings suits. Some bad stuff might have happened that night, but before all that, we were having a really good time and making everyone uncomfortable. I know there are more copies, but this is the one Kat signed for me, like it was a celebrity photo or something, and I hate to leave it behind.

Still. There's no room for it.

And there's no room for the watercolor painting of a Velociraptor in a top hat having a tea party that Riley made me, or Damien II, my old teddy bear from when I was a kid, which I only recently liberated from Xavier. And then there's Dr. Wiggles, Kat's old dancing flower toy she gave me for my sixteenth birthday. Well, his remains, anyway. We duct taped him back together after Amelia murdered him. He was kind of my only friend when I first moved in here, and now that I'm leaving, it seems weird to abandon him.

I tell myself I can't take any of it, even if I don't know when I'll be back. Or *if* I'll be back.

I grab a piece of paper from my binder. My hand

shakes as I write my note to Gordon, making my words
jittery and hard to read.

*Dad,*
*Thanks for letting me stay here and stuff.*

Ugh. That's terrible. I want to get a new piece and start
over, but I know if I take too long, I'll lose my nerve.

*Sorry. I don't know how to say this. I mean, you're*
*reading this letter, so you can probably figure out that*
*I'm gone. I had to leave. I know you didn't want me to,*
*but you don't understand how dangerous I am. And*
*yeah, that sounds dramatic, but it's also true. I can't put*
*you guys in that kind of danger, either from me or from*
*the League. So I know you'll be pissed at me for doing*
*this, but I have to. Because if something happened to*
*you guys, I couldn't live with myself.*
*Don't hate me, okay? This is the right thing to do.*

I consider adding that I'll be back as soon as it's safe,
that I hope this isn't permanent, but I don't want to give
them false hope. Because what if things never go back to
normal? And, besides, part of me worries that Gordon will
be too upset after this to ever take me back. So maybe I'm
the one I don't want to have false hope.

I sign the letter, then add:

*P.S. Please don't let Amelia touch my stuff.*

Because even if I'm not coming back, some things are sacred. I fold the letter in half and write *Dad* across it, so it doesn't get mistaken for a random piece of paper.

My shoes are downstairs, along with my toothbrush and my coat. So I guess this is it. I glance around my room one last time, to make sure I'm not forgetting anything important. Nope, nothing. Other than my whole life, that is.

I make my way downstairs. The one thing I won't miss about this place, besides living in the attic, is these stupid stairs. And even though I avoid the worst steps, they all seem to creak extra loud tonight. It's past eleven, so Gordon and Helen are at least in bed—hopefully asleep—but the last thing I need is for them to hear me sneaking out and try to stop me. Well, okay, no. The *last* thing I need is for the staircase to collapse under me while I'm making my escape.

But I make it to the bottom with both me and the staircase still intact. I creep across the living room and into the bathroom, so I can grab my toothbrush and deodorant and stuff. I cram them into my bag, which barely wants to zip closed, it's so full. Then I go get a hooded sweatshirt from the closet.

I'm pulling it over my head and wondering if I should wear another coat on top of it when I hear Amelia snicker and say, "Going to *Riley's* again tonight?"

Maybe it's the way I gasp in surprise, or the completely shocked look I give her before it sinks in that she doesn't know where I'm going, but her eyebrows scrunch up as she reassesses the situation.

Damn it. I thought she was up in her room. I didn't know she was down here.

I decide I'd better skip the second coat after all. I swing my backpack onto my shoulders, and now all that's left are my shoes. And leaving my letter for Gordon.

Amelia notices me clutching it. I turn it over so she can't see the name on it, but I think she already did.

"Where are you going?" she asks, scowling at my overly full backpack and the note in my hand.

"Okay, fine. You got me. I'm going to Kat's."

"It's a weeknight."

"So? She needs me. I mean, *really* needs me. Sexual urges don't just happen on the weekend."

"*Gross.*" Amelia makes a disgusted face. She takes a step away from me, like she might cut her losses and go back upstairs rather than subject herself to any more details about my love life. But then she folds her arms and says, "It's eleven thirty. There's no train past eleven."

I hesitate. A little too long. "I'm getting a ride."

"What's that?" She tries to reach for the letter in my hand.

I hold it away from her so she can't touch it and use her power to steal it from me. "It's nothing."

"You're leaving Dad a note? About you sneaking out?" Even she can tell that that doesn't add up.

"It's none of your business." Great. I can't even leave the note now, because Amelia will read it as soon I'm not looking.

"You have a lot of stuff in your bag."

I swallow. "Go back to your room."

"Why? I could call for Dad, you know. And then—"

"*Don't.* This is important, Amelia. So just leave it."

"You're not really going to Kat's, are you?" Her voice comes out hushed, almost afraid.

I shake my head.

"Then where?"

"Doesn't matter. I can't stay here."

Her eyes go wide. "You can't just leave!"

"Shh. You don't understand. I could have hurt Alex today. And it doesn't matter that I didn't, because I couldn't control it." I clench my fists. "It can't happen again. I can't let it."

"You wouldn't hurt anybody. Not on purpose. You lost control at Homecoming, and you didn't hurt anybody then."

"People know who I am. All I did today was go outside, and the League busted me like that was actually a threat to people."

"So don't go outside. Mom and Dad won't make you go to school."

"It's not that simple. I shouldn't have to stay inside just because the League says so."

"You shouldn't leave here because of them, either."

"What if the League decides to harass me at home? It wouldn't be that hard for them to find out where the Crimson Flash lives—they must have his address on file or something. The whole city knows I'm his son."

"They wouldn't do that. They're only doing this because of that stupid video you were in. If the Truth stops attacking them, then the League will stop attacking villains."

She makes it sound so simple, like that line of thinking isn't totally messed up. "Maybe they won't come here, maybe they'll stop at not trusting villains to be out in public"—which I really doubt—"but if I wait to find out the hard way, it'll be too late. You've seen what I can do, Amelia. Especially when threatened. I can't stay here." I bend down to put my sneakers on.

"When are you coming back?"

I shrug while tying my shoe. I can't say it out loud.

She makes a surprised, choking sound. "You can't abandon us. I won't let you." Her face is drawn and her voice is shaking.

"You can't stop me."

"I'll take your phone. You won't leave without your phone."

"I'm going. I have to."

"No. You don't."

I hand her the letter. "Give this to Gordon. And tell him I'm sorry he's going to miss another birthday." Maybe all of them.

Amelia stares at the paper in her hand, horrified and unmoving, like she's gone numb. Then she snaps out of it. Her mouth twists up and she glares at me and practically spits out the words, "Fine. *Leave.* I'm not even going to miss you. I never wanted you here in the first place!"

"Good. Then you'll keep your mouth shut until morning."

Her eyes are wet. Her jaw trembles. "I hate you."

"Yeah, I know." I put my arms around her. She resists

hugging me back, but only for a second, and then she squeezes me really hard. "Bye, Amelia."

She pulls away, not saying anything.

I put my hood on and readjust my backpack, stalling for time. As soon as I open the door, a gust of cold air hits me. It's freezing outside, and I don't want to go.

"If you leave, I'll never forgive you," Amelia says from behind me.

I wince. But I can't let them get hurt because of me.

So I don't look back. I just leave.

$$X \cdot X \cdot X$$

I wait until I'm a couple blocks away, to make sure no one's coming after me. Then I slip my phone out of my pocket and call Grandpa. It's late, almost midnight, and I don't know if he'll be up. And I haven't talked to him since his party, because he was screening my calls.

"Damien?"

He sounds awake, and not like he was asleep. "Sorry, Grandpa. I know it's a weird time to call."

"Don't be sorry. You can call me anytime—you know that."

"I just wanted to know if your offer still stands."

"Which offer was that?"

"You said you would have taken me in, after Mom kicked me out. I thought maybe I could stay with you guys for a while. I mean, unless it's a problem or something. Because I don't want to bother you, and I could always just—"

"Where are you? I'll come get you. Gladys!" he shouts, away from the phone. "Get your coat on—we have to go pick up the boy!"

"I can get to your house, Grandpa. It's no problem." The buses are still running.

"Nonsense. No grandson of mine is going to trek all over town in the middle of the night when it's freezing cold out. Send me your coordinates. I have GPS on this thing."

"Okay. And... thanks."

"No need to thank us. We're happy to have you here."

"You're sure it's all right if I stay?"

"It's insulting that you'd even ask me that. You can stay with us as long as you like, and I don't want to hear another word about it. Now you sit tight and text me those coordinates. We'll be there as soon as we can."

# CHAPTER 22

I wake up pretty late the next day. There's a moment of panic when I look at the alarm clock and see that school started over two hours ago. And then I remember that it doesn't matter. I'm at Grandma and Grandpa's house, and I'm sure as hell not going to school. Or doing any stupid worksheets. And I don't have to look out for letterist douchebags in the halls, or deal with equally letterist teachers who think I shouldn't be there, either.

Which is kind of a huge relief.

I turned my phone off last night. It's sitting on the nightstand, dark and silent, and I wonder how many messages and missed calls I have. Gordon must know I'm gone by now. He must have tried to call me a million times.

A ball of guilt forms in my stomach. It feels like I swallowed a rock.

A good son would turn on his phone and at least listen to the messages. He'd face the fact that he ran out in the night and left his father devastated—or pissed off, or whatever Gordon's feeling right now—even if he knew there was nothing he could do about it. Maybe this hypothetical good son would even call his father *back*, just to say he was okay. It would mean hearing his dad's upset voice and telling him in real time that he wasn't coming home, and it would be hard, but he'd do it anyway.

I am not a good son.

The thought of turning on my phone and even seeing that I have missed calls fills me with dread. I know I'll have to look eventually, but it doesn't have to be right now. Or even today.

I get dressed and go out into the living room. Grandpa's sitting at the table, reading the newspaper. He tells me to eat up, because we have work to do today, whatever that means. There's lunch meat in the fridge, and I end up scarfing down two sandwiches and a glass of milk.

After breakfast—which is really more like lunch—we go out into the backyard.

"We'll start with something basic," Grandpa says. "To see where you're at. Watch carefully." He holds his hands out in front of him, palms together. Lightning sparks between them as he pulls them apart. He turns his wrists so the lightning arcs in a rainbow shape, like when he was showing off at Mom's wedding. Then he moves his hands father out, widening the arc, then brings them back in again before letting his lightning disappear. "All right, kid. Your turn. Show me what you got."

"Wait, this is the work we're doing?"

"Yep. I saw those videos of you last fall. I know you've

got a lot of oomph. But I can't assess your skills unless I see them in person."

"I know how to use my lightning. We don't have to do this."

He folds his arms and gives me this look of pure disbelief. "Afraid you'll embarrass yourself in front of your old grandfather? Or that I won't be as easily impressed as all those heroes you know?"

I roll my eyes at him. "You mean Zach? Because he's pretty much the *only* one who's impressed." Well, other than the people who pay twenty bucks to get their picture taken with me while my hands are all electric. But that doesn't count. "Everybody else is…"

"Afraid?"

"I was going to say disgusted, but that, too."

"And now you're too ashamed of your power to even show me."

"It's not like that. I—"

"Like hell it's not. They're the ones who should be ashamed. There's nothing wrong with having lightning. You're a villain. But they make you feel like it's something to hide from. To pretend you don't have. I saw some of the garbage they spouted off about it on the news when you took down that superhero. You'd think you'd murdered him in cold blood, the way they went on about it. Bet that father of yours wasn't too happy, either."

I shove my hands in my pockets and stare down at my shoes. "He's trying, okay? It's not easy for him."

"Not easy for *him*? You're sixteen years old."

"I'm almost seventeen."

"Living with heroes. That's hard enough. And he has to go and make you feel ashamed of who you are. Like you're not good enough."

I swallow. "He doesn't. Not on purpose."

"And you're making excuses for him. Some father he is. But you're living with me now. And you're sure as hell good enough for me."

He doesn't put a hand on my shoulder, like Gordon would, or even make a point of looking me in the eyes, to show how serious he is. He just says it, and means it, and that's enough. I kind of hate to admit it, but it feels really good to hear. "Thanks, Grandpa."

"I'm just stating a fact. No need to thank me for that. But you're welcome anyway. Now, you can show me your lightning, or we can stand here all day, but you can't ignore it forever. It's in your blood. It's who you are."

"I'm not ignoring it." Especially compared to the way I'm ignoring my flying power.

"Then show me. And don't hold back."

"Okay. Fine." I hold my hands out in front of me. Lightning zaps between my palms, and I move them outward, the line of electricity stretching between them. I've never tried to make an arc before, but it can't be that hard. Even if Grandpa's been doing this for over forty years and I've only been doing it for five months. It takes me a second of concentrating, but then I make the same rainbow shape he did. No problem.

I look to Grandpa for confirmation that he severely underestimated me and should have started out with a harder challenge, but he's shaking his head. "I told you not to hold back."

"Uh, I wasn't. Maybe you weren't watching."

"I was watching. Do it again, and put more power into it this time."

Whatever. I do what he says, focusing more energy into the arc. It gets all bright and crackly. "Happy?"

"I suppose it'll do. For now. Just hold it like that as long as you can."

Okay, so much for him not underestimating me. "What's the point of this?"

"The point is you've got a lot of power. But it's no good if you don't know how to use it. And keep going—don't let up on that arc."

"I'm *not*." Except maybe I was, just a little. I refocus my energy so the power level stays steady. It takes more effort to maintain than I thought, and sweat already prickles along my back. "And you say they overreacted in the news about me, but now you're acting like I can't control my lightning, either. But I didn't hurt that guy, even though I wanted to—I knew what I was doing."

"And if you'd needed to hurt him?"

"I blew a hole in the gym. I think I can stop a bad guy if things get out of hand."

"You could obliterate him, you mean. Those are your options right now—barely touching someone or completely annihilating them. One won't always be enough, the other might be too much."

Might be? My arc falters again, and I push more energy into it. Sweat beads on my forehead, and it's taking so much concentration that I can hardly talk. "I'm not... I don't want to hurt anyone."

"That's not the point. You should be able to control your ability at any output. And you should be able to defend yourself without worrying about taking out the whole block."

Not having to worry about killing somebody every time some crazy hero points a gun at me? It sounds almost too good to be true, and the thought breaks my concentration. My lightning suddenly fizzles and the arc falls apart.

"Not as easy as it looks, is it?" he says, with that really annoying look adults get when they think they know more than you.

"You caught me off guard." Though I'm not sure how much longer I could have kept it up, because, yeah, he's right. It's a lot harder than it looks.

"Not bad for your first try. But I know you were still holding back."

"So, if I practice like this, I won't be dangerous anymore?"

He sighs. "It's not that simple. You'll always be dangerous. It comes with the territory."

"But you can teach me how to, like, keep my lightning in check?"

He gives me a suspicious look. "Suppressing it isn't the answer. If you want to control your power, you have to embrace it."

The back door opens, and Grandma pokes her head out. "You've got a phone call," she says. For a second, I think she's talking to me, and I don't know if I'm disappointed or relieved when she addresses Grandpa instead. "There's been an attack. Three of our people have been injured and taken in. You'd better come quick."

## X·X·X

I go with Grandma and Grandpa to the League's interrogation site—the secret one where they take villains for questioning. Because it's not like they could do that at headquarters, where they pretend that they're above that kind of thing. I mean, some of the League members *are* above it—people like Gordon who didn't know it was going on—but still.

We meet up with three other Truth members behind a beige, nondescript office building that no one would ever suspect was used by the League to torture villains. Grandpa keeps his voice low, but still commanding, as he lays out the plan. "We're going in two teams. Pain Wave, you're with me and Gladys. Cheshire Spider, you take the Reflector and Damien. Go through the back entrance and find our guys. You know where to look. We'll go around the front and distract them. I want a lot of firepower for that, in case things get ugly. But you'll have Damien to take out the security cameras."

Everyone looks at me. I'm definitely the youngest of the group, and probably the least experienced. And also the most famous for going to hero school and generally being an all-around screwup, just in case anyone's keeping track. So it's not too surprising that the Reflector curls her lip in skepticism or that the Cheshire Spider makes eye contact with Grandpa, silently asking if he's serious about this.

"I can do it," I assure them, even though I'm not exactly sure what I'm supposed to do.

"You get our people out of there and bring them to the van," Grandpa says, addressing the Cheshire Spider. "If we're not back yet, you go anyway—get them help. It's likely they'll need immediate medical treatment."

"You want us to leave you behind?" the Cheshire Spider asks.

I was wondering the same thing.

Grandpa waves a hand. "Don't worry about us—we know what we're doing."

Hopefully that isn't code for "Don't worry about us—we'll already be dead." But I figure Grandpa really does know what he's doing, since he's got a lot of experience with this kind of thing and is also really badass.

Gordon might not want me to be like my grandpa, but I could do a hell of a lot worse.

Grandpa signals for us to get going, and I guess this is it. I go with the Cheshire Spider and the Reflector, heading around to the back of the building.

"Whoa." The Cheshire Spider grabs my arm as I'm about to turn the corner. "What do you think you're doing?"

I'm not sure how to answer that, since it's pretty obvious I'm doing what Grandpa said.

"*Cameras*," the Reflector whispers, pointing them out to me. "You have to take them out before you go walking in front of them." She exchanges an exasperated look with the Cheshire Spider.

"I didn't sign up to be a goddamned babysitter," he

mutters under his breath, but still plenty loud enough for me to hear. "I don't know what he's thinking, during an *emergency*."

Great. They think I'm some stupid kid who's only here because my grandpa's their leader. Which I guess is kind of true. My face heats up, and a hot, prickly feeling spreads through my chest. But I ignore it—or at least try to—and zap the three security cameras. I blast them a little harder than necessary, both because I'm pissed off and because I want to make sure there's no doubt in anyone's mind that I did it right.

Neither of them acknowledges me or my accomplishment. They hurry around the corner and over to a door. It has a card reader instead of a normal lock.

"Your job's done," the Cheshire Spider says to me, while the Reflector gets out a plastic ID card to swipe. "You can go wait in the van."

"What? No way. Grandpa said—"

"He said for you to take out the security cameras. You did that. I don't need some *hero* kid getting in our way in there. Last I heard, you were on their side. And if I can't trust you, then—"

"It's not working," the Reflector says, interrupting him. She swipes the card again, even though she just did it three times in a row. She swears and looks like she's about to try and kick the door down in frustration.

The Cheshire Spider takes the card and tries again. "They must have reconfigured it." There's a note of desperation in his voice. He glances back the way we came, like Grandpa and the others might be there with an answer. Or like he's thinking of making his escape, but I'm going to assume Grandpa has better people working with him than that, even if this guy is kind of a douche.

"I can open it." I glare at the Cheshire Spider and don't look away, daring him to tell me I should just go back to the van again.

He raises his eyebrows. "Open it, or blast it to smithereens?"

The Reflector folds her arms. "What difference does it make? We need to get in there. *Now.*"

"If we blast it down, we'll have heroes all over us, like *that.*" He snaps his fingers. "We might as well have left the security cameras on."

"I don't have to blast it," I tell them, even though I didn't know I was going to say that until it came out of my mouth. "I can take out the knob. Melt it, I mean." I know Grandpa's done it before. Or, at least, I'm pretty sure he's told me he has. I've never actually seen him do it.

The Cheshire Spider snorts in disbelief.

"Let him try it," the Reflector says. "Unless you have a better idea. We're running out of time."

"And if we get caught, we're all dead. Do you understand that, kid?" he says, staring me down. "You screw this up, and rescuing those guys will be the least of our worries. So you'd better be damn sure you can do this."

Crap. I glance over at the doorknob. I'm *not* sure. Not completely. But what choice do I have? I stare right back at him and say, "I've done it before. I've got this." Which is a total lie, and I don't even think I'm fooling anyone with it.

But he must realize there's no other option, because he steps aside and gestures to the door.

I don't hesitate. I pretend I really have done this before and hold my hand in front of the knob. I turn on my lightning, making electricity surge between my palm and the metal. It's not enough—I know it's not—and I concentrate, focusing more power into it. I remember what Grandpa said earlier, about not holding back. The truth is, I don't know what that feels like, except in extreme situations, like when someone's trying to kill me or the people I care about. I can't recreate that, and even if I could, it would be too much.

It doesn't help that the Cheshire Spider and the Reflector are practically breathing down my neck, watching and waiting for me to screw up. And it doesn't help that there are Truth members trapped inside this building, depending on us to rescue them from the League. And if I can't do this, they're going to die, and we're all probably going to get caught. Then the next time Gordon sees me, it'll be on the local news, with some douchey guy from the League bragging about how they always knew I'd go back to my villain roots and that it was just a matter of time.

I push those thoughts away, because even if it's all true, it's not making this any easier. Instead, I concentrate on increasing my power. Electricity crackles in the air, and I can feel the heat radiating back at me from the doorknob. Sweat prickles along my back from the effort, and I realize I'm clenching my jaw.

But then the knob starts to melt. Slowly. And it's just the very front, not even the whole knob, and certainly not the mechanism inside. But it's happening.

I don't know how much time passes as I watch it disappear. It feels like forever. And then, just like that, it's over. The knob is gone, the mechanism in the middle melts out, and there's a clang as the other half drops to the floor.

The door swings open, and we're in.

## X·X·X

The dark, grainy video clips of the interrogation-site basement didn't do it justice. It's the creepiest place I've ever seen. The above-ground part of the building might look like an office, but down here looks like a prison. There are actually cells. It's obvious there are people in some of them, even though the cells don't have any windows, because of the moaning and crying. A few prisoners bang on their doors when we creep by and scream to be let out.

The video didn't capture all that, or the smell. It's like the worst bathroom ever, mixed with rotting blood and vomit. When I caught my first whiff of it, I had to try not to gag.

The Cheshire Spider and the Reflector hurry past the cells, heading straight for the actual room where the League does its interrogating. And even though I knew the League was bad news, and even though I didn't have any doubts about that video footage being real, I still can't believe this. It's too horrible to be true.

The Reflector listens with her ear pressed to the door, then nods. "They're in there."

The Cheshire Spider pulls a set of lockpicks out of his pocket and gets to work. He winces when there's a shout inside the room, like he's afraid he's been caught already, but it's followed by screaming, and no one comes over.

A chill washes over me, and the hair on my arms stands on end. This has been going on for years. *Years.* And nobody cared. Or at least not enough to do anything.

There's another shout, and this time I can make out the words. "Tell us their names! A list of names and powers, and all this goes away!"

The Cheshire Spider fumbles with the lockpicks, his hands shaking.

"They've been trained," the Reflector whispers. "To resist torture. They won't give anything up."

I raise an eyebrow at her. "And if they don't? Then what?" I'm pretty sure I already know the answer, but I ask it anyway.

"Then they're dead."

The Cheshire Spider suddenly motions for us to be quiet and stops working on the lock. He sits perfectly still, his head tilted toward the hallway, listening.

The Reflector listens, too. "Footsteps."

He nods. "Someone's coming. We have to get in there *now*. Blast it open!"

It takes me a second to realize he means *me*. I put my ear to the door real quick to make sure no one's standing right behind it. Which is hard to tell, but I have to at least try.

"What are you doing?" the Cheshire Spider hisses. "Do you want to die? Is that it?"

I glare at him. "You need me, so shut up."

His jaw clenches and his whole face turns red.

I take a step back from the door and hold up my hands. Lightning sparks along my arms. The footsteps are getting closer. Two guys, talking about the news. They don't know we're here yet, but any second they're going to turn the corner and find us. Or hear the door explode. Either way, we're in serious trouble.

I channel my fear over getting caught—and of what might happen afterward—and my anger at the fact that this place even exists. People like Gordon and Riley and Sarah, they *believe* in the League. And I might never have cared about it, but they do, and I hate whoever started all this and let them down. They deserve an institution that actually honors its ideals, even if those ideals are really stupid.

"*Now,*" the Cheshire Spider says through clenched teeth. "If you don't, we're—"

I blast the door as hard as I can. I don't know if I can destroy the whole door at once, and I only have one shot before they know we're here, so I aim for the knob. There's a loud crack and a booming noise. The knob and a huge chunk of the door explode inward.

There's immediate shouting, both inside the interrogation room and down the hall. We run inside the room. A superhero shoots an ice beam directly at us. The Reflector throws her hands up in front of her, and the ice beam hits some kind of energy shield and disintegrates.

I look around, noticing that there's only one prisoner in here, not three. There are, however, three superheroes in here now, since the two from the hall came running when they heard the blast. "How did they get in here?!" one of them shouts.

"Cover me!" the Cheshire Spider says as he makes a run for the prisoner, who's chained to the wall.

The prisoner desperately shakes his head, even though he's got blood on his face and one of his hands is black with frostbite. "They have the others! They're in the holding cells—you have to help *them*, not me! They've got Larissa!" That last part comes out a sob.

The Reflector backs toward him and deflects another ice beam. "For God's sake, *shoot them*!" she screams, practically knocking me over as she spins to block an energy blast from one of the other heroes.

My heart races. Time feels like it's moving too fast and too slow at the same time. I wish more than anything that my friends were here instead of these strangers. But they're not. I have to make it through this on my own.

One of the superheroes from the hallway takes off running for the exit, saying something about getting backup. I don't think and I don't hesitate—I hold up my hand and zap him. It's just enough to knock him to the floor, where he lands hard but is still moving. His friend shoots more energy at us, and I attack him, too, except I only get him in the arm. Still, he cries out and stops using his power on us, at least for now.

"What the hell was that?" the Reflector says. "You call

that helping?!" Sweat glistens on her forehead, and the effort of using her energy shield so much is obviously taking its toll.

But I don't want to kill these people, even if they've done terrible things and probably deserve it. Not unless I absolutely have to.

And I realize that Grandpa's right—I only have two modes, and just zapping people a little isn't enough.

I aim at the superhero with the ice powers. Just as I'm about to blast him, the Reflector's energy shield flickers and stops working. She shoves me to the floor, saving both of us from getting hit, while also making my lightning miss its target. It's way stronger than I meant it to be, thanks to her startling me, and it tears a chunk out of the wall.

"We have to go!" she calls over her shoulder to the Cheshire Spider.

"Not yet!" he says. "I've almost got it!"

"There's no time!"

"Please," the prisoner sobs, "you have to find Larissa."

The Reflector's right, there isn't time. I don't know how we're going to get out of here as it is. And whatever the Cheshire Spider's doing to free the prisoner is taking too long. I glance over at the chains attached to the wall. There's not enough space—they'll get hit with some of the debris—but it's better than what these heroes are going to do to us.

I try one more time to hit the guy with ice powers. I'm getting tired and my nerves are shot, and it would be so easy to just blast him as hard as I can. But I don't. My lightning hits him in the foot, which isn't where I was aiming, but it messes him up enough to buy me some time.

"Watch out!" I tell the others, and then I blast the chains on the wall. Bits of brick and metal rain down on the Cheshire Spider and the prisoner, but they're alive, and it works. He's free.

There's a clang on the other side of the room. I move to zap the hero with ice powers again, but it's not him. A door fell out of its frame, and Grandpa and Grandma and their other team member come rushing in. Grandpa quickly assesses the situation and takes out the heroes, using just the right amount of power to disable them and not kill them. Though I'm only assuming that last part.

"Time to hightail it," Grandpa says. "This whole place knows we're here by now."

"The others," the prisoner whimpers. "You have to save the others."

Grandpa looks at him with pity, but he shakes his head, because it's obvious there's no time to save anyone else. My stomach twists at the thought of leaving anyone behind. I don't know these people, but I imagine if it was Kat, or Riley, or even Amelia, and how desperate I would be to get them out, even if it meant risking everything.

"There's no time," Grandpa says, as if he can tell what I'm thinking. Or maybe he's thinking it, too, because he must hate losing some of his people, especially like this, and it can't be an easy decision. But he makes it anyway, because it's us or them, and gives the order for us to make our escape.

# CHAPTER 23

There's a loud knock on the door later that afternoon. Grandpa's in his office, making hushed phone calls, and Grandma's out visiting the families of the people we left behind. It doesn't feel real. Not any of it. The knock comes again, more urgent this time. It seems weird to answer the door at someone else's house, but I figure it's someone important that Grandpa's going to want to talk to once he's off the phone.

I get up from the couch, where I was pretending to read a book I found, just so it would seem like I was doing something normal and not freaking the hell out about what happened earlier. Though the book is apparently about managing menopause, with a special section on how hormone changes affect superpowers, so I'm not sure it would have fooled anyone if they'd come to check on me.

Kat's standing outside on the porch. Speaking of things that don't feel real. I blink at her. "*Kat?* What are you doing here?"

"Me? What am *I* doing here? What the hell are *you* doing here?!" She folds her arms, looking seriously pissed. "You know what? Don't even answer that. I know what you're doing here. What I don't know is why you ran away from home and *didn't tell me.*"

Oops. I scratch my ear and stare at my feet. "I didn't think about it. I mean, I had to get out of there, and then I turned my phone off—"

"Oh, I know. I know you've had your phone off, because I only tried to call you about a zillion times!"

I take a step back. Kat's so angry, she's shaking. I don't know if I've ever seen her this mad—at least, not at me. "I'm sorry, Kat. I would have called you, but…" I swallow. "I'm kind of avoiding my phone right now."

"That doesn't make it okay! Because instead of hearing from you that you ran away, I had to hear it from freaking Sarah!"

Well, at least that explains why she's so pissed, though I have no idea how Sarah found out.

A neighbor lady gapes at us from across the street, conveniently letting her dog stop to sniff some bushes so she has an excuse to keep listening in. Not that we're exactly being discreet or anything.

"Er, maybe we should go inside."

Kat glances over her shoulder at the neighbor lady, then pushes past me into the house. She stands awkwardly in the middle of the living room, scowling at everything with her hands clenched into fists. I gesture for her to follow me into the guest room.

I lean my back against the door to close it, feeling a

little better now that we're alone. Or maybe kind of terrified, since Kat looks like she might actually kill me. "I don't know what you heard, but I didn't tell Sarah anything. I didn't really tell anyone."

"Yeah, well, your dad called Riley, freaking out because you ran away. He didn't have anyone else's number, and I think he only had Riley's because of Amelia. So then Riley called Sarah, to see if she knew where you were, and Sarah emailed me. I'd tried to call you earlier, and I thought it was weird that you had your phone off—you *never* have your phone off—but I thought maybe you forgot to charge it. Or that you accidentally fried it or something." She holds up her hands, mimicking me using my lightning. "Then I had to hear from Sarah that you ran away. Because some superheroes attacked you in the park, and luckily your best friend *Cosine* was there to save her old pal *Renegade*." Kat makes a disgusted face when she says our superhero names, like they leave the worst taste ever in her mouth. "She actually thought it was okay to email me and call you that."

"I thought you were deleting all her emails?"

"This one said *Urgent—Damien's Missing* in the subject line. And that's not the point."

"How did you know where I was?"

"I figured it out. There weren't a lot of places you could go, and you weren't with me." She shrugs and sinks down on the bed, her chin in her hands. "I shouldn't be the last person to find out you got attacked by some douchebag superheroes and then ran away from home, and I really shouldn't have to hear it from your *ex*."

"Whoa, Kat. Sarah's not my ex." I sit down next to her on the bed, even though she glares at me. "I mean, she is, technically, but I don't think of her like that. She's just my friend."

"No, Damien, not just your friend. She's your sidekick. You were begging her to be part of your future, and that would have hurt even if you hadn't made out with her before. And then apparently she saved your life in the park yesterday. It sounded really serious—serious enough for you to feel like you had to leave home—and not once during all this did you think to call me and let me know what was going on or that you were okay."

When she puts it like that... "I'm sorry, Kat. It all happened really fast."

"Yeah, and you look so busy here."

"I have my phone off for a reason, but I'm avoiding Gordon, not you. And if I'd known you were worrying about me, I would have called. I swear." I slip my hand into hers, hoping she won't just pull away.

"Everyone's worried about you, Damien. Not just me."

"So, what were you calling me about?"

"You're really going to try and change the subject right now?"

"I know everyone's pissed at me. But I had to do it, and I'm not going back, so there's nothing to say."

She raises her eyebrows. "I said *worried*, not *pissed*. I can't believe you'd do this to them."

I look away. "This is hard enough as it is. I don't think I could take it if I knew— Hey!" She reaches for my phone on the nightstand. I make a grab for her and pull her toward me, so the phone's out of reach, but she just uses her shapeshifting power to make her arm longer.

Kat presses the button to power up my phone.

All my insides go cold, and I want to be anywhere but here right now. I get up from the bed and pace the room. "I can guess what they're going to say. I don't need to actually hear it. Gordon's not going to be all, 'Hey, I understand, son. You're doing what's best for the family, even if it's really difficult for you, and I admire that.'"

Kat looks up from the screen. "Great Crimson Flash impression."

"Just delete all my messages. When all this is over and I'm ready to go back home, I want to be able to say I didn't hear Gordon disown me or tell me not to bother coming back."

"He's not going to say that, Damien. And I'm not deleting anything for you. You've got, let's see, twelve missed calls from me, eighteen from your dad, seven from Riley, four from Zach, and five from Sarah. And you've got fifteen texts, six emails, and..." She swipes her finger across the phone, then scrolls down. "One, two, three, four, five, six, seven, *eight* voicemails. You're going to have to tell them something. You can't let everybody worry about you like this."

"I know." I sigh and sit back down on the bed.

Kat drops my phone in my lap. "If it makes you feel any better, I get why you did it."

"Thanks." Everyone's always telling me how wrong I am—it's nice to hear the opposite for a change. "I've seen what the League does to people. Not just in those videos, but in real life. Some members of the Truth got captured, and Grandma and Grandpa went on a rescue mission earlier. They took me with them. Me and some other people. I saw the interrogation room, and I saw how they treat villains and what they do to them. I can't let that happen to anyone I care about. Even if they don't understand why I left, and even if it means they end up hating me, I can't put them in danger like that."

"So, if you're not going home, what are you going to do?"

"I don't really have a plan."

She rolls her eyes. "You *always* have a plan."

"My plan was for superheroes to *not* point weapons at me in the park and try and steal my little brother. But that didn't exactly work out. So, you know, I quit school and abandoned my friends and family. Like you do."

"Naturally."

"And now..." I take a deep breath. "I don't have a lot of options left. Grandpa was right when he said the heroes don't need me. They don't, and they don't even want me. I don't mean my friends and family," I add, when she gives me a look, "but just in general. And normally I would take that as a challenge, and I wouldn't back down." I guess that's kind of what I've been doing. "But now the League's decided to openly harass and attack anyone they even suspect might be a villain, and that's not okay. Someone has to stand up to them."

"It doesn't have to be you."

"Yeah, Kat, it does. The Truth needs me. The heroes don't. It's a pretty clear choice."

# CHAPTER 24

Me and Grandma and Grandpa are eating dinner a few nights later when Mom comes over. Unannounced, of course. She has Xavier with her and an overnight bag.

"I'm so sorry to have to do this," she says, not sounding sorry at all, "but our other sitter canceled, and Taylor and I have a big date night planned. This is the—"

"Damien!" Xavier screams, trying to tear himself loose from Mom's grip so he can come glomp me.

Mom acts like she hadn't noticed me until just now. Maybe she hadn't. "Oh, Damien, what are you doing here?"

Apparently she's the only person on the planet who didn't get the memo about me running away from home.

"The boy's staying with us for a while," Grandpa says, his tone not inviting any questions about it.

"Yep," I tell Mom. "That means the guest room is occupied. There's no room for anyone else. Too bad."

"You're always so dramatic. Of course there's room. My little sweetiekins doesn't take up much space. No, he doesn't." She says that last part in full-on baby talk, while tickling Xavier in the stomach until he giggles uncontrollably.

One side of Grandma's mouth twitches in disgust. "You're interrupting dinner, Marianna. We were in the middle of eating."

"I won't stay long. I'm just dropping Xavier off for the night. I know it's last minute, but like I started to say, our other sitter had to cancel, and Taylor and I have plans."

I can't believe her. "For a date night? Maybe *you* should cancel. He's your kid."

Mom laughs. "Cancel! Honestly. You couldn't possibly understand at your age what it's like to have a small child in the house. Taylor and I *need* our time together. We're still newlyweds."

Gross. "Maybe you should have thought of that before you had a baby. And wasn't having 'time together' what caused the problem in the first place?"

She ignores me. "It's only for one night. I've got everything in the bag. His pajamas, his special formula—"

"What? You're not still giving him that growth stuff, are you?"

"I need it!" Xavier screeches. "It's mine, and you can't have any. Mommy makes it just for me, because she loves me so much."

I share a look with Grandma and Grandpa.

"Marianna," Grandpa says, in a half-scolding, half-warning sort of way.

"We have *reservations*! Booked weeks in advance. And that bed in the guest room is big enough for both of my boys, and if it's not, Damien can sleep on the couch."

"I can *what*?"

"Anyway, make sure he has his special formula before bedtime. I want him to grow up big and strong. Show them how strong you are, sweetie."

Xavier makes an attempt to flex his biceps.

"There's a change of clothes in there, just in case, along with his *you-know-whats*." She fake whispers that part. "He's still having the occasional accident. Make sure he puts on his big-boy diaper before bed. And that he doesn't take it off when you're not looking."

"I don't want to wear it," Xavier whines. "Only babies wear diapers."

"But these are big-boy diapers. Only big boys can wear them."

Oh, my God. This is not happening. "Wait, are you saying he wets the bed? And you want me to share with him? Are you out of your freaking mind?!"

Mom glares at me. "You only have one brother, and you should think of him as a gift."

"No, I have two brothers. I *wish* I had one."

"You have two brothers?" Xavier asks, an edge of suspicion in his voice. "You *can't*. Only I can be your brother! Just me!"

"Now look what you've done," Mom says. "You always have to upset him, don't you?" She drops his overnight bag on the floor and holds up her hands. "That's it. I can't take all this chaos. I'll be by in the morning to pick up my little sweetiekins. My favorite little boy in the whole wide world." She leans down and kisses Xavier loudly on the cheek, then makes a run for the door.

Grandma and Grandpa both sigh.

"One of these days," Grandpa says, "I'm going to put my foot down."

Grandma makes air quotes. "Her 'other sitter' canceled, my ass. That other sitter doesn't exist."

$$X \cdot X \cdot X$$

"*Off.*" I point to the floor and glare at Xavier as he tries to get up on the bed for the hundredth time. It's only eight o'clock, but apparently that's when Xavier has to go to bed. And he has to have the lights on, all night. And even though Grandma got out a little air mattress for him, he keeps trying to get into the bed. It's nowhere near my bedtime, but after what Mom said about him having "accidents," I'm not taking any chances by leaving the bed unguarded.

Xavier scowls. His "big-boy diaper" makes crinkling sounds as he slumps down on his mattress. "That's *my* bed. I could tell Grandma you're not allowed to use it."

"Yeah? Good luck with that." I keep scrolling through Facebook on my phone. Kat posted a new pic of First Mate Suckers. He's at a seafood restaurant, staring longingly at a framed photo of a boat on the wall. I hesitate before clicking *like*, but then I decide being off the grid is overrated. Not that I'm really off the grid, anyway, since I called Gordon my second day here to let him know I'm not dead.

And by "called Gordon," I mean I dialed the house phone during the middle of the day, when I knew no one would be home, and left a message on the machine. I didn't tell him where I was, because I don't need him trying to track down where my grandparents live, but I said I was safe and doing okay.

"If you're not nicer to me," Xavier says, "I'm not going to invite you to my birthday party."

"I'll take that deal."

His mouth falls open, like that was the last thing he expected me to say.

My phone chimes and a new text pops up. I don't recognize the sender, and obviously it's not anybody already in my phone, because then it would say a name.

*Your friends are worried about you.*

What? I start to type *Who the hell is this?* but before I can finish, a new message comes in.

*This is Mason, btw.*

Rage floods my chest, and lightning burns beneath my skin. Riley's new-old BFF is seriously texting me to tell me my friends are worried about me? They should be worried about *him*, because if I ever see him again, I'm pretty sure I'll murder him.

"You're going to be sorry if you miss my birthday," Xavier says in his shrill, annoying voice.

I ignore him and write, *How did you get this number??*

*From Ry. He's worried about you. Zach is, too. And they know I'm an experienced mediator.*

I have so many things to say to that. So many that I just

sit there, fuming, trying to figure out where to start. I mean, seriously, who does he think he is? Just because he's best friends with "Ry" doesn't mean he's allowed to text me and say all this crap. And bringing Zach into it? Zach doesn't even like Mason, and I can't picture him asking for his help. Mason just wants me to think that I'm so awful, even Zach is desperate to find some way to deal with me. Which would never happen. Not in a million years.

Right?

"We're going to have a pony," Xavier goes on. "With blue hair. And only I get to ride it."

"Ponies don't have blue hair. And your birthday's not for over half a year, so shut up about it."

"They do, too! If I want them to, they do. And my birthday's in a couple *weeks*. I'm going to be six months old."

His birthday's in a couple weeks? *My* birthday's in a couple weeks.

*If Zach and Riley want to talk to me,* I write, *they can text me themselves.*

"If you miss my party, you won't get to see the pony. And you won't get to watch me and my friends play in the bouncy castle."

I look up from my phone long enough to raise an eyebrow at him. "What friends?" There's no way Xavier has friends. And if he does, while I have to be "mediated" by this douchebag because my friends don't know how to talk to me anymore, I'm going to be seriously pissed.

Another text comes in from Mason.

*They tried, but you wouldn't answer. I told them you're going through a tough time right now—running away from home is a high-stress event, similar to a bad breakup or having to start over at a new school. You've obviously got some trauma going on in your life, and they're hurt by your actions, so I'm stepping in to make things right.*

The only way he could even remotely make things right is if he steps *off* and leaves all of us alone.

"My *friends*," Xavier says, as if that explains everything. "I have lots of them."

"Imaginary ones don't count."

His nostrils flare, and he clenches his fists and stands up on his air mattress. "My friends are real!"

Sure they are. Xavier supposedly has a bunch of friends, who somehow put up with him and would still come to his birthday, even though he's the only one who gets to ride the pony? "How much does Mom have to pay them to hang out with you?"

He totally misses my meaning. "Everyone gets a party-favor bag. With candy and a toy pony."

So they can remember the one they didn't get to ride?

*Are you still there, Damien?* Mason writes. *I know this is hard for you, but that's why I'm here. Talk to me. The healing process can't begin until you express your true feelings.*

Baaaarf. God, I hate him so much. I open up my contacts list and find Riley. I'm about to text him when I think better of it and dial his number instead. This calls for telling him off in real time.

"I have a birthday party every month." Xavier's creeping toward the bed again, as if I won't notice. I wish

I had a spray bottle. "Because I'm growing up so big and strong."

Ugh. I pretend I don't hear him and listen to the phone ringing instead, willing Riley to pick up. If he doesn't, I'm going to be so pissed at him. It's already not cool that he gave Mason my number, and now he doesn't even have the decency to answer his phone when I call to tell him where he can shove it?

"X?" Riley sounds almost skeptical.

"What the hell, Perkins?!"

He breathes a sigh of relief. "You're okay."

"No, I'm not 'okay.' You want to know why? Wait, he's not there with you, is he?"

"Who?"

"Oh, *come on*. You know exactly who I'm talking about."

Xavier makes a noise that I can only guess is supposed to be him clearing his throat. He screeches extra loud, trying to talk over my conversation. "I was telling you about my birthday party! You're supposed to listen!"

I plug my other ear with my finger. "This is unforgivable. You gave Mason my phone number!"

"Unforgivable? You mean like you running away from home? You just left everyone, X! And then you wouldn't even answer your phone."

"That doesn't mean you're allowed to get Mason involved!"

"It got you to call me, didn't it?" There's a smile in his voice. A smug one.

Damn it. I consider hanging up on him.

"Last time," Xavier says, "I had a Samurai Squids party. Like the show. They live underwater, and—"

"I *know* what Samurai Squids is." It used to be my favorite cartoon when I was a kid. I didn't realize it was still on TV. They must air the reruns. "I had a Samurai Squids party, too." I can't help sounding defensive. But I hate that we have something in common, and I hate that Mom lets him watch my favorite TV show from back in the day. It feels like when she gave him Damien II, my teddy bear, like my childhood doesn't matter to her and she really does want him to replace me.

"I used to watch that show," Riley says on the phone. "I had all the action figures."

"Me, too. But don't think you can distract me from what you did. Giving Mason my number is never okay."

"I just wanted you to stop avoiding me. I figured you wouldn't answer my texts, but getting Mason involved would piss you off so much you'd finally call me back."

"And what if it hadn't?"

"Then I would have had to rely on his excellent mediator skills."

I *think* he's joking. At least, he'd better be.

Xavier's still trying to tell me about his stupid birthday party. "We had a Samurai Squids tablecloth, and paper plates, and a pin-the-tentacle on the squid game. I won, 'cause I'm the best."

I had all those things, too. Mom must have reused the stuff from my party, even though it's all ten years old. And made of paper. How cheap is that? And he thinks she's getting him a pony and a bouncy castle next month?

"So," I say to Riley, "what you're telling me is you *used* your best friend?"

"I wasn't using you. Maybe I manipulated you a little bit, but I was just trying to get you to talk to me."

"No, I meant Mason."

"Oh." There's a pause, and then he clears his throat. Gearing up to tell me that *I'm* his best friend, not that douchebag, I hope. "I told him there was a chance that you hearing from him would get us talking again."

"He was *in on it*?" I can't believe this.

"I wouldn't say it like that."

"How would you say it? That you and your new best friend conspired against me? Is that how you'd put it?!"

"Hey. You were the one who disappeared and wouldn't answer any of my messages. And I didn't tell him you'd call because you'd be pissed. I said that reaching out like this might get through to you. That's all."

Xavier climbs up onto the bed. His diaper actually grazes my arm, and he gives me this nasty smile, like he's just daring me to tell him to get down again. I wish I was back home, where all I have to deal with is telling Amelia to turn down her TV. Or at Kat's dorm, where there aren't any siblings at all.

"Get off the bed. *Now*."

Either he can't feel the electric charge building up in the air, or he's willing to risk getting shocked, because he doesn't move. "We also had a Samurai Squids *cake*. It was shaped like a rectangle, but it had a drawing of a squid on it. Except one of its legs was missing, because the idiot at the bakery doesn't know how many legs they have."

Something about that sounds really familiar, and then I remember that I had a Samurai Squids cake at my party, exactly as he described. One of its legs was missing, and Mom complained that whoever was working at the grocery-store bakery was an idiot.

Something weird is going on. Mom might have saved all the party stuff from way back when, but how could she have gotten the exact same cake?

"I get why you left," Riley says. "And I get why you were ignoring everyone's calls. But you don't have to, okay?"

"You didn't have to get Mason involved."

"You kind of proved that I did."

Xavier pokes me. When I don't respond, he does it a bunch of times in a row, until I get fed up and grab his hand. There's a spark when I do, and he whines and starts squealing.

"Get *down*."

"Noooo! Let me go!" He squirms and kicks, making horrible high-pitched noises. I drag him off the bed, in case all this struggling causes him to have one of his "accidents." "I just wanted to tell you about my birthday party!"

"Yeah, right." To Riley, I say, "I don't know why I'm even talking to you. First you ditch me for Mason, and now you get him to trick me into calling you."

"It wasn't supposed to be a trick. I just wanted to make sure you're okay. I know you left that message for your dad, but I wanted to hear it for myself. That's all."

Xavier's face is red from his tantrum. He takes short,

hiccuping breaths and says, "It was the funnest party ever! I'm glad you weren't there! Mommy loves me best, so she got me lots of presents. I got a stuffed shark *and* a Samurai Squids underwater playset for the bathtub that came with a gold trading card. And we had so much ice cream, one of my friends threw up and had to go home."

I sit down and grip the edge of the bed, because it feels like the floor's falling out from under me. That happened at *my* party, and Mom got me those same presents. They don't even make the underwater playset anymore, not just because it was limited edition, but because they got recalled, due to some people having an allergic reaction to the plastic they used.

"I have to go," I tell Riley before hanging up. Then, to Xavier, "I have news for you. Those weren't your presents. They were mine." So much for 'Mommy' loving him best.

"Nuh-uh. Mommy gave them to me!"

"And the name of the kid who had to go home? It was Kyle, wasn't it?"

"He's my friend."

I'm going to kill Mom. "Nope. He was my friend. That was my party. I had the same stuff, the same cake, and those were my presents." I knew she was giving him fake memories at night while he sleeps, but I didn't know they'd be *mine*.

"It was *my* party," Xavier screeches. "I was there!"

"Were you? Have you ever used the playset?"

"Yes! It's fun!"

"Yeah? When?"

"I..." He pauses to think about that.

"You've never played with it, because it wasn't yours. It doesn't exist anymore. And that shark was mine, too. I named him Timothy." Timothy the Tooth, to be exact—it was his street name.

Xavier's mouth drops open. "Did Mommy tell you that?"

"She didn't need to—I was there, not you." Though she does have a lot of explaining to do. "Mom never threw you a party."

"Yes, she did! You don't know what you're talking about!"

"She faked it. She used details from one of my birthday parties and made you think it happened to you. You don't have that playset, and you don't have Timothy, and you don't have any friends."

Xavier's eyes water. His whole face screws up in a mixture of horror and spite. "You're jealous! You're jealous because Mommy loves me best! She *told* me so!"

"She *what*?"

The door bursts open and Grandpa gives us both stern looks. "What's all the fuss in here?"

"Damien's being mean!" Xavier wails. "He said Mommy lied about my birthday, but she wouldn't do that."

"You've known her for five months," I tell him. "You have no idea what she's capable of."

Grandpa looks like he agrees with that, but he doesn't back me up on it.

"She loves me more than anything! And that means more than *you*."

I feel sick. It shouldn't matter, because it's not like I

think I'm number one on Mom's list of favorite people. Or even on the list at all. But she used to say she loved *me* more than anything. Now she's replaced me with Xavier, and she's giving him my memories. And I wonder if it was ever true, if she ever really did love me more than anything, or if that was as much a lie as Xavier's Samurai Squids party.

And I should let it go, because he's just a stupid kid, and it doesn't matter what he thinks. But what he said struck a nerve, and it feels too raw. "If she loves you so much more than me, then why is she giving you *my* memories? I'm the one she threw birthday parties for. Yours weren't even real."

Xavier starts crying, in that half-screaming way of his.

"That's enough," Grandpa says, frowning at me. Xavier runs up to him and holds up his arms, begging to be picked up. Grandpa ignores that part, but he does pat his back. "Come on. You'd better sleep in our room tonight." He doesn't sound happy about that. "But if you take off that diaper, so help me, God..."

He drags Xavier out of the room and closes the door. Maybe it's the sudden quiet in here, now that Xavier's gone, but it sounds really loud when it hits the doorjamb.

# CHAPTER 25

I thought I was over seeing myself on TV. After everything that happened last fall, and over the past few months, I figured it wouldn't be weird anymore. But I was wrong. And even though this time I actually volunteered for it, and I'm not saying anything embarrassing or too personal, I still kind of want to go hide under the bed rather than watch myself on the screen.

Especially since all of Grandpa's friends are over. He's having a private viewing party of our first commercial for the Truth, though his idea of a "private party" apparently involves having twenty of his closest friends come over. And Kat couldn't make it, because she has school—though she promised she'd watch it secretly in class and text me—so I don't know anyone here except my grandparents. But everyone *acts* like they know me. Patting me on the back and saying, "Good job, kiddo," and stuff. I don't know what Grandpa's said to them, but they keep giving me these looks, like I'm a piece of junk they just found out is worth a million dollars. It's cool that they're celebrating what I've done for the Truth, but it would be even cooler if they kept their hands to themselves while they did it.

And also if they didn't act so weird.

Or call me "kiddo," what with me being almost seventeen and not, like, five.

On the bright side, at least Mom wasn't invited to this. Not that she knows anything about the commercial, or that it's airing today, but as Grandma said, "Nothing ruins a good time faster than your mother and that little hellspawn of hers."

"Seats, people!" Grandpa shouts. "We've got two minutes till show time."

Everyone crowds around the TV in the living room. There aren't nearly enough spaces, even with the dining chairs and a couple of fold-out seats Grandma borrowed from the neighbors.

I'm thinking maybe I can get away with just standing around in the back, where no one can see me, when Grandpa puts a hand on my shoulder and gestures toward the center of the couch. "Everybody scoot over for my grandson, the guest of honor!"

There are already three people sitting on the couch, but they beam at me and squish themselves toward the edges to make room.

"That's okay, Grandpa. I was going to stand, so—"

"This is the moment we've been waiting for. You're going to want to sit down." He grins at me and wiggles his eyebrows, like we're both in on some big secret. Like the next thirty seconds really are going to change my whole life.

As if my life hasn't changed enough as it is.

I sit down on the couch, sardined in between two people I've never met before. They're an older couple, around Grandma and Grandpa's age, and they seem to be married to each other, which makes it even weirder that I'm sitting between them.

Grandpa looks at his watch and then double-checks that the TV is on the right channel. There's a shampoo commercial playing, but as soon as it's over, ours comes up.

And I use the term *ours* pretty loosely here. Even if Grandpa's the one who came up with the idea to make these and organized the whole thing, *I'm* the only one in them. I'm the one people are going to see and associate with the Truth.

"Right on time," Grandpa says, turning up the TV.

Everyone leans forward as I appear on the screen.

"When you think of the word *hero*," I say in the commercial—and yeah, hearing my voice in it is still weird, too—"do you imagine someone who drags innocent people off the streets? Someone who *tortures* them? Because that's what *hero* means today, thanks to the League."

The camera jumps to some footage taken at the League's interrogation site, like in Grandpa's original launch video, with my voice playing over it.

"The Truth is speaking out for villain rights. Because somebody has to. Because we can't let the League get away with hurting people just because they don't have an *H* on their thumb. This isn't only a problem for villains—it's a problem for everyone." The camera switches back to me, looking solemn and kind of intense. "The Truth doesn't grab people off the street. We don't torture anyone. And we don't claim to follow a set of rules but then look the other way whenever it's convenient. The Truth is here to give villains a voice. Now"—I wince in real life as the camera zooms in on my face—"what do *you* have to say?"

The commercial ends, and another one takes its place, this time featuring some gigantic car that fits the whole family. But no one's paying attention to that, because they're all clapping and cheering. *For me.* Everyone looks really pleased, and even though I kind of want to sink into the couch cushions and disappear, it feels good to be appreciated.

Grandpa beams at me. "Couldn't have said it better myself!"

"Definitely not," Grandma agrees.

The old woman on my left actually puts her hand on my knee—who told her she could do that?—and says, "You're going to do big things for us."

Across the room, Grandpa holds up his drink for a toast. "To Damien, the best grandson anyone could ask for. I want everyone to know how proud I am of you today. You did good—not just for me, but for all of us. And this is just the beginning. To Damien!" he says again, and this time everyone else repeats it, and anyone with a glass starts clinking them together.

# X·X·X

"Are you watching this?" Riley asks when I answer the phone a couple days later. No *hello*, no "I know I'm not pro-Truth or anything, but wow, those commercials you did are pretty excellent." The second one aired yesterday, and the third one's supposed to be on tomorrow. And there's no way Riley hasn't seen the first two, but does he congratulate me on them? Nope. Nothing.

"Am I watching what?"

"Turn on Channel Five. *Now.*"

"Geez, Perkins. We're barely back on speaking terms, and you're ordering me around?" But I head into the living room and turn on the TV.

"We're not— We're what? I mean, you're talking to me right now, and I *wasn't* ordering you around. It's just that you'll want—you *need*—to see this. You won't like it, though." He says that last part kind of quiet.

"You want to tell me what's—" But I don't need to finish that sentence. As soon as I flip to Channel Five, I know exactly what he's talking about.

My *dad* is on TV. And okay, that's not really that unusual, since he has his own show and is kind of famous and all. But this is different. He's on some kind of talk show, being interviewed. He's dressed as the Crimson Flash, of course, and he's talking about *me*.

The hostess, who's wearing a couple pounds of makeup and smiling way too hard, says, "How do you feel about allegations that your son has been secretly working for the

Truth this whole time?"

This whole time? As in, as long as I've lived with Gordon? Or as long as the Truth has existed?

Gordon—er, I mean, the Crimson Flash—doesn't smile back at her. He looks way too serious for that. "I don't believe that. Not for a minute. Damien's a good kid, and he means well." He turns his head to look directly into the camera for this, like he knows I'm watching. "But he's wrong this time."

He says "this time" as if he actually thinks I've been right before. As if he isn't constantly telling me how wrong I am.

"X?" Riley says.

"I'm watching it."

"What did you mean we're *back* on speaking terms?"

"I wasn't talking to you, remember?"

"You weren't answering your phone. Nobody could get a hold of you. That's different."

On screen, the hostess gives the Crimson Flash a pouty, sympathetic look, to show that she feels for him having to put up with my existence. "We've all seen your son's commercials for the Truth. He makes some awfully harsh statements about the League and what it means to be a hero. That's got to be difficult for you and your family. How are you holding up?"

"Can you believe this?" I ask Riley.

"X, seriously, when were you not talking to me?"

The Crimson Flash folds his hands together. "It hasn't been easy, Barbara. Having one of your children run away from home... It's been a strain on all of us. I don't agree with the changes the League's implemented lately to deal with the Truth. Something has to be done, but there has to be a better way than challenging people on the street."

I tighten my grip on my phone. "What the hell? That's what *I* said!" Only when I say it, I'm supposedly wrong.

"These kinds of tactics are only making things worse. That's why a group of us at the League are petitioning to stop this violence. The Truth is trying to egg us on—we can show them we're still in control by simply ignoring them. The more seriously we take them, the longer it will be before this problem sorts itself out."

"*What?!*" I shout at the TV. "Are you kidding me?!"

"Come on, X," Riley says. "When were you not talking to me?"

"You gave Mason my phone number!"

"Yeah, and that's *when* you called me again. We were on speaking terms."

"Fine. It was before that."

"When you weren't speaking to anyone? Because—"

"Be quiet for a minute, will you?"

He shuts up just as the hostess, Barbara, finishes asking the Crimson Flash what one thing he'd really like to say to me, if he had the chance.

On TV, the Crimson Flash swallows and looks pleadingly at the camera. "If I could tell him anything, I'd say he needs to give up this crusade with the Truth before anyone else gets hurt. I've spent my whole life believing in the League, and I know that things are going to get straightened out. What it means to be a hero hasn't changed—not in my book, anyway. And I'd tell him...

Damien, if you're watching this, we all want you to come home. I don't care what you've done—none of us do. We just want you back with us, and we'll figure things out together. As a *family*."

Wow. He's laying it on kind of thick with that "as a family" crap. Like they should all get to take a vote on my every move, while we pile into our family-sized all-terrain suburban vehicle to go on a picnic in the park, where we'll take lots of candid shots of us all getting along and then post them on our family blog and send links to all our friends and relatives.

I turn off the TV and hurl the remote at the couch, because I've heard enough. He thinks I'm wrong—big surprise. He thinks the League will somehow have the answer to all this, despite the horrible things they've done, and that they should ignore us until we go away? He thinks I should just shut up and come home? It's not exactly a compelling argument. And he doesn't care "what I've done"? Is he talking about the commercial, or does he think I've been going around committing crimes?

"It's like he doesn't know me at all."

"X."

"Okay, okay." I run a hand through my hair on my way back to my room. "When I wasn't talking to anyone, I was pretty sure you were the last person who'd want to hear from me."

"That's not the same as not being on speaking terms."

"Right. But I thought you'd be mad. Or..." *Disappointed.* Disappointed in me for running out on everybody, but maybe kind of relieved, too, because at least he'd know he made the right choice, choosing Mason. And at least he wouldn't have to deal with being friends with a half villain who picks fights at school, and who he's not even supposed to talk to anymore. "I just thought you'd be mad at me, so I was mad at you first."

"So, you were pissed at me because you imagined I'd be pissed at you? That's stupid. I was *worried* about you, like everybody else. And, yeah, once I knew you were okay, I was kind of mad. But only because you were avoiding me."

"And then you went and gave Mason my number."

Riley clears his throat, ignoring my last comment. "Your dad being on TV wasn't the only reason I called. You know the Heroes' Gala that's coming up next weekend?"

"No."

"That was a rhetorical question. *Everybody* knows about the Heroes' Gala. It's, like, the biggest event of the year."

"I'm half villain, remember? I've never heard of it."

"Seriously? Okay, well, it's this big fancy party where they announce all the important awards. Like Most Beloved Superhero. You do know your dad wins that one every year, right?"

"*Yes.* I'm not stupid." Though I did just find that out last semester, after having lived with him for months. "Let me guess—he's not even nominated this time, because of me."

"He's still in the running. Your commercials probably didn't help, but he's also getting a lot of sympathy for them. Because he still supports the League and all that.

But, listen, you know that award Mrs. Deeds nominated me for? At Heroesworth?"

"Yeah, I remember." How could I forget?

"Well, they do a couple big student awards at the Gala, too, and that's one of them. It's kind of a big deal, and I've got tickets. Me and Sarah are going to be there, and Zach and Amelia. And I thought—"

"Are you seriously inviting me to watch you win some stupid award at the *Heroes'* Gala? And I thought Amelia was banned from all things Perkins."

"She was, but then, after you left... Well, Zach was pretty upset, so Mom decided to ease up."

"You mean Curtis decided. Because I wasn't around to be a bad influence anymore, right?"

"It wasn't like that."

"Sure it wasn't."

"I have five guest tickets. Amelia doesn't need one, because she's getting one through your parents, and if you don't take the other one, then Mom's going to bring *Curtis*."

"Great. Good to know I still rank above that douchebag. Is that the only reason you're inviting me, or did you need someone to make runs to the refreshments table so you don't miss your big moment?"

Riley makes a frustrated sound. "I'm inviting you because you're my *friend*. Because maybe something really cool is happening to me, and I actually want you to be there. But if you're going to be a jerk about it—"

"I'm the spokesperson for the Truth. The League already tried to haul me off just for walking through the park. Showing up at their big awards ceremony would probably be, like, triple red alert."

"You're half superhero. We're all going to be there, and we're not going to let them do anything to you. Plus, your dad will be there. They're not going to nab you in front of the Crimson Flash."

I'm not so sure about that. "You really think I can just walk into the Heroes' Gala?"

"You'd have a ticket, right? And I know you could probably get one through your dad, too, but I figured since you're *actually* not talking to him, that you wouldn't want to ask. And it doesn't matter anyway, as long as Mom thinks there's no extra ticket. I'm still not technically supposed to hang out with you, but she doesn't have to know who I'm saving it for."

"Who has the other one?" I tap my fingers against the edge of the bed, doing the math.

"What?"

"You said you have five tickets. You're only inviting four people. Your mom, Zach, Sarah, and me, because you said Amelia doesn't need one. So, Perkins, who else did you invite that you were just conveniently not going to tell me about and hope I didn't notice?"

He sucks in a breath, obviously annoyed that I wasn't fooled. "Mason was *there*. He's the reason I got nominated for this award in the first place."

"Because he wrote about what you did at the museum in his report. He didn't lift a finger to actually *help* you."

"He's my friend, X. Just like you. I want the people who are important to me to be there. And I get that you don't like Mason—"

"Don't *like* him? That's sugarcoating it."

"—and I get that you're working with the Truth, and you don't think you can show up. But for once in your life will you just *listen* to me?! Will you stop thinking about yourself and what you want for five freaking seconds?!"

"Hey, I didn't—"

"You never care what I have to say, or what the consequences will be for anyone but yourself. That's how this whole thing started, right? During our final last semester. *You* chose to zap that superhero. *You* didn't listen to me—you didn't care what I thought or what might happen to me because of your actions. So I had to partner up with Mason. And you know what? If the situation was reversed, he wouldn't be giving me crap about it. If I'd made plans with him and had to change them for some reason—and not getting kicked out of school is a pretty good reason—he would have *understood*. He wouldn't have tried to make me feel bad about it every single chance he got for the next couple months, or for the rest of your life, or however long you're going to hold this stupid grudge! Because you know what? That's what friends do. *Real* friends, anyway."

"Perkins. I *am* your real friend."

"Yeah, when it's convenient for you. You might think this whole awards ceremony is stupid, but it's important to me. It's next Saturday night at the Grand Park Hotel. Seven o'clock, black tie. I'll leave your ticket at will call. If you can get over yourself by then, you should come."

# CHAPTER 26

I t's Wednesday afternoon, exactly two weeks since the incident in the park, when those superheroes attacked me and tried to steal Alex. And now I'm sitting in my grandparents' living room with my phone, watching response videos to the commercials we made.

At first, most of the responses were people crying with relief that they could finally talk about what heroes had done to them and the people they cared about. Or they were angry people, railing against the League and their new policies—both the policy of capturing villains and asking questions later, and the one of completely ignoring us. Those were the extremes, but in the last couple days, the response video thing has really caught on, and now everyone's coming out of the woodwork to tell their stories or just to thank the Truth for making all this possible.

And to thank *me*, since I'm their spokesperson. It's kind of weird, but really cool, too. Gordon can go on TV and say I'm wrong all he wants, but what I'm doing is actually helping people. Helping *villains*.

A notification pops up on my phone, and I switch over to the chat window. There's a message from Kat, along with another video link. *My friends made this for you. :)*

*It's not one of the crazy ones where some girl says she wants to marry me and/or have my baby, is it?*

*It better not be. Though Jordan did tell me he thinks you're hot.*

I hit the link, and the video starts up. A bunch of Kat's friends are all crowded together, smiling at the camera. It's pretty much everyone who was at her party I went to, minus Tristan, of course.

Kat's suitemates, Tasha and Liv, are in the front, along with June, the girl who told me about her mom getting taken by the League. They're holding up a homemade banner that says, *We luv u, Damien!* The guys—Jordon, Cameron, Blake, and Nathan—are all in the back. Liv counts off, "One, two, three," and then the whole group shouts at the same time, "Thanks for telling us the *Truth*!"

They're not the first ones to say that—it's become part of the trend with these videos—but they are the first people to say it that I've actually met. And who it would maybe be cool to be friends with. I mean, we'll probably never play Monopoly again, after the way I kicked their asses, but we could still hang out.

I thumbs up the video and hit *replay*, right as Grandpa walks in from his office. He stretches his back and looms over the couch, squinting at my phone. "I don't know how you can see that thing. You'll ruin your eyes."

I shrug. "It's fine."

"The public has really taken to you, you know." He grins at me.

I raise my eyebrows. "I thought you couldn't see it?"

"I can *hear* it. And everyone's been sending me links on the computer. I watched a couple of them. A lot of good things are happening because of you."

"It wasn't *just* me. But thanks, Grandpa."

He points a finger at me. "You practice your lightning yet today?"

"Yes. Geez."

"Good. And Gladys wants you to get to work cleaning out the garage soon. It's almost planting season, and all her tools are in there. Somewhere."

"I'm getting to it. Tomorrow," I add, when he tilts his head. "And it's only February. The ground's still frozen."

"She's starting them inside. And anyway, she said if you clean the garage like I do, you're going to need at least a month's head start."

"You should just stop putting so much crap in there."

He laughs, as if that's the most ridiculous thing he's ever heard. "I've got something I need you to do for me. Since you're not busy."

I glance at him, then at my phone. "I was going to call Kat, but I guess it can wait."

"I need you to shoot another commercial. We're going to put this one up on that internet site."

"You mean YouTube?"

He waves that away, like he can't be bothered to remember. "I got a PR guy. He says this online stuff is the fastest way to get a message out. So I need you to tell everyone about a rally we're having Saturday night."

"*This* Saturday?"

"Of course this Saturday. What's the matter? You got somewhere to be?"

Yep. Not that I can actually go to Riley's stupid awards ceremony. "It's kind of short notice."

"That's why we're using the internet. But don't you worry—I've had this planned for weeks. We don't want people to get all fired up about it, then have to wait and let their enthusiasm die down. And the longer people know about it, the longer those damn heroes have to try and stop it. But now we've got to get the word out. All these kids making videos because of you—"

"They're not all kids."

"Well, whoever's doing it, these are the people I want coming to this rally. Villains who've got something to say. Who want to do something."

"I don't know."

"What don't you know?"

"Maybe someone else should make the video this time. Because if I do it, then everyone's going to expect to see me there."

"And?"

"And you're right, I have plans."

"You'll bring Kat to the rally. It's not the best place for a date, but you can go anywhere you want afterward. Say the word, and I'll make you a reservation. I've got connections with half the four-star restaurants in town."

"Um, yeah, me and Kat don't really do fancy

restaurants." Especially not if Grandpa wants to stay on friendly terms with his "connections." I've been officially banned from two of the swankiest places downtown. One of them because I brought my own ketchup bottle and poured it all over my plate when the chef came out to personally see how we were enjoying the meal. And one because we were making out in public, and when the waiter asked us to stop, Kat gestured to all the octopus decor—it was a seafood restaurant—and shouted, "How do you expect anyone to control themselves with all these *tentacles* everywhere?" I couldn't stop laughing, but the waiter's face turned bright red, and he threatened to get the manager if we didn't pay up and leave on the spot, even though we hadn't even gotten our food yet.

"I'm buying," Grandpa says.

I consider it, just for a second. "I can't. I promised a friend I'd be somewhere." Okay, I didn't promise. Actually, I said I wasn't going. And I'm not at all sure that I'd get through the door, even if I do have a ticket. But if I get turned away, at least I can say I tried. That counts as being a real friend, right? Even if I'm a half-villain spokesperson for the Truth and the Heroes' Gala is probably the last place I should be.

Grandpa narrows his eyes. "A new friend? Because as far as I'm aware, Kat's the only villain you hang around with."

"A different friend."

"A *hero* friend, you mean."

"It doesn't matter who I'm hanging out with. I can't be there, okay? And that means it would be hypocritical if I told people to come to the rally." Not to mention false advertising.

He takes a deep breath. "This is important. I need those people there, and you're the one they'll listen to."

"I can do it next weekend."

"No. It has to happen this Saturday. Tell your hero friend you've got something more important to do. If they're really your friend, they'll reschedule."

"That's not... We have tickets. To a thing. There's no rescheduling." I'm not about to tell him where I'm actually going. "Why can't you reschedule? You haven't even told anyone about it yet."

"Damn it, kid. It's got to be *this Saturday*, or else there's no point!"

I flinch when he yells at me. Grandpa never yells at me. Not like that, anyway. Not like he means it.

"I'm sorry, Damien," he says, after he gets a hold of himself. "I'm just under a lot of stress here."

I glare at him. "If it's really so important, why did you wait until the last minute to ask me? You said you've been planning it for weeks." We could have filmed it when we did the other commercials. I could have told Riley I had other plans—unbreakable ones—and then he couldn't really blame me for having to miss the awards ceremony. I mean, he probably still would have, but at least he'd know I had a good reason for not showing up.

"I didn't think I had to worry about whether or not you'd do it. I didn't pick you to be our spokesperson just because you're famous, you know."

"Being your spokesperson doesn't mean I don't have a

life."

He ignores me. "I'm not saying it doesn't help, but it's not the real reason. You're a natural leader, like me. You know how to make people listen. How to make them follow you. It's part of who you are. And you're dedicated to the cause. You don't have to look very far to see you're already inspiring that dedication in others. The Truth needs you. I need you. And you have to trust me that this weekend is important."

"It's just a rally." I'm not even sure what people *do* in those.

"It's not just a rally—it's the first one. This is the first time that villains from all over Golden City are going to come together, regardless of their differences, and tell each other their stories. I know you think that's what they've been doing online, but talking from behind a computer isn't the same as getting out there and meeting other villains who share similar experiences. This is a chance for the Truth to reach out to real people and bring them together for one goal. And the heroes are going to be busy with their big gala Saturday night. It's our best chance to do this without getting interrupted and without putting people in danger. You know how the heroes feel about us, and what their policy is right now. Saturday night's the only time I can risk getting that many villains together in a public place. We need this to happen, and we need you to be there. The people who come to this thing are going to expect to see you, whether you do the commercial or not. You've got a lot of fans, and you're the one who's brought them this far. They're counting on you,

Damien, and so am I."

"Wow. You really think... all that?" It's flattering. In a "that's a hell of a lot of pressure" sort of way.

"I really do. And whatever else you have planned, I just don't see how it compares. So, what do you say we go film ourselves another commercial?"

# CHAPTER 27

It's five thirty on Saturday. The Heroes' Gala starts in an hour and a half, but so does the Truth rally. I really only need to be at the gala for, like, five minutes. I just don't know which five minutes. Not that it matters anyway because I can't exactly be seen at the Heroes' Gala the same night as the rally. Or, like, at all. And the villains need me. The heroes don't even want me at their event, and they wouldn't have even if I hadn't become a spokesperson for the Truth.

Except Riley wants me to be there.

I stop outside the back entrance to the laundromat. Well, to Grandpa's secret offices behind the laundromat. He's here, getting ready for the rally tonight, and I figured telling him I might not be there for the *entire* event was better done in person. Or at least it sounded like a better idea when I was contemplating calling him. Now that I'm actually here, I think I would have preferred the phone.

I go inside—Grandpa gave me a key—and dial Riley's

number. Maybe I don't have to talk to Grandpa about this at all. Maybe—

"Hey, X." Riley answers on the first ring. He sounds hopeful. It's a tentative hopeful, but it's still enough to make me feel like a jerk for what I'm about to say.

"Hey."

"We're all getting ready at my house." There's some noise in the background, and I hear Zach shouting something that must be hilarious, because then Amelia cracks up.

Sarah's laughing, too, until she says to Riley, "Tell Renegade he *better* be there."

"Sarah says—"

"I heard her."

There's a pause, and then the background noise gets quiet, and I hear Riley's door close. "You should come over. Curtis isn't here, and I think... Maybe my mom would make an exception."

"For the spokesperson for the Truth? I don't think so." If she didn't want me over there before, there's no way she wants me there now. "Anyway, I can't."

"But you're going to be there tonight." He says it as a statement, not a question, as if that will make it true.

"About that."

"Come on. Don't—"

"Just hear me out, Perkins. You're better off if I don't show up. If I go, it's going to turn into some scandal. People will be staring all night, shooting dirty looks at our group and taking bad pictures that will be all over the internet. It's your big night. You don't want that."

"You mean *you* don't want that."

"You've got everybody else going. Sarah and Zach and Amelia and... Mason." His BFF. "Your mom's actually leaving the douchebag at home. You really don't need me there, ruining everything."

"You already told me you weren't going. You didn't need to call again to rub it in."

"Look, you got that nomination because you were working with Mason, not me. You don't need me there when you win it, either."

"Who said I was going to win? And anyway, it's not about that."

"I screw things up for you, okay? At school, at home, in the field. I know I already told you I wasn't going, but I didn't call to rub it in. I called to tell you I'm s—"

The door flings open so hard, the handle smacks against the wall. Two of grandpa's thugs shove another guy through the doorway. He's blindfolded and his mouth is duct taped shut. He's got on a red-white-and-blue spandex costume. I've never seen him before, but it's pretty obvious he's a superhero, what with the patriotic colors. He looks like one of those Popsicles you can buy around the Fourth of July.

"You're what, X?" Riley sounds worn out and more than a little pissed at me. "If you have something to say, just say it already."

The thugs shove the superhero, hard, and he trips, sprawling forward on the floor. His wrists and knees land with a loud *smack*. He cries out, but his voice is muffled by the duct tape.

What the hell? The two thugs notice me standing there right as Grandpa shouts, "Get him off the ground and into that room! We need him talking! We don't have time to—"

Grandpa swears when he sees me.

I hang up my phone without looking and slip it into my back pocket.

"What are you doing here?" Grandpa asks, practically growling the words, like he's not at all pleased to see me. He turns to his thugs before I can answer. "What are you standing around for? Get him out of here!"

They haul the superhero to his feet and march him down the hall.

"What am *I* doing here?" I glare at Grandpa. "I could ask you the same thing."

"You shouldn't be here."

"Neither should that superhero!" Electricity fizzes along my spine and up the back of my neck. My blood runs cold, and I feel sick. Not just in my stomach, but all over, like the realization of what I just saw is a poison spreading through me.

Grandpa's expression is grim. He shakes his head and says, "You really weren't supposed to see that."

X·X·X

I don't say anything when Grandpa insists on driving me home. Or when we get in the car. He keeps scowling at the clock on the dashboard, like me discovering that superhero and him having to take time out of his busy schedule to make sure I'm not hanging around his office, stumbling onto more secrets, is a huge annoyance.

Not, like, the end of his favorite grandson ever trusting him again, but just really annoying.

"Well?" He sounds extra put out, and he doesn't look at me. "You going to just sit there, or are you going to ask me about it?"

I press my hands against my knees to stop them from shaking, and because I don't know what else to do with them. I don't know how to exist in the same space as him after what he did. "What do you want me to ask? Why you *betrayed* me? Or why you don't seem to care that you did, just that I found out?"

"You're sixteen."

"So? Why is that everyone's answer to everything? Whenever I call an adult on their crap, that's their excuse. *You're only sixteen. You wouldn't understand.* Like hell I don't."

"You're full of ideals. And you still believe you can get them without compromising." He glances over at me. "I didn't want to take that away from you. Not yet. You've got plenty of time to learn the truth."

"The truth? The truth about what? That my grandpa's a liar?"

"I was protecting you."

"Yeah, right."

"The Truth is still giving villains a voice. We're helping a lot of people. That hasn't changed. And it means a lot to you, that we're helping them. That you're part of it. Don't think I don't know that. You get in front of that camera, and anyone can see you've got conviction. You believe every word you're saying. You couldn't have done that if you knew."

"So you were just using me." It's such an awful statement, even the words taste bad.

"I did what was right." He says that like he actually believes it. Maybe he does.

I glare at him. "You made me lie to everyone! I said that the Truth doesn't capture and torture superheroes! The whole city already thinks I'm a liar, that I'm just some half-villain screwup. Or at least they did. And now I finally do something important, something that made me feel like more than just a screwup, like I might actually have some kind of future, and it turns out they were *right.*"

"You're not a liar, and you're sure as hell not a screwup."

"Why should I believe you? Why should I believe you about anything ever again?"

He clenches his jaw, keeping his eyes focused on the road as he turns a corner. "I never intended to let things go this far. But I was retired for years—I was out of the game for too long. I forgot how ruthless you've got to be to succeed in this business. Exposing the truth only gets you so far. I wish that was really all it took, but as long as the heroes are going to get violent, the villains have to, too. Things weren't that peaceful to start with, and we're inciting a revolution here. You had to know things would get dicey."

"I'm not an idiot. It's not like I thought the Truth was all about peace and rainbows or some crap. But kidnapping superheroes? Torturing them? That's what *they're* doing to us, and if you're doing it, too, then you're no better than they are."

He laughs. "We're going for equal rights here. We can't be equal if we keep letting them oppress us. Or ignore us. I'm not sure which is worse."

"I went on TV and I said we weren't doing that! I said we didn't pretend to stick to some rules, then break them when it's convenient! You wrote those commercials. You lied to everyone, and you used me to do it."

"I might have written those words, but you said them better than I ever could. You wanted to make a difference for villains—I gave you that opportunity." He pulls into the driveway and cuts the engine. "Meeting your goals in life while maintaining your ideals is a luxury. You'll find that out soon enough as you get older."

"Being a decent human being isn't an *ideal*."

He ignores me and gets out of the car. "We can talk more about it later, but right now, we have an important rally to get ready for. I know this is a lot to take in, and if you're not comfortable giving a speech—"

I slam the passenger side door as I get out, interrupting him.

He lets out a deep breath, like I'm the one being unreasonable and he shouldn't have to put up with it. "If you're not comfortable giving a speech, you can just say a few words. I'll put together some phrases for sound bites, and you'll stick to those. All you have to do tonight is look good and smile. You think you can do that?"

Is he serious? I turn my back on him and stomp off into the house. I kind of want to slam the front door, too, but I don't because I don't want to upset Grandma. Who probably also knew about what Grandpa was doing and didn't tell me.

Grandpa follows me inside, his own footsteps pretty heavy, if not also stomping. "You can lose your temper and do the sullen teenager thing tomorrow, when you don't have a crowd of people waiting for you."

"I'm not going to the stupid rally! I don't know how you can even think that after what just happened!"

"Because what happened doesn't change our goals. And it doesn't change how important tonight is!"

Grandma comes in from the kitchen. She's obviously been to the salon today, because her hair's a stunning red now—more like her natural color I've seen in pictures—instead of pink. "What is going on here?"

"The boy found out," Grandpa says.

"*The boy* is right here!" I shout.

Grandma's mouth shrinks into an *O* shape for a moment. Then she recovers. "Honestly, Alistair, it's about time. You couldn't keep him in the dark forever."

"I could try. And tonight! Why did it have to be tonight? The last thing we need at the rally is our spokesperson sulking and acting out."

"Great," I tell him, "because I'm not going."

"It's not up for debate."

"I already told you I had plans tonight. With a superhero friend. My *best* friend. And you know what? He wouldn't lie to me." Give Mason my number to trick me into calling him? Sure. But at least he's honest. "Tonight's important to him, too, and I was actually going to ditch him for your stupid rally." Which I'm pretty sure makes me the worst person in the world. Or at least the worst half-villain ex superhero partner.

"Damien. You're going to that rally tonight, or else you're not going anywhere."

"You don't get to tell me what I can and can't do. I'm going out. To the Heroes' Gala," I add, just to see how much that pisses him off.

"*No.*" Grandpa's expression darkens, and a muscle on the side of his face twitches. He exchanges a worried look with Grandma, and I get the feeling they're still keeping something from me.

Grandma gives me the kind of stern look she usually reserves for Xavier. "You're absolutely not going to the Heroes' Gala."

"I *am* going, and if the spokesperson for the Truth ditching your rally to go to the hero awards looks bad, then maybe you should have thought of that before you guys lied to me."

"You're staying here," Grandpa says. "For your own safety."

"You think the League's going to attack me in the middle of their gala?" I actually kind of do think that, despite what Riley said, but I'll take the risk.

"Damn it, this isn't about the League." Grandpa grabs my shoulders, gripping them too hard. "You *promise* me you won't go anywhere near that gala tonight. You hear me?"

"*Ow.*" Not only does he have my shoulders in a vice grip, but sparks fly from his hands and actually zap me.

Grandpa *never* loses control of his lightning, not even a little bit, so either he meant to shock me, or... "Grandpa." I swallow, my throat suddenly tight, and take a step back. "What's happening at the gala tonight?"

"I didn't hear a promise."

"I'm not promising you anything! My *friends* are going to be there! And my family!"

He shuts his eyes, looking really tired. "I hate to do this, Damien. I really do."

"Do what?" My voice is shaking. "Whatever you've got planned, I'm not going to let you hurt them!"

"But you can't stop me, either. Don't make me use my power on you. I'd hate to do it, but I think we both know which one of us would win."

"What are you talking about?"

"You're staying here tonight, whether you want to or not. It's for your own good." He takes something out of his pocket, then holds it up so I can see, and I recognize Sarah's alert bracelet. "I got this from a friend of mine at the retirement home."

Damn it.

"Put this on, and if you try to use your power, you won't be able to stop, so—"

"I *know* how it works." I guess Sarah's friends at the retirement home couldn't fix it, either.

He raises his eyebrows, like he doesn't see how that's possible and thinks I'm just being impatient.

"My friend made it."

"Well, it's had a few adjustments. Those guys at the retirement home, they don't have a whole lot to do over there. A couple of them got together and did some tweaking. This is their donation to the cause. So, I want you to understand what will happen if you use your power while you have this on." He looks me in the eyes, all serious. "It's amped up. Your lightning will go full blast, nonstop, until you've got nothing left. You understand what that means?"

I nod. This is just great—another one of Sarah's inventions that's going to drain me to death. So much for her "friends" trying to help her with it. I guess I'm not the only one who got betrayed by a retired villain.

"That's if you don't burn the house down first. You might be immune to your lightning, but you won't be immune to fire. I know you don't believe this, but this isn't how I wanted things to go. But I know you, and I know that if I don't take precautions, you're going to go out there and get yourself killed tonight. And I'd do anything to make sure that doesn't happen."

He straps the bracelet onto my wrist. The rubbery material kind of chafes against my skin.

"What about my family? And my friends? You think I wouldn't do anything to make sure nothing happens to *them*?!"

"I know you would. That's why I'm doing this. I can't let you get hurt, and I can't let you ruin our plans. All those heroes are going to be in the same place at the same time, and I've got a crowd of fired-up villains ready to take them on. I'm sorry, Damien. If it makes you feel any better, I've got a machine in place that's going to knock them all out first. They won't feel a thing."

"*What?* What does that mean? Grandpa, you *can't.*" I feel the familiar electrical twitch underneath my skin, and I remember the alert bracelet just in time to force myself not to let my lightning start up.

"This is the Truth's big chance to show them we mean business. Once we take some of their most prominent heroes captive, they won't be able to ignore us anymore."

"You could still stop it. You don't have to—"

"It's already set to go off. At seven thirty tonight, everyone at the gala will be knocked out cold, and we'll be ready."

Tears prickle the backs of my eyes, though I refuse to let them water in front of him, let alone cry. "And what, you thought I was just going to go along with this if I came to the rally? You knew that at least my dad would be at the gala—he's there every year—and you thought I'd have *anything* to do with this?"

"No, I didn't. That's what the bracelet was for. I just didn't think I'd have to use it this early."

# CHAPTER 28

If being with Kat at her dorm was the best moment of my life, I think this is probably the worst. Grandpa takes my phone—not that I could reach it to call anyone, anyway—and handcuffs me to the radiator in the corner of the living room. He winds the chain through as many of the bars on the radiator as will fit, so my hands can't reach each other, and then leaves for the rally. I'm forced to sit on the floor, unable to really move. At least he turned the heat off.

I lean forward, trying to get at the alert bracelet with my teeth, but of course it's too far. Not that I think I could actually chew through it or unbuckle it or anything. But at least trying gives me something to do besides freak the hell out. It's taking all my concentration not to let my lightning spark up, since Grandpa made it extremely clear that if I do, I'll die of exhaustion. But, you know, only if accidentally lighting the house on fire while I'm trapped here doesn't kill me first.

This can't be happening. I let my head fall forward against the radiator with a metallic *thump*. A ball of fear and frustration gnaws at my stomach. Riley, and Sarah, and Zach, and Amelia, and Gordon, and probably the rest of my family are going to be at that gala. Riley's going to be waiting to see if he won, thinking it's his big night. They all are. And he's going to think I ditched him after all. That I didn't care enough to show up. And then Grandpa's machine is going to go off, and...

I never even got to say I'm sorry. Because even if I still think I did the right thing, stopping that fake kidnapper during our final, Riley's right—I wasn't thinking about what it would mean for him. I wasn't listening. We were supposed to be *partners*, and I acted like I was working alone. And, okay, I'm not sure what I'd do differently if it happened again, but maybe we could figure it out together somehow.

Though, just for the record, I'm *not* sorry I gave him crap about choosing Mason over me.

Not that any of it matters now, because Grandpa's going to...

I swallow down a lump in my throat. He's going to knock them all out. *They won't feel a thing.* I know what that sounds like, and even if all he intends to do is capture a few people, there's no way that all those angry villains from the rally attacking all those knocked-out heroes ends well. He must know that, because there's a reason he locked me up and didn't want me anywhere near the gala. And I'm the one who made that commercial for him, encouraging people to show up tonight. They're at that rally because of *me*. Grandpa might have used me to lie to everyone, but I'm the reason they believe in the Truth.

Now my friends and family are going to get hurt—probably worse—because of what I did, and there's nothing I can do to stop it, or even to warn them.

I shut my eyes. Maybe I should risk it. Turn on my lightning and hope Grandpa was wrong and it doesn't kill me. Except I know he wasn't wrong. And me dying isn't going to save anybody, and—

"Yoohoo?" Mom calls from the other room, opening the front door. "Is anybody home?"

Oh. My. God. I never thought I'd be so happy for her to show up. She can't see me yet, since the front room is around the corner from the living room, and I'm on the far edge, but all she has to do is come a little farther into the house. "Mom!" I scream. "*Over here!*"

"Oh, thank God someone's home," Mom shouts, still by the front door. "I thought you'd all be gone, because of the rally. Do you hear that, sweetiekins? Damien's going to watch you. And he's going to turn on the heat, because *brrr*, it's freezing in here. We don't want my little baby to catch a little cold."

Ugh, she must be talking to Xavier. "*Mom!*" My voice is raw with desperation. She has to hear that, right? "Come in here!"

"I really can't, Damien." I hear her hurrying to set down Xavier's stuff, practically throwing it onto the floor. "I've got to go, but I'll just be a few hours! I have a few errands to run, and then Taylor and I are going to dinner. We've got a bottle of wine at home, and who knows where that might lead? I swear, we never have a moment to ourselves. But we still love our little Xavier sweetiekins, the bestest boy in the whole wide world, yes we do."

Gag. It's bad enough that practically everyone I know is going to freaking *die* tonight if I don't get out of here, but now I have to listen to this, too? "*Mom!* You have to help me!"

"I hate to rush off, but if we're going to make our reservations tonight, then I've just *got* to get out of here."

"No! *Mom!*" I rattle the handcuff chain against the radiator, trying to get her attention.

"Whatever it is, I'm sure my two boys can figure it out! You behave for your brother, sweetie." She kisses Xavier, really loudly, and then practically slams the front door.

"Mom!" I shout again, even though I know it's useless.

Xavier peers around the corner. "Mommy left, so she and Daddy can be newlyweds. That means you *have* to watch me."

"Yeah, sure, just *get over here*." I would have preferred Mom, since she's a lot more capable, and, knowing her, she probably has an extra set of handcuff keys on her. But I guess Xavier is better than chewing my own arm off.

He comes closer, stopping just short of the radiator and staring at me. "What are you doing?"

*Trying really hard not to freak out and get us killed.* "What does it look like I'm doing? I'm stuck. You have to help me."

"I *don't.*"

"Uh, yeah, you do."

"Nuh-uh. Because I'm not talking to you."

"You don't have to talk to me—you just have to do what I tell you."

"Because I'm *mad* at you." He pauses, presumably giving me a chance to ask him why, which I don't. "Because you were mean."

"I wasn't. So just get over here and take this bracelet off my arm."

"No!" His voice is a high-pitched screech, and I wish my hands were free so I could cover my ears. Or murder him. "You *were* mean. You said Mommy didn't throw me any birthday parties, but she said you lied."

"She what?" I take a deep breath in through my nose, trying to stay calm. It doesn't matter what Mom said. Not if getting pissed about it is going to get me killed. "Look, Xavier, we can talk about it later. After you unbuckle this alert bracelet."

"I might do it. I might *think* about it. If you said you were sorry."

"I'm sorry, okay? So now—"

"You didn't mean it!" He stomps his foot, his nostrils flaring. "You have to say it for reals."

"I..." I brace myself, trying to make this sound genuine. "I'm sorry I was mean to you."

He bites his lip, thinking that over. "Now say you're sorry you lied."

"Look, I apologized for hurting your feelings or whatever. That's going to have to be enough, because I didn't lie. Mom's the one who faked all your birthdays." Worse than that, she stole them from me.

Xavier's face starts turning red, and he sucks in a bunch

of air, getting ready to scream. "That's *not* true!"

Too bad the neighbors are probably used to hearing him wailing and screeching all the time by now and won't hear the noise and, like, come rescue me.

"Fine. I'm sorry I lied. Happy now?"

He shakes his head. "I don't believe you. You didn't—"

"Mean it? Yeah, and I'm never going to, because I didn't do it."

"Yes, you did! Mommy always tells me the truth, because I'm her special little miracle. And if you aren't sorry about lying to me, then you're not sorry about being mean to me, either."

I really, really hate him. "If I'm the liar, then where are all these friends you supposedly have, huh? And why do they have the same names as the friends *I* had when I was a kid?"

"Because you're just saying that to make me feel bad. Because Mommy loves me more than you, and you're jealous that I'm growing up so big and strong."

I clench my jaw until my teeth grind together. I have to concentrate really hard on keeping my lightning from sparking. "That is the last thing I'm jealous of. And I don't care if Mom loves you more, because at least my childhood was *real*."

"She told me I'm her second chance, and now she's doing everything right."

"She... she *what*?"

Xavier gets this snotty grin on his face. "Mommy said a precious little angel like me only comes around once, and she's got to make sure nothing happens to me. And that we have big parties for all my birthdays, and I get lots of presents and everybody loves me."

I'm trying really hard not to lose it. Really, *really* hard. "Great. That's—"

"And I asked Mommy if someday I'd have to leave and go live somewhere else, like you did, but she said *no way*. She said she would *never* give me up, not in a million, billion years. That's a lot."

Give him up? As opposed to me? Because Mom actually thinks of it that way, that she *gave me up*?

A surge of emotions rushes through me, and I can't stop it this time. The sparks that have been building beneath my skin suddenly zap across my arms.

A jolt of adrenaline hits me in the instant before the bracelet kicks on and kills us both. Ice water floods my veins. And I think, this is it, I'm going to die. I'm not getting out of here, I'm not going to get the chance to warn my friends or to stop Grandpa. Everything ends now, and I didn't even get to say good-bye to Kat, and—

And nothing happens.

Okay, not nothing. The bracelet makes a *zzzzt* noise and stops my power from working, just like Sarah intended it to.

I take a deep breath, still not completely convinced I'm not dead. Maybe this is what being dead feels like.

Except that it feels an awful lot like being chained to a radiator in my grandparents' living room, so probably not.

Xavier wrinkles his eyebrows at me, like he thinks I'm acting crazy.

Grandpa was wrong about the bracelet. Or he lied

about it.

Maybe the guys at the retirement home didn't betray Sarah. Maybe they actually did what they said they were going to do and fixed it. So either they lied to Grandpa, which doesn't seem likely—they didn't have to donate the bracelet, after all—or he lied to me. Which wouldn't be the first time.

Maybe he thought I could create a big enough burst of power in that split second before the bracelet kicked in to actually get away. *He* probably could, though I'm pretty sure that's still way beyond my level. Or maybe he just wanted to scare me that much, to keep me too worried about burning the house down to think of a way to escape.

Whatever his reasoning, it's a relief that he didn't leave me here to accidentally get myself killed. Even if it doesn't make up for everything else he's doing tonight.

"Well?" Xavier asks. "Are you sorry yet?"

"Yeah." Sorry he was ever born. "And as far as I'm concerned, we're even." I might have been mean to him before, when Mom was the one I should have been mad at, but he didn't have to say all that stuff about her loving him more and never giving him up. He didn't have to rub it in, and he really didn't have to look so happy when he did it. "So take this bracelet off me *right now*, and then stand the hell back."

$$X \cdot X \cdot X$$

"Can't this thing go any faster?!" I ask Kat. We're in her car, racing to the gala. Only *racing* isn't really the right word when we're barely going the speed limit.

"This *thing* has a name." Kat pats the top of her dashboard. "And no, Ol' Bluebell here is already at top speed."

"Slow down!" Xavier screeches from the back seat. Because, unfortunately, we couldn't just leave him alone at the house. I mean, we *could have*, but I don't trust that he wouldn't burn the place down just for spite. Or trash my stuff or pee in my bed. "You're going to make me throw up!"

Kat glares at him in the rearview mirror. "If you throw up in here, you're *dead*."

I fidget with Sarah's alert bracelet, which is in my sweatshirt pocket—I didn't exactly want to leave it out of my sight after getting attacked with it earlier—and check the time on my phone, which I snagged from Grandpa's office after I used my lightning to bust free. "It's almost seven." Everyone must already be at the gala, because they all have their phones turned off. I know because I've tried calling them a million times. Amelia's was the only one that went through, but she didn't answer, and when I tried to call back, it went straight to voicemail. So I guess she's not over the whole me running away from home thing.

At least Kat answered when I called her. And was home from Vilmore this weekend.

"We'll make it," Kat says. "We're almost there. We'll have plenty of time."

I nod, even though I'm not sure that's true. I have to get into the gala, find my friends, and somehow evacuate the entire building, all before seven thirty. And hope nobody recognizes me and hands me over to the League.

"When we get to the hotel, just drop me off at the front entrance."

"What? *No.*" She glances over at me, then back at the road. "You're not going in alone."

Xavier kicks my seat. "You can't leave me here! You have to *watch* me!"

"I wish I could just murder him and get it over with," I tell her, ignoring Xavier's screech of protest as I say that. "But we can't leave him in the car alone."

"You think I want to be stuck in here with him? You can't do that to me. And you can't go into that gala on your own. How are you even going to get in? And don't say you have a ticket, because we both know that's not going to work. Plus, it's black tie, right? You're wearing jeans and a sweatshirt."

"I..." Fine, so maybe I haven't thought this through. "I'll think of something. But pretty much everyone I care about is going to be in danger. I don't need to add you to that list. Because it's bad enough all my friends might get killed tonight, but if something happened to you, too... I couldn't handle that."

Kat slams on her brakes as the light in front of us turns red.

"You're not being gentle!" Xavier screams.

We both ignore him.

"Damien," Kat says, "you don't even know how you'll get in. You might get captured by the League before you get a chance to warn everybody. You need me. And I couldn't handle losing you, either, so don't even try to tell me to *wait in the car* while you go get yourself killed!"

"And what are we supposed to do with him?" I jerk my head toward the backseat. "Bring him with us?" Having to drag Xavier along on a rescue mission, one where I'm trying not to draw attention to myself, sounds like the worst idea ever.

Kat sighs. "I guess we have to."

"And how are we supposed to get in?"

"Leave that to me," she says. "I think I know what to do."

# CHAPTER 29

Kat tries to park illegally, so we can be as close to the gala as possible, but there are so many people here, even the illegal spots are taken. We end up having to park in a nearby parking garage, which is still pretty close, but it costs twenty bucks, and Kat seems a little disappointed that she didn't get to park in some badass way, like in the movies.

But still. We ditch the car and make a run for it. It's 7:03 by the time we get there. Twenty-seven minutes to stop Grandpa and save everyone I know.

Even though the ceremony started at seven, there are still people milling around outside the entrance. Some of them are obviously reporters, though some of them are guests who just showed up late. I pull the hood of my sweatshirt up as we approach, because I really don't need someone from the press recognizing me and telling the whole world I'm here. Not before I get inside and warn everybody, anyway. Thankfully, it's pretty dark out, and none of the people just getting here seem to be celebrities, so no one's paying too much attention.

No one except the two guys standing in front of the door, checking tickets, or the security guys wandering around outside, keeping an eye on the crowd. They're all wearing official badges from the League, even if they're not in costume. I've never been to one of these things, and it might just be because I'm trying to sneak in, but it seems like a lot of security.

"Be ready," Kat whispers. "I'm going to cause a distraction. You go in while no one's looking. I'll meet you inside."

"A distraction? That's your plan?"

"Yep. And don't give me that look—this is going to work." She grabs Xavier's hand, trying not to make a disgusted face, but totally failing.

I raise my eyebrows at her in a silent question.

She mouths, *Play along.* Then, out loud, to Xavier, "Your mom's in there. We're going to go surprise her."

He squints at her, not quite buying it. "Mommy's on a date, being newlyweds."

"Right. But this is where she's on her date."

"I thought we were going to the Heroes' Gala." He glances up at me for confirmation.

"Don't look at me. I can't keep up with Mom's plans. All I know is that she, uh, texted me to say she'd be here, and she really wants—er, needs—to see you."

Xavier frowns, thinking about that, and Kat motions for me to keep talking.

"Because... she thought she could go a few hours

without seeing her special"—I practically choke on the words—"angel miracle, but she was wrong. And she wants to set the record straight about our—*your*—birthdays."

He takes that in, then slowly nods, like that makes sense. He also gets that smug grin on his face again. "She's going to tell you you're wrong *and* a liar."

"And probably that she likes you more."

"She *loves* me more, because I'm her special little bestest boy in the whole wide world."

Ughhhh. "Yeah, and I don't really want to be there for that. So Kat's taking you inside to see her."

He perks up, actually buying it now. "Okay, let's go."

Kat exchanges a look with me. She shapeshifts her thumb, and it shimmers a little as her *V* changes to an *H*. "Here goes."

"Let's go *now*!" Xavier tugs on her hand and stomps his foot.

People are already starting to glance over at us, so maybe this really *is* going to work.

Kat takes Xavier up to the entrance, where the two ticket-takers are.

"Hi. Excuse me," she says.

"Tickets, please." The one on the right holds out a hand. He frowns when he sees that she's not dressed up.

"I don't have—"

"I'm sorry. If you don't have tickets, I'm going to have to ask you to leave." He doesn't sound that sorry about it.

"I'm babysitting this little guy"—she pulls Xavier forward a step—"and he really, *really* needs to see his mom. So—"

The ticket-taker holds up a hand, as if Kat is really stupid and needs visual cues that he doesn't want her coming in. "The best I can do is have someone give her a message."

"I want my mommy!" Xavier screeches.

Both ticket-takers wince at his nails-on-the-chalkboard voice.

"You see," Kat says, "it's just really important that we get in and see her real quick."

"I can't let you in. If you'll give me her name and—"

"Do you hear that?" Kat asks Xavier. "This guy doesn't want you to see your mom. He doesn't want her to get to tell you how much she loves you."

"Wh-what?!" Xavier's face is already turning red.

"He thinks your mom should be able to go hours and hours without seeing you, like she could just *forget* about you."

"That's not true!" Xavier glares at the ticket-taker and screams, "You're *lying*!"

The ticket-taker looks bewildered. "I didn't say any of that!" He has to raise his voice to be heard above Xavier's wailing. "Now, if you'll just step to the side, we can—"

"*No!*" Xavier screeches. "You have to let me see my mommy!" His face is almost as red as his hair now, and he takes big, gasping breaths as tears slide down his cheeks.

Kat sighs. "Come on." She tries to drag him away from the door. "You heard him. We have to go. Your mom's just going to have to be heartbroken that she didn't get to see you."

"You can't do that!" It's unclear who Xavier's yelling at

at this point—Kat for trying to drag him away, or the ticket-taker for not letting them in—but he's so loud, and his voice so ear-splitting, that *everyone* turns to stare at him. Even all the security guys from the League. He tries to shout something else, but he's crying too hard now, and his words aren't exactly intelligible.

Especially when he drops to the ground in full-on tantrum mode and starts kicking and flailing and screaming bloody murder.

The guys in front of the door actually kneel down—I think because they're worried he's having a seizure or something—and someone in the crowd asks if they should call 911.

"You see?!" Kat shouts. "This is what I've had to put up with all night!"

With everyone's attention turned to Xavier, this is totally my chance. I pretend like I'm part of the crowd of freaked-out bystanders, then slip past the ticket-takers when nobody's looking.

## X·X·X

Everyone at this thing is dressed way fancier than me, especially since, as Kat pointed out, I'm wearing jeans and a sweatshirt. With the hood pulled up, no less. Everyone else is in tuxes and fancy dresses, and they keep glancing at me as I walk by, like they can tell I'm not supposed to be here, even if they don't know who I am.

The awards ceremony is taking place in the grand ballroom. There are round tables all over, covered with red tablecloths and flickering candles as the centerpieces. There's some hero I don't recognize—but who sounds really full of himself—up on the stage, doing an introduction speech.

I find Riley and everyone sitting at a table near the back.

Amelia's the first one to spot me. She scowls and pinches Zach's arm, directing his attention to me.

"*Ow.* Hey, what did I—" Zach trails off when he sees me. I can't tell if he's stunned or angry.

"You made it," Riley says, sounding pretty shocked.

Sarah's wearing a dark-blue dress with little fake roses in her hair that are dyed to match. She pulls out the empty seat next to her. "It's about time."

"I can't stay. I—"

"Oh, great." Riley exchanges a look with Mason, like they've been talking about me—probably about how I wouldn't really show up for this.

Sarah purses her lips in thought. Amelia makes a *hmph* noise. Zach swallows and stares down at the table.

"Riley," his mom says, "you didn't tell me this is who you were saving that ticket for." She sounds nervous. I wonder if she'll try to ban me from their table, or if she'll let it go, since it's Riley's big night and all. And because Curtis isn't here to remind everyone how horrible he thinks I am.

"Look, I can't stay, because—"

"Save it," Riley says, keeping his voice hushed. "I don't want to hear what your excuse is. If you don't want to be here, then just *leave.*"

"But—"

"Ry's tried several times to communicate with you," Mason says. "But you're not open to that connection. It's obvious you're still not thinking about how he—"

"*Cosine.*" I turn to Sarah, ignoring Mason. And Riley. And the way everyone's looking at me, except for Zach, who isn't looking at all. "We have an emergency."

"I knew it," Sarah says, sounding almost happy about that. "Your body language was all wrong for an awards ceremony."

"An emergency?" Riley asks.

I check my phone. It's 7:07. "In exactly twenty-three minutes, the Truth is going to attack this place. I mean, my grandpa's machine is going to go off, and everyone here is going to be knocked out. And then all these villains are going to storm the place, and it's not going to be pretty."

Mason sighs and tries to exchange another look with Riley. "Convenient that this story puts all the focus back on him. This is typical behavior for his personality type, making up elaborate scenarios to make himself the center of attention."

I really want to tell Mason to shut up, or maybe just zap him. Judging from the way Sarah opens her mouth and the way her eyebrows come together, I'm pretty sure she wants to, too.

But Riley beats us both to it. "He's *not* making it up." He's already getting to his feet as he says that. "What do we do? We really only have twenty-three minutes?"

"Twenty-two, now," Sarah corrects him.

"We have to warn the League or whoever's in charge. And..." I run my hands through my hair, trying to think fast. "We have to get everyone out of here. Amelia, you—"

"Did you hear something?" Amelia asks Zach. "Because I *didn't.*"

"*Amelia.*"

"I'm not talking to you."

"Seriously? Now?"

Kat hurries over to the table, dragging Xavier with her. His face is still red, though he's stopped crying. "Give him your phone," Kat says, slightly out of breath. "To call your mom."

"They let you in?" I ask her.

"We're supposed to have an escort, but I ditched him between the bathroom and the concession stand. And if the hellspawn doesn't get to talk to your mom in, like, the next five seconds, he's going to have another meltdown. So, phone. *Now.*"

I get out my phone and find Mom's number, then hand it to Xavier. Not that I want him using my phone— especially so Mom can call him some gooey, disgusting pet name and tell him how great he supposedly is—but the last thing I need is for him to throw another fit and get us kicked out. I shove him down into my empty seat. "Zach, you and Amelia watch my brother—"

"Your *brother*?" Amelia gapes at me and Xavier, apparently forgetting that she's not speaking to me. "You have a *brother*?"

"—and find Gordon and the rest of my family. Get them and your mom out of here, and don't stick around."

"What?" their mom says. "And where are *you* going?" She looks at Riley, then at Sarah, who's already on her feet, then at Mason, who reluctantly gets up from the table, as if anyone asked him to join us.

"We'll be okay," Riley assures her. "Just do what he says and get out of here."

X·X·X

This is bad. Like, really bad.

All five of us are standing in the head of security's office. We raced over here after Kat used her shapeshifting power to transform into someone official looking to get directions. I just finished explaining to this guy that the Truth plans to attack tonight and that he needs to evacuate this place as soon as possible.

And he just kind of scoffed in response, like it's no big deal.

"Didn't you hear him?" Sarah adjusts her glasses and glares at the security guy. He's in a suit, but also wearing one of those League badges, and looks maybe ten years older than us. His nametag says *Wooster Shine*, which I'm guessing must be his superhero name.

"Did I hear the spokesperson for the Truth tell me they plan to attack? I was sitting right here—it would have been hard to miss." His phone buzzes, and he actually picks it up to check his texts.

"Wow," Kat mutters.

See, this is why Grandpa's attacking tonight in the first place. Because the League thinks they don't need to take villains seriously, like if they just ignore us, we'll get tired of fighting to be heard and shut up.

Er, not that I agree with what Grandpa's doing, but it doesn't help that this security guy is totally proving his point.

"So, if you heard him," Riley says slowly, like he's talking to someone really stupid, "then you know you need to get everyone out of here."

Wooster Shine glances up from his phone, amused. "We don't need you to tell us that the villains are going to attack. We're not idiots. It's taken care of."

"I don't think it is," I tell him. "You don't understand. People are going to get hurt. Or worse."

"No, *you* don't understand. You're half villain, right? I liked that video you did for your dad. I'm a big Crimson Flash fan. I keep up with the tabloids, and I'm pretty sure he cares about you, despite all the ways you've messed up lately. So I'm going to do you a favor and give you some advice—*get out of here.*"

"But—"

"Look, if you don't want people to get hurt, go back to the Truth and tell them to stand down. Because if they come here tonight, they're not going to get very far."

"What's that supposed to mean?"

"It means I wouldn't want to be a villain at the Heroes' Gala. We've taken precautions."

"You expect me to leave, to abandon everybody when I know they're in danger, because you've 'taken precautions'? I'm going to need a better reason than that."

"We all are," Riley says.

"You guys will be fine," Wooster Shine tells the rest of the group. Everyone except me. "But *you* have villain DNA. So I wouldn't want to be you when the Truth attempts to attack."

"I don't know what that means, but I'm not leaving until you *listen* to me! Whatever you have planned, it's not good enough. You have to get everyone out of here, and you have to do it now."

"No, really, we've got it under control, and you need to not be here. We've got villain-targeting lasers placed in the ceiling. Remote access. This whole place is being closely monitored, and we've got people on the outside ready to hit the button if a bunch of villains show up. Or if the cameras go dark," he adds, like he thought I might have been getting ideas about it. "Those lasers go live, and any villains stupid enough to be in range are toast. That includes half villains."

"And what about the person standing next to them?" Sarah asks. "That kind of targeting from that distance isn't very accurate. A lot of people could get hurt, and not just villains."

"That's a risk we're going to have to take. The Truth is bringing this on themselves, and if a few of our people get hurt because of them, then maybe the public will realize what we're dealing with. And if you're so concerned about it, like I said, get the Truth to stand down. The people monitoring the gala have their orders, and I have mine, and we're proceeding as planned. No evacuation."

# CHAPTER 30

Mason puts a hand on my arm when we get out into the hallway. "If you need help talking to the Truth and getting them to see that attacking tonight is only going to end in misery, I'm here."

I jerk my arm away. "No one's talking to the Truth."

"But you heard what he said. Getting them to stand down is the only way to stop all this violence."

"That would never work," Kat says, looking just about as disgusted with Mason as she did with Xavier. "If we even had time for that, which we don't."

Mason's face goes pale. He swallows. "What are we going to do? We can't just let this happen."

"Easy," I tell him. "We stop the weapons." Except I'm pretty sure *easy* is the last thing it will be. But it's the obvious answer, and the only one that gives us any chance of success. "Sarah, if you had a machine that was supposed to knock everybody out, where would you put it?"

"The roof," she says, not even having to think about it. Then, seeing me flinch a little, "Or the basement."

Great. I know what kind of luck I have. There's no way that thing's in the basement. Because if there's any chance at all that it'll be on the roof, then that's where it is. "We'll split up. It's—" I reach for my phone out of habit, forgetting that I left it with Xavier.

Riley checks his instead. "It's seven fifteen."

"We have fifteen minutes. Kat, you and Sarah find the lasers."

"*What?*" Kat folds her arms and glares at Sarah, then at me. "Damien, I'm going with you."

I shake my head. "You need to figure out where to go to disarm the lasers or where to cut the power or whatever. That means shapeshifting again and asking the right people. And Sarah's the only one of us who can actually disable them. You can do that, right?"

Sarah nods. "We could cut the power, but the League will have thought of that. They probably have a backup generator. Our best bet is to take out the receiver or to disconnect the laser system from the rest of the grid."

"So it has to be you two. And me and Riley will find Grandpa's machine, and..." I press the heels of my palms to my forehead, trying to think this through. "If we disable the machine, then no one gets knocked out. But that still means a battle."

"We need to postpone it, not disarm it," Riley says. "If we can set it to go off after the villains get here, then maybe no one has to get hurt."

"Unless we fail," Kat says. "If we can't turn the lasers

off, then that means all those knocked-out villains will be sitting ducks."

"We won't." Sarah smooths out the sides of her dress. "I can turn the lasers off. You just have to trust me."

Kat looks like that's about the last thing she wants to do, but she keeps it to herself.

"If you need to get in touch with us, call Riley's phone," I tell them. "And no matter what happens, be outside by seven forty."

"We'll meet back up at my house afterward." Riley checks the time again and frowns. "Thirteen minutes."

"Okay, let's—"

"You forgot me." Mason has a sour look on his face, like he doesn't understand how I could possibly forget the importance of having a human light bulb around in a crisis. "I'm coming with you."

I really want to argue with him on that, but we don't have time. So instead I just nod and say, "Let's go."

## X·X·X

"You sure you want to do this?" Riley asks as we wait for the elevator. "You don't have to go up there. We could try the basement."

"Maybe we should have split up into three teams," Mason says. "Ry and I could go to one location and you could go to the other."

He means he and Riley could ditch me again. "It's not going to be in the basement. And we don't have time to start second guessing." Plus, one person going off by themselves doesn't really count as being a "team," and I don't hear Mason volunteering for it.

"You might need backup," Riley says. "And if you want me and Mason to check the roof—"

"I have to do this. I got us into this mess."

The elevator doors finally open, and all three of us step inside. There's no stop that takes us directly to the roof, so I hit the button for the fifth floor. The doors take forever to close again, and then we begin slowly going up.

"Why would we check the roof?" Mason asks. He doesn't know about my problem with heights. Or with falling off of buildings.

"Come on, X," Riley says, totally ignoring Mason's question. "It's not your— Well, it's not *all* your fault."

"None of this would have happened if it wasn't for me. And..." I shrug. "Look, Perkins, I'm sorry, all right? That's what I was trying to say on the phone to you earlier."

"You mean when you hung up on me?"

"I'm sorry I didn't listen to you during our final. Not because I think what I did was wrong or anything, and I really don't care that I broke the rules, or—"

"Geez. If this is your apology, no wonder you hung up."

I scowl at him. "My point is, I don't care about any of that stuff, but you're my friend. And we were supposed to be working together. I shouldn't have acted like it was just me."

The elevator stops at the third floor. The doors take a million years to open, and then an old man with a rolling suitcase tries to get on. I hold up a hand to stop him and start hitting the button to close the doors. "Sorry, we're, um, at full capacity already."

He frowns at the three of us and all the space left on the elevator. "But—"

"It's an old elevator," Riley says. "You have to be careful. It's already making a weird knocking sound."

"Wait, it's what?!" I would have noticed if there was some knocking noise. He's got to be making that up.

The old man starts to say something else, but then the doors *finally* close again and we continue on our way. I clutch the bar around the edge this time, listening hard for the supposed knocking sound.

Riley lets out a slow breath. "You didn't know about my scholarship, or what would happen to me because you broke the rules. It sucks that you screwed up, but it's not like you did it on purpose."

"Yeah, but..." I glance over at Mason, who's watching this conversation play out. And I hate that I have to say this, especially in front of him, but there's a not-so-small chance I might get obliterated by some villain-targeting lasers tonight—or by this elevator, because I definitely heard a creak, if not a knock—so it's kind of now or never. "But I guess I can kind of maybe see why you wouldn't have wanted to work with me anymore. I don't like it, but I get it."

The elevator dings, and the doors slowly open. I practically jump out into the hallway of the fifth floor. It's got the same fancy carpeting as the rest of the hotel, with this swirly red pattern in it, and the walls are painted the same off-white color. The only difference between this hallway and any others in the building is that there's a door to a stairwell with a sign on it that says, *Roof Access*.

Mason pulls the handle, but it doesn't budge. "It's locked. Now what?"

"Move." I motion for him to get out of my way. Then I step up to the door and use my lightning on the handle.

"It's not that I didn't want to work with you, X," Riley says.

Sweat beads on my forehead as I focus my electricity enough to make the handle start to melt. Even though I've been practicing my skills, it still takes a lot of concentration. "Kind of busy here."

"The truth is, I actually admire what you did. When you zapped that kidnapper."

"You *what*?" Me and Mason both say that at the same time—ugh—though probably for completely different reasons.

"Don't get me wrong, it still really pisses me off that you didn't listen to me, or consider the consequences of your actions, or that you don't care what happens to anybody but yourself."

"Hey. Not true."

"But it's not like I didn't want to catch that guy, when I thought he was a kidnapper. And what you did? It was against the rules, but it was also really badass. You weren't afraid to do what you thought was right."

"Yeah, well, that's great and all, but it doesn't change anything. Maybe you wanted to work with me"—I pause, concentrating on melting the last bit of the handle—"but you made the right decision." Other than the fact that he picked Mason as his partner, of course. "I would have gotten you in trouble. More trouble, I mean. And—"

The handle finally gives, and the roof access door swings open. I wipe the sweat off my forehead onto my sleeve. It's not a whole lot of stairs between here and the roof, but the thought of going up them and being out in the open, on top of a building again, makes my stomach clench.

Mason hurries up the stairs, though Riley hangs back a little. "And?"

"You're better off without me." I hold the railing tight and force myself to take a step. I don't even want to know how little time we have left, but if we don't make it, my fear of heights *cannot* be the reason.

"X—"

"I mean it. Being badass and stopping some fake kidnapper even though it's against the rules might be cool, but it doesn't make me a good partner." I grit my teeth and take another step. I kind of wish Riley would just go on without me, instead of watching this. "I put you in a bad situation, and, let's face it, if you kept working with me, you probably would have been kicked out of school by now. You need to have a partner who doesn't get you into trouble on a daily basis." Not that it was every day, but still. Obviously he and Mason really are on the same page.

Mason's already at the top of the stairs, staring out at the roof. I'm pretty sure he hears our conversation, though other than glancing over his shoulder at us, he stays out of it. But he also looks pretty worried about something, though that may just be our impending doom. "It's not there."

"It's there." I have to stop myself from rolling my eyes at him. I focus on taking another step instead and try really hard not to show how much effort it takes. "You just missed it."

"No. I can see the whole roof, and there's nothing."

Yeah, right.

Riley practically runs up the last few steps and joins him at the top. "I don't see it, either."

They both stand there and stare at me as I painstakingly make my way up. And, okay, once I'm at the top, I have to admit that I *can* see pretty much the entire roof, and I really don't see a machine. But it's got to be here.

"I told you we should have split up," Mason says.

I step out onto the roof, even though it's just about the last thing I want to do. The wind hits me, making my ears and nose cold. I consider putting my hood up, but having it on gets in the way of my peripheral vision, and I'll take the cold over accidentally not seeing a ledge and falling to my death.

I mean, I *can* fly, if I have to, so I guess I wouldn't die. But I really don't need any more trauma related to falling off of buildings.

"Maybe it's over here." Riley has to shout to be heard over the wind. He checks behind the enclosed area that houses the staircase. I start to follow him, but he reappears a second later. "There's no machine."

"That's what I said." Mason sounds really put out about me not listening to him.

"It must be in the basement," Riley says.

"Or neither of those places." Mason folds his arms. "Sarah was only guessing where it would be. It could be anywhere, and we might not even find it."

I look out across the roof one more time, just in case it's possible we missed it. But the roof is flat, with nowhere for a machine to hide. And if Riley says it wasn't behind the stairwell house, then I trust that it wasn't. "Let's go back inside. We don't have time to—"

"What are you kids doing up here?!" someone shouts as a couple security guards from the League appear in the doorway. They look us over, taking in Riley and Mason in their tuxes, and then me, in my sweatshirt and jeans.

The security guard on the left's eyes widen when she realizes who I am. "We've got a villain up here!" She whips out a raygun and points it at me. "Don't move!"

Her partner does the same thing.

"He has a ticket!" Riley shouts.

"I don't think they care about that, Perkins!"

"Call for backup," the first security guard tells her partner. "We're bringing him in." Her eyes dart from me to Riley, then over to Mason. She squints at them, like she thinks they must be guilty by association, even though none of us has done anything. Other than trespassing on the roof, I mean. "We're bringing *all* of them in."

Crap. We don't have time for this. I flex my hands, thinking about zapping the security guards. Because if they haul us in right now, and we can't get to Grandpa's machine to stop it, then a lot of people are going to get hurt. We're going to have to fight our way out of this.

Riley must be thinking the same thing, because before I can decide to actually zap them, he turns invisible and says, "Mase! Your light!"

Mason has a deer-in-the-headlights look at first, and then he gets it, and I have just enough time to remember to close my eyes and fling my arm over them as he uses his power.

The two security guards cry out in surprise, temporarily blinded.

"Come on!" Riley shouts.

I can't see him, but I don't need to. All three of us hurry for the stairwell, pushing past the security guards while they're still too stunned to stop us. One of them actually shoots their raygun, completely missing us, but tearing a chunk out of the rooftop.

"Were they *shooting* at us?!" Mason cries.

I pause at the top of the stairs. Adrenaline floods my veins, and I know I have to do this.

Before I can take a step, though, Riley turns visible and grabs my hand, pulling me down the stairs against my will.

And if I thought I was full of adrenaline before, I *really* am now. Lightning crackles across my whole body, and Riley cries out and lets go.

We stumble down the last few steps. I don't know if I should thank him—which, even if I should, is *so* not going to happen—or punch him in the face. "What the hell, Perkins?! You can't just drag someone down the freaking *stairs*! Were you trying to kill me?"

"I was saving your life." He shoves something into my

hand. It's his phone. "Take this. Mason's number is in there, and so is Sarah's. Get down to the basement. We'll hold them off."

Mason makes a strangled cry of surprise at that, but he doesn't argue.

"Perkins, you can't—"

"We can! Now go!" He shoves me toward the elevator.

I press the down button. The doors open immediately this time, and I step inside and hit *B* for *basement*. The doors close again, right as the superheroes come running down the stairs, weapons pointed at my best friend.

# CHAPTER 31

The basement isn't as straightforward as the roof. I was picturing one big room, dark and full of junk, but there's actually a well lit hallway with several doors leading off of it. Thankfully, there's no one here. There are no stairs or ledges to fall off of, either, and I run to each door, hoping they're not locked. Because if I have to blast through all of them...

I check the time on Riley's phone. *Three minutes.*

The first door is locked, but the second and third ones aren't. The third room is some kind of storage, full of folded up tables and stacks of extra chairs. And there, in the middle of the room, is a big metal box with a keypad on it.

Unless someone else just happens to also be attacking the Heroes' Gala tonight, this has to be it. I walk up to it, wondering how I'm going to stop it from going off, let alone reprogram it. Maybe if I call Sarah, she can walk me through it. If she isn't too busy disarming those lasers.

There's no big obvious button that says *Power* or *Reset*, so I hit one of the numbers on the keypad. Nothing happens. I hit a couple more until it makes an angry beep at me.

This isn't going to work. I have *three freaking minutes* left, and no idea what to do. Panic twitches in my chest. I can fry this thing. I can at least shut it down, but if I do, then there's still going to be a battle. There's still going to be—

"Damien."

I jump, a wave of electricity crackling up my spine.

Grandpa steps out of the shadows, a look of extreme disappointment on his face.

"Don't scare me like that!" Maybe I'm just on edge, on account of having less than three minutes left of consciousness, or maybe it's because I got attacked by superheroes—*again*—and dragged down the stairs, but him showing up out of nowhere really freaks me out. "What are you doing here?" He's supposed to be at the rally, getting all the villains I inspired for him ready to come murder everyone I care about.

"I knew I'd find you here." He sighs, really hitting home the disappointment. "Your mother called. Apparently she spoke to Xavier and found out the two of you were at the Heroes' Gala, where I *specifically* told you not to go. I locked you up for a reason—for your own safety—and it wasn't so you could show up here and attempt to destroy all my hard work."

"I'm preventing a *massacre*."

He snorts. "We're capturing a few prominent heroes to

show the League they can't just ignore us. We're not—"

"You're leading an angry mob here! You're knocking everyone out, making them vulnerable, and then bringing in hundreds of strangers who hate heroes! What do you think is going to happen?"

His eyebrows come together. "You're too soft when it comes to them, you know that?"

"My friends and my family are here. You used me, and now a lot of people are going to get hurt because of it."

"And what do you think is going to happen if you destroy my machine? You think the heroes will come quietly when the Truth shows up? You're not preventing anyone from getting hurt by doing that. You're making it worse. And you're right—those villains are coming here because of you. Is this what you want for them? To have to fight for their lives?"

I glare at him, and I can't help the lightning that surges along my arms and collects in my palms. I think about Sarah's alert bracelet still in my pocket and wonder if I should put it on, so I don't accidentally lose control and hurt the machine. Maybe if Grandpa wasn't here, I would. But then again, if he wasn't here, I wouldn't need to.

"Don't try anything," Grandpa warns. "I can take you down before you even think about it."

"Just listen to me. We've got, like, two minutes before that thing goes off, and... What?"

"You think I'd be standing here if I really only had two minutes left? I reset it, gave it an extra ten. Xavier's already out. Twelve minutes is plenty of time for us to do the same and get far away from here." He holds up his hands, electricity crackling. "I'll take you out of here by force if I have to."

"No, wait! You have to listen to me! The heroes have villain-targeting lasers set up. They're going to turn them on if they see a bunch of villains coming. They've got remote access, and it won't matter if everyone in this building is knocked out."

"All the more reason to get you out of here!" He takes a step forward, the lightning in his hands growing brighter.

"Grandpa, wait!" Sweat prickles along my back. My heart races. Even if I use my lightning and make myself immune, it only goes so far. I don't doubt that he can overpower me.

"This isn't up for discussion. And we don't have time to stand around—we're leaving. *Now.*" He grabs my arm. There's a surge of electricity as our two powers meet.

Before I know what I'm doing, I've got Sarah's alert bracelet in my hand. I slap it around Grandpa's wrist and hold it there.

There's a loud *zzzzzt* noise as the bracelet cancels out both of our powers. Grandpa gasps and pulls away from me, the bracelet slipping off his arm. I couldn't keep it there forever. Even if I managed to close the clasp, he could take it off again. And even without his power, he could probably still drag me out of here. He's a lot stronger than you'd expect for someone in their sixties.

But the bracelet stopping his power like that startles him. Enough so that he stops trying to force me to leave and actually pays attention.

"You can still call this off!" I tell him. "It's not too late."

He's staring at the bracelet in my hand, like he can't believe it did that to him. Then he comes to his senses. "I've got hundreds of riled up villains waiting for me. They might not know my exact plan tonight, but they know this is their chance to stand up and be taken seriously. To make a change. They're ready to face their oppressors, and I can't just call that off."

"Face their oppressors? They're coming in here and attacking people who are unconscious—that's not 'facing' anyone! If they come here, they're going to get hurt. A lot of people are. I know you, and I know that you care about these villains. They're trusting you. And... and maybe they came to that rally because they trusted me, but those were your words I was saying in those commercials. You didn't just start the Truth for me, or for yourself. You did it for *them*. So villains could finally have a voice. And I know—I *know*—that you don't want them to get slaughtered. Because that's what's going to happen if you don't call it off. All those people, looking for a way to be heard, who trusted you... You can't betray them like this!"

"You've got good leadership potential, Damien. Just like I said. But you've never been in charge of this many people. I might have started the Truth, but if I want to keep it going, I can't afford to look weak. I can't go around getting people charged up and ready to attack and then calling it off at the last second. This is the first rally, the first chance for us to show the heroes that they need to take us seriously. Letting them scare us off with their lasers?" He shakes his head. "I'd never live that down. And no, I don't want anyone to get hurt, but the Truth needs me. It's still a new organization, and starting a revolution... It's fragile. People might get hurt tonight, but the Truth will go on to do a lot more good in the long run. So, come on, let's get out of here. You weren't going to do anyone any good by destroying my machine, anyway."

"I wasn't trying to destroy it. I was going to reprogram it. To delay it, so it doesn't come on until the villains are here, too. Just hear me out!" I say when he scowls at that, his electricity crackling again. "We're taking down the lasers. I mean, my friend Sarah is. She's the one who made this bracelet. She knows what she's doing, and if you just help me reset the time on this thing, then no one has to get hurt tonight."

"Or your friend can take down the lasers, and I can still let my machine go off as planned. None of my guys are in danger, and we still show the heroes we mean business."

"You can't do that. Everyone in the world who's important to me is here tonight, in this building. Maybe you hate heroes, and maybe you think you have to prove something to them. But all this attack is going to do is prove that we're exactly who they thought we were— dangerous and untrustable."

"We *are* dangerous. Especially when we're being ignored. Villains aren't going away. We're not a problem to be swept under the rug, and they need to know that."

"Yeah, but... Look, maybe your plan tonight would work. Maybe it would make them take you more seriously." Not in a good way, but still. "But I lost Mom, okay? I lost her, and my dad thinks I'm crazy, my sister isn't talking to me, and... Everyone I love is here. *Kat* is here. And if you hurt them, if you let all this crap get in the way of seeing reason and you bring in some crazed mob, I'm not just going to lose them—I'm going to lose you, too."

"Damien—"

"*No.* Just shut up! I thought Mom cared about me, but it turned out she didn't. I wanted to protect my hero family from her, and she abandoned me at the drop of a hat. She *gave me up*, because she didn't really care. And now you come along and you act like you care about me, despite me having an *X* and not going to Vilmore and all that. You used me. And maybe you did care, but... It's happening again. You might not be abandoning me in the same way she did, but if you hurt my family, or my friends, then you might as well be. Because we can't come back from that."

My eyes are wet. Just a little. I'm torn between wiping them on the back of my hand and doing nothing in the hopes that he doesn't notice.

"You going to let me talk now?" Grandpa says.

I nod, though I guess it depends on what he has to say.

"Damien, I'm not abandoning you. I did things that were for your own good without consulting you, and, yes, putting it plain and simple, I used you. But I'm not your mother. One disagreement isn't going to send me packing. I love you, and nothing's going to change that, all right? If it means that much to you, I'd call this whole thing off and take the risk. I would, but it's too late."

"What? What do you mean, it's too late?"

"I told my seconds that if I wasn't back before seven

thirty to lead the attack without me. It's seven thirty-two. They're already on their way. They'll be here in about fifteen minutes."

"Can't you call them?!"

"I can try, but there's no guarantee they'll pick up. It's loud over there. And once you get an angry mob going, it's not that easy to stop them."

"Okay. So, we stick to my plan. We reset the machine so it goes off after they get here. It knocks everyone out, including the mob, and nobody gets hurt."

He frowns at that. "That plan leaves my people completely defenseless. It's one thing if they're awake and can fight back against these lasers, or try to avoid them, but unconscious? That's a lot of death warrants you're signing, there."

"Sarah can turn them off. She *can*. Tell me how to reprogram the machine—give us until seven fifty. Nobody has to know you helped me. You don't even have to lose face with the Truth."

"If I do this and that mob shows up here, only to be knocked out and murdered by the League..." He shudders. "If the Truth is still around after that, I won't be leading it. And you'll have a lot of angry villain families crying for blood. So you'd better be damn sure you can do this."

"I am. I swear, Grandpa. You just have to trust me."

# CHAPTER 32

The elevator doors open, and I almost run into Amelia as I hurry inside. She was on her way out, and her forehead bonks into my chin.

"*Ow!*" She glares at me and puts a hand to her head.

"What the hell are you doing here? I told you to—"

"Warn Mom and Dad? I did. That only took about two seconds. Then I called Sarah, and she said you were either on the roof or in the basement. It wasn't hard to guess which one of those *you'd* be in."

"I also told you to get out of here. And since when do you have Sarah's number?"

"Uh, since she gave it to me? We got our hair done together before we went to Zach's house."

I glance over at Amelia's hair. It looks a little shinier, but otherwise exactly the same. "That still doesn't explain what you're doing here." I get out Riley's phone and dial Sarah's number to tell her I did my part and that she's got until 7:50. Er, well, she's got until the mob of angry villains shows up, I mean, since that's when the heroes will turn on their lasers.

"I'm here," Amelia says, "because you don't get to tell me what to do."

"I told you to get out of here so you wouldn't get hurt."

"Yeah, like I'm completely useless."

"Riley?" Sarah says, answering the phone after a couple rings. She sounds kind of panicked. "Where are you? Is—"

"It's me."

"Oh, Renegade." Then, presumably to Kat, "It's Rene— I mean, it's Damien. Your boyfriend."

"I reset the machine. You've got until seven fifty, but the villains are on their way."

"That's— Watch out!" There's the sound of a raygun blasting, and then something exploding.

"Sarah?! What's going on?"

"Damien?" It's Kat this time. "You guys have to get over here! We were on our way to the control room, to turn off the lasers, and—" There's another exploding sound.

"*Kat?!*"

"I'm here. Anyway, someone saw me shapeshift, and we got stopped by security, and then your crazy-ass sidekick pulled out a megaphone—"

"It wasn't a megaphone!" Sarah shouts in the background. "It was a stupefication gun!"

"Okay, your crazy-ass sidekick pulled out a *gun*, and aimed it at security, and then it exploded."

There's a muffled noise as Sarah takes the phone back. She sounds out of breath. "I made some adjustments on this new model, but I overcompensated, and I didn't have a chance to test it. So— Kat! The door!"

"Got it!"

"Sarah, what the hell is going on?!"

"Basically, some superheroes think I attacked them—"

"Because you *did*," Kat says.

"—and they pulled actual rayguns on us, so we had to run. Now we're barricaded in a hotel room, and I'm trying to fix the stupefication gun. We're holding them off, but you guys need to get here, *now*!"

"Where are you?"

"Fourth floor. I don't know the room number, but it'll be obvious which one, since it's the one all the superheroes are shooting at!"

"Okay, I'll—"

"I have to go! Just get here!"

She hangs up. I press the button for the fourth floor. The elevator starts to ascend, and I brace myself against the railing, since I'm still not sure Riley was joking about that knocking sound. "I don't have time to drop you off," I tell Amelia, "but as soon as I get off this thing, you're going to the lobby and getting out of here."

"I'm going with you," she says, even though her voice wavers a little and she looks kind of like going with me is the last thing she wants to do. "I'm *not* useless. And you don't get to tell me what to do, because you *left*."

"Amelia, I—"

"You left, and you didn't tell anyone where you were going! You weren't even going to tell anyone you were leaving! Everybody was worried, and they were all mad at me, because I kind of knew about it. I felt sick for days. And you *lied* to me. A bunch of times. You lied about what happened on our mission, and you lied about that awful red-headed kid being your *brother*."

"That's only twice. And if he was your brother, you'd lie about it, too."

She glares at me. "But those are just the ones I know about. You've probably lied about a bunch more things. And then you show up here and tell everybody what to do, and you think you can just send me off to babysit and warn people. You didn't even consider the fact that I could really do something."

Since when is that a fact? "Warning people is important. You know you're not exactly the best at fieldwork, and this is an emergency. I don't have time to babysit anybody, least of all you."

She gives off an angry noise that makes her sound kind of like an elephant. "At least I'm here, and I'm not leaving, unlike *some* people."

"I *had* to leave, okay? I had to! You guys could have gotten hurt. Which is why I don't want you here now."

"But you didn't even ask us!"

"Because if I had, you would have told me to stay, and it was hard enough to leave as it was. But Alex almost got kidnapped, and if something else had happened, I couldn't take it."

"So you left because of *you*. Because you couldn't take it. Don't pretend it was for us."

The elevator stops. There's a ding, and then the doors open. I step into the fourth-floor hallway, and Amelia makes a big point of doing the same.

"*Amelia.* Get back on the elevator. I don't have time for this." We're at what looks like the end of the hall, which branches off in different directions. I can hear the sounds of fighting in the distance to the right.

"Who knows how many superheroes there are? You can't face them alone. You need me."

I hold up my hands and make electricity wash over them. "Yes, I can. What are you going to do, throw eggnog on them? And anyway, Riley's around somewhere. Just get back in there and call Mason"—I shove Riley's phone into her hands—"and tell them to get over here."

She starts to scroll through Riley's contacts, actually listening to me for once—or half listening, since she stays put in the hallway—but then we both jump as the stairwell door next to us flies open.

Mason comes tearing out of it. He's out of breath, like he's been running a long time. And despite the way his face is red from exertion, he looks kind of green. Like he's about to be sick. His eyes go wide when he sees us, and he tries to push past me into the elevator.

"Whoa." I reach out to stop him, and Amelia moves to block the doors. "What happened? Where's Riley?"

"They were shooting at us! They were *superheroes*, and they were *shooting* at us!"

"That doesn't answer my question!"

"Slap him," Amelia says. "That always works in the movies."

I grab Mason by the collar with one hand and make the other go all electric. "Tell me what the hell happened!"

Mason lets out a whimper and tries to twist out of my grasp.

I hold my electric hand closer to his face.

His words come out all jumbled together, so that it takes me a second to realize what he said. "Ry-got-hurt-and-I-couldn't-do-anything-and-we're-running-out-of-time-and-I-can't-be-here!"

"Wait, he what? And you left him?!"

"They were shooting at us!" There's a bright flash as Mason suddenly uses his power.

I let go of him, instinctively putting my hands to my face to cover my eyes. I can't see anything, just bright blobs of color. Amelia cries out at the same time, so I'm guessing she can't see anything, either.

"Mason, what happened to Riley? *Mason?!*"

"He's gone," Amelia says. "He pushed past me to get into the elevator, and then I heard it start moving."

My blood runs cold, and my stomach flops. I can't believe this. "We have to go up there."

"What about Kat and Sarah?"

"They can hold off those superheroes for a little longer." I hope. But there's no way Amelia could fight her way to them, and I can't be in two places at once.

"What about the lasers?"

"We'll get to them in time."

"But—"

"Riley's hurt. I don't know what happened, but we're *not* leaving him."

"Okay."

I rub my eyes, trying to make the blobs go away. My

vision's getting a little better. "Where are you? Can you hit the button?"

Amelia hesitates. "The elevator's *really* slow, and Mason's already on it. He must be going to the lobby, so he can get out of here. That means it would take forever to come back."

Damn it. "But I can't…"

"I'm coming over to you. Don't zap me."

A whole flight of stairs. And I can hardly see. But Riley's hurt. The superheroes were *shooting* at them, and now he's hurt.

Amelia's hand reaches for me, then grabs my arm. "Come on. He didn't get me too bad—I can mostly see stuff again."

"I'm too slow. Slower than waiting for the elevator. I can't—"

"You have to!" She takes a deep breath. "If I was better at fieldwork, I could go up there by myself, but you're right—I'm not good at it."

"I shouldn't have said that."

She drags me toward the stairs and opens the door. "But it's true. I got us caught during our mission, and if I hadn't, none of this would have happened."

I laugh. "My Grandpa would have told me about it eventually. He wanted me to join—that's part of why he made the Truth in the first place."

We get to the stairs. My vision's mostly cleared up, though there are still a few spots. I shake off Amelia's arm and look up. The stairs spiral around with a landing at each corner. I can't actually see the top, and it has nothing to do with the spots in my eyes. "This is impossible. The elevator will be faster, even if we have to wait."

"Come on." Amelia grabs my arm again.

I jerk away from her. "The last person who touched me while I was on the stairs got zapped, so hands off."

She screws up her face and glares at me. "I know I don't have a cool power, and I can't, like, shoot people like you can. I'm not good at fieldwork, and I'll probably never be good enough to join the League like Mom and Dad, but I can do this! I can make you go up these stupid stairs, and I don't care if you zap me!" Her nostrils flare in and out, and she wraps her arms around one of mine and pulls.

I go up one step, then another. My heart's racing, partly because of my fear of heights, but mostly because I know I don't have time for this. I make the mistake of looking up again, and a spark of electricity runs through me.

Amelia winces, but she doesn't lose her grip. She continues walking backwards up the stairs, as if it's no big deal. "Just look down at the step in front of you. Pretend there's just the one. One step up from the ground isn't very high. Just keep imagining that each step is the first one."

"It's not that easy."

"You're not going to fall, okay? I'm not letting go, no matter what."

"So then we'll both fall." But we're halfway to the first landing already, so maybe this is working.

"Neither of us is going to do that. You're on the ground, remember? Just one step up."

I grit my teeth. I hate this. My best friend is hurt, and I don't even know how badly, but Mason looked pretty freaked out, and he said it was bad enough that there was nothing he could do. Which could mean anything. It could mean something very, *very* bad. And I hate that Amelia's seeing me like this. "You're wrong, you know," I tell her. "You have a pretty cool power."

"Not as cool as flying. Or turning invisible. Or even having lightning."

"Gee, thanks." I don't raise my foot quite high enough, and my toe scuffs against the edge of the next step, throwing me off balance a little. There's a split second where I *know* I'm going to fall, and it feels like my heart stops, like everything stops, but then Amelia pulls me forward.

The ground is flat, and I realize we're at the first landing.

"We're almost there," Amelia lies. She speeds up as we get to the second set of stairs, dragging me with her.

"You have a cool power, and maybe you did botch our mission, but you also managed to steal the key and get into the back room. So you can't be as bad at fieldwork as you think."

"Yeah, right. We both know I'm not that great at it."

"Okay, but you've got potential. And... maybe if I'd been helping you instead of standing around texting, things would have gone differently." I kind of mumble that part, and I keep my eyes on my feet, and not just because it's helping me not freak out too much.

"You want to know something?" Amelia says. "I don't

even know if I like fieldwork. And I'm never going to be good enough to join the League. I've wanted to forever, but I didn't really think about what it would mean. And I thought I'd get flying power, and that I'd just be able to do stuff."

"It doesn't work like that."

"You're slowing down. Come on." She picks up the pace, keeping her death grip on my arm and forcing me to keep up.

"I wasn't a very good partner to you."

"Or a good brother."

I guess I deserve that. "I shouldn't have lied."

"Second landing," Amelia says. "One more to go."

I nod. I don't want to think about how many stairs that means are below us, or what it would mean to fall right now. "But my grandpa asked me to keep the Truth a secret. I couldn't betray him."

Amelia scoffs at that. "And what about having a whole *brother* I didn't know about?"

"It wasn't really any of your business."

"But it hurt when I found out you lied about him. Like you don't trust me."

I'm about to say that I don't, but it seems kind of contradictory, what with me trusting her to lead me up the stairs and all. "Mom had him after she kicked me out. She used some weird growth formula on him, so even though he looks like he's Alex's age, he's actually not even six months old. He's all villain, and he even looks like her. She didn't want me, and now she has a replacement. It's not exactly something I go around telling people."

"I only spent a couple minutes with him, but he's really terrible. You're way better than him, and if your mom doesn't know that, then she must have something wrong with her."

"Mom got married. Xavier has both his parents around, and I never thought I cared about stuff like that, but maybe I do. I only ever have one or the other. And now it's like she has this completely new family, and I'm not part of it. She doesn't *want* me to be part of it."

"You have a family she's not part of, too. A much bigger one, and we would never act like she does. I know I got mad when you left, but you're still my brother, and I didn't really mean it when I said I'd never forgive you. It just really hurt when you left. I couldn't say anything to make you stay, and then you walked out, and—"

Amelia slips as she steps backward onto the third landing, like she lost track and wasn't expecting the ground to be flat. It throws me off balance, and I lose my footing. A jolt of adrenaline rushes through me, and before I can stop it, a burst of lightning races across my skin.

Amelia cries out in pain, but she doesn't let go.

I can feel myself falling backward. Then Amelia recovers and pulls me up.

We're at the top, both of us out of breath and kind of freaked out. Now that we're safe, she drops my arm and rubs her hand. She checks her phone. "We made good time. You *almost* went up the stairs like a normal person. Faster than if we waited for the stupid elevator, and who knows if it would have even come straight up."

"You're not useless, Amelia. You know that?"

"That's what I've been trying to tell you." She rolls her eyes at me, but her cheeks turn a little pink at the compliment.

# CHAPTER 33

The fifth floor looks like a war zone. Or at least what we can see of it. There's a cave-in a little ways down the hall. It looks like a beam from the roof collapsed, along with the wall next to it. There's debris all over and dust in the air. Whatever happened, the superheroes must be stuck on the other side, because there's no sign of them, and they didn't follow Mason down the stairs.

But there's no sign of Riley, either.

"Oh, my God," Amelia says, gasping at all the rubble. "Do you think—"

"*No.* Don't even say it." He has to be okay. He has to *be here*, and he has to be okay. Because if he was on the other side, with those superheroes, or if he was under the beam when it collapsed...

Something flickers on the floor by the cave-in. There's a body—no, a person—propped against the wall, trying and failing to stay invisible. "Perkins?!" I rush over to him and kneel down on the floor.

"X?" His voice is faint, and he says it like he doesn't believe it, like he might just be delirious and imagining anyone else is here. His right leg is pinned under a giant chunk of debris.

"What happened?"

"My leg hurts. I can't move." His face is really pale, and it's obviously taking a lot of effort to talk. "Did you find the machine?"

"Yeah, don't worry about it. Everything's going to be okay." Except for the fact that Kat and Sarah are trapped in a fight with some superheroes and haven't turned the lasers off yet and the Truth is still on its way. But other than that, everything's just fine.

"The superheroes were shooting at us, and then the ceiling was coming down. Mason pushed me to get past. I fell, and then I was on the ground and my leg hurt. The superheroes couldn't get through—I think they went to find another way down. But I couldn't move, and Mason *left*. He just left."

"I know. We ran into him." I should have killed him.

"He pushed you?" Amelia says, her eyes wide.

"He panicked." Riley coughs from all the dust and then winces.

"Not as much as he's going to panic the next time I see him." I half expect Riley to argue against that, to try and defend Mason even after what he did, but thankfully he doesn't.

"What are we going to do?" Amelia gets out her phone and frowns at the time. "The villains will be here any minute."

"What?" Riley asks. "What about the lasers?"

"Sarah and Kat are trapped in a hotel room," Amelia says. "They haven't gotten to the lasers yet."

I glare at her. "Amelia. Shut up."

"What? It's *true*."

I jerk my head toward Riley, trying to silently communicate to her that he doesn't need to hear all that.

"They're what?" Riley sucks in a breath in surprise and ends up coughing again. His eyes water from the pain. "X, you have to get out of here."

"I'm not abandoning you." Those superheroes will be back, plus Riley doesn't look too good. I move to inspect the debris that's on his leg. There's a big chunk from the ceiling, but thankfully the beam missed him, and the chunk's not *too* big.

Okay, it's kind of really big, and it looks really heavy, and I don't have super strength.

"Amelia. You're going to have to use your power to move this thing."

"*That?*" Amelia gapes at the chunk of rubble. "I can't call that!"

"Yes, you can."

She's shaking her head. "I can only summon up small things. I tried to use my power to call a dining chair into the kitchen the other day, so I could reach the top shelf in the cupboard, but it just shuddered really hard and fell. I can't—"

"Amelia, you have to! Just concentrate, okay?"

"It's bigger than a chair. And it looks a lot heavier. I'm still working my way up to that. The biggest thing I've moved so far was Tiffany's lamp that's shaped like a turtle, and it was mostly hollow. If I do this, Riley's just going to get hurt worse. Because of me!"

"You have to try! We can't leave him like that, and we don't have time to argue! Please, Amelia. If I could do it, I would, but I can't lift it, and I don't have your power. So, please—"

"Okay, I guess, if I have to... I'll do what I can." She sets her mouth into a grim line and presses her hand to the chunk of debris. Then she stands back. She takes a deep breath and holds her hands out face down, moving them closer to the floor, so the chunk won't have as far to drop if she succeeds.

When. I mean *when* she succeeds.

I kneel down next to Riley. "This is going to hurt like hell, Perkins." More than it already does. "So, just... I don't know. I don't know what else to do, but I'm going to be right here, and I'm not going anywhere." I grab his hand, because I really *don't* know what else to do.

Riley nods. He looks absolutely terrified. "I'm sorry, X. I'm sorry we weren't partners this semester."

"It's okay. It doesn't matter now."

"But if we don't make it out of here—"

"We're going to make it! All of us! So don't start apologizing to me like we're never going to see each other again. Amelia, call it! Do it now!"

I glance over my shoulder at her. Her face twists up in concentration. "Nothing's happening. I don't—"

"You can do this! It doesn't matter what you have or haven't done in the past—this is now, and right now, *you can do this.*"

She takes a deep breath and focuses again.

A scream tears through Riley as the chunk of debris disappears from on top of his leg and crashes down in front of Amelia. He squeezes my hand so hard, I feel like my fingers are going to break.

"Oh, my God! I did it!" Amelia looks shocked, like she really didn't think it was going to happen.

"Yeah, you did. Now get over here and help me get him off the floor. Perkins, put your arm around my shoulders. I'm going to support you on this side, with your bad leg. Amelia's going to get the other one."

"No." Tears drip down Riley's face. He almost can't get the words out, he's crying so hard. "I can't. I can't do this. Just leave me here!"

I motion for Amelia to get into place. "I don't suppose you've touched any painkillers you can call up?"

She looks sick. "Maybe we shouldn't move him. It's going to hurt a lot."

"In case you haven't noticed, everything's gone to hell tonight. Those superheroes are going to come back. They already did *this*." I indicate the cave-in and Riley's injury. "I don't even want to know what else they're going to do if they find him again. So, come on, and help me already!"

Amelia doesn't look completely convinced, but she does what I say and gets Riley's other arm around her. I count off again and we stand up, hauling Riley up between us. He screams and starts muttering incoherently. I try to keep most of his weight on me. It's not easy. All of my muscles strain just to keep us standing.

"Where are we taking him?" Amelia asks. She sounds a little out of breath already. "We don't have much time, and we still have to help Sarah and Kat."

"This way." I indicate the closest hotel room. "We just have to get him inside, and then you're going to stay with him."

"Me?! But what if the superheroes come back?"

Right as she says that, the stairwell door bangs open, and a security guard from the League steps into the hallway. He holds out his hand like a weapon and says, "Nobody move!"

And I know I have to zap him. Even before he reaches for the walkie-talkie on his belt to call for backup, I know. Because we don't have time for this. The Truth is going to be here any minute. Those lasers are still hooked up, and I promised Grandpa I could do this. And I don't know if the lasers are only in the ballroom, where the awards ceremony is, or if they're all over the hotel, but I don't really want to find out. I have villain DNA, and so does Kat, and I kind of want both of us to stay alive.

Not to mention that Riley's in a hell of a lot of pain right now, and me and Amelia can't keep holding him up like this.

And now some superhero douchebag thinks he can show up here, point his stupid hand at us, and we'll just do whatever he says? Because tonight hasn't been awful enough.

Electricity crackles in my palm, and I don't think I could stop it even if I wanted to. I have to force myself to hold back, because I just need to incapacitate this guy, not kill him. Grandpa's right, I need to learn something in between barely touching someone and totally obliterating them, but right now it's all I can do to avoid that second option.

The superhero charges up his own power—a burning ray of destruction. My electricity hits him before he fires, knocking him off balance, so that his blast hits the ceiling instead. More debris rains down on us, but at least we're not dead.

And I must have held back more than I thought, because the superhero's on the ground but still moving. He shouts into his walkie-talkie, "I found them! You've got to get up here—"

I zap him again, and this time he loses consciousness.

"If anybody asks, you guys didn't see that. Especially you, Perkins." I readjust Riley's arm around my shoulder, making sure I have a good hold of him, then move toward the hotel room. "Use your power to take out the lock," I tell Amelia. "Once I'm gone, barricade the door."

"That guy called somebody," Amelia says. "More of them are going to come. You can't leave me."

"You'll be safe in here. And I'm trusting you to stay with Riley."

"They're going to figure out where we are!"

"They won't." I hope.

"And if they do?"

"You remember when one of Grandpa's goons had that raygun to your head?"

"Uh, yeah. How could I forget?"

"Call it."

Her eyes go wide. "And then what? I'm not like you, Damien. I can't... I can't shoot a superhero!"

"You won't have to. Just make them believe you will long enough to stall until Grandpa's machine goes off, and then it won't matter anymore."

X·X·X

I take the elevator back down to the fourth floor. I check the time on Riley's phone—7:44.

Kat and Sarah have been stuck in that room for over ten minutes. If they're still there. If those superheroes didn't bust their way in and capture them. And if they did, then that's it. I don't know where the control room is, and even if there was time to find out, I have no idea how to turn off the lasers. Without Sarah, we're screwed.

But I still hear shouting and rayguns blasting off to the right. I never thought hearing that would be a good thing, but it means the girls are still under siege.

Er, not that that should be a good thing, either, but at least I'm not too late.

I race down the hall toward the sounds. Electricity crackles across my skin. I have no idea what I'm going to find, only that I have to be prepared to fight. I round the corner and see five superheroes crowding the hallway, all focused on the same hotel-room door. There are holes in the walls from them shooting their rayguns. It's not as much of a war zone as the fifth floor, but it's not good, either.

One of them was shouting, "Last warning!" at the door,

but he stops when I come running and they all turn to look at me.

Maybe it's because they recognize me, or maybe it's because I'm covered in electricity, but it seems like they barely have a chance to register any of that stuff before they start shooting at me. And I don't care what Gordon says about still believing in the League—they've totally lost it.

I jump to the right to dodge a raygun beam and zap the nearest superhero. It's difficult to control how much power I'm using, especially when they're *shooting at me*, but I try to hold back. Maybe I shouldn't be, because they seem like they're trying to kill me, and after everything the heroes have been doing tonight, they don't exactly deserve the benefit of the doubt. But I'm not a killer.

Even if there are five heroes attacking me all at once and I'm pretty sure I'm going to die.

I dodge another beam. It hits the wall to my right, blasting out a chunk that hits my arm. The superhero I got with my lightning is on the floor, so at least that's one down. Maybe I should run and try to lead them away from Kat and Sarah and hope they notice that the hall's clear. But there's no way I can turn my back to my attackers and live to tell about it, so my only option is to stay and fight.

I zap another one. I wish Grandpa was here to take them all down. I wish I'd had more time to train with him and learn how to do it myself.

"Eliminate him! He's a villain!" one of them yells. It's the same one who was shouting at the hotel-room door, and I figure he's their leader.

*Eliminate* really sounds so final. I duck to avoid another shot. Fighting for my life kind of makes my electricity harder to control, but I don't have much choice. I aim for another hero, and if I zap them harder than I mean to, it's because I don't have the luxury of holding back anymore.

But right as I zap them, a raygun beam hits my left arm. There's an explosion of white-hot pain, and for a moment, it's all I'm aware of, and I can't make sense of what's happening. My lightning misses its mark, hitting the wall instead.

The pain slows down my reaction time, and another blast almost gets me. I lash out, holding up my right hand and not caring how much power I hit them with. It's them or me.

Right then the hotel-room door flies open, and Kat and Sarah burst out, screaming some war cry. Sarah's holding out her stupefication gun—it has some wires hanging out of it, and she must have managed to fix it—and Kat's wielding a small coffee pot full of boiling water and holding a little rubber garbage can like a shield.

They're standing behind the heroes and almost get hit by my electricity. Kat swears and drops her coffee pot, nearly splashing herself with it, as she pushes Sarah out of the way, so that they both narrowly avoid getting electrocuted.

"It's about time you showed up!" Kat shouts. Now that her right hand is free, she shapeshifts it into a sword.

The three remaining superheroes are shooting at all of us. I blast another one, and Sarah fires her stupefication gun at the other two. There's a loud click, and nothing happens. Kat throws her garbage can at them. Sarah fires again, and this time there's a whirring noise and a *pop* as the gun sort of explodes. But it worked this time. The heroes lower their weapons and stand there, confused.

I zap them before there's any time for it to wear off. They fall to the floor, and I kind of feel like joining them.

"Oh, my God," Kat says. "You're bleeding!" She ducks down and grabs one of the knocked-out heroes' rayguns.

"I'm fine." I think. I press my right hand to the wound on my left arm. It burns like hell, but it's not too deep.

Sarah's eyes flick back and forth, taking everything in. "Where's Riley? And Mason? What took you so long?"

"Mason left. And Riley... He's going to be okay."

"What? What happened?!"

"I'll tell you later—we have to go!"

There are footsteps in the hall, coming from the direction of the elevator. One of the superheroes must have called for backup.

Sarah opens her mouth to argue, but Kat grabs her arm and starts running. "Come on! The control room should be down here."

I hurry after them.

Kat stops in front of a door labeled *Networking/Storage: Authorized Personnel Only*. "It's an old building," Kat says. "They converted an old janitor's closet into a control room for the network when they got internet. Or at least that's what the manager told us. I had to look *really* official—I turned into the head of the League, based on a thumbnail from his bio I looked up on my phone." She tries the handle, but it's locked.

Down the hall, I hear shouting. They must have discovered all the superheroes on the floor.

"Hold on—I've got this." Kat starts to transform her hand into lockpicks.

"There's no time!" I hold up my hand, and she nods and gets out of the way so I can blast it.

"Tell me now, Damien." Sarah's voice is flat. I don't know if I've ever heard her sound so freaked out before. "What happened to Riley?"

"If he says he's going to be fine," Kat says, "then he is."

"If it was your boyfriend, you'd want to know. Don't tell me you wouldn't."

"His leg's broken," I tell her. "But he's going to be fine. Amelia's with him now."

Sarah breathes a little easier, but then frowns. "There's something you're not telling me."

"Sarah, we don't have time for this!" She's right, I'm not exactly giving her the whole story, but it's going to have to be enough. I step forward, ready to blast the door.

"Wait!" Sarah shouts. "Be careful—don't fry any of the equipment. We don't know what we're dealing with yet."

I aim for the knob. My arm is killing me, and I'm both worn out from everything that's happened tonight and high on adrenaline. I don't have a lot of control left over my lightning, and I know that if we don't get in there, we're in serious trouble. Everyone in this building is. So I hit it with everything I've got and hope.

The whole right side of the door explodes, and what's left of it falls open.

"I said don't fry anything!" Sarah scowls at me and

rushes inside.

Kat stands next to me, almost shoulder to shoulder, as we brace ourselves for the incoming superheroes. She glances down at my arm. "That looks bad, Damien."

"It's nothing compared to—" I stop myself from saying *It's nothing compared to what happened to Perkins.*

But I think Sarah must know anyway, because her voice shakes when she says, "It's—everything looks fine. The equipment's still working."

The first superhero rounds the bend. "Over here!" he shouts to the others, pointing a raygun at us.

I try and zap him, but I'm too slow, and he dodges. My electricity hits the guy coming up behind him. That guys falls, and the other superheroes cry out and start shooting.

Kat aims her stolen raygun at them and fires. "You know," she says, "this is really *not* how I planned to spend my Saturday night."

"No more dates involving gun fights—got it." I manage to zap the first guy, but only in the leg. It brings him to the floor, but it doesn't knock him out. "Got those lasers disarmed yet?" I ask Sarah, not looking away from the fight.

"There are a lot of controls here. I don't..." Sarah's voice trails off. She doesn't sound like herself—she sounds like she's about to cry.

"She's losing it," Kat says out the side of her mouth. She shoots the floor in front of one of the superheroes, forcing them back a step. A raygun blast almost hits her in the shoulder, but she shapeshifts out of the way just in time. It explodes part of the wall behind us.

I take another hero down with my electricity. "Sarah, he's going to be fine! I care about him, too, okay? I wouldn't lie about this!"

"Right." Sarah's voice comes out a squeak. "Unless you were keeping the worst from me until after I disarm these lasers."

"Come on, Cosine! This is an emergency!" I use her sidekick name in the hopes that it will snap her out of this. Then I glance over at Kat, hoping she's not too pissed about it. Especially since she's got a raygun in her hand.

Kat's face is lined with concentration as she aims and fires at another hero. She hits him in the shoulder, making him drop his weapon. If she cares that I referred to Sarah as Cosine, she isn't showing it.

Another superhero comes running toward us. He doesn't have a raygun and instead fires a blast of ice. Me and Kat both dive in opposite directions to avoid it. He shoots at me again, and I have to roll out of the way. I don't have time to zap him.

"Over here!" Kat shouts. She fires her raygun at the ice guy, her beam just grazing his arm. He cries out and blasts more ice at us. Kat drops to the floor, still shooting. "Damien! Take him out!"

I do what she says and hit him with my electricity. Maybe a little harder than I meant to, but it gets the job done. He looks like he's twitching a little, so I'm pretty sure he's not dead.

One of the heroes' walkie-talkies makes a static noise, and then a voice says, "The villains are here! I repeat, the villains are here! All available League members to the ground floor!"

This is it. Grandpa's mob has arrived, and the heroes are going to set off the lasers. "Sarah! Any time now!"

"I'm trying! But I don't know which one it is. There are too many options. I don't know what to do!" There are tears in her voice, and panic, and maybe it's from all the stress of tonight, but it's probably because of Riley, and maybe I should have flat out lied to her. I should have said he and Mason were outside, waiting for us.

But it's Sarah. She would have seen through that.

"You can do this!" Kat says. She fires her raygun again, but this time it sort of half blasts, then fizzles out. "Damn it—I'm out of charge!" She throws the now useless gun on the floor and ducks behind me.

I zap a hero who takes aim at us.

"I can't!" Sarah cries. "I can't make sense of anything! I need more time!"

"This is your thing!" Kat tells her. "You know what you're doing, even if you don't think you do. We're out of time—trust your instincts and just pick one!"

"But—"

"It'll be the right one! I promise!"

I'm not sure how Kat can make that promise, but it doesn't really matter, because Sarah says, "Okay," and types something into the keyboard.

Right as Grandpa's machine goes off and we all lose consciousness.

# CHAPTER 34

I t's kind of fitting that I sneak back home in the middle of the night, since that's how I left when I ran away. It's two in the morning by the time I get there, and the house is quiet. Thankfully. I don't really even know if Gordon's going to let me stay here. I mean, he said on TV that he wanted me to come home, but what if he changed his mind since then? What if he blames me for what happened tonight?

Even if he does want me back, he's probably got a lot to say about me leaving. A lot to say that might also take the form of yelling, and right now, I don't think I can take it. I can't take him being mad at me or the whole family gawking at me like they've never seen a prodigal son before. Today was one of the worst days of my life, and after everything I've been through—including my grandpa betraying me, finding Riley in that pile of rubble, getting shot by superheroes, and spending hours in the emergency room—I just want to crash and try not to think about it.

It takes me forever to get up the attic stairs, and I keep thinking someone's going to wake up and find me there, but they don't. I get to my room and crawl into bed. I don't even get undressed. My pajamas, along with everything else I took with me, are still at my grandparents' house. I could find something else to wear, but it doesn't matter—I don't have the energy to bother changing anyway.

I'm *so* tired, but as soon as I lie down, the enormity of everything that happened today hits me. More than it already had. I curl up into a ball and press my face against my pillow as tears fill my eyes.

There's a knock at the door. I expect it to be Amelia, but it's Gordon who pokes his head in and says, "Damien? I thought I heard you come in."

I don't move. Maybe he won't know I'm here and will go away. If he asks tomorrow, I can say I must have been asleep.

He turns on the light and sighs with relief.

I quickly wipe my eyes on the blanket and sit up, blinking against the sudden brightness.

Gordon rushes over and pulls me into a hug. Which is kind of the opposite of yelling at me.

"*Ow.* Dad, watch the arm!"

He lets me go and sits on the edge of the bed, frowning at my bandage. "What happened?"

"It's nothing."

"Damien."

"I got blasted by a raygun, okay?"

"You what?! Amelia didn't mention that."

"It happened after the last time I saw her." Though I know she made it home all right, and that she and Riley didn't die or anything, because she texted me earlier on his phone. I'll have to get her to use her power to get mine back in the morning. Assuming Xavier hasn't done something to completely ruin it. "They patched me up at the hospital."

"At the *hospital*? Why didn't anybody call me?!"

"It still hurts, but it'll be okay. And they did call you, but it was after midnight, and you didn't answer. And can you keep it down? We don't need to wake the whole house."

"I must not have heard it. After we took Amelia home, I went back to help get things straightened out at the gala. I actually only got back here myself about an hour ago."

"I didn't mean to wake you up. You can go back to bed."

"I wasn't asleep. I was worried about you."

"So you were just sitting around, hoping I'd show up? Wait, does that mean you knew I was here and you were *listening* to me go up the stairs?"

He looks away. "I know having an audience for that makes you uncomfortable, so I thought I'd wait until you got to your room. I didn't want to scare you off when you'd finally come home."

"Uh, yeah, that doesn't make any sense. What did you think I was going to do? Run back down them and out the door?"

"I was trying to give you some space." He runs a hand through his hair and lets out a deep breath. "I know I'm a big reason why you left."

"Amelia was *supposed* to give you my letter. I left because—"

"Because you were trying to protect us. I know. I read your letter about a thousand times."

"Okay, then you know it didn't have anything to do with you."

He shakes his head. "You shouldn't feel like you have to run away from home to keep us safe. I shouldn't have *let* you feel like that. You're my son, and you're only sixteen. It's not your job."

"Hey, I'll be seventeen on Friday."

He gives me a look. "You know what I mean. You tried to tell me how you felt, and I didn't listen."

"Yeah, well, that's not exactly anything new. And I saw that interview you did. You went on TV and told everyone I was wrong. You said villains should be *ignored*, that we would just go away."

He flinches on the *we*. "Damien, I didn't mean—"

"Yes, you did. And that was after I left home. So you'd already had your revelation that you weren't listening to me, right? But you still went on TV and did a whole interview about how much you disagreed with me."

"My son had joined *the Truth*. You better believe I disagreed with that."

There it is. Now he's starting to sound pissed. Part of me wants him to go away and not have this conversation, and the other part of me wants to piss him off more and just have it out. "So, nothing's changed."

"You're home. And since you didn't go back to your

grandparents' house, I'm assuming you're not with the Truth anymore."

"You figured out where I was?"

"Not exactly. I had my suspicions, but I didn't know for sure. Not until I called your mother."

"You called *Mom*? How did you even get her number?"

"I found it on a wedding invitation."

"You went through my stuff?!"

"Well... Amelia got it for me."

"Wow. Didn't you pay *any* attention to what I wrote in my letter?" I specifically told him not to let her touch anything. "But just because I'm not with the Truth anymore doesn't mean I don't care about villain rights. And it doesn't change the fact that you think villains should just be ignored, or that you still think it's okay to be part of the League after everything they've done."

"Not everyone in the League agrees with their current policies, or with what they've been doing to villains."

I hold up my bandaged arm. "You mean like shooting your son? That's the difference between us. When the Truth started attacking heroes, I *left*. But the League practically kidnapped Alex and tried to haul me in off the street, and you didn't care. And now they actually shot me. And yeah, I was zapping them, too, but only because they'd totally lost it. They had Kat and Sarah trapped, and they were attacking them. And they almost killed Riley."

"What happened to you guys tonight wasn't okay. But you have to believe me when I say that those people don't represent all of the League. And the Truth did have an attack planned."

435

"I can't believe you're actually defending them right now. Didn't you hear me? They almost *killed* my best friend. And he's a hero. He has an *H* on his thumb, and he didn't point any weapons at them. But I guess seeing him with me was enough."

"I wasn't one of those people."

"Yeah, and I wasn't hurting anyone while I was in the Truth, but that doesn't mean you were cool with me being part of it."

"I've been with the League for almost twenty years. Maybe it's not what I thought it was, but I still believe in what it stands for. Or what I've always *thought* it stood for."

"They tried to kill me! But you obviously care more about them than you do about me!" I press my palms over my eyes. I didn't mean to say that, and now I can't look at him.

"Damien. That's not true. I care a lot about you. You have to know that."

"So what? So does Grandpa. I thought Mom just didn't actually care, that that's why she gave me up. And maybe she didn't, but Grandma and Grandpa do. Probably more than they care about anybody else. And they still betrayed me."

"I'm not them. And I'm not those people in the League who were shooting at you."

"Grandpa actually listens to me. He *loves* me." Great, now I sound like Xavier. "I can actually talk to him. Or, at least, I could. But things still didn't work out, and if I couldn't trust *him*, then how am I supposed to trust *you*?"

Gordon's silent. I still have my hands over my eyes, so I have no idea what his expression is or what he might be thinking.

"Damien, do you... do you think I don't love you?"

I shrug, still not lowering my hands. "It's okay if you don't. You've only known me a year, and I'm always doing stuff that pisses you off."

"You're my *son*, and I— Will you look at me?"

Slowly, I let my hands fall to my lap.

"You're my son, and of course I love you."

"You say that"—though this is the first I'm hearing about it—"but you think it's okay to be part of an organization that wants to drag me in off the street and kill me."

"I don't think it's okay, all right? But I can't quit the League. I'd lose my job. How would we put food on the table or keep a roof over your heads? I know this situation looks black and white to you. You're young, and... Let's just say that part of being an adult is having to make compromises."

"That sounds a lot like something Grandpa said." Right before he locked me up.

Gordon sighs. He doesn't look happy about being compared to Grandpa. "Even if I could quit the League, I don't know if I would. I *want* to be able to believe in it."

"I've seen the place where they torture villains. It's real, and it's even worse than it looked on TV. Whatever you think the League stands for, it's not true."

"It's more complicated than that. There are a lot of us who didn't know that was going on and who want to make the League what we always thought it was. It's going to take time to sort this out. There's even talk of splitting into two factions."

"Let me guess, one faction tortures villains, and the other one ignores them?"

"I can't say what's going to happen with the League. Everything's up in the air right now, and it's clear that ignoring the Truth isn't going to make it go away."

"No kidding."

"And that goes for ignoring the truth, lowercase. I've made a lot of mistakes. And the two of us"—he gestures to me and him, as if I could possibly have thought he meant anyone else—"don't always listen to each other."

"I listen, all right? I just don't like what you have to say."

He laughs at that. "We're too alike."

"Don't say that." Can't he see I've been through enough? Does he really have to insult me on top of it?

"It's true. And unfortunately that means that we don't always get along. But it doesn't mean I don't love you, even when we're not seeing eye to eye. I want you to be able to trust me. I know that's going to take time. You've put your trust in people who've let you down, and I've probably contributed to that more than I realize. But I want things to be different."

"That's great, Dad. Good luck with that." I'll believe it when I see it.

"Damien, I mean it."

"Sure, you do. And I mean it when I say I want a million dollars, but it doesn't mean it's going to happen."

"Maybe I can't quit the League, but I can do my best to make sure it's not the kind of organization that shoots at teenagers, for God's sake, or that tortures innocent people, no matter what letter's on their thumb. And that starts tonight, with you telling me what you saw. At that interrogation site, at the hotel, all of it."

"Right. And have you interrupting every five seconds to tell me how the League would never do that? I don't think so."

"I promise I won't. You're going to tell me what happened, and I'm going to listen. *Really* listen. Okay?"

"Okay, but one thing."

"What's that?"

"Can it wait until morning? It's a long story, and I can barely keep my eyes open."

He smiles and pats my knee. "Tomorrow, then." He gets up to leave, but then hesitates. "Are you sure you're okay?"

"You mean my arm?"

"I mean all of it."

"I'm—" I start to say *I'm fine*, but I stop myself. "You want the truth?"

"Yes, I do."

"Everyone I care about almost died tonight. A lot of things are messed up. My arms hurts, and I can't stop hearing Riley's screams from when we had to dig him out of that rubble and move him with a broken leg. I had to zap a lot of people tonight, and I know you think I don't care about stuff like that, that I don't feel anything about it, but I *do*. And I don't want something like tonight to ever happen again, but I'm pretty sure it will, because heroes and villains still hate each other. That's not going to change anytime soon, and the heroes aren't going to just let villains have a voice. I prevented a battle, but I didn't prevent a war. And I finally felt like I had a future, when I was with the Truth. I was helping people and making a difference. But now I'm back to where I was before, with no future and no idea what I'm supposed to do. I'm not a hero and I'm not a villain. I can't be part of the League, and I can't be part of the Truth. So where does that leave me?"

"That's... a lot to think about."

"Well, you asked."

"You don't have to have your future figured out. Certainly not *tonight*. Not even this year. And you don't have to be part of the Truth to make a difference."

"Everyone else has a plan except me. I *always* have a plan. But Sarah's going to college, Kat's going to get some cool villain job, and everybody else is joining the League." Or at least they were, before the League went all crazy. But if it's not the League, then it'll be something else like it. "And I'm just... not."

"You'll figure it out."

"What if I don't?" Grandpa's right—I wouldn't really be happy being a trophy husband/Kat's part-time sex slave. I mean, there are worse career choices I could make, but that's not the point.

"I may have only known you a year, but that's long enough to know that you never settle for anything you don't want. If the right place for you doesn't exist, you'll make one, because that's just who you are. And as for everything else… I won't pretend I know what it feels like to have gone through everything that happened to you tonight. But everyone made it out of there, and they're going to be okay. You saved a lot of people, heroes *and* villains, and you should be proud of that."

"Thanks."

"Try and get some sleep, all right? It won't feel as bad in the morning. And if you need me, you know where I am."

"If I need you? I said I was turning *seventeen*, not seven."

He laughs. "Goodnight, Damien."

"Goodnight, Dad."

He starts to leave. His hand is on the lightswitch when I say, "Dad? I'm sorry I left. I mean, I had to do it, but I'm sorry you were worried about me."

"It's okay." He says it in a tone that means it's not really, but that maybe it will be. "I'm just glad to have you back."

## X·X·X

Riley's propped up on his bed when I come in. He's wearing an old T-shirt and a pair of sweats with one leg cut off to fit over his cast. A pair of crutches are leaning against the wall. There's a prescription bottle on his nightstand, along with a bottle of water, a thousand-page fantasy novel that looks like it weighs three tons, a sketchpad, some colored pencils, a stack of comic books, and a couple textbooks from school. I set his phone on top of them.

"Textbooks? Seriously?" At least he's watching TV right now and not, like, trying to do homework. Though he's watching the news, which doesn't really count as relaxing.

He glances over at the nightstand. "Those were already there."

"So, you just keep textbooks by your bed, ready to go? I'm not sure that's any better."

The segment on the news is about what happened last night. All the news stations have pretty much been going over it nonstop. Right now they're showing footage of all the destruction, while the Channel Four news lady says, "The League's being charged with damages to the Grand Park Hotel, one of Golden City's oldest historical landmarks. For the first time in the sixty-eight years since the League's creation, the city government has had to step in and institute regulations on the once-trusted organization. Only time will tell what the repercussions—"

Riley picks up the remote and turns it off. He notices the bandage on my arm. "What happened?"

"It's nothing. How's your leg?"

"Sore, but better than last night." He sighs. "They had to do surgery on it to screw the bones back together. I won't be able to walk on it for a couple months. So, fieldwork is out." He sounds pretty upset about that.

"I can say firsthand that the alternative assignment sucks, but at least you won't have to do it alone."

He perks up. "You're coming back to school?"

I shrug and sit down at the foot of the bed. "The news

442

said we were heroes. They even said I was 'largely responsible for preventing a massacre.'" They heard that from Amelia, who has a big mouth, plus mentioning my name kind of guaranteed that her interview ended up on TV. You'd think mentioning that she's the daughter of the Crimson Flash—which she did about five times—would have done it, but no. "So, I think there's a good chance Heroesworth will take me back. Plus, I never officially left. I've just got two weeks' worth of unexplained absences, and probably a whole lot of detention." And Gordon said he would talk to them if they gave me any trouble.

"Does this mean you're home, too?"

"Since last night." I still need to get my stuff from Grandma and Grandpa's house. But staying with them has lost its appeal, for obvious reasons. Plus, the League's not allowed to haul in random villains off the street anymore, thanks to the city stepping in, so my family should be safe again.

"What about your dad? What about all that stuff he said? Are you—"

"Look, Perkins, I just came by to see if you're okay. You kind of scared me last night."

He swallows. "Thanks, X. For everything you did. You saved my life."

"I didn't abandon you, like that douchebag Mason, but you would have been okay."

"No, I wouldn't." He grips the bedspread beneath him and stares at the edge of the bed. "There was another cave-in last night while we were all knocked out. More of the roof fell in, and if I'd still been in the hallway, I would have been crushed. So, um…"

"Where's Sarah? I thought she'd be here."

"Hey. I'm trying to tell you something important."

Zach comes in from the hall. "Sarah *spent the night*. She went home to take a shower."

"*Zach.*" Riley glares at him. "Shut *up*. Mom might hear you."

"Wow, Perkins." I raise my eyebrows at him. "And after they had to screw your leg back together."

His face turns bright red. "We didn't *do* anything. Sarah was worried about me and didn't want to leave, so…" He clears his throat. "Nothing happened. And I was on a lot of painkillers. I fell asleep right away."

Me and Zach exchange a look. He rolls his eyes.

"She should be back soon," Riley says. "And, anyway, I just wanted to say that you're, um… You're my best friend, X. And maybe, if you're coming back to school, we could be partners again?"

"I should go. You're probably tired or something."

"X. Come on."

"You really want to do this right now? You're pretty messed up, and you're supposed to be taking it easy. So don't make me have to say it."

"Have to say what? Isn't this what you wanted?"

"If me saving your life is the reason you want to work together again, then the answer's no." He only wants to work with me because Mason let him down. And by *let him down*, I mean *totally screwed him over*. But I'm still his second choice.

Riley shakes his head. "That's not—"

"What the hell is he doing here?!" Curtis suddenly appears in the doorway, looking seriously pissed to see me. "Didn't you learn your lesson last night? This"—he waves at Riley's cast—"is exactly why I didn't want you hanging out with him!"

Riley gapes at him, taken by surprise, but Zach looks like he's *this close* to punching Curtis in the face, even though he doesn't even come up to his shoulder. "You don't know anything!" Zach shouts. "Damien didn't do this!"

"Zach," Riley says.

"What? You know he didn't! Are you just going to let him say that?!"

"You think I don't know anything?" Curtis folds his arms. "I'm trying to teach you boys something. Your mother and I told you we didn't want you hanging out with him for a reason. He's a villain, and he's working for the Truth. You saw what they did last night. You can't count on someone like him. Not when you're out in the field."

Riley sits up a little higher against his pillows. He glares at Curtis. "*Villains* didn't do this to me. Heroes did."

"Heroes who saw you with *him*. What were they supposed to think? Everyone in Golden City knows what he is. I'm so disappointed in you, Riley. I thought I was finally getting through to you, and then you go and put your trust in him again, and look what happens."

"*Curtis.*" Their mom comes in from the hallway, along with Sarah, who must have just gotten back. Her hair's wet and she's changed into jeans and a sweater. "Riley's supposed to be resting. Is this really the time?"

"Yes, Win. I know it's harsh, but the boys need to learn." He turns to Riley again. "Heroes, your own people, couldn't trust you because you were working with him. That should tell you something."

"Damien isn't the reason I got hurt." Riley's voice is low, and he sounds really tired, like all this stress is wearing him out.

"You stayed behind to protect him. You had his back, but he didn't have yours."

"That's not—"

"I don't want to hear it! I know I'm not your father, but I'm the closest thing you've got. Your dad and I worked together for years, and I know he wouldn't want this for you. You were there last night because you got nominated for an award at Heroesworth, and you're lucky the school isn't suspending you or reporting you to the scholarship committee."

"Suspending me? For what? Getting shot at by the League?"

"They must have had a reason. And you're already on probation. You've only got that scholarship because of Miles's sacrifice. You don't seem to realize that."

"Yes, I do! You only remind me every chance you get."

"And I'm going to keep reminding you until it sinks in. What are people supposed to think when they see his son working with a villain? What kind of legacy is that? You're one step away from getting kicked out of school, and now you almost get yourself killed fighting for the wrong side."

446

*"What?"* I can't believe him. Okay, I can, because it's not like I didn't already know he was a total douche, but still. He's acting like Riley told off the League and joined the Truth instead of trying to save everyone from both of them.

Curtis points a finger at me. "You stay out of this."

"Curtis, please," Riley's mom says.

He ignores her and goes back to lecturing Riley. "And then I find that you've deliberately disobeyed me and let him into the house, even after everything that's happened. If your father were still alive, he wouldn't stand for this. You should have seen him that day, climbing into that bus. He was terrified, but he wasn't going to let that stop him. He was one of the best in the League, and I had high hopes for you, Riley. I still do. It's up to me to make sure that Miles's boys grow up right and follow in his footsteps, but—"

"What did you say?" Sarah takes a step forward, squinting at him.

Curtis scowls at her for interrupting. "I said it's up to me to make sure his boys follow in his footsteps. Miles isn't here to teach Riley and Zach what it means to be a hero, so I've got to do it for him."

"Not that. You said 'you should have seen him that day, climbing into that bus.' But I thought you were late for work that morning. You weren't there, right?"

"What?" Curtis looks up, then his eyes dart from side to side, like he's thinking about something. "I meant figuratively, of course. Miles was always so brave. The situation didn't matter, or how scared he was. He always did what needed to be done. And I'm sure that the day he died was no exception."

"No." Sarah puts her hands on her hips. "That's not what you meant. You said it like *you were there*. Like *you saw him* on that bus that day."

Everyone looks at Curtis. Zach gasps a little. Riley's face is pale, his expression cold.

Curtis tries to laugh it off, but it sounds really fake. "You just misunderstood. You shouldn't take things so literally."

Riley's mom is watching Curtis like she's never seen him before. "We all heard you. And it sounded like..." She puts a hand to her chest. "My God. Were you *there*?"

"Win, come on, you know I wasn't. I was just—"

"Sarah's right." Riley's voice wavers, thick with emotion. "You meant what you said just now, about seeing Dad climbing into the bus, didn't you?"

Curtis waves that away. "It's a story. I was embellishing a little."

"*No*. This isn't one of your stories! You don't get to make things up about this."

"You were there?" Zach says. "You've been lying to us this whole time? Did you kill our dad?!"

"What?! No!" Curtis holds up his hands. He looks to their mom. "You have to believe me. He was my best friend! We were *partners*."

She takes a step back, horrified.

Sarah makes eye contact with me and jerks her head toward the doorway. At first I think maybe she's telling me we should get out of here and miss this—which is *so* not going to happen—but then I realize she wants me to get between the door and Curtis, in case he makes a run for it. I indicate Sarah's purse and mime shooting a gun, but she shakes her head. I find it really hard to believe she's not armed, but I do what she wants and move toward the doorway.

And as tired as I am of getting accused of shooting superheroes, I kind of hope he does run, because zapping him would be really, really satisfying.

Zach clenches his fists. "If you didn't kill him, then why would you lie about it?"

"I—I panicked." Curtis puts his hands to his temples, like getting found out gives him a headache. "You weren't there! You don't know what it was like. We had orders to stop the bus. It was coming into the city, and we had intel that there was a bomb on it. It was going to explode when it reached the convention center. We tried to flag it down, but the driver didn't see us at first. He had to swerve and ended up in the ditch. One second we were on a routine mission, and the next, the bus was on its side. The door was against the ground, and nobody could get out. The front was smashed against a telephone pole, the power lines were down, and the gas tank was leaking. The bus caught fire, and there was a *bomb* on it. It was impossible to know how much time we had."

"But our dad got on that bus," Riley says. "And you, what?"

"Miles didn't care that it was on fire. He was always like that, you know. He didn't care about his own safety, only that there were all those helpless people trapped inside." He shuts his eyes for a second, reliving it. "He climbed up onto the top and got a window open, then went in. He wanted me to help pull people out. I should have done it. I know that now. But I *couldn't*. I'm not like him."

Riley makes a disgusted sound. "No, you're not."

"I told him to leave them, but he wouldn't. He had you kids to think about, and you, Win. But you know how he was. He couldn't have lived with himself if he didn't try."

"And what were you doing?" their mom asks. "What were you doing while my *husband*, your *partner*, was dying?!"

Curtis winces and doesn't look at her. "I ran. I had to get out of there. Later, of course, I heard that Miles got everyone else off the bus. The last person he helped almost didn't get away fast enough—he was treated for burns from the explosion. I read all the interviews with them, though I couldn't bring myself to talk to any of them in person. Not after what I did. If I'd stayed, we could have gotten them all out of there in plenty of time. But there was no way to know that when I was looking at a burning bus with a bomb on it."

"So you lied about it?"

"I deserted my partner. No one would have ever forgotten that. And I knew that if I'd stayed, Miles wouldn't be dead." He pauses after he says that, like finally getting it off his chest is a huge relief. "You don't know how awful it's been, keeping that a secret these past few years. There were so many times I wanted to tell you the truth. You and the boys. But it was too late. Too much time had passed."

"Get out of my house." Her voice is full of barely subdued rage, and I'm glad she doesn't have laser eyes like my mom, or we'd probably all be dead.

Curtis holds his hands out, pleading. "Win, listen. You're overreacting. Can't we talk about this?"

"I said *get out*." She points to the door.

I step out of the way, staying just close enough to zap him a little as he walks by.

"*Ow*." He glares at me.

"Must have been static." I flash him a fake smile. "That happens when you build up too much douchebaggery. Or is that when you rub your feet on the carpet?"

"It's douchebaggery," Zach says, coming to stand next to me, "and there's more where that came from."

Curtis glances at their mom one last time, but she just stares him down until he finally actually leaves.

As soon as the front door closes, she puts her hands to her face and starts to cry.

# CHAPTER 35

"**P**retend I'm at your house," Riley says when I answer the phone Monday afternoon.

I just walked through the door after getting home from my first day back at Heroesworth. Which was unpleasant, to say the least. "Yeah, sure. If anyone asks, you're at my house." Though I'm not sure how he supposedly got here, since he can barely get out of bed. I take my coat off and put it in the hall closet. "You're going to have a problem, though, because Amelia said she was going over to your place. Where are you really?"

"What? I'm at home."

"If you're at home, then who am I supposed to lie to?"

"No one. Just, for the purposes of this conversation, pretend I'm at your house, okay? Because this is important, and if I could, you know, walk and stuff, I would have come over to say it."

"Okay, Perkins, but if you're about to declare your love for me, you should know that my heart already belongs to

Zach."

He makes a frustrated sound. "Will you shut up and *listen to me*? This is serious."

"All right, all right. I'm listening." I was going to go into the kitchen and find something to eat, but he sounds like he means it, so I flop down on the couch instead. Gordon's at work, Alex's school doesn't get out yet, and Helen must be at the antique shop with Jess, because the house is completely silent. It feels really awkward, like I'm not supposed to be here. I kind of wish they were all home already, just so they could stare at me and get it over with.

"You know what you said yesterday?" Riley asks.

"I said a lot of things yesterday. You're going to have to be more specific."

"About us not being partners. You said if the reason I wanted to work with you was because you saved my life, then the answer was no. But that's not the only reason."

"Uh-huh. Mason turning out to be the complete and total douchebag I said he was doesn't count, either. If that's all you have to say, I've got important sandwiches to make, so—"

"This is why I wanted to be there in person. So you couldn't hang up on me."

"I'm not hanging up on you. But there's nothing to talk about, okay? This whole semester, you've been telling me how great Mason is and why we can't work together. And now that you finally know he sucks, you've conveniently realized that we should be partners again? I don't think so."

"I was wrong. I thought it would be easier to work with someone who followed the rules."

"And it was. You won that award. Congratulations, by the way." The awards ceremony was a bust, but they posted the winners online. Amelia looked them up to see if Gordon won Most Beloved Superhero again. He came in second, which isn't too bad, considering all the scandals I've caused recently.

"Thanks." Riley doesn't sound very excited about it. "But I almost *died*. It wasn't worth it."

"See, it all comes back to me saving your life. You might be happy about that now, but who knows when some old BFF of yours is going to show up again, and then you won't care anymore."

"I won't care about you saving my life? I think I'm always going to care about *being alive*."

"Yeah, but that's not the point. Not everyone who follows the rules and is 'on the same page' as you is going to be a douchebag."

Riley scoffs. "I was wrong about that, too. Me and Mason were never on the same page."

"You don't want to be partners with a half villain who gets you in trouble all the time. Saving your life doesn't change that. And if working with you means I'm always going to feel like you're looking for my replacement, then I'd rather stick with Amelia."

"Mason left me. I was hurt really bad, and he knew that, and he couldn't get away fast enough. I wouldn't have even gotten trapped under that rubble if he hadn't pushed me. Some things matter more than following the rules. You didn't leave me. And you were right—if you'd been at that museum, you would have gone chasing after the bad guy with me. I wouldn't have gotten nominated or won that award, but that doesn't really compare to having a partner I can count on."

I get up from the couch and pace the living room. "Unless I zapped that guy. Then you would have lost your scholarship and gotten kicked out of school. We've been over this, and nothing's any different, so let's just drop it."

"Curtis abandoned my dad. He chickened out and ran away when he needed him the most. Dad got killed because of him. Curtis said that you didn't have my back, that you weren't watching out for me, and that I couldn't trust you. But *he's* the one who couldn't be trusted. You've always had my back, X. And, okay, maybe you don't always follow the rules, but I trust you with my life, and that's kind of more important. The two of *us* are the ones who are on the same page, because if we'd been there with that bus, there wouldn't have been any question of whether or not we were going in. Neither of us would have had to worry about the other running off, no matter how bad the circumstances were. And I thought the stuff Mason did when he was overseas was really cool, but you were right. He wasn't in any danger, and he just turned his power on. Anyone could do that. And maybe everyone here's trying to be a hero, but like you said, we're better at it than them."

I smile at that, and I'm kind of glad he can't see me, because he might think that means I'm giving in. "What about your scholarship? And the League?"

He's quiet for a second, and then his voice wavers a little. "How can you even ask me that?"

"Uh, because you're practically their poster boy? It's your whole future."

"The League tried to kill me. They're the reason my leg had to be *screwed back together*. And they tried to kill my best friend."

"Yeah, but you can't really blame them. I wanted to kill Mason as soon as I met him, too."

"I'm talking about *you*. They tried to kill you—they freaking *shot* you—and they tried to hurt Sarah. And Kat."

"Because you guys were with me. I mean, okay, maybe they figured out Kat was a villain, and Sarah sort of pulled a gun on them. But your only crime was being seen with me. Working together's not really going to fix that."

"It doesn't need to be fixed! You didn't do anything to them. And even if last night never happened, they tried to kidnap you in the park. They were going to take you away to who knows where and do who knows what to you, just because you're half villain. And... maybe six months ago I would have thought that was okay. I hate that I was that person, because it's *not*. It's *so* not okay. It makes me sick that they're paying for me to go to Heroesworth, and maybe things will be different by the time we graduate, but I don't know how I can join an organization who would do that to you."

I stop pacing and just stand there, taking that in. I don't know what to say.

"X? Are you still there?" He sounds kind of nervous, like he thinks I might have hung up on him.

"They must have you on an awful lot of painkillers."

"I mean it."

"You've been preparing to join your whole life. You can't just—"

"Yeah, I can. I don't know what I'll do, and I'm not ready to lose my scholarship or drop out of school or anything, but I know I can't be part of something like that. And I don't care what Curtis says—I don't think my dad would want me to be, either. So, what do you say, X? Can we go back to being partners again?"

# CHAPTER 36

"That's the Damien Locke?" I wrinkle my nose in disgust as the waitress at the superhero-themed diner sets a steaming plate of meatloaf in front of Kat. The diner was so grateful that I saved them from that armed robbery that they decided to name something after me. Unfortunately, they went with what the waitress was serving at the time, or at least what she was trying to serve, before that robber pointed a gun at her. The sliced-up meatloaf is grayish brown and has chunks of rice and some kind of red thing all over it. It smells horrible, and even the side of mashed potatoes and gravy looks kind of congealed and unappetizing, though that might just be because of its proximity to the meatloaf.

"It's not the Damien Locke," Kat corrects me. "It's the Son of Flash."

"Not in my menu." Not after I found a pen and changed it, anyway.

The waitress glares at me as she finishes setting

everybody else's food in front of them.

"They should have called it the Renegade X," Sarah says. "Maybe we should talk to the manager about it."

"This doesn't have sauce on it, right?" Amelia inspects her sandwich, which really obviously has sauce on it. "I wanted a *Crimson Flash*, but without the sauce. I'm his daughter."

I roll my eyes at her. "You mean you wanted a turkey sandwich. You should have just ordered that."

"I got a chicken sandwich," Zach says. "We could trade. I don't mind."

Amelia bites her lip. "It's not the same."

The waitress sighs. "Anyone else have a problem?" She makes eye contact with everyone, from me all the way around the booth to Riley.

"I have a problem with Kat's food." I jerk my thumb at her plate of meatloaf. "Does that count?"

Kat punches me in the shoulder. "It's not every day they name something after you. I'm going to try it at least once."

"Yeah, but on my birthday?"

"It doesn't look that bad," Riley says, though he doesn't sound very convincing.

The waitress takes Amelia's plate and heads back to the kitchen.

"Nobody eat anything yet." Kat gets out her phone. She uses her shapeshifting power to stretch her arm out far enough to get everybody in the picture.

"But my food's not here," Amelia whines. "Nobody will know I had the Crimson Flash."

"They wouldn't know that anyway," I tell her, "because you didn't."

Kat finishes taking the picture, then elbows me and indicates I should get out of the booth. She sets up First Mate Suckers in front of her plate and positions a couple of his arms so it looks like he's about to pick up the silverware.

"Come on, Kat. Don't drag First Mate Suckers into this. He has a reputation to uphold."

"First Mate Suckers has a wide and eclectic palate. His tastes know no bounds." She snaps a couple pictures of him before sitting down again.

Sarah takes a bite of her chicken-fried steak. "Wow, this is really good. But not as good as the one your grandma—" She stops herself and looks down at her plate, though she was obviously talking to Kat.

I guess it took getting shot at together for her to finally realize Kat hates her guts. Or, um, something like that.

"As the one my grandma makes?" Kat asks. She doesn't sound super happy about it, but she doesn't sound too pissed, either.

Sarah nods. "It was Feed Your Grandkids night at the retirement home, and they invited me and Riley for dinner."

Kat suddenly glares at them.

Riley's mouth drops open a little, like he wasn't expecting Sarah to implicate him in this. He closes his mouth and swallows the bite of hamburger he was eating. "Hers *was* really good," he mutters.

"You were probably busy," I tell Kat. "With, like, finals

or something."

Sarah shakes her head as she takes a drink of her lemonade. "You were home that weekend, but your grandma said you were out 'fornicating with that boy' and couldn't be bothered."

"She *what*?" Kat's face turns red, and she slumps down in her seat.

I point at Sarah with one of my Justice Fries. "'That boy' has a name."

"Yeah," Zach says, "he's called Son of Flash."

"And *fornicating* sounds so cheap. Like we weren't having a good time. I happen to know I provide a quality service."

Amelia makes a face. "*Gross.*"

"Don't worry," Sarah says. "I told her things are changing for young women these days and that she doesn't need to make you feel ashamed of your sexuality."

"Oh, my God." Kat presses her palms to her forehead and sticks her fingers through her hair. "You didn't."

"We had a long talk about it. I think she's coming around. And it was very informative. Your grandmother knows a lot about—"

"*No.* No, she doesn't. And you're not allowed to talk to her about my..." She swallows. "You know. My sex life. And not his, either." She gestures to me, like she thought Sarah might try and talk about my sex life instead as some kind of loophole. "Got it?"

"Okay. If that's how you feel about it."

"It is. It's how *everyone* feels about it."

"But it's obvious you get really self-conscious about the

fact that you enjoy sex, even though it's perfectly—"

"*Sarah.*" I try to kick her under the table and accidentally get Riley instead, though luckily it's his good leg, not the broken one. He still cries out and glares at me, though. "You're killing me, here."

"Well, it is."

"It's also my *birthday*, if you know what I mean. So *shut up.*"

Sarah frowns and opens her mouth to say something else, but Riley hurries and changes the subject before she has the chance.

"So," he says, "I'm coming back to school on Monday."

"It's about time," I tell him. "You're only going to have that elevator pass until your leg gets better. And as your new partner, I will of course take time out of my busy schedule to escort you to all your classes."

He rolls his eyes at me. "You know not all our classes are on the same floor, right?"

"You guys aren't really partners," Amelia says. "You're both doing the alternative assignment. Individually."

"Not the point." I take a drink of my birthday-cake flavored milkshake. "And there's always next year."

"You mean summer school, when you flunk Advanced Heroism." She cranes her neck, trying to look toward the kitchen. "What's taking so long?"

Zach offers her the second half of his sandwich. "Are you sure you don't want any? It's pretty good."

"Maybe just a little." She chomps into it, like she's trying to set the world's record for the most sandwich eaten in one bite. Then, while chewing, she asks Riley,

"Isn't it going to be weird seeing Mason again?"

I'm starting to forget why I even invited her.

Riley sighs and sets down his hamburger. "He tried to call a couple times, but I didn't talk to him."

"He won't be bothering you," Sarah says. "I took care of it."

Everyone stops eating and stares at her.

"What does that mean?" Riley asks.

"He came by your house the other day. You were asleep, but I was there, so I told him I know where he lives. And that I'm officially back from my hiatus. He didn't know what that meant, so I explained that I make dangerous weaponry that tends to explode. I said that if he ever even tries to talk to you again, a broken leg would be the least of his worries."

"Props to that," Kat says.

"And I mentioned that he should probably stay away from Damien, because getting electrocuted really hurts, and he doesn't look like he has a very high pain tolerance. And he said you wouldn't do that because you'd get kicked out of school, and I said that getting punched in the face hurts a lot, too, even off of school property. I might have implied you were kind of unstable." She shrugs.

Amelia finishes stuffing the rest of Zach's sandwich into her face. "Mrs. Deeds tried to make me work with him, since both of you are out, but I refused."

I gasp in fake awe. "Wow, Amelia. How do you handle being so brave?"

"Shut up." Bits of Zach's sandwich fly out of her mouth and land all over. "I know it's not as cool as what Sarah

463

did."

"*Badass* is the word you're looking for."

"But I told the teacher what he did to Riley, really loud, so the whole class could hear, and I said I couldn't work with someone like that. So she put me in a different group, and he just had to stand there, looking stupid."

"He better not have ended up with the alternative assignment." I haven't seen him in the library, where I've been banished to work on my stupid binder full of really biased essay questions, and I'd like to keep it that way.

Amelia shakes her head. "He got assigned to another group, too. But they didn't look very happy about it."

The waitress finally comes back with the turkey sandwich. Amelia hands half of it to Zach, who asks the waitress if he can get some sauce for it.

"The girls in my new group are really nice," Amelia goes on. "They call themselves Team Glitter, and they made up fun names. Melissa goes by Sapphire Sparkle, and Hilary—we call her Hil—she goes by Ruby Red. I'm going to be Diamond Dancer."

"Sorry to be the one to break this to you," I tell her, "but you don't dance."

She makes an outraged squeak. "Yes, I do. Just not in front of you, because you're my brother, and I know you'd make fun of me. But I practice all the time. Tell him, Zach."

"What?" Zach pauses in mid bite and has that deer-in-the-headlights look. "I, um... Do you?"

"*Yes.* I told you about it, remember? Anyway, Melissa and Hil asked me to help them design costumes for us, since I have an important role in costume club."

"You're treasurer," I tell her.

"It's still important. And we're going to come up with a synchronized dance routine."

"Wow. That will really come in handy the next time someone points a raygun at you." I finish the last bite of my hamburger, along with my last fry, and slurp up the last bit of my milkshake. "You must have a really busy schedule. How do you find time to work on catching those pirates?"

Amelia flicks her hand, waving that away. "First of all, they're *not* pirates. And second, we have one notebook for our research, and one for the important stuff, like ideas for costume accessories. Mrs. Deeds says our notes for our assignment are the most organized in the whole class. We color-coded them and everything. But Melissa and Hil don't really care about being the ones who get to capture the bad guys, and neither do I. It's a lot more fun this way."

"So, you're not upset that I switched partners?"

"Um, *no*. And you didn't 'switch' because you'd have to actually have a partner to do that, and Mrs. Deeds gave you the alternative assignment, which you're supposed to do alone. But Melissa and Hil care about the same things I do, and they have really good fashion sense."

"Right. The most important quality in a superhero partner." I look over at Riley, taking in the Christmas sweater he's wearing. In February. "On second thought, Perkins, we might have to rethink this renewed partnership thing."

He glances down at the reindeer and snowflakes on his sweater. "What?"

"Christmas was two months ago."

"It's *wintry*. It's still winter. And it was cold out, and this is what Mom grabbed for me when I asked her to get me something, so I wouldn't have to hobble on my crutches all the way back to my room, since we were about to leave."

"Uh-huh. Letting your mom pick out clothes for you? We're going to have to work on that."

Kat finishes off the last of her meatloaf—I can't believe she actually ate any of it, let alone *all* of it—and pushes her plate away. "Hey, are you ready for your present now?"

I raise my eyebrows at her. "Geez, Kat. In front of everyone? It's great that you're not ashamed of your sexuality and all, but I kind of thought we'd wait until we were alone for that."

She smacks my arm. "Your *other* present." She reaches down by her feet and pulls up a birthday-themed gift bag. "Happy birthday, Damien."

I pull out all the purple tissue paper until I get to the actual present. It's a stuffed octopus, kind of like First Mate Suckers, only this one is pink and has little hearts all over it.

"I found her around Valentine's Day," Kat says. "Her name's Octavia Suckers. She's First Mate Suckers's wife."

"Obviously." One of her tentacles has a sticker at the end that says *Press here!* I squeeze the button, and she starts singing a song by Super Star, which is a cheesy pop

466

band that also happens to be my favorite. "Thanks, Kat. She's really awesome."

The waitress comes back with Zach's sauce. She scowls at all the tissue paper everywhere as she clears away some of our plates. "I'll bring the check."

Sarah holds up a finger. "Separate checks, please."

The waitress mutters something under her breath and storms off.

"It's supposedly bad luck to have a woman on board a pirate ship," Kat says, "but First Mate Suckers and Octavia defy the rules, because their love can't be tamed."

"And yet, they live apart. So tragic." I look around at everyone. "That's two amazing presents from Kat"—even if her second present hasn't happened yet, I think it's safe to assume it will be amazing—"and zero from the rest of you."

"My leg's broken," Riley says. "It's hard to get anywhere."

"That's your excuse for everything these days. And you might have heard of this thing called the internet? You can use it to order presents from the comfort of your own home."

"I got you something, too," Zach says, "but I left it at the house."

"Convenient."

"It's from both of us," Amelia adds.

"Right. So, you didn't get me anything, either. My own sister."

"I'm still working on your present," Sarah says. "I'm a little rusty after my hiatus, but the guys at the retirement home have been giving me some pointers, and I think my skills are really improving."

"Does this present explode? No, wait, don't tell me. You'll ruin the surprise."

"What did your parents get you?" Kat asks.

"Me and Gordon are going to see *Super*, that new musical that's coming to town."

Amelia makes a little yelp. "Not fair. *I* wanted to see that. I've been talking about it all week!"

"It's starring… Wait, let me think. Who's in it?"

"Joanna Jones! She's only my favorite actress. And singer."

"Oh, *is she*? I had no idea."

"Yes, you did! You saw me putting that picture of her up on my wall, the one from my magazine. Maybe Dad will take me, too."

"It's only playing for three nights—it's a special showing—and the tickets are sold out already. Plus, it's not your birthday. Too bad."

"*Uh!*" Amelia gives me a really sour look. "You're doing this on purpose, aren't you?"

"Doing what on purpose? Turning seventeen and letting Gordon, who's missed every one of my birthdays so far, finally give me a birthday present? Yeah, wow, that's really devious of me."

"You knew I was *dying* to see that! And it's a romantic comedy."

"So?"

"So, it's something I would like. It's for *girls*. There's a song in it about her getting her superpower *and* realizing her power as a woman on the same day."

"And boys can't enjoy that? Way to be sexist."

"I've never even heard you say you like musicals, and now you're making Dad take you to the one you know I wanted to go to?"

"I'm not *making* him. He wanted to do something together. Just the two of us. He said I could pick anything."

"And you couldn't pick something that you actually like?"

"Who said I don't like it?" Plus, going to this will annoy the hell out of her for a long time. It's the gift that keeps on giving.

"I take back what I said. Zach's present *isn't* from both of us."

"Oh, no. Anything but that."

The waitress comes back with our checks. Sarah glances at them and starts passing them out. We all get our money out to pay, though none of us moves to leave yet.

"Just think," Kat says, "a year ago, you didn't even know you had a dad. And now you're going to your first women's musical together."

"First *Heroes on Ice*, and now this," Amelia whines.

"Yeah, at this rate, by my next birthday, I'll have done everything you want to do. Probably twice." I look meaningfully at Zach.

He wiggles his eyebrows. "Only twice?"

"I don't want to cheapen our relationship. I respect you too much. Quality over quantity."

"*Hey*," Kat says.

"Aw, you know you're always quality." I pull her close to me and kiss the side of her head. "And I respect you way too much to deprive you of all this." I gesture to myself.

Kat laughs. "You'd better."

"I do. But if you need me to prove it to you, the backseat of your car is right outside."

"*Ew*," Amelia says. "I sat there on the way here."

"Relax. We've never actually done it in the car."

"Well, not in *my* car," Kat says.

"Whose?" Riley asks, narrowing his eyes at me.

"Not yours, Perkins. Geez. You're so paranoid." Though we did make out pretty hard in there once.

"It was my parents' car," Kat mumbles, sounding a little embarrassed.

"Oh." Sarah's eyes light up. "You and your grandma have that in—"

I stand up, clapping my hands together. "All right, that's it! Party's over. Thanks for coming. Being seventeen is great. Sarah, you're not invited next year."

# ACKNOWLEDGMENTS

Special thanks goes out to my beta readers, Chloë Tisdale, Karen Kincy, and Ryan Hayes, who all insisted this book was awesome, even when I couldn't see it. You guys were right, of course.

Thanks also to Phillip Russell Newman and Daniel Warneke, the narrator/producer team behind the Renegade X audiobooks. When I set out to find the right voice for Damien, I never imagined I'd find someone as perfect for it as Phil.

And thanks to Raul Allen, who makes the most amazing book covers.

And last—but definitely not least—thanks to all my readers who fell in love with this series and keep asking for more. Yes, there will be another book.

# SPECIAL THANKS TO THE FOLLOWING CITIZENS OF GOLDEN CITY

| Name and Alignment | Power |
| --- | --- |
| Sales Man, V | Compels ~~subjects~~ *valued patrons* that they haven't lived until they've tried this overpriced product. Spell can only be broken by violating the warranty |
| Shadow Zap, V | Electricity |
| Breeze, V | Tornado breath |
| Accelerator Ray, H | Kinetic manipulation |
| Crimson Leopard, H | Firebreathing, super agility |
| Uamada, H | Patience |
| Fusion, H | Transforms into human/animal hybrid |
| Nano of the North, V | Swarm army (swarmy, if you will) of refrigerant nanobots |
| Violet Smoke, H | Teleportation |
| The Librarian, H | Able to silence villains with a single book |
| Caymen, V | Body morphing |

| | |
|---|---|
| Nature Woman, H | Able to communicate with, and control the actions of, animals |
| Kesal Exuo, V | Technopath |
| The Plaid Matter, H | Can turn anything plaid |
| The Deaf Lemon, V | Able to communicate with citrus fruit |
| Ah-hoo, V | Excessively violent sneezing. These sneezes can be summoned at a moment's notice, propelling the sneezer up and back a distance of 15-20 ft. as a concussive shock wave flattens anyone or anything in front of her. Unfortunately these sneezes move the sneezer regardless of any structures in her way, and she does not have unbreakable bones, so she generally relies on stealth and obsessive observation to accomplish her goals |
| Sourpuss, V | Able to curdle dairy |
| MK the Pig-Tailed Overlord, V | The power to freeze things and people |

| | |
|---|---|
| Dragonstar, H | Energy manipulation |
| Ryoku Mourn, H | Teleportation |
| Lord Wilco, V | Grand technomancer |
| Bibliotheca, H | Literary teleportation |
| The Late Ace, H | Tardiness |
| N/A, V | Able to bypass required fields in a single bound |
| Lord Keffingstar, V | Shoots landsharks out of his eyes |
| Tasha "Queen Esther" Lennhoff, H | Healing |
| Talia, V | The ability to make everyone eat too much sugar |
| Master Sculptor, V | Body/mind molding |
| Pryoscream, V | Flight and pyrokinesis |
| Light Em Up, V | Controls light to generate concussive blasts from his palms and moves at light speed by adjusting the properties of the light around him |
| Storm Cat, H | Weather control |
| The Amazing Sponge Man, H | The ability to absorb liquids and get squishy |

| | |
|---|---|
| The Ingenious Mrs. H, H | People can't use improper grammar around her |
| The Mysterious Lady N, V | Teleportation |
| Super Jymn, H | Fast typist |
| Bookdragon, H | The ability to hoard and protect books |
| Kravix, V | Able to make multiple copies of himself and all gear he is wearing |
| Thud, H | Invulnerability. (Good thing, too, as he is ridiculously clumsy.) Most all his villain captures are the result of him falling on them. He waits on top of tall buildings, and, as he leaps from one to the next, when villainy occurs, his luck kicks in. He trips and plummets down to make the capture with his trademark THUD! |
| Chris "Warcabbit" Hare, H | Super-coordination |
| Scantrontb, V | Power of indecision |
| Clockwork Rose, H | Inventor |
| The ExoFlasher, V | Can control clothing |

| | |
|---|---|
| The Engineer, H | Technical detective |
| Lustra, H | Her beams of light convert anyone hit by them into a friendly pacifist |
| Dark Thea, H | Can morph into any animal |
| Kensei, H | The ability to see spirits |
| Single Entendre Man, H | People always get his meaning |
| "Cinder Ellie" Harrison, H | Fire princess |
| Miki the Dabbler Girl, H | Can do anything once |
| Professor Photosynthesis, H | Making plants grow |
| Dark Deviance, V | Able to manipulate the confidence and insecurities of those within a five-foot radius |
| Indigo, H | Weaver of illusions and dreams |
| Thunderin, V | Controls thunder and lightning |
| Rhel ná DecVandé, H | Logistics |
| Jargon, V | Confuses enemies by spewing technical jargon at them |
| Mutagen, H | Adaptive shapeshifting |
| Gertjan, V | In de weg staan |

| | |
|---|---|
| Ion, H | Electrical |
| Raziel, H | Indestructible, also has the power of flight |
| Phantom Photon, H | Ability to turn matter into light and light into matter |
| Equivocator, V | Web of confusion |
| Revanp, H | Alters reality (slightly) |
| Captain Sunlight, H | X-ray vision on Lego models |
| Pschye, V | Brings soulmates together, or keeps them apart, depending on her mood |
| The Toymaker, H | Making toys come to life |
| Captain Page, V | Ability to control and manipulate paper |
| Simpleton, H | Common sense |
| Fzz, V | Magic |
| Chad Bowden, V | Can transform into any animal |
| Absolute Shelving, H | Library clairvoyance |
| Wolf, H | Possesses the senses, instincts, agility, and stamina of a canine. He also frequently chases cats up trees and attacks mailmen |

| | |
|---|---|
| Possibly, V | Manipulates chance, increasing the probability of a particular event's outcome. Results can range unpredictably from lucky guessing safe combinations to evading police due to a collision with an overturned fruit cart and a flock of unexpected emus |
| Stormfire, V | Control over fire |
| Sumasuun, V | The ability to customize/modify inanimate objects |
| Al A Bi, V | Didn't do it |
| Quantum Scourge, V | Ability to change space-time |
| Indigo Crusader, H | Teleportation |
| Azure Flame, H | Pyrokinesis |
| Tubthumper, H | Always gets back up no matter the damage. His first death/terrible injury was in the tub. Everyone thought he was dead with the odd angle of his neck. Then he got back up again good as new. His family jokingly nicknamed him from the sound he made that fateful night |
| The Antikytheran, V | Technokinesis |
| Simina, H | Superpower-less |

| | |
|---|---|
| MasterMouse, H | Shapeshifting |
| Captain Punch, H | Teleportation |
| Collateral Damage Man, H | Earthquakes |
| The Procrastinator, V | Will think of it later |
| The Grad Student, V | The ability to turn coffee into mathematical theorems |
| The Fantastic Feline, H | Flight |
| Zephyr, H | Aerokinesis |
| Daimadoshi, V | Teleportation |
| Charter, V | When he says "hit by a bus," a bus falls out of the sky on his target |
| Anomaly, H | Loses his power every few weeks, then develops a new one after a few days |
| Ms. Liberty, H | Kicking Ass |
| Raven King, H | Flight |
| Forge, H | Creates physical constructs with his mind |
| Sofer, H | The ability to pluck magical items/weapons from books |

| | |
|---|---|
| Amazing Mandy Wultsch, H | Speed reading |
| Mr. Zero, V | Probability |
| Rhea Silver, H | Healing |
| The Rockstar V, H | Creates ultrasonic waves |
| Airy Harvester, V | Uses wind to carry away objects within 10 meters |
| Titaniumman, H | Strength |
| James Pratt, H | Can fix anything |
| Autumn Pratt, H | Has a green thumb |
| Zzzzzzzzzzzz!, V | Showing up last in the thank-you section of the book |

# ABOUT THE AUTHOR

CHELSEA M. CAMPBELL grew up in the Pacific Northwest, where it rains a lot. And then rains some more. She finished her first novel when she was twelve, sent it out, and promptly got rejected. Since then, she's earned a degree in Latin and Ancient Greek, become an obsessive knitter and fiber artist, and started a collection of glass grapes.

Besides writing, studying ancient languages, and collecting useless objects, Chelsea is a pop-culture fangirl at heart and can often be found rewatching episodes of *Buffy the Vampire Slayer*, *Parks and Recreation*, or dying a lot in *Dark Souls*. You can visit her online at www.chelseamcampbell.com.